# The Binding Tempest

BY

## Steven Rudy

MYSTICHAWK
PRESS

THE BINDING TEMPEST

Edited by O.L. Faulkner

Cover Design by Sara Oliver

Cover Illustration by Sara Oliver

Map Illustrations by Steven Rudy, using (Wonderdraft and Adobe Suite)

Interior Illustration following Chapter 15 by Екатерина Витковская

Published by MysticHawk Press LLC

ISBN- 978-1-7370652-1-0 (paperback)

ISBN- 978-1-7370652-0-3 (ebook)

First Edition: May 2021

*For D*

# ACKNOWLEDGMENTS

First, I must thank my beautiful and brilliant wife for pushing me to pursue my dream, but more so for putting up with me while I found my way through this. Your help was essential in getting this thing across the finish line.

I want to express my love and complete admiration for my three wonderful children. Caleb, Quinn, and Avery; you are all an endless source of creativity, love, compassion, perseverance and strength. I love each of you for the beautiful beings you are and your unique spirits. Thank you for inspiring me.

I want to thank my parents who are indescribably amazing. I can never repay you for your love and unflinching support. My love for both of you is unending.

I want to thank all my early draft readers, including my editor, who are all brave souls for traversing the chaos of my world before it was inhabitable. You helped me immensely. May you all live well and prosper.

Lastly to all the creative souls in this world. Art is the spirit of life as essential as the magnificence of nature, it is an energy that reaches deep and unites us. Go forth and create.

"Everything is Light...

Matter is an expression of infinite forms of Light, because energy is older than it."

NIKOLA TESLA

# CONTENTS

# ILLUSTRATIONS

# PROLOGUE

*The Sagean Empire ruled for two thousand years.*
*Until The Great War when the Empire fell.*
*Leaving a frontier of alchemy, magic, and machines, adrift*
*&*
*A generation struggling, broken and vulnerable.*

## 39 Years After the Great War

The wind-borne clouds of sand were colliding on themselves in a fog of misdirection when he reached the ancient city. The ruins had been withering away unseen for centuries, in a lifeless land a hundred leagues north of the Cracked Lands. Gusts of frigid breath from that frozen abyss, were slowly blowing the ancient city out of existence, and it whistled through the remnants in an eerie howl.

Qudin dismounted from his horse, tied the rein off and walked among the scattered graveyard of stone shards. He found the artifact he sought resting in the middle of what was once an old courtyard. The ancient gate was surrounded by broken stone columns that had long ago crumbled into the dirt. The monolith had an ominous appearance amongst the surrounding debris and decay, because it looked untouched by the passage of time. A dulled polish on the metal components was the only sign of wear or corrosion on the relic. Everything from the Eckwyn Age had disappeared and Qudin had spent a lifetime trying to uncover what was lost. Now, finally, something substantial was within his reach.

He placed his satchel on the ground and walked around the gateway to study the components. The gate had a series of layered metal arches held up by tapered stone plinths at each end. Together, they held a paneled circle, with a worn golden gleam. The circle gradually stepped in thickness from the center out, a retracting aperture akin to a human eye.

Qudin stepped closer to run his hand along the cold stone edge. Though he hadn't used his powers in many years, they were always awaiting his call. He took a deep breath, and without a second thought, exhaled and channeled an effluence of energy into the metal frame. The gate reverberated and hummed, but the energy recoiled and snapped back into him.

His senses flooded and a bright flash blinded his vision. Qudin stumbled backward to the ground. The back surge of electrical current burned as a harsh reminder that humans made fragile capacitors. A pain in his head compressed behind his eyes, and something wet emerged at his ears. Suspecting it was blood, Qudin wiped at it with his hand. He looked for confirmation, to see blood at his fingers. The glow fading rapidly as it dried.

Climbing to his feet, Qudin put his outstretched hand against a stone fragment for balance. He could feel the energy in his veins oscillate with fury and fire. The torrent radiated through him in waves, while the gate remained static and unchanged. He streamed the destructive surge from his body and into the broken column beneath his palm. Qudin was a luminary and it was a simple task, but old ways are easily forgotten by an idle mind. He had imprisoned his abilities and wondered if they were now a muscle in atrophy.

The surrounding scents in the air returned with the smell of noxious brown weeds mixed with the stale odor from the fine granulates of clay in the ground. Qudin's thoughts became clear, and the solution presented itself.

Desperation had made him blind; he couldn't help himself. Every artifact he collected, every tomb he uncovered, map or text he had studied, every bit of the Ancients he dug up had brought him closer to the one item he longed to find more than any other. Something that could explain what had happened the night he killed the Sagean Emperor.

Qudin rummaged through his satchel until he spotted the shimmer of colored glass peeking out from the bottom of his bag. Pushing aside an old tattered journal, he grabbed the goggles. With the inside of his shirt, he gently cleaned the optics before putting them on. The goggles diffused the emissions of light, into a visual spectrum of energy particles. They were fashioned with tetra-chromic glass that he had discovered in a buried chamber near Echo Canyon, and he hated to wear them. The chromatic diffusion sometimes made him sick, but they would see what his eyes had missed.

He approached the gate once more with the goggles on. With his right hand he rotated the tiny gears at his temple. His thumb turned the dials a single notch at a time and tuned the optics until his vision cleared; exposing waves of colored particles that radiated from the gate in large pulsing ripples throughout the air. Scanning the full area, the sight of the surrounding ruins stopped his breath. The entire city was being swallowed into a deep micro-fluorescent blackness, cloaked in strange effervescent purple that consumed all the light. Whatever it was, he suspected it was gathered there because of the gate and his instinct was to fear it.

Qudin turned his eyes back to examine the artifact with a new sense of urgency. At his feet he could see a faint red emission buried below the ground. He dug and swept the sand away, until his hands felt something solid. With his fingertips, he traced the smooth edge of the glowing red metal symbol inlaid beneath. Qudin had knowledge of symbols and sigils, and their various powers, this was something new.

He took a deep breath and started to pull the energy he sensed beneath the land. Older than all, and crafted in creation, pulling from the territh was arduous. Every energy source was different and each had a unique vibration, a signature. But all were tempestuous. He wasn't sure if their true nature was chaotic or just in confluence with forces beyond him.

First, Qudin had to attune to the energy and then he could focus the disorder. The effort of drawing energy through obstacles of matter took strength, but it was the best source at the moment. Qudin drew in what he could, binding the energy to his own. Once captured, he could convert it to uses other than the original form he drew upon. Heat could become light, and light could become motion. With the captured energy, he streamed a trickle of electricity into the symbol.

The gate erupted to life. It pulsed and vibrated like an awakened ocean kraken. It began to discharge arcs of blinding blue-white lighting that whipped and crashed around the ancient courtyard in sixteen-foot lengths of unpredictable lashing bursts. Each blast destroyed the silence of the cold wasteland. Then the gate's moving parts of metal arches began scraping alive, and it groaned in its resurrection. The coarse desert sand compressed out of the grooves and flew into the air.

The energy was mounting, and the ground started to shake. Building fragments broke free and crashed nearby. With his satchel in hand, he ran to get his horse. He found it in a frantic state, trying desperately to pull and gnaw at the tie. The horse's muscles flexed with each tug, while his hooves stamped and dug for leverage. Qudin approached him with caution. Slowly he placed his hand on the proud animal, moved his face in close, and whispered gently in a rhythmic tone. A faint glow from Qudin's hand cast out as he patted the upper shoulder. The horse calmed. He plodded the horse back in the direction they had first arrived and set him free. He was confident that the horse had a good enough memory to make it back to civilization.

When Qudin returned to the gate, the gold-plated center was slowly retracting to reveal a vertical mirror of liquid light suspended in the gateway's eye. The glowing white pool of refracting light reflected in his goggles, with colors that flared at the edges. He lifted the strap of his satchel over his head, and with a growing grin on his face, Qudin stepped into the light.

# CHAPTER ONE

## ELLARIA ARRIVES

*SORROW IS A TREE THAT GROWS FROM THE SOIL OF WISDOM. IF THERE WAS such a thing as truth in this world, that was hers,* Ellaria thought idly. She was being reflective; long journeys had that effect on her, and she found the curious circumstances that had her coming home were weighing heavily on her mind. She had a keen sense of the snare before it was sprung, but she had yet to devise the real reason why she was being called to the Ascendancy Tower this time. These were suspicious times and Ellaria was suspicious by nature and she hated the idea that she was being lured into a trap. Ellaria was uncommonly resilient, not because she was strong, but because she was flexible. She had learned to bend with the wind to endure the storm. This time, she was having trouble anticipating what was on the horizon. The state of the world had only grown more chaotic in the forty years following the fall of the Empire, and it felt like she was about to find herself once again in the whirlwind.

Ellaria watched the coach wheels roll through the stone tracks and splash the overnight rain out of the grooves. The Imperial Road went through the valley of Tavillore, directly connecting the largest cities on the eastern shore of the Anamic Ocean. It was a smart piece of engineering and one of the first projects after the Great War. Made of limestone, the road had a series of channeled out tracks for the coach wheels to guide along in. Simple. Of course simple engineering is the smartest form of engineering. At over five-hundred leagues long, it took eight years to complete. Unifying the wounded nations reeling from the war by connecting them, providing faster travel, and better supply opportunities beyond the Uhanni river. It provided jobs and good pay for thousands of people. Ellaria looked at it and rolled her eyes in exasperation.

She helped to push the idea and see it to fruition, but the politics fought her at every turn. The stone for the road should have come from the Free Cities in the New World to establish a working relationship across the ocean. Political bargaining and backroom dealing took over, as it always did. A common enough occurrence that the Tavillorean people started calling the Coalition of Nations, 'the encumbrance'. Their faith in the process obviously shaken as the voice that was once promised them was increasingly ignored and dismissed.

The people had the right of it; it was a game of lies and corruption. In this new scientific era, 'the encumbrance' was a machine all on its own, and it exhausted Ellaria. Every city in the world was home to a different syndicate of organized crime, but they were all small-time crooks compared to the Coalition. In the end, the limestone came from across the Warhawk Mountains to the west, where it had cost more to transport over Thorn Pass than it would have from across the ocean. The stone was a white and it was beautiful, but because of its inherent softness, it cracked all the time and needed constant repairs or had to be fully replaced. The big joke, was that all of it would be obsolete in ten years when more train lines became operational.

Ellaria tried to control her pessimism, but old age left her less inclined to contain her frustration. The first train line had opened two years ago from Adalon to Andal up north, but the rail lines being laid to the south and west had progressed far more slowly. Ellaria suspected it was because of land rights. The Coalition of Nations had been squabbling over the land in the valley for years. In the west, Rodaire had completed their train line almost twice as fast, but all the tracks were laid on the ground; whereas the train from Adalon to Andal was suspended off elevated rails to navigate the terrain of rivers, rocky coastline and unreliable soils.

Ellaria wished she could have taken a train this time. Coach rides were unpleasant – even the nicest ones were hot and cramped. She had initially declined Delvette's invitation to attend the Council's court meeting in Adalon. But her friend was adamant. Delvette even sent tickets for a cloudparter that Ellaria had to refuse outright, on account of her fear of heights. Her friend's persistence was the beginning of Ellaria's trepidation, and that uneasiness had accompanied her on the road as though it were a burdensome piece of luggage.

It was possible the meeting was about drawing the border lines between the nations. Land itself had never been more valuable. As the world became more accurately mapped in the last forty years, the arguments of the exact boundaries of land were more meticulously contested. Under the Empire's rule, there was only a general understanding of the extent of each nation because the Sagean Empire ruled all of it. Like everything else since the fall of the Empire, it was just another unresolved issue causing turmoil. Somehow, Ellaria knew that probably wasn't the meeting's purpose.

Most of the Coalition was still sore over the Free Cities of the New World and the autonomy given them after the war. Some of the ambassadors were eager to claim the territory and the resources. The court meeting was probably more trade bargaining and disputes, but that didn't explain why Delvette wanted Ellaria there.

As her stagecoach rolled on, she looked at the book in her hands that still lay open to the same page for the past hour. She wrinkled her nose at the words and adjusted her sitting position again. She glanced at the passenger across from her, who sat behind the driver's position. He had on a black suit with a black long coat neatly folded in his lap. His legs were crossed and he diligently kept his boots from hitting against the cabin's interior wood paneling when the bumps from the coach jostled them about. They were a polished black with a patterned overlay at the top, and clean, like they had just come from a box. His dark hair was neatly cut and he wore gold spectacles with shaded lenses. He was younger than Ellaria, if only slightly. Everything about him was precise and in order, but she had a feeling this was the nicest suit he owned. He sat too stiffly in it as though afraid to wrinkle or wear it in.

She pushed open the coach window to let a breeze pass through the cabin, the blast of fresh air was a pleasant relief. It became stagnant in the small coach compartment with more than one passenger. She had been lucky to have the stagecoach to herself for most of her trip through the valley. It had taken eleven days to reach Adalon from Eloveen. Before the Imperial Road, the same trip took twenty days and broken axles were common. When the rail was complete, the trip would take only two days. A comforting thought for Ellaria who relished the idea of crossing Tavillore quickly all the while staying on the ground.

They kept to a regimented travel pattern, always stopping just before dark. The Imperial Road had waypoint cities at regular intervals along the road to stop and rest for the night. Some were large cities and some only had a small inn and outpost. All of them had a fort tower with a stone torch basin at the top, burning blue throughout the night, and manned by at least three guardsmen.

It was unsafe to travel at night and unwise to stop between the waypoints. The deadliest beasts were driven out of the cities after the war; but the open country, forests and mountains were a different story. The wild beasts - the bonelarks, wolveracks and ravinors - prowled in the unsettled land preying on wayward travelers, livestock and even unprotected small dwellings. She had paid extra for a coach master with his own blast rifle due to rumors suggesting escalating activity of beast attacks, though the trip had been quiet on that front.

They had picked up the man across from her this morning at the last stop outside of the city. They hadn't spoken since their simple greetings when the man had introduced himself as Haden Mathis. Ellaria made a point not to talk too much, especially in confined spaces. Some people thought women talked needlessly. She found the real truth was that women were the superiorly intelligent beings, and men felt ashamedly unable to offer anything of meaning. The origin of any such a notion was simply a deflection of their own inadequacies. Though Ellaria did agree that it was in poor taste to prattle. She also lacked the proclivity for shining people on, as others did and could. She had a greater probability of annoying or angering someone. When Ellaria was younger, she would have already made this stranger into a great friend and ally. But she had lost that skill overtime. Age takes a lot from you and your patience is one of the first things to go. Besides, most conversations between strangers were typically so shallow *honestly what was the point*; however, seeing this man's lack of luggage and the journal he kept in his hand, she was curious to find out more. She closed the book in her hand with a snap.

"Excuse me, what time do you have?" She asked the man. He did not look surprised she had said something to him. *Had he seen her staring?* She hated that. She had a tendency to look at things intensely.

"Twenty-two minutes past the hour," he said, with a gruff edge to his voice.

"Are you going home to Adalon or to work?" she asked.

"Work."

"Ah, you're a professor then?" she postulated. Watching his eyes for confirmation she found her deduction had surprised him.

"I am," he confirmed.

"At the Arcana?" she followed up.

"Of course. Only the desperate seek learning at the Paravin Schools."

His view of the small trade schools that helped students find apprenticeships, was not unique, but something about his tone agitated her.

4

"Interesting. I've always found the ones most desperate to learn are the ones worth teaching," she said.

He scowled at her and turned his attention back to looking outside his window. Ellaria took that as a concession and smiled to herself. Then, he turned back to her.

"Miss Moonstone, I presume?" he asked.

"Yes, that's right," she said, slightly shocked by the redirect more than the recognition.

"Well, your reputation precedes you."

"I know. It's like a shadow I try to step on when I can. It can be elusive though," she said with a smile.

"Uh hum," he muttered and shook his head before turning it away again.

Apparently, he was a man not easily charmed, and the fighter in her wanted to keep sparring, but the carriage was passing over the Ash Gate and into Adalon City. The rattle of the wheels crossing over to the stone bridge clacked in repetition, and the cabin swayed with the transition. Ellaria put aside her rising disdain for this man to watch their approach. In many ways, it was the capital of the world. As one of the largest cities, it was also a scientific epicenter and the former location of the now abandoned Emperor's palace.

They passed by the brass held cylindrical gas lamps still holding a trickle of orange light in the glass, where a small amount of sodium vapor remained charged. The liveliness of the city was full of uniquely crafted charms, glowing glass spheres, brass clockworks, and rotating stair lifts with giant powered wheels.

Adalon City was built at the heart of the Mainsolis Sea, where the concave eastern seaboard cradled the Anamic Ocean, and two estuaries met the sea from the west. Four hundred years ago men had connected the two rivers with a spillway off the western rise. The artificial spillway was mostly a shallow moat dwarfed below rocky cliffs and towering city walls. The walls rose high with the land, and higher still as a stone fortification, and at various points along the wall, water flowed out of the city and into the moat below.

Her coach crossed up through the bands of various beltways spreading from the city center. The streets that encircled the city, like rings, were crowded with small steam powered dollop cars. They reminded her of a baby carriage with room enough for two passengers in a small shell sitting over the steam engine. The small contraptions were known to explode on long rides, but from the looks of it, they had become very popular within the city.

As they reached the heart of Adalon the shadows of the Prevalence Spires spread far across the streets. Three buildings of great renown; the Ascendancy Tower, which was the governing center, the Arcana University, and the Craftcore, a building devoted to scientific advancements and experimentation. All of them built of tungsten metal, stone and glass. The Craftcore was the employer of the world's foremost thinkers, tinkers, machinists, physicists, mathematicians, and alchemists. Buildings on the lower belts were just as large as the spires, not as tall typically, more sprawling, stoic and less grand.

The stagecoach pulled to a stop and both Ellaria and Mathis got out. She was glad to exit, and waved off the coach master's hand stepping down onto the cobblestone sidewalk. The air cooled against her back and legs where sweat lived under her garments.

She fixed her skirt and adjusted her black hat. It had a wide sweeping brim and a diamond crown with a green ribbon trim and colored feathers including a large green peacock's feather flowing backwards. Big cities of the world in these modern times were just a procession of hats, and she loved hers. Her dress was another matter. She preferred trousers, but they were terribly uncomfortable for traveling in the stuffy coach cabins. So, she wore a full black skirt and a fitted red blouse with black buttons, as was the fashion. The fit of the blouse was less than ideal, but she liked to portray a bit of attitude and flaunt how she was winning her fight against old age. The impending onslaught of her sixties were only a few years away, and she didn't think her fight would last much longer.

On the sidewalk, she cast her eyes around, assessing the atmosphere. Every place in the world had a different feel to it. The culture of the people dominated some, and some were dominated by the architecture or climate. Adalon city could have a different temperament every day. There was a feel to the hustle and chaos, a sound and a breath to the natural order. You could sense if something chaotic was in the air, or if the people were grumpier than usual. A quick observation told her the typical bustling city was in a casual beat– grumpy and preoccupied. The smell of baked bread lingered in the air from the bakery a few paces off and overtook the typical stale smell of metal and stone that the city always had near the core, where the smell of the sea didn't wash it out.

"Ms. Moonstone, we will deliver your baggage to the address you gave us. Is there anything you need from out of your luggage?" the coach master inquired.

She double checked her leather handbag, shook her head no, and handed him a small bag of talons for his service. The amber coins glinted in the light as she tipped him extra. They had mostly left her alone, and she appreciated that. A hint of cigar smoke passed in the air and she turned to find the source, but couldn't locate it and wound-up catching Mathis watching her.

"You don't stay in the consulates housing in the Ascendancy Tower?" he asked.

"No, I don't enjoy being so easily called on," she answered him, more aggressively than she meant to.

"I assume you're here for the coalition meeting?" he asked.

"I am."

"Well, enjoy your stay. I trust the meeting will be satisfactory."

"What do you know about it?" she asked.

"Oh, I wouldn't want to ruin the surprise. Good day," Mathis said and he tipped his black top hat and walked away down the block.

She had been containing her anxiety over the meeting and Mathis had just made it bloom. She needed to find her friend, Delvette, tonight before court tomorrow and see if she could tell her anything. Ellaria knew of a certain spot she frequented and headed there.

ELLARIA ARRIVED AT THE TWINES KNOT BAR JUST AS A GROUP OF ARCANA students were pulling out. Ellaria called them youngsters even though they were university age. When she was younger than that she was already entrenched in the Resistance efforts, which would soon be the Great War. She felt a slight tinge of jealousy at their youthful bounce and shine.

One of the young men bumped into her on accident and she lost a handle on her handbag, the contents dropped onto the cobbled stone road.

"Ander, you mule, you ran into her," a young man said. He had feathered golden blonde hair and was attractive in his youthfulness. It surprised Ellaria that he had stopped to jog back and help her pick up her things. The young were typically so indifferent.

"Sorry, Ander is slow of mind," he said, kneeling down to help.

"Well, I appreciate the assistance," she responded, taking the ruby fountain pen of hers from his hand. She noted his mechanical forearm wrap and assumed it was a weapon of some sort. Looking at him, she got lost in his calm and confident blue eyes. There was a pleasantness and an honesty to him.

"Again. I apologize for him. Of course, I think Ander would have been more careful and come back to help if he knew how beautiful you were," he said.

Ellaria laughed out loud; she had to in order to hide a blush from within. *Was he flirting with her?* For honest and nice, he was also cavalier. She was thrice his age. It was just flattery she supposed, but he had a bravado about him she appreciated; and she liked him instantly.

"Thank you, young man. You tell your friend to keep his head up, so he doesn't mistake a punch to the face for a handshake."

He smiled and said, "I will. My name's Wade, what's yours?"

"Ella," she said and almost gasped. *Why had she told him her first name?*

"Nice to meet you, Ella. We were just on our way to the Frog Leg Tavern down the block. Would you care to join us?"

"No. I'm meeting a friend here," she said with a smile.

"Here? Are you a professor?"

"No, now you should hurry. Your friends are leaving you."

"Oh, they'll save me a spot, I'm sure. Why don't you come? It's a friendly atmosphere, with poets and music too. Bring your friend. Or don't you believe in the pursuit of happiness?" Wade asked with a light smile that Ellaria was sure worked for him most of the time.

"To pursue something so fleeting, is a young person's game. Thanks for giving me a laugh, but it's time for you to run along."

"Well good evening to you Ella, I'm sure we'll meet again."

He smiled again. It was a smile that brightened his appearance more than she thought possible. Then he turned and jogged after his party, running past an older man with sideburns who leaned against the brick corner column with a cane and rounder hat. The man watched Wade through shaded spectacles as he jogged past and out of sight. Ellaria just laughed to herself as she walked into the coffee bar. She spotted her friend near the front, who was already standing up to greet her.

"Ella, how are you? I saw you out on the street and I got up, but you were talking with Wade Duval."

"That was embarrassing. Do you know that young man?" Ellaria asked.

"I've never taught him. I've seen him before and heard others talk about his skill with mechanics, and alchemy. I believe that was your area of expertise, remember Ella?"

"How could I forget?"

"Well, tell me you're ready to take me up on my offer, and I'll let it go."

"Sorry, I've been so busy trying to get the Southport University in Eloveen opened. I honestly hadn't thought about it."

"Would you consider speaking to our graduates or maybe an end of year seminar on alchemy?"

"No to the first, but I'll think about the seminar."

Delvette had been after Ellaria for years to teach alchemy at the Arcana. Ellaria would visit from time to time and occasionally do seminars, but she had never felt the calling to teach. They had been friends for almost fifteen years now, and Delvette probably asked every time they talked going back long before her appointment as the Scholar's Regent.

The Guild was set up after the war as the international institute in charge of education throughout the world, and had anonymity outside of the Coalition of Nations. The Regent was a position that sometimes-caused friction. Ellaria was seen as a radical by some and never was considered for the position. She had worried that her friend would be a pushover as Regent, but her soft touch had been successful.

"What are we walking into tomorrow, Delvette?" she asked her friend.

Delvette leaned closer into the table, "I've only heard rumors, mind you, and they're not good. The Coalition wants to elect a Prime Commander, and I hear that they're intent on finding Qudin Lightweaver."

"What!" Ellaria blurted.

"Shhh! I told you it's just rumors, but where there's smoke . . ."

"There's fire, yes. Well, they've been searching for Q for years. That's no secret. Why a Prime, they must be crazy? I can't imagine the Free Cities of the New World agreeing to this, there's no way Danehin won't fight it. If it is true, then I fear the influence of the Scholar's Guild may have slipped further than I thought."

"I'm not sure what the Peace King will make of it. I think they have grown resentful of his position, always keeping them in check," Delvette said, speaking of Danehin the ruler of the New World and the Coalition's most powerful ambassador.

Ellaria rubbed her temple with her fingers and brushed a stray hair away from her face before it dawned on her. "Thorns! If they're thinking of electing a Prime, does that mean they have found a new Sagean?" Ellaria asked.

"No, I don't think so."

"That's a relief. The only thing worse than a Prime Commander would be a new Sagean Lord, claiming divine right by the Light and mad with luminary powers. Wait, then why would the Coalition freely relinquish their power?" Ellaria followed up.

"Well, the Prime would only be in charge of the collective. Under the rules of the charter, each nation would still keep their power to govern their own lands. It's possible the ambassadors think we need a head figure to mediate the Coalition," Delvette suggested.

"Delvette, it's just a step away from another dictator!" Ellaria said sharply, and Delvette had a look of shame upon hearing her friend's outburst. "Sorry, old friend, you know how passionate I can get," Ellaria apologized.

"I understand you're frustrated Ellaria. I just think you forget how hard it is to navigate the Coalition."

"You're right. I could never handle the encumbrance."

"Are you using the people's word for us now too? Don't worry, Ellaria. Whatever happens tomorrow the Guild will maintain the rights you fought for."

"I hope so."

"You know, sometimes I think you should have been the Regent instead of me," Delvette said.

"It was never a possibility and you know it," Ellaria said dismissively, sipping her tea and wondering how differently everything would have gone.

"Only because you have to be so combative with the ambassadors. Our own guild is afraid of you sometimes," Delvette said.

"Delvette, you have to be the ever-present bitch they think you are. You can't cede any ground, or they will walk all over you," Ellaria replied. She still hoped one day her friend would grow a backbone, but feeling herself getting frustrated, she left the conversation at that and changed the subject. "I wanted to ask you. Do you know a professor named Haden Mathis?" she asked.

"Not personally. We hired him last year to teach mathematics and chemical calculations"

"I see. That's why he has a general disdain for alchemists then," Ellaria said.

"Probably. Most of the professors in the Natural World Department have only a modicum of patience for the other schools," Delvette agreed. "Why, how do you know him?"

"Oh, I had the pleasure of his company on the coach ride into the city," Ellaria said in her best sarcastic tone.

They sat at the modestly sized round table for a while catching up before Ellaria decided she needed to get some rest for the next day's trials. She couldn't stop thinking about why the council would bring her all the way here to tell her that the Coalition was going to elect a Prime. They knew she would be one of the strongest opponents. It was obvious they wanted her out, but by what means and why? She didn't have any real power beyond her reputation. She feared something else was going on.

It was getting dark on the streets as they said their goodbyes. The sun was casting a pink-orange glow across the wispy clouds, and a lamplighter was already working. The man carried two large poles. One for lighting the traditional lamps and one that he used to power the electric lamps. Ellaria watched as he used the staff's copper arch to spark and charge the metal jar capacitors that provided the electric current for the lamps.

Outside the bar's patio table and chairs, Ellaria and Delvette parted in opposite directions and she watched her friend walk away ready to retire for the evening. Ellaria noticed the man she saw before with sideburns was still lurking down the street. Still suspiciously lingering down the block smoking a small cigar. A short-walk cigar, as it was called, and there were more than a few at his feet. A sickening feeling that she was being followed settled in her stomach.

Ellaria turned up the street, and almost stumbled into the lamplighter working the corner. She passed him and chanced a glance behind her. The man had thrown his cigar and was chasing after her. She rounded the building corner and ran.

Her knowledge of this section of the city was good enough she believed she could make it to her apartment without an altercation. Rushing from block to block, she struggled to understand why she was being watched. Alone on the streets with night creeping in, she felt vulnerable. A feeling she despised.

She could tell Delvette had been holding something back, afraid to say anything more. Ellaria had tried to angle for additional scraps of information throughout their conversation as delicately as she could, but Delvette wouldn't bite. With what she had said and the realization that someone was having her followed, Ellaria decided she needed to send a message to her two closest friends. Wherever they were, she knew she could always count on Kovan and Qudin.

There were magnotype stations where she could send messages to different posts throughout all the major cities, but they were easily intercepted. She required something more covert. Also, she didn't exactly know where either of her old friends were.

Kovan was probably on some wild crusade fighting someone, or something, or dueling in Amara. Most likely he was in jail somewhere. They hadn't spoken in years, which was still painful to think of. It had been even longer since she had heard from Qudin. She knew that neither were dead, because both were too stubborn to die.

The secret messengers of the Whisper Chain were her best and only chance to reach them. Their vast network of spies could find people almost anywhere.

After circling around a few blocks of similar looking buildings, she found the door she remembered. With no sign of her pursuer, she stepped to the landing and knocked. It was a rather indistinguishable wood door with a small bronze placard embedded in the adjacent wall. Their symbol engraved – two flowing lines knotted in the middle. The door was a paneled dark stained mahogany with a gold knocker, but no handle on the outside.

A metal plate behind a screening window slid open and Ellaria saw only a set of eyes inspecting her. She caught her breath and showed them a medallion from her handbag. A woman opened the door wearing a high collar purple shirt, and Ellaria walked inside without a word being spoken. The amber medallions were impossible to replicate, difficult to come by, and hers was one of the oldest around.

Inside was dimly lit by lanterns hung on the walls. The floor was a wide plank hardwood with a fair bit of shine, and they had covered the walls with a patterned paper in dark-gray and gold filigree. She walked past the leather lounge chairs, that sat empty, and up to the exchange counter. The place smelled of oil, machinery, and warm glue.

"I have a package that needs delivered."

"By hand or by whisper?" the teller asked.

"Both probably, I need to send a message to a Thelmaria postbox and to Rylabyre, but location unknown."

"Thelmaria could be done by magnotype. Are you sure you want the Chain to do that?"

"Yes."

"Rylabyre, unknown. Trickier. But our hearing is very good out west."

The postmaster handed Ellaria two forms to fill out and a self-contained ink fountain pen. It was a fluted black metal and the ink streamed forth perfectly. She noticed for the first time how sweaty her hands were and wiped them on her leg before she filled out the forms and wrote her messages on the rolled parchment they provided. She handed the scrolls back to the postmaster behind the counter when she had finished. Reluctantly, the pen too. He took it without losing her eye contact and held out his other hand for payment. She paid and left.

Ellaria stepped back out into the streets. The night had taken hold, and she suddenly felt more exposed. The streets were mostly deserted and as she made her way to her quarter-house, the sound of her boots clacking against the cobblestone street pavers was like a beacon announcing her position. She wove in, and around buildings the best she could and through courtyards in a direct but obscure path to her residence.

She stopped at the corner short of her building and paused in the shadows of a set of brick stairs. Breathing fast, she peered around the brick half wall for anyone suspicious. Her building was an elongated mass wedged into the lot with the front ending in a large, rounded corner. While the apartments were on the upper floors, a small flower shop took up the first floor and always had beautiful storefront displays. When Ellaria decided that nothing looked amiss, she darted for the building quarters entrance. She passed through the lobby and rushed up the three flights of stairs to her room without incident.

She leaned up against the back of her door and slid down to the floor. Her heart racing, she felt oddly exhilarated. It was good to have her old blood pumping again. Being watched, sending secret messages, this was something she was good at. Her spontaneity may have dried up and fallen off like a useless limb, years ago, but somewhere inside she still knew how to be the general and war hero she once was. Tomorrow, she would have to go back to doing something she was bad at: convincing people to do what was right.

# CHAPTER TWO

## WADE

Wade leaned back in his chair, with his legs crossed and his feet propped up, carefully studying the cards fanned out in his hand. The Frog Leg Tavern was a good mix of stained wood, leather, energetic crowds and live acts. The ceilings, undercut by thick rough sawn wooden beams, spread out above him. The scrapes of the saw's teeth were visible in the joists that spanned low enough that a Hazon man would have to duck under them. Wade had found the tavern at the start of his first week at the Arcana last fall, but only decided to go inside this spring after passing by it at least twenty times. When you're new to a place it takes a long time to venture into strange buildings. Odd taverns or shops are daunting when you don't know the natural order of their inner workings. It was the funny sign out front that finally convinced him and his friends it might be a place for them. The tavern moniker was a frog biting its own leg.

This night at the Frog went as usual with the regular smattering of mostly bad but enjoyable entertainment playing to a cheerful crowd from the corner stage. Wade's friends maintained their predictable behaviors. Ander drank until he was half-rats and proceeded to run amok all night, heckling stage performers and somehow making friends with everyone at the bar. Lyka and Vargas argued and jabbed at each other constantly, while Wade and Stasia played the city favorite card game, Reckoner. Simultaneously, they passed the time by teasing each other in a game of deviant matchmaker, where each of them challenged the other to flirt with strangers of their choosing.

While Wade was friends with this group, they weren't exactly close knit. Of them, he only considered Stasia as his close friend. They had met a year ago on their way to Adalon and were friends ever since. Something about two scarred kids from the south coming to the grand city had bonded them.

"Are you sure you want to stay in the city through the summer?" Stasia asked and placed her card face up into her graveyard pile, keeping the new card, she drew in her reserves.

Stasia Mimnark was probably one of the smartest people Wade had ever met. She easily outperformed Wade in most of their studies, except Mechanical Dynamics. She had straightened blond hair which she tied back with small round clasps, leaving a short angular cut piece neatly styled just over her left eye and complimenting her soft triangular face. She had full lips and startlingly blue eyes. Wade thought she was beautiful, but he never told her so. She would say her favorite feature was her thin-angled eyebrows. Which made Wade laugh at the silliness of eyebrows being anyone's favorite feature. She was joyful and fierce, but sometimes let her insecurities affect her friendships.

Neither Stasia nor Wade, had much of a yearning to go back home when sessions ended in a week. They preferred to live in the Arcana's quarters instead. As he understood it, Stasia was content to never return home if she could help it. Wade didn't pry. One of the first things he figured out after leaving home was that family meant different things to different people. His own home was chaotic, but pleasantly so.

"Definitely. I have three brothers and two sisters. Besides my older sister Tara will be there, and it makes for a crowded house. I can only hope they help my parents on the farm without me. Besides, if I left, who would you annoy all summer?" he teased and drew a Zenoch's shield card. He replaced his sentry in the field and discarded it to his graveyard pile, with an audible groan from Stasia.

"I don't know why I play Reckoner with you, Wade. You are the luckiest person I know."

"What are you talking about? If the reckoning comes in the next spin, you win at the moment."

"It only looks that way. I know you're holding a resurrecting card in your reserves. Which one is it, the Tregorean healer or the Sagean, Herron the Wise?"

"I'm not looking to save any cards from the graveyard," he told her. Though he didn't have the heart to tell her his head card was a Sagean lord and essentially unbeatable. The game of Reckoner strategically deployed four cards in the field under the leadership of the head card. With one of the three unbeatable head cards currently face down on his side, he could essentially build the field for power instead of balance. The reckoning would come eventually on the spin of the action turner.

Stasia pulled a card and found it useless and discarded it straight to the beyond. Then she looked up with seriousness to her eyes, "Please don't stay in Adalon because of me," she said.

"I'm not, I promise. Now, Mims, how about the poet?" Wade asked. Stasia had reluctantly earned the nickname when Wade shortened her last name and found it annoyed her.

"Which one, the wordy one with dark hair?" she replied.

"No, the portly gentlemen with the beard."

"The one that rhymed 'gone with mom' and played the screeching flute at the end?" she said and shook her head in disgust, "No, no, and no. Besides, I think he was a comedy act not a poet."

Wade laughed, Stasia had a tendency to correct any inaccurate statement. "Well, your selection is dwindling by the minute, Mims. It's the flute guy or whoever that guy is that Ander's been talking with at the bar," he said. Stasia turned to look, but the many wood columns in the bar made it hard to see all the way to the back.

"I can't see him. I do see Harlow coming over, finally."

They had intentionally hung back to talk with their friend, Harlow, who they met the first night they came into the bar. She made the Frog feel like home. She wasn't much older than them but had a big sister sentimentality.

"Good, I'm tired of beating you at cards," Wade said as the reckoning eyes spun up. Neither played their reserves nor resurrected a graveyard card. So, Stasia revealed her head card as a Menodarin priest. It was a good card to lead her field, and if she had picked up a Luminary card at some point, she could have beaten him. He turned over his Sagean Empress with her shadow scepter and Stasia's face scrunched up and she came as close to cursing as he had ever seen.

"I hate playing with the Empire era deck. Those Lords of Light are unfair," she said. Wade didn't disagree, but he also knew she just hated to lose.

Stasia gathered the cards and slid them back into the action turner and set them in the diamond groove at the center of the wood table. Wade looked up to see Harlow joining them.

"Sorry guys," Harlow said, knocking Wade's feet out of the side chair and sitting down.

"Busy night?" Wade asked.

"Yeah, one of the new ones knocked over a stand and we were cleaning that up forever."

"We heard the crash. Sorry," Stasia said.

"I'm sorry, it's so late. Thanks for sticking around. I was dying to talk with you, Wade," Harlow said.

"Me?"

"Yes. I can't believe you were talking to Ellaria Moonstone."

"Who?" Wade asked, confused.

"When?" Stasia jumped in.

"Outside the Twine Bar up the road, when you guys were walking over here tonight. Do you know her?"

"Oh, the lady," Wade motioned, snapped his fingers and pointed at Ander. "Ander ran into her and I helped pick up her things. She told me her name was Ella."

"What?" Stasia blurted out.

"Yeah, why? Who is Ellaria Moonstone?" Wade asked.

"Ellaria Moonstone, you thickhead," Harlow said.

"The war hero, alchemist and pioneer for arts and science. She was a strategist and general in the Great War. She even fought in battles herself. Come on, Wade?" Stasia exclaimed.

"No way. That couldn't have been her. She looked way too young to have been a general in the war," Wade said, waving their words away with his hand.

"That's because she was the youngest general in the war," Harlow said.

"And she said to call her Ella?" Stasia said indignantly; Harlow just laughed.

"Wait, how do you know it was her?" Wade wondered.

"Because I know what she looks like. She visited the Arcana when I was there. A few times, actually. She also wears that amazing hat that no woman should be able to pull off, but she can," Harlow told them.

"What else did you say to her, Wade?" Stasia asked with a tinge of irritation.

"Nothing," Wade said innocently, trying to brush off the question.

"Oh no, you hit on her!" Stasia said. Reaching over and punching Wade in the arm.

"I . . . I was nice."

"You two make me laugh," Harlow told them, "Well, I have to get going," she said standing up.

"Us too," Wade said.

They all prepared to leave the tavern, with Ander still meandering in the back. Wade told Stacy, Vargas, and Lyka to go on ahead while he rounded up Ander. Wade just had to stop him from talking to the fellow at the bar first.

THEY LEFT THE BAR SOON AFTER THE OTHERS AND HEADED TOWARD THE residence halls. Wade had to tow Ander out into the streets with his hand partly pulling and holding up his friend who continued to chat with strangers all the way out the door. It was very early morning, and the sunrise was still some time away. The electric gas lanterns were dimming with the diminishing charge nearly exhausted. The faded orange glow barely lit the walks and road, leaving gaps of shadows between the lights. Up ahead, a man was approaching them on the otherwise deserted cobblestone street. He seemed to recognize Wade as he deliberately crossed over and headed toward him. He had sideburns and a rounded hat, and Wade was sure he did not know the man.

"What did she hand you?" the man demanded.

"What, who?" Wade asked, confused.

"Moonstone. I saw her hand you something," he repeated, and his body seemed to shake.

"I think you have the wrong guy. Go home and sleep it off," Wade said and proceeded to walk away, trusting the conversation was over. The man reached out and grabbed Wade's shoulder, with a fist full of Wade's shirt he tugged and turned him around. Ander perked up and shoved the man away.

"Get out here!" Ander sneered.

The man flourished his arms and coat, and something flashed in the darkness. He had drawn a short sword in his right hand and a long, curved knife in his left. Ander backed away as he didn't carry a weapon.

"Stop!" Wade yelled, and the man paused in motion and seemed to consider his options

"Hand over what she gave you. Was it a message?"

"I'm telling you – I don't know what you're talking about! Ander ran into her and I helped her up. That's all I know," Wade said while slowly retreating. The man muttered something under his breath Wade couldn't quite hear about returning empty-handed. Then the stranger made a movement toward Ander. Wade quickly put his hand to his right forearm and the mechanical gauntlet strapped there. He triggered the safety

18

release switch, and a short blade sprung out of the mechanism with a strident clang.

"Stop!" Wade yelled again.

The man froze at the distinctive ringing sound of the blade releasing from the gauntlet. Ander took the moment and moved behind Wade.

"Wade, don't," Ander mumbled at the back of his neck.

"If he attacks go get help," Wade said.

The stranger pitched and shuffled his feet, positioning to attack. Wade pushed Ander back with his left hand and turned the blade arm up in defense — just as the attack came.

The man came in high with his sword and followed it up with a strike from his knife. Wade clashed and swept away the sword's vault but had to jump back from the slashing knife. Fighting a duel-wielding opponent was not the same as someone with a single sword, a sword and knife combination were different still.

Ander ran off to get help. The clatter of his boots faded and left Wade's pounding heart as his last companion.

The man swung wildly, and Wade pivoted around him. The best way to fight a two-handed blade was to keep circling, forcing the second hand to overreach and maintaining only one active attack hand. The man attacked again and again, with simple forms and Wade deflected them.

So far, the strategy was working. Wade had little choice, he had to hope that he could keep up the volley until help arrived. Wade's gauntlet blade really was a defensive weapon. It was cumbersome and limited, making it hard to attack with it. Wade heard footsteps running on the stone toward them and tried to back away, hoping the man would see the others arriving and come to his senses and stop. They both looked over to the newcomers. Ander had returned with the tavern's peacekeeper. Wade thought his name was Enric. He slowed from a run to a walk and drew his sword.

"This is over . . ." but before Enric had finished his sentence, the stranger lashed out in an attack more ferocious and yet more focused than before. He swiped and made dash attacks at both Wade and Enric simultaneously, showing more skill than before. He swung hard at Enric with the knife, then spun and surprised Wade with a back-slashing sword. Wade raised his arm as fast as he could. Even blocked, the blow of force knocked Wade to the ground. Most of the blade clashed against his forearm gauntlet, except the finishing arch cut a long gash in Wade's arm just above his elbow. Wade screamed out in pain.

When he hit the ground, he immediately rolled away. At the same moment, Enric pressed his attack. Ander grabbed at Wade to help him up. Wade instinctively retracked his blade, so he didn't accidentally cut Ander, then peered back at the fight. Enric and the stranger clashed swords high, then the man dipped and slashed with the rounded knife, cutting into Enric's thigh.

Wade scrambled out of Ander's arms to help. He ran and tackled the stranger. The man's sword went clanging to the ground nearby as they collided on the stone street. Wade's arms hooked under the stranger as they rolled. Then Wade heard the unmistakable sound of his gauntlets release pin flip and snap. The blade sprang out in all its mechanical force. Right through the stranger's neck and chiseling off the cobblestone at the tip. Wade's panic peaked, and he disentangled himself from the man who now lay motionless. Wade unlatched the cuff from his wrist and the sudden pain of his own wound flared.

Ander rushed to Wade and pulled him away from the corpse. Enric was writhing and moaning in pain a few feet away. More footsteps came running their way, echoing in the cavern of buildings. Two greencoats had finally arrived on the scene, both carrying pulsators, one already drawn.

While one man attended to Enric, the other took Wade aside a short distance and left him by himself. Then he returned to investigate the dead man. He said a quick word to the other greencoat and came back to Wade. Wade answered his questions and explained the whole incident. After the greencoat went back and compared stories with his fellow officer, they let Wade go. They suggested he follow Enric to the hospital, but Wade insisted on going to the Arcana's medic instead.

Wade couldn't stop shaking as he and Ander walked back to the Arcana. Eventually, his breathing returned to normal by the time his key hit the lock on his room. He had a feeling he had just gotten in the middle of something he didn't want any part of.

# CHAPTER THREE

## KOVAN'S CELL

WATER TRICKLED ACROSS THE GRIME COATED CEILING OF KOVAN'S CELL where it pooled in the corner and dripped down to the cold moss-ridden floor, dripping incessantly. Each drop produced the same predictable soft patter of sound. It was so monotonously drab the sound seemed amplified and made his skin crawl. The prison was on the western cliff of the island of Ravenvyre in Rodaire. The salty ocean air from the Brovic below was strong enough to taste, but Kovan was grateful for it as it masked the fouler stenches. The horrible mix of human waste, body odor, and blood baked into the disgusting black stone was repugnant. It was a kind of moist smell that clung to his throat and refused to go away. It was enough to turn your stomach, and he wanted to retch but then he would be stuck sleeping next to that too.

The prison was built into the cliffside and you could hear the ocean waves break and crash against the rock below with a grunted rumble. There were no windows anywhere on the block, and the only light was cast from five lanterns that hung in the corridor on chains. Only three were lit. The lanterns were simple metal bowls and covered with years of spilled wax. The light from the candles flickered and danced, mostly just illuminating the raised ceiling where they were strung from one end of the walkway to the other. The west wind was loud as it wailed against the outside stone façade.The largest and most forceful gusts caused the hanging lanterns to rock sporadically. Their chains groaned softly with each sway.

There were eighteen cells on this block, nine in each row. One or two men in each. Kovan wasn't entirely sure. Most of the prisoners kept to the darkest parts of the interior. Kovan shared the third cell from the front. Of all the jails in the world that Kovan had visited, he knew Ravenvyre was supposed to house the worst one. At least the worst still in operation. The Coalition had closed the Red Dune in Echo Canyon after the war. Either way, this was certainly not the Ravenvyre pit. A small part of him was slightly offended. The way he looked at it, it was like dating an attractive woman who was slightly crazy. Yet, you always heard her sister was twice as dazzling. There was an allure there, but you were now sure the sister was definitely a complete lunatic, and it was best to stay away from the entire family.

When they brought Kovan in, they came through a hallway that split in two directions. Left or right, darkness concealed both. They had gone left, down a flight of ten steps and into a guard station room. It didn't have a window either. They took his long coat from him and escorted him to his cell. Kovan doubted they had stored much in that room. Getting to the room, finding his guns to shoot his way out would not be happening. He wondered what they *had* done with his pulsators. It had taken him quite some time to put them together and get them working just how he liked. They had the z-series magnetic flux inductors and brand-new electron flashtubes which were not cheap. The high-end modifications on the Alvir Elite pulsator body with a higher quality charged joulestone would've been perfect.

The small guard's room only had a table and chairs, two small cots, and two doors. One door to enter, and one to exit to the holding cells. A boarded oak with cross-wood construction made up the first door, and a man could break it down fairly easily. However, at Kovan's age he would probably break his foot or dislocate his shoulder. The inner door, the one to the cells, was reinforced with a metal plate. It would be much harder to bust. There was also no armory or wall hung weaponry, suggesting that the only weapons on the wing, were the ones the guards carried.

Kovan had counted nine guards when they brought him in. Two at the outside gate, one in the courtyard, two stationed inside the main entrance, two in the guard's room, one walking the corridor, and the one who walked him inside. All of them carried the same belt strapped thin-bladed sword with steel that subtly arched from the small circular guard to the straight cut tip. A meiyoma blade was not the most intimidating sword, but the Rodairean's took exceptional care of their weapons. He could be sure every blade could cleave and cut with ease, if put to use with bad intentions. He estimated six paces to the guard's room, ten more to exit the building. Maybe thirty paces to get out of the complex entirely.

A hundred feet to freedom. Kovan was sure they manned the courtyard with archers, though he hadn't seen them stalking about. It could be worse: he could be dating the insane sister.

They had put Kovan in a cell with another man though they had yet to speak to each other. He was of medium height and build, and they had worked him over. His swollen face was discolored with blood and dirt caked into his skin and beard. He had thick black hair, tan skin, and Kovan thought he was from Nahadon by the looks of him. The man sat to the far side with his head in his hands, while Kovan stood at the front bars to keep from pacing, with his forehead pressed against the cold, corroded bars of his cell. They smelled of chemical rust and felt like stalactite rock in his hand. Drip, drip, drip . . .

"Ok. All right! I did it! Now can someone fix this god damn water leak!" Kovan yelled down the corridor. Every drip was like a clock tick, it was maddening.

"They can't hear you, sayzon," his cellmate said from the darkness. Kovan glanced back at him, tilted his head, squinted, and remembered sayzon meant friend in the Zacaren language still spoken in remote parts of Zawarin. Then he went back to ranting.

"Someone! Anyone! Guard, guard, let me out of here!"

"Shut up, little man," a deep voice in a heavy accent echoed out from down the corridor.

Kovan adjusted his head to see as best he could to the cell down the hall and the giant shadow moving in it.

"Sacred death, you're a big one. What did they bring you in for, eating your village?" Kovan jabbed.

"Hazon's don't eat humans. T's a foul thing. The God Amadazumi would cast your soul to Daraku."

"Who is Amazuie?"

"Just be quiet, little man, or I will rip the bars off and put them through your head."

"Hey, hey big guy. Wait, is that really possible Gigantore? Tell you what, you get to breaking things, and I'll give you a free shot once we're out of here. Deal."

"You're crazy sayzon, that Hazon man will crush you," his cellmate offered.

"The Hazon's are rags!" Kovan exclaimed loudly and across the block. "They're just a lot of pus-filled, twig-collecting, sheep herders. They're weak."

"I'll show you, little man, who is weak."

"How Gigantore? How are you going to do that from a cell? Tell me when showtime begins so I don't miss it, Turd-Face."

"Have you ever seen a Hazon lose his temper?" his cellmate asked.

"Yes, I have," Kovan said unconsciously scratching at the gray stubble on his chin. Hazon was an island in the far north, on the northeast coast of Tavillore. The man was a long way from home, but so was Kovan. The Hazon men were not giants, though they were bigger than most men. Their land was harsh and beautiful with an abundance of monarch trees that grew to incredible heights. Each with forty-foot-wide trunks you had to walk around. Kovan had a lot of respect for their country.

He glimpsed back over to his cellmate and asked, "What's your name?"

"I am Erann Thanheralas."

"How about I call you Thann? Sound good?"

"It matters not."

"Well, Thann, what are you doing in Ravenvyre? Besides drowning in this cell with me, that is? What did they get you for?" By the man's slight accent, Kovan knew he had been right. He was from a land a thousand leagues to the south called Nahadon.

"I was here for trade, but the man I came to trade with stole my spices and refused to pay. I ask him to pay what's fair, but he kills my men instead. So, I killed him with his own sword."

"That sounds like the honorable response. Why did they lock you up?"

"The man was a prominent official's son. So, they put me in here and I'm sure they mean to hang me."

"Yeah, they're not fond of foreigners killing locals."

"Have you killed a man too?"

"I've killed my share. This particular entanglement, I broke Rodaire's stupid honor code when I shot the men down with my pulsators."

"Did they deserve it?"

"Not sure. Just a couple of road raiders I caught stealing a coach from a man and his daughters. The man wisely let them take his coach in exchange for his life. I heard the girls crying and stopped. They told me what happened. When I caught up with the raiders down the road. I gave them the chance to surrender. They made a bad choice."

"Why not just kill them with a sword?"

"I didn't know I was inside the border. Plus, I'm not the best with a sword, so I don't carry one. Besides, I…" Kovan paused as he heard the door at the end of the chamber open.

Two guards entered the walkway, one stayed at the door after it had closed and the second approached Kovan.

"Are you the one making all the racket?" the guard asked.

"Yeah, that's me and you're just the guy I wanted to see. Do you know who I have to talk with to get this cursed leak fixed?" Kovan asked and pointed to the gathering water.

The guard stared at Kovan for a moment, then struck him with the end of his club. The blow to Kovan's chest was minor, but only because Kovan had expected it. Better to let him hit Kovan through the bars, then to make him come into the cell. At least for now, Kovan played up the pain a bit, so as not to encourage more or worse. Wheezing and moaning while watching the guard's reaction. He didn't look to the other guard for help, and he didn't look around at the other inmates. He obviously enjoyed hurting people. The other guard didn't react either.

"Now be quiet!" the guard yelled and stalked away.

Kovan eased backward into the cell, wanting to say something else but not wanting to push his luck. He watched the guards return, the one that stood at the door knocked lightly on the door with three beats. The door opened. That explained why he had yet to see a set of keys. After the guards were back in their room, Kovan turned to Thann.

"So, do they always patrol in pairs, with one at the door?" he asked.

"Yes, there's always three or four inside the room too, beyond the door," Thann said.

"From what I can tell, we're only in their low security cells. I know these can't be the black pits I heard about," Kovan said.

"You're right. Those are through a different hall and down a set of winding stairs. Much further down then the stairs to these cells. They started taking me there two nights ago. Just as a riot in the pit erupted, they changed their minds and so they brought me over here. Lucky me."

"Ah, and lucky me, my new friend. Tell me about this riot and tell me what the guards did exactly? Don't leave anything out," He said, and he sat down with a wild idea forming that could get him out of there with hopes this stranger, who was also a murderer, could help him escape. Kovan always found himself surrounded by the strangest company.

SITTING ON THE GROUND IN THE DARKNESS, KOVAN HAD NO ACTUAL SENSE of time. When they walked him through, it had been just after midday, three days ago. When the guard's patrols tapered off, he assumed that was during the night, but it was tough to tell the difference between protocol and shift changes. As time wore on, Kovan settled on a plan of action, he just needed the right opening. He knew from talking with Thann there was a second level off a set of stairs in the right corridor, where armed men flooded out to deal with riots. A series of bells accompanied their scramble. Most likely a guard operated pull at the first sign of unrest, and not any sort of contraption or mechanism. Thann wasn't sure, he also couldn't say whether the alarms were set off for minor scrapes between cellmates.

While Kovan weighed the loose ends, the sound of the guard's door creaked open at the end of the corridor. This time, the soft puttering sound that shuffled towards him was from two sets of boots instead of the typical one. Kovan stood up in the cell when he was sure they were coming for him, but he kept to the recessed shadows. When the two intruders stopped outside his cell, he had to do a double take. One was a guard with a manicured black beard he had only seen once before upon his arrival. The other was a young woman with her face hidden under a black hood. The guard didn't say a word or even look at him, but the young woman approached the bars. For the briefest moment, he glimpsed her face and found her eyes were studying him, until she shifted her head slightly and hid herself into her hood again. She wasn't as young as Kovan first thought, but still she couldn't be more than twenty with her dark hair and dark calculating eyes, he figured she must be a local.

"Kovan Rainer?" she said in a soft earnest whisper.

"Yes," Kovan answered.

The young woman's hand came up to the boundary of metal bars. She was careful not to go beyond them. Her delicate fingers held a small piece of rolled parchment. Kovan took the message and the guard and young woman turned and walked away.

Kovan watched them walk back the length of the corridor and close the door before kneeling down to unroll the parchment. The ends of the roll were meticulously turned and tucked, and the edge was sealed with a purple wax stamp in the emblem of two strings knotted in the middle. He broke the seal and as it unrolled a small red crystal fell out into his palm. It was the size of a bean, and though it didn't shimmer in the candlelight, he could tell there was something inside. Kovan rolled the gem between his fingers and thumb, held it to his nose to smell it and then read the note . . .

*"In Adalon, someone's after me. I need you. They're going to dissolve the Coalition. Q still missing."*

*Ella.*

Kovan read the message over a few times, looking for any codes. When he was satisfied there weren't any, he moved over to the pool of water in the corner. Placing the red gem inside his pocket and the parchment inside the puddle. As he expected, the paper dissolved in a swirl. Then it dawned on him what the crystal might have inside and what it could do for him. A new plan formed in his mind. Ellaria had used the Whisper Chain to find him, so she must have been desperate. He needed to get to her, as he promised he always would if she needed him. First, he needed to get out of the cell.

# CHAPTER FOUR

## TALHALEANNA

Tali disliked delivering messages to the prison. The place was vile and the entire structure creaked and moaned on the cliffside, ready to fall apart at any moment and plummet to the ocean below. Between the smell and the darkness, she didn't understand how the guards worked there, but she was grateful for them. The cages were full of thieves and killers. Prison messages were the worst kind, but the chance to meet a living legend was too much to pass up, though she shouldn't have let him see her face. Tali had been trained to hide herself into her hood, to make quick glances. To look when others weren't. It was reckless, but there was nothing she could do about it now. She needed to hurry to get across the city and back to her link.

The streets of Ravenvyre were a rat's dream. A maze of colored stone roads weaving through jumbled neighborhoods and landmarks all over, all intersecting. There were unexpected dead ends and alleyways so narrow she could barely slip through them. To get around, Tali sometimes had to climb from roof to roof. The low sloping tiled roofs were easy enough to get on to, but dangerous to walk atop. The tiles had a tendency to come loose, so she learned to spot the vulnerable ones. Sometimes they already had cracks, or they were just slightly out of line, sometimes they had a water stain. All negotiable as long as you avoided all out running on them.

It was a habit she picked up as a kid, except now the sight of a grown woman of nineteen climbing on rooftops was awkward. Tali was still slight enough to move swiftly and light enough on her feet that the people inside didn't notice. Every once in a while, someone would poke their head out of a window after she had passed.

Mostly she navigated by the landmarks. The Sun Bridge to the southeast, the Ancient Palace of Redvine to the north, the Thunderbreak Cliffs to the west, and of course, the famous Amatori market to the South. That was where she needed to get to before dark, to help her mother cook for the dinner service. First, she had to get to the Clock Heart District, which was in the center of the island. The name came from a towering four-sided clock that rose high above a small courtyard of businesses, mostly crafting merchants, makers and tinkers. Her Link would be waiting for her there.

The Whisper Chain's network of messengers was established at the end of the war to deliver highly secure letters. It was rumored they used an alchemist's creation, called the melodicure, to find anyone they wanted anywhere, but the headquarters in Marathal were supposed to be well guarded. A single Link in the Chain employed her, and besides her Link, the only other member she knew was Maki. He was the courier captain who had trained her. Though Maki was probably not his name. Most Rodairean's had intolerably long first names and went by some shortened version of it. Like Talhaleanna. It was a mouthful, even for her. So, she went by Tali. Her Link knew her as Rue.

In Rodaire, her lower Order and her gender had closed a lot of doors. After watching her friends go away to universities or apprenticeships that took them off the island, she was happy to have a job. Before the Whisper Chain found her, she was spending most of her time pestering the tinkers in the hope that one of them would take her on as an apprentice.

She dreamed of going to the Arcana in Adalon, but until then, she lived with her mother and aunt. Constantly in fear she would end up just like them. Only worse, with no siblings, Tali would be an old lady drinking tea around an empty table, and she was too restless for such a fate. Her mother called her a searcher and said she should follow her instincts. Her mother was a very unselfish woman. Some mothers can be magnificent like that. She told her that the cleverest ravens are bold and listen to the pulls of the territh. Of course, ravens could fly, and Tali was stuck on the ground.

Being a messenger was simple and Tali found she was good at it. She could swiftly appear, hand off the message, and disappear. Without being remembered. Until today, that is.

When she had found out the message was for Kovan Rainer she was beyond excited to meet a true war hero here in Ravenvyre. Then when she learned he was being held in the prison she was confused and oddly compelled to act. Everyone her age had grown up learning about the war and the great war heroes like Kovan Rainer, Ellaria Moonstone, Maclin the Mad, Flynn the Silver Captain and of course Qudin Lightweaver. She couldn't just let one rot in jail.

To be sure if it was the actual Kovan Rainer, Tali had to look into his eyes. The eyes would tell her all she needed to know, and they did. It was all there as she imagined. His gaze was calculating, and full of the fire and energy Tali expected. They were also full of shadows, and the cracked age lines added to a haunted weariness and exhaustion in them. He was a man with a past and his eyes couldn't hide that.

Moving swiftly through the alleyways she emerged into the Clock-heart courtyard to find it more crowded than it should have been with people gathered around something in the square. When Tali was close enough to see the source of excitement, she realized it should have been obvious. An argument had escalated into a duel, again. She shook her head and grimaced trying to decide which party disgusted her more, the duelers or the blood thirsty crowd.

It had taken her most of the afternoon to get back here from the prison and she needed to be quick. Tali's mother would be starting the dinner service soon by herself, and Tali would never hear the end of it. Which meant cleaning duty.

Her Link, Daric, stood with his back against the red brick tower, tapping his silver cane against the surface. He wore a low rounded black hat with a short brim and a black coat with a high collar. She neared and leaned against the adjacent side of the tower. Above her the notches and flutters of the exposed brass mechanisms omitted a steady clatter.

"Message delivered," she said.

"Any problems?" Daric asked without looking up.

"None, other than the stench."

"Rue, bad men smell."

"Those did."

"Did the guards require the entire payment?"

"No, I talked them into it for less than the sum."

"Good for you. Consider that a bonus."

"A bonus? Maki told me to never accept a bonus. There's always strings attached."

"No strings."

"Even so, here," She reached into her cloak and reluctantly handed Daric a small coin purse. He eyed it and took it. Then she pointed to the crowd. "Are you going to do anything about that, or just watch?" She asked.

"What is there to do. Men duel, and men die. I don't see the problem."

"I'm sure you don't. Farewell Daric," Tali said, lifting her back from the masonry to leave.

"Until next time, Rue," Daric said.

"Sure," Tali said, and strolled over to the crowd. Rodairean's were always quick to clash swords and you couldn't stop every one of them, but the size of this crowd had her worried that the violence could transform into destruction that might carry into the tinker shops she so dearly loved.

She took a deep breath and exhaled a grunt of annoyance before squeezing through. She had to nudge herself within the throng to get to the men arguing inside. It was fairly easy for her with her slender frame but maneuvering around shouting strangers was unpleasant. When crowds became blood thirsty like this, the people at the very front were there because they wanted to fight as well. The promise of blood was as a proxy for the caged violence in the spectator's hearts. Duels serviced the worse parts of human nature, best summed as violence excusing violence. It was an ugly sight and she needed to avoid aggravating them if she had any hope of stopping this thing.

The two men in the center who had been shouting at each other stammered, their curses catching in their throats, as Tali appeared. She could tell by the look of them, their short coats, unbuttoned sleeves and scruff, that they were gamblers from the gaming den nearby. One man already had his meiyoma blade drawn. Tali addressed him first.

"What's the problem?"

"Get out of the killing ring, girl," the man spat with rage clouded vision.

"You two can duel and both kill each other for all I care, but could you leave the Clock Heart to do it?"

"Get out of here I said!"

More shouts from the angered onlookers cursed her to leave and let the duel commence, but she ignored them and tried a different tactic, "If you fight this fellow, you will lose. Trust me. So why are you determined to die at this man's hand?" She asked.

The man with his weapon drawn, scowled, "How do you know he will beat me?"

"He has four maybe five inches of height on you and more importantly he hasn't drawn his weapon yet. He has no fear of you. You would see this if you weren't blinded by anger. Again, what's the transgression?"

"This lout stole coins from me at the den. He denies it, but I saw him pocket my amber."

"I did not. Why don't you dry-up, you stoneless death-worm?" The second man called out.

"How much?" Tali asked, her voice rising above their jabs.

"Two talons."

Tali sagged her head and took a deep breath. Death over two talons was idiotic. Still if a few talons from her own pocket kept this mess from playing out, she was happy to pay. Besides she adored the patterned tile of the square and hated to see it blood stained. Tali moved to an equal distance between the men, contemplating how best to trick them.

"Right, here's what we're going to do," she said, and pointed at the accused, "You."

"Mazer," he said.

"Mazer. I'm going to do my friend over here a favor. You see, I'm an alchemist's apprentice and I have a few magical abilities and I hate to see this man die when I could do a simple spell and solve the problem," Tali said. At the sound of the words, alchemy and magic, the crowd began to quiet and pay closer attention. The quizzical look on Mazer's face made her nervous, but up to the ankle, up to the nose, as they say. So, she pressed on.

"All I need is one of the amber coins you're accused of stealing. I will use my abilities and turn it into three. Therefore, you both get your money, and no blood gets spilled in the square."

Mazer laughed and shook his head. At first Tali thought he was going to deny her, but he reached in his side pocket and retrieved the coin.

"Here, but only because I'm curious to see you fail girl."

Tali took the coin and slid it into her right hand. With a retention move and flash of her hand, she kept the coin in her right hand but appeared to move it to her left. Shifting the coin behind her fingers and out of view. The sleight of hand tricks her father taught her as a kid coming in handy. One of the few things she recalled about him. Then she waved her open hands to show that the coin had disappeared. She snapped her fingers and clapped her hands. Clasping them tightly together like she was massaging the coin. Then quickly pulled her hands free to reveal two coins. The men stared at her and the one named Mazer laughed louder. She flicked him back his original coin and did the flourish again. Producing the third coin. She walked back to the first man and held them up.

He eagerly went to grab them, but she pulled back slightly and motioned for him to sheath his blade. When the exchange was made. The accuser seemed satisfied, and the tension left his shoulders. The crowd started to disperse, some with resentment for having their entertainment taken from them.

Tali swiftly tried to file out of the square, careful not to appear like she was in a hurry, even though she was. In the scattering, she could see Daric still watching from the tower. She left the square with empty pockets but breathing easier.

About an hour later, she reached the Amatori Market, and the colorful patterned lanterns that strung back and forth between all the merchant tents and food stands. The market had everything from food grains, and spices, to elixirs, candles, trinkets, small – geared devices, jewelry, and clothing. There was even a crystal and gem merchant, who had the best selection of gems outside of the Jade District where the alchemists clustered in the north of the island. He even carried joulestone crystals that could hold an electric charge. Though Tali preferred the tiny hollow glass jewels like the one she slipped to Kovan, called verium crystals. Once smashed, the crystalline – glass structure broke down into mostly a fine powder.

All and all, Amatori Market was the place to find the strangest things from all over the world. Though not from the west, across the Brovic. No one sailed the Brovic Ocean past the Dire.

Tali crossed the intersecting paths to her mother's stand, avoiding the patrons filing in. The market was always packed, but especially at night, when the lanterns were lit and all the food stations were firing. She walked to her mother's food stand and found her mother beginning to clean a large butterfish. The silver and golden scaled fish had big black eyes, green fins, and a mouth that went up in a sort of grin. When Tali cleaned them, a mess inevitably unfolded, with the shinny scales going everywhere with each scrape.

Tali smiled at her mother and hurriedly removed her cloak. She washed her hands in the small basins and quickly pinned her black hair back. Then she presented herself ready to help. Her mother nodded toward the large pan, as an obvious gesture to start the noodles. Instead, Tali pointed at the knife in her mother's hand. Because as much as Tali disliked preparing the fish, her mother loathed it. It was a small gesture to say she was sorry for being late.

A classic scowl crested her mother's face but then she shrugged and handed Tali the long thin serrated knife. The fish laid there on the board, smiling up at Tali. She lifted the cold butterfish up by the gills, apologized, and sliced into it.

# CHAPTER FIVE

## LEARON

The crickets were chirping and the blackbird's song whistled as the sun crested the mountain and over the tree line, where Learon slept. He heard the sounds of the morning robins and the leaves in the trees around him rustling, but it was the grass beetle on his neck that woke him up. Swiping at the insect, he sat up, opened and closed his eyes a few times to adjust his sight. The smell of the fresh tree bark and wildflowers awakened his senses. The harmless pebble-sized beetles were a nuisance prevalent in this part of the West Meadow woods. Last night, he had wrapped himself in his traveling cloak as he slept, to keep the bugs out. There usually weren't too many insects in the night, if a person knew what trees and ground to avoid sleeping nearby. The grass beetle was inescapable, though.

A day ago, he had hiked into the mountain from Garner's lodge. The lodge rested at the foot of White Hawk mountain outside the mouth of a ravine. Learon had left his horse there to hike in on foot, as the terrain required. It was a hike he had made many times. His father brought him when he was young. After his father died, when he was eight, his uncle began to bring him. When his uncle injured his foot and could no longer hike in, Learon started coming up by himself. Even with his experience in the woods, it was foolhardy to venture in alone. There were plenty of beasts more dangerous than bears or mountain lions here.

He had come up this time to retrieve something from his father's old hunting cabin. While he was at it, he hoped to harvest a buck and haul it back to town. Selling the meat would get him the extra money he needed to make it to Adalon. Learon was determined to gain access to the archives of the Arcana and research his father's shipwreck. The silva-meat of large free roaming animals had become more and more lucrative since the war forty years ago, when beasts invaded the natural habitat. The beasts people thought were myths, attacked Resistance soldiers; and after the war retreated all over the country, into the thick forests and the mountains. The challenge was not in avoiding the beasts on the hunt but bringing the catch home. Most of the beasts were smart enough to avoid humans, but blood attracted them. You had to either field dress your animal on the spot or carry it out in a transport litter by wrapping it tight in something to mask the scent. Field dressing on the spot was difficult. It was not something you wanted to rush, but you had to be fast and then be on your way. The harvesting site would usually attract the beast first, but you could bet they would pick up the scent. Either way, you had to take special care not to injure yourself.

The West Meadow Woods had both wolveracks and bonelarks, but not the more deadly ravinors. Learon was more familiar with the wolveracks. They were larger than a typical wolf by two and the hair on their head and mane was full and wiry, but the hair from their chest to their tail was short. They were gray, almost green colored, and their tails were almost three feet long. But it was their eyes that stuck with him; the yellow eyes that seemed to glow with rage.

After getting up, he dusted himself off and checked his field wiring. The line was taut, and nothing had moved it. Learon always set a warning wire around his campsite to feel more protected. The only thing known to keep the beasts away were campfires burning either anthracite or drooping pine bark. The anthracite was a hard black rock that was difficult to ignite but it helped sustain the fire embers all night. It didn't give off any smoke, but it produced a blue flame and almost no discernible smell to humans. All travelers carried it or the pine bark, and it made packs cumbersome. Curiously, the drooping pine bark also gave off a blue flame, but because it was a soft wood, the pine burned quickly, and you had to keep throwing on bundles throughout the night. Everyone had their preference, and Learon preferred the anthracite when he wanted a long night's sleep. People who preferred the drooping pine believed the smoke and smell helped safeguard them. In Learon's experience, belief and truth rarely shared the same reality.

He quickly disentangled his dull silver wire, assessed the site for tracks and retrieved his supplies. Learon relied on the essentials for hunting that his father taught him: mask your smell, know your terrain, and play the wind. He had a large two compartment bag that strapped to his back. It was a soft, worn green color he got specifically for hunting trips as it had nice leather straps that stored his bow and quiver on the outside face. Out of habit, he checked the bend in his bow and adjusted the arrows in the quiver before attaching them to the pack. With everything sealed up for the hike, he hefted the pack over his shoulder and re-tightened the brown leather belt to his hip sword before heading out. The hip sword annoyed him as he hiked the incline of rock and tall grass. It was extra weight and restricted his movement, but he still set a pace he thought would allow him to reach the cabin in four hours.

THE SUN WAS GETTING INTO THE BLUE, THE MIDDAY HOURS WHEN IT WAS highest in the sky, and Learon had been hiking up the north slope for most of the morning. Sweat had collected on his neck and forehead. He wiped his brow with his arm and shirt, then he rolled up the sleeve past his elbow. Cresting the ridge, he had come to the clearing he was looking for. A beautifully tucked away corner of the world. Just a day and a half hike from the ravine's mouth where the mountain plateaued and cradled a small meadow. There was a lake at the center and a lot of natural grasses, greener than elsewhere on the trail. His father's cabin sat nestled in the back with a small grouping of trees.

The timing of his trip meant he would need to get to the cabin today. Then to the hunting tree tomorrow, an hour before the sun rose. If he wasn't in his spot by then, he would be out of luck. Most of the animals would be up, moving around at the first sign of brightening. Learon knew how to be slow and how to take measure of each movement. The moment can move extremely fast, only slow, deliberate, soft movements can withstand the currents of time. Learon had developed a gift for it and felt at home amongst the trees.

Inside the meadow the first thing Learon saw was the bright sun shimmering off the surface of the small lake. His father had called it 'the pool'. One of the oldest memories Learon had of his father was camping in the night up here. They sat on the bank of the lake discussing how the moon reflected off the still surface water of the lake. His father said the moon swam in it like a pool and they called it the pool ever since.

As he delighted in the moment's serenity, Learon realized the woods were eerily silent here and his instincts told him something was amiss. The side slopes surrounding the meadow usually put a slight amplification to the birds and wind. Then he heard the low-muffled, howling growl of beasts in the distance, wolveracks.

Learon kicked himself for not noticing their howl before getting up here. It was a distinct growl, and ravenous sound, like a high-toned dog's growl. He quickly unsheathed his sword as silently as he could manage. It was as old, dull, and plain a sword as swords came and he wasn't much good with it. He scanned around but found no immediate threat. Unmistakably, the sound was coming from across the lake near the cabin. He slowly walked closer to the shore to see across the other side. It wasn't a big lake, but the distance was far enough that he could only just make out the wolveracks.

They were scratching relentlessly at the cabin's exterior wood slats. Their claws dragged across the weathered wood in a louder peel than their howl. They had obviously trapped something in the cabin they wanted very badly. Learon needed to end their howls quickly. Regardless of whatever animal they trapped inside, the howls would bring other wolveracks. They were not a diplomatic species.

He scanned the side slopes of the surrounding landscape for options. He spotted a grouping of rocks he thought might give him a good vantage point, and a good wind for a bow shot. He sheathed his sword and armed his bow, nocking a heavier high wind arrow from his quiver. Holding both the arrow and bow in his left hand, he stalked into position as swiftly as he could without causing notice. His heart pounded in his chest. The collection of rocks were big enough for stabilizing his body and hopefully his shot.

As he got closer, he could see one of the wolveracks had its head through a broken hole in the wood door. It had scratched and chewed away a small hole, but the jagged splinters of the wood cut into the beast as it jammed its head in. The other one bounced around behind it. Their long tails whipping furiously.

The key to bow hunting was patience, which he didn't have the luxury of here. He needed to make his first shot count. The wolveracks were bloodthirsty. The wind was at Learon's back, blowing toward the beasts. They would soon smell him if they hadn't already. He needed to take his shot before their interests changed. He wanted to shoot the one farthest from the cabin first. Since the other one at the door, was too ensconced to attack him. But the one in back was moving frantically. He quickly aimed for the one at the door.

Decision made.

He wiped the moisture from his palm, pulled the arrow to cheek and chin. Took a breath, exhaled, and released.

The arrow struck the wolverack in the high side of its mane, it stopped gnawing at the door and slumped to the dirt. He hoped it was a heart kill. Learon reached for his sword, expecting the other one to turn and attack him, he planned to use the rocks to help his defense. Instead of attacking him though, the second wolverack grabbed the one slumped at the door. It sunk its jaw into its back with a wet crunch. It ripped and growled, and drug it away from the cabin. Then, it too, bounded into the cabin door. Learon nocked a second arrow.

Aimed. Exhaled. Released.

The arrow struck the second wolverack a fraction lower in the body than the first, in the beast's short-haired middle back. It yelped, staggered backward, and away from the cabin door. It finally fell about ten feet away. Learon put his bow around his shoulder, grabbed his sword, and slowly descended from the rocks to investigate.

Learon had been with others when they had taken down a wolverack, but had never done it himself. A hunting party tracked two into the woods last fall after the wolveracks had killed some livestock and a horse at a farm near town. Those had taken two arrows to bring down and the hunters quickly stormed the beasts and drove swords through them to make sure they were dead. Learon warily approached the cabin and the beasts. As he drew closer, he heard sounds coming from inside the cabin. Someone was inside.

He tried the doorknob, but the door was jammed. He threw his shoulder into it, and it gave on the second attempt, the beasts had been close to getting through. The door slammed back against the cabin wall and rattled some contents. Learon came through the opening with his sword out front.

A man was on the floor, half-hunched up against the far side wall. His leg was bleeding, and a trail of blood smeared the floor from the door to where he laid. He was alive and struggling to sit up with one hand. His other hand was outstretched in defense with his fingers stretched wide, he winced like the sun was in his eyes. As Learon studied him, there was a movement from behind.

The second wolverack was back on its feet and charging at Learon. He turned and moved inside the cabin. The wolverack reeled up on its hind legs like a bear and swiped at him with its long claws. Learon's heart hammered, he retreated frantically backward and tripped over something in the cabin and tumbled to the floor. His head hit with a smack and his eyes closed in reflex. A white light burst in his vision as he impacted the floor. He felt a rush or vibration in the air and then he heard the beast crumple. Learon rolled and bounded up back to his feet, grabbing the sword he momentarily dropped when he hit the floor. Without a second thought, he drove the point of his sword through the wolverack. Then he stepped outside and drove it through the other one for good measure.

"We need to hurry, kid. More will be on the way," the man in the cabin spoke, his voice was gruff and muddled and he obviously needed water.

"Let me find something to wrap your leg. Then we'll see if you can walk," Learon said, and he bounded over to the lone cupboard in the cabin. There was always a bandage and ointment in there, but almost nothing else other than a pan and a fishing pole. He grabbed what he needed and walked over to the man to treat him. He cut away the blood-stained pants first. The wound appeared bad, but not life threatening. Not yet anyway, but Learon was no expert.

"Thank you, kid," he said, and then gestured toward the door. "In my bag there's some water."

Learon retrieved the water from the bag and returned, handing it to the man. He drew a small sip and gave it back.

"Clean the wound before dressing it," he told Learon.

"Right," he said.

After they dressed the wound, he helped the man to his feet.

"Sorry it's the best I can do. Can you walk?"

"Yes, but not fast."

"I saw a long branch out there you can use for support."

Learon had a thousand questions for the man, but now didn't seem like the time for discussing them. He helped him out of the small square cabin and pointed the direction of their best route out of the meadow.

"See the point where the two slopes meet on the other side of the lake? That's our path out of the meadow and down the mountain," Learon said.

He turned and went back into the cabin, stepping over the dead wolverack just inside the door, where dark blood pooled on the dirt-covered wooden floorboards. He went to the single bed in the corner and moved it out of the way. Using his boot knife, Learon started prying at a floorboard there by placing his knife point in-between two boards. Digging his knife into the hilt, he levered a board free and then another. He replaced his knife and reached into the hole to the dirt below. His entire arm stretched below the floor until the wooden boards dug into his

40

armpit. He extended out with his fingers, but all he could feel was damp dirt. Finally, he found something at the tip of his pinky finger. He moved his hand until he could grab what he was searching for, stuffed it into his pack, got off the floor, and left with the stranger.

THEY HIKED IN SILENCE, NOT WANTING TO GIVE AWAY THEIR POSITION ANY more than they already were. Descending the mountain back toward Garner's lodge, with one man carrying two packs worth of gear and another lame, minimizing their sound was a chore. The sun had already slipped over the summit above them, and now the last rays of sunlight were disappearing in the sky. With the light waning, Learon knew their progress would slow. He had not spoken to the stranger since leaving the cabin. Instead, their communications were resigned to small hand gestures and head nods. Learon would point out the best routes or he would flash the man a thumbs up from time to time to check on him. The stranger always nodded yes in reply. Learon took it as confirmation to keep going.

For an older man, with a leg that had been chewed-on by one of the most wicked beasts in Tavillore, he hiked without being winded and showed no sign of pain. No winces or grunts escaped his throat, and Learon had been watching him closely. He suspected he was the same age as his uncle, but his face told the story of someone much older. Not in its ruggedness, but its weariness. There were a few moments where Learon could hear his breathing, not the sucking of wind from exhaustion, but the sound you make before you release an arrow. A calming, steadying of his breath. He had messy gray hair that sometimes covered his eyes and Learon hadn't noticed at first, but the man had a second injury marked by a bandage wrapped across his palm and wrist, though it didn't show any blood staining.

With darkness coming on, the bugs started coming out. The sounds of the woods crept in on them, and their own footfalls seemed louder as the coarse ground crunched under the weight of their steps. Learon checked on the man again, and again he received a reassuring nod to keep going. He was initially afraid the man wouldn't make it down the mountain, and now he feared the man was pushing himself too far. They had already traveled further than Learon thought they would, passed through the ravine where a grove of wild, twisted pine trees grew. It was a marker of sorts that Learon used to gauge how far they still were from Garner's lodge. Curiously, in the middle of the twisted trees, the stranger paused. Learon thought that they were finally going to stop, but it was only momentary, and they kept pushing on.

Learon's legs had grown heavy and only his focus on the next step kept him from calling for a stop, but his mind started to wander. Overhead, the moonlight filtered through the tree bows to the dirt below, and he thought about how he would need to find another way to fund his journey east. He was coming home without the buck he had planned, and a hobbling old man instead.

He thought about his mother who had fallen ill and began slowly losing her mind two seasons back. How she had waited to give Learon his father's journal. She must have waited because of the things it hinted at. When she gave it to him, Learon had been furious. It had felt more like she had kept him in the dark. Looking back, he couldn't believe the horrible things he said to her. After all it was her husband's journal. He had no claim to it, and his father addressed her in almost every entry. In his father's lonely hours, when he sat down to write, she was always ever present in his mind. It was his way of continuing conversations they were having, or new ones he meant to have with her later. It was probably her most cherished possession, and Learon had actually been mad when she shared it with him.

Learon supposed that meant he shouldn't sell this thing he had just risked his life retrieving from the cabin. He didn't actually know what it was or what it did. His father's journal was cryptically vague about it. Learon wasn't sure he cared what it was, anyway. He was far more interested in the suspicious nature of his father's death than artifacts from his father's last excavation. Some passages from the journal were always on his mind . . .

\*

. . . We don't know a lot, Cara, but I can say we know for sure there are great energies in this world capable of many things. We are certain the ancients knew a lot more about these powers than we do. Why that knowledge was lost is unknown. I don't think we lost it, Cara, I think it was kept from us. It seems likely it was the lone reason for the last thousand years of oppression by the Sagean's. From the things we found in our dig, the ancients had crafted things from and for these energies. I think the Zosmus text is true. There were five amulets held originally by five guardians. I think we've been studying one here, but the one we have is cracked beyond repair. Large chunks of the blue azurite are missing. Some of these artifacts have amazing properties, but we don't know yet how any of them work.

- 5th of Shadal, 44e23

. . .Cara, I'm getting worried about our project. The coalition doesn't know we are working on it. I ran into our friend Lavaren Brugo and he didn't know what I was talking about. How can the Scholar's Guild Regent not know?

- 29th of Shadal, 44e23

. . .A man came in today asking about our research. Specifically asking about the artifacts and our experiments with them. I got the distinct impression he was looking for a certain one. The one I told you about. I don't like the gentleman. I think he's from the Citadel. At least I think he's military. He's got a pleasant smile, but when he looks at me it's like he's looking through me.

- 18th of Savon, 44e23

. . .The one artifact that fascinated me the most. I think it's in a safe place now. Where the light and the shadow can't touch it, asleep in the meadow by the pool of the moon.

- 25th of Savon, 44e23

. . .The man came back today. Stalking through the halls with his black cloak billowing out. His eyes are soulless, Cara. He was furious about the accident, and he didn't believe that some things were destroyed completely. Hopefully, this means I'll be coming home soon.

- 3rd of Deluand, 44e23

\*

WHEN THE MAN FINALLY PUT HIS HAND OUT FLAT IN A GESTURE TO STOP, Learon nearly missed it. His brain and body were in a sort of sleepwalking state by this point, and it took another three paces before everything snapped back.

"I can't go any further," the man said. Then he walked over to the nearest tree and scavenged wood for a fire.

"Good me either," Learon said. He had been carrying a lot of weight for a long time and his shoulders ached. He retrieved his flint and the anthracite.

When they had gathered the wood for the fire, Learon arranged it into place, got the fire started, and then got his bedroll situated.

"Do you think we're safe now?" Learon asked as they settled into their spots opposite the fire.

"From the wolveracks, yes," he said.

"My name is Learon, what's yours?"

"Elias,"

"Well, Elias, I have a thousand questions for you."

"Sure, I owe you that and more for back there. Thank you. I'm usually good at not finding myself in such a compromised state. One condition though."

"What's that?"

"Do you have a white quartz stone on you? Most hunters have them for luck."

"Yes, of course. Why?"

"Can I borrow it for the night?"

"I guess so, I'll want it back, but why? Do you think it can help heal you?" Learon questioned. He reached beneath his shirt and pulled a necklace out. It was a tanned piece of thin leather knotted at one end and cross tied over a white quartz crystal about the size of his eye. There was a faint shine to it even in the dark. There was an old myth that it brought luck or health, and hunters more than most carried them. Learon walked it over and handed it to Elias. He took it with a nod of appreciation.

"Something like that. Sometimes, myths are just truths we've forgotten," Elias said, and laid back to stare at the stars above, "Go ahead, ask away. But I have to warn you I'm tired, I might fall asleep."

"Right, well first, how is your leg?"

"It will be fine, still have full movement. I was lucky."

"What happened? How did you find yourself in that cabin chased by wolveracks? It's not an easy place to find."

"I was up near Hawk's Perch, further west. But when I got there, I was feeling extremely sick and dizzy," Elias said.

"That makes sense, it's very high up there."

"Yes, well, while making my way down, I ended up slipping on the shale slopes. Tearing this long gash in my ankle in the process."

"Oh, I thought you had been bitten?" Learon asked.

"No. If they had bitten me, I would be much worse off. Either way, I was in terrible shape after the fall and then the wolveracks came. So, I scrambled down the mountain as fast as I could. I came over a short ridge and saw the meadow and the sunlight reflecting off the lake. When I got to the meadow and spotted the lodge, I figured I would make my stand there. That's when you found me."

"A stand? I didn't see you had a weapon?" Learon asked. Elias slowly rolled to the side and flipped his coat away to reveal a short skinny sword at his hip. Learon had never seen anything like it. The whole sword couldn't have been much over two feet long, and the hilt was a good third of it. The cross guard was only a small round lip, and the blade had a patterning in the steel. Elias had it hooked to his hip, upside down from his waist up. With the tip up to his shoulder, it was strapped in place by an odd-looking clasp. Everything was the complete opposite way you typically sheathed and drew a sword.

"What kind of sword is that?" Learon asked.

"It's called an elum blade. It's old. I would have been shocked if you had seen one before."

"From the war?"

"No, the design is older than that," Elias said.

"Interesting, do you live in Atava?"

"No."

"Oh, we don't get many people further than Atava to come in here."

"I'm fairly nomadic."

"What I don't get is how did you get up to Hawk's Perch? That peak is higher than White Hawk mountain. There's not much up there," Learon stated.

"More than you think. But how I got there is a very long story. I promise I'll tell you sometime, as it is a good one. But I'm too tired to tell it tonight. If you don't mind, I need some rest."

"Sure, I understand."

"Learon, have you ever killed a wolverack before today?" Elias asked somewhat obscurely.

"Never by myself, no."

"It was a superb shot. Thank you again. I think we should be up and gone before that fire goes out," Elias said, and he turned over and fell asleep instantly.

Learon stayed up thinking over the day's events for a moment. Then he wrapped his cloak around himself and shut his eyes. His last thought was that the fire wouldn't last very long.

# ADALON

1. ASCENDANCY SPIER
2. ARCANA SPIER
3. CRAFTCORE SPIER
4. ROOFTOP WALKWAYS
5. TWINE KNOT BAR
6. FROG LEG TAVERN
7. ELLARIA'S QUARTTERS
8. FISHERMAN'S MARKET
9. WHISPER CHAIN
10. SAGEAN'S PALACE
11. THE WATCHMEN'S PORT
12. THE MERCHANTS BELT

TAWER RIVER

MAINSOLIS SEA

SAGEAN'S PALACE

SPILLWAY

ARENA

GREENBELT

WATERFRONT BRIDGE

THE CRESCENT PIER

TRAYDE RIVER

# CHAPTER SIX

## COUNCIL'S COURT (ELLARIA)

Ellaria awoke in her tipped back chair under the window in the rounded corner of her quarters, where it overlooked the street below. Her soft-knit gold blanket lay crumpled on the floor, only a corner still hanging on and draped over her leg. She opened her eyes to the sounds of rattling garbage in the alley. The intrusive clatter was a reminder of Adalon's grit.

She had fallen asleep beneath the window, watching for signs of her stalker. She had taken great pains to keep the location of her quarter house a secret. In the first five years after the war, the Coalition and the Guild constantly called on her. She learned a long time ago the hard lesson that it took effort to maintain her privacy.

She had a small stone cottage across the ocean once, on the coasts near Illumeen in the New World. She hadn't been back there in a long time. It was comfortably small, with a great river stone fireplace, and doors out onto a long porch that overlooked the Anamic ocean. In the evening, when the sun set, the whole place would glow with orange rays of light. It was muddy during high tide, but that was part of its charm. It stayed cool all year round. The western wind would blow off the cold ocean water and up the rocky shore. The surrounding fields rolled high and green, and in the winter, the tall grass turned golden brown and rippled in patterns with the wind. That was home once, a place where she shared a life with Kovan, but that was a long time ago when she was another person.

Ellaria got up, stretched and rolled the drapes closed. There was a sinking pit in her stomach that had nothing to do with her flight through the city last night. The Coalition's meeting was today, and she wanted to be early. Truth be told, she always wanted to be early to everything. Today, she wanted to watch how the other ambassadors acted when they arrived. Who was consorting with who, and what was their general attitude? Their appearances also told her a lot about what each ambassador thought about the meeting and its importance; overtly cultural attire and possibly they were ready to stand up for their nation more. Did they wear a hat, shaded spectacles, carry a cane, or even arrive with guards? All of it spoke something about them. Ellaria used to get very worked up about her own look, until she figured out the right outfit that told everyone else not to mess with her. Her hat helped a lot. She wore variations on the same outfit now with scant care for outside opinions. With age came an impatience to be anyone but herself, even if that person doesn't please everyone. Worrying about others is time wasted and time lost, because the flame burns regardless of who sees the glow, but it doesn't burn forever. She never thought of herself as a war hero, even though she was one of the few women who had fought in battles. It took going to the universities and meeting with students to learn that they saw her as an iconoclast mutineer.

Ellaria made sure she brought her wrist wrap today as she left her place. It was an ornately detailed sleeve with layers of dark gray, gold, and green lace. A large intricately carved watch attached with gold exposed gears and stretched from her wrist to an attached metal ring on her second finger, shaped like a phoenix. It was extravagant, but Ellaria liked it because under the clock face was a small, secret compartment that held small vials of shadow dust and firespark. Sewn into the underside was a knife hold, where she concealed a light wooden handled knife Kovan had given her when they were younger. She double checked the draw and hoped she wouldn't need it.

She made her way to the rooftop walkways above her. The raised cable bridges connected the entire city, and instead of having to navigate the belts, she could take the ways directly to the Spires. The walkways arched above the ground level, from roof to roof and sometimes up against and around the sides of taller buildings. Sections when unsupported by roofs, were held up by columns from below. They periodically stretched up and formed archways of stone above the walkway. When the fog rolled in off the sea, as it often did, the city became a maze of high-rise paths, stone streets and arched overpasses shrouded in the clouds.

When Ellaria got on the bridge, she was disappointed to find it mostly empty. From the wash of light on the surface she realized the sun was going into the blue. For the two hours that the sun was at the apex in the sky, and the sun turned blue, the city would break from whatever they were doing. It was a time to eat a midday meal, rest, and worship depending on what part of the world you were in. Some saw the blue sun as the thinning of the veil between our world and the Risen World—the spirit world. Many considered the color blue sacred, and rare blue azurite crystals were extremely valuable as a result. Ellaria was fairly agnostic on it all. She understood the realities of other worlds, but questioned the validity of connecting to them or being governed by them.

She stopped on her walk and got a hazelberry tea and ice from a walkway vendor. The high vantage point on the elevated walkways allowed her to see all the way out to the Mainsolis Sea and the Crescent Pier in the east. In the thin channel between Adalon and the crescent-shaped island, there was a group of fishing vessels that typically populated the water under the bridges. She walked the rest of the way to the Spires, enjoying the sun and mild weather. The heat of the zenithal season was arriving.

As the Ascendancy Spire came into view, she realized she wasn't as early as she thought she would be. The activity outside the Spire's grand stairs had already dwindled to only a few people.

Ellaria found the nearest stair tower to exit down to the street level. The cylindrical tower of gray stone had a band of wooden framed openings that followed the rise of the stairs. Ellaria's short cuff boots took the steps in a swift rhythmic clacking. She looked through the opening on her climb down and spotted Delvette. She was standing next to a man Ellaria did not recognize. They were both waiting for her outside of the Spire's main entrance, at the foot of a grand set of marble stairs that cascaded up to the main doors.

The man was tall with dark hair and had clear spectacles with a reflective silver frame.. He wore an elegant dark blue suit and freshly shined shoes and carried a dark tanned leather satchel. He didn't wear a hat, unlike a lot of men in the city, but he looked comfortable in his own skin and he was handsome. They both smiled as she approached.

"Waiting long?" Ellaria asked when she got to them.

"No," Delvette said. Then she motioned to the man standing to her left. "Ellaria, this is Edward Knox. The new headmaster at the Arcana."

"Oh!" Ellaria said, surprised. "Nice to meet you, Mr. Knox."

"Please, call me Edward," he said in a friendly tone. It was tough for Ellaria to tell his age. She suspected they were close to the same age, but he was younger.

"Sorry, I forgotten Mr. Callahan might retire. I didn't know it was official," Ellaria told him.

"No need to apologize, Miss Moonstone."

"Ellaria," she corrected him. She still hadn't decided how comfortable she was with this man.

"Ellaria. I'm sure you have quite a lot on your mind. Delvette tells me you've heard the terrible rumors?" Edward asked.

"Only just recently. Anything else I should know before we go in there?"

"Well, I hear they're going to legalize guns in the city," Delvette said tentatively. She knew it was an issue of contention for Ellaria. Every nation allowed you to carry swords or knives, but only a few allowed their citizens to carry firearms openly in the city.

"That's a mistake. It just invites the lawlessness that goes on in Amera or Nahadon. Obviously, the Citadel's influence has grown. Not in Ravenvyre though, I suspect?" Ellaria asked. They had the strictest laws against firearms of any other nation, it was part of their honor code. They basically considered guns vulgar and a sign of weakness, Kovan hated it there.

"No, not there," Delvette confirmed.

"So, Ellaria. Delvette tells me you're one of the foremost historians we have?" Edward asked.

"I'm not sure. I doubt there are many that have read more than I have, but I don't know."

"And you have traveled extensively, correct?" Edward asked.

"I've traveled more than most. I'm not sure any of that makes me the expert," Ellaria said, uncertain where the line of questioning was going.

"Well, if not you. Who?" Edward asked.

Ellaria let his question hang in the air. She felt like he was fishing for something, possibly dancing around asking her about Qudin. It was a line of questioning most people pursued.

"Let me ask you, what do you think of this book?" he asked her, and he pulled a book from his satchel and held the binding of the textbook for her to read. The Ancient World Forgotten by Tabor Nolan.

"Honestly?" she asked.

"Please."

"It's a fairly derivative reinterpretation of others' work with very little research or new insights to offer. Just information that everyone already knows. How Territhmina was named by the people long before the

Ancients, meaning the land of all. Which shortened to territh over time. If you're after something on the Ancients and the Eckwyn Age, I would suggest Arlene Kent's work. It is better researched and more extensive by far. Of course, the best texts are located inside the Arcana's restricted section."

"Yes, I agree. However, Mr. Nolan is seeking a position at the Arcana. I was reviewing his work. I don't think Ms. Kent is seeking employment. Last I heard, she was living in Ioka," Edward said.

Ellaria felt slightly embarrassed by her honesty, though every word was true, "Yes. Arlene will be working for the university there when it opens," she told him.

"Interesting, I didn't know that the Ioka university was near opening or even that construction for a building was underway," he said.

"Edward was the professor of geology, and of course, one of the lead scientists on the metallurgy team that was allowed to survey the Crystal Cave in Kotalla," Delvette said unprompted, which jogged Ellaria's memory. That was where she had heard his name. He had led the team some years ago that discovered the uses of quandinium and its conductive properties. An astonishing achievement, no one was allowed to go to Kotalla. Which made him a rare person.

"Of course," Ellaria said. She noticed they were being approached by Queen Rotha, Durrone from Andal, and two others. The Queen and Ellaria went back a long way, and they were no longer friendly with each other. Which made the smile on her face unsettling.

"Your grace," Delvette said, but the Queen of Andal ignored her and looked at Ellaria only. Ellaria could tell one of the young men with her was obviously her son based on his blonde hair and sharp facial features, but the other man she did not recognize.

"Ellaria, I'm glad you made it today," Queen Durrone said.

"Rotha, how are you, is this your son Evrick?" Ellaria replied.

"It is. He's joining the rolls at the Arcana next year, and I thought he should witness the day's events."

"Is that so?" Ellaria said arching her eyebrows.

"Splendid, I can see by the look on your face that you don't know what you're walking into. Well why would you? This world is ruled by lineage, which you know nothing about. You will recall Ellaria, that last time we spoke I told you I would see you ruined. That day has come. Neither you, nor your friends can stand against this. I will enjoy watching you squirm."

Ellaria, cognizant of Delvette and Edward's eyes on her, merely removed her hat, smiled and bowed. The Queen stalked away up the stairs, while her son snickered like an idiot.

"What was that about?" Edward asked.

"Just an old rivalry," Ellaria said, and began ascending the marble steps. As Delvette and Edward followed her she heard Edward take a deep breath like he was also dreading the meeting.

ELLARIA SAT IN A SIDE CHAIR, LOOKING AROUND THE COUNCIL'S COURT with light shining through from the massive windows to her left. Four glass panels were positioned between buttressing wing walls. It had been a long time since she had attended a council meeting, and it took a moment to familiarize herself again. The room was a large rectangle where the dark wood floor sunk down three steps in an oval shape. The first step had benches that curved with the oval: the delegates' pews. Each section of pew had a wood front with a tiny writing surface, and there were also two stations at the ends of the oval. One for the meeting's Chair, and the other for the Scholar's Guild. Two steps down from that was the open wood floor area of the speaker's stage. When it was not used for speaking, they brought in a table to the stage to review materials or maps. Ellaria saw that there were no maps down there today, making it unlikely to be a simple meeting over borders then.

Each ambassador could go down to the stage to speak whenever they wanted, but the law allowed for only two ambassadors on the stage at a time. An ambassador couldn't return to the stage after they had left it, unless someone called them back, or at least two people went between turns.

At the far ends of the room, there were chairs against the wall for the ambassador's supporters, called the Confidence Members. Ellaria was sitting in one of those chairs, next to Edward, both of them behind Delvette. In addition to Rotha's threats, her observations made her think this was going to go worse than she first thought. She could see more whispered conversations between ambassadors, and very few looked to be clenching their fists like she was. Ellaria rolled the lace of her wrist wrap between her thumb and forefinger, turning her attention to admiring the beautiful glass sphere of electric light that hung in the middle of the room.

It was a great enormous ball of glass with electrically charged gas inside. It must have been krypton gas because the color was bright white, blue. Held in place by brass frames wrapping around it and back to the ceiling. The sun drowned the light out, but still it hung in the center of the room as if it was the collective energy of the surrounding assembly.

As she waited, Ellaria thought about how badly she had wanted the coalition to succeed when they first put it together. The Resistance had wanted a new republic that valued knowledge and science, art, life and each other. The United Coalition of Nations was meant to be a sovereignty that unified the world, one that let each nation rule itself. Many countries experienced an incredible amount of upheaval after the war, but while the faces of the leaders may have changed, the corruption remained. The rich before the war, were rich after it. The only difference was the wealthy now had power they never had under the Empire.

As more of the ambassadors arrived, Ellaria looked around the room and feared history was repeating itself like a great gear of time. Grinding and cranking out the same play, with the same roles, only with new players. Doomed to play their part until the gears revolved anew.

Repeating the mistakes of the past seemed inevitable. The Empire had destroyed all historical records. There was no map to follow and no guiding light to lead them through the broken world.

The Empire had reigned for fifteen spans, or close to fifteen hundred years, and had controlled the entire territh. Under the Sagean's rule there had been no higher learning, and no freely shared knowledge. This should have been enough reason for people to rebel, but it wasn't. Over the ages, the Empire had instituted a law for a common currency and language. Destroying cultural traditions in the process, all in the name of the Rule of Harmony. Still, it took physical abuse of cruel proportions, to finally tip the scales.

While the continent across the Anamic Ocean was known to exist, it had never been colonized. The New World provided the opportunity for a passive rebellion. People began to travel across the Anamic in droves, hoping distance would weaken the grip of the Empire. It had. As more people escaped there, the Sagean made it a crime. The Resistance was born. One of the biggest reasons the Resistance had won the war, besides Qudin, was that the New World was on their side. A land unified by one goal, to end the rule of the Sagean Lords.

After the war, when the nations came together, the Resistance was idealistic and innocent. Ellaria, too. It had been their moment to command more, and they gave it up in the name of unification. Ellaria now realized the Resistance should have made more stipulations. Sometimes she wished she would have just persuaded Qudin to lead.

The one thing they demanded was control over education. Every nation signed a pact called the Freedom of Mind Act. It entrusted the future of education to the scientists and scholars. The Resistance became the United Scholar's Guild. It gave them a seat at the Council's Table, a Regent, and two additional confidence chairs. Delvette was the Scholar's Guild Regent and Ellaria and Edward her confidence.

A series of loud slams echoed out, when the doors to the outside hall were closed by the standing attendants. Ellaria quickly regained composure. Apparently, all the ambassadors had arrived. However, two seats remained empty, and Ellaria's eyes darted around trying to determine who was missing. Her stomach dropped when she figured it out. The Ambassadors for The Free Cities of the New World were missing. Where was Danehin, the Peace King? She eyed the doors in a primal instinct for survival.

"Ambassadors I call to order this court of the United Coalition of Nations, on this day the twenty-fifth of Jovost, in the year 54 so endowed of the 23rd epoch," said the ambassador from Adalon, Lavic Dunne. He had called the meeting to order, meaning he was also the oval's hearing officer, and the one who would keep order for the proceedings. He was allowed to speak, recognize or dismiss other speakers. This position was always chosen by the ambassador who called for the hearing. *So, who had called the hearing?* she wondered.

"We are here today," Dunne continued, "To usher in a new order and a return to the greatness of a harmonic life. We come together to recognize the appointment of a Primordial. We have been floundering in this unity without leadership . . ."

"Wait!" Ellaria shouted. She had rushed to the speaking stage as soon as she heard the word Primordial. The room erupted in murmurs and aghast breaths. It was highly irregular, but not strictly forbidden for a confidence to speak, but it was an insult to interrupt the opening statement.

"Yes, Ms. Moonstone?" Dunne said with complete disdain and stepped out of the oval.

Ellaria gathered herself and spoke to the full assembly.

"We cannot seriously be considering going through with this. I realize that the Coalition has had issues, but we are still young. The young make mistakes in order for them to grow and succeed. Don't . . ." she faltered a moment as an ambassador got out of his chair and sat on a step before the speaking stage. It was the customary place to sit and wait to speak next.

"Don't throw away what we earned. The world earned this right to speak freely and for every nation to govern their own people in a way that best represents them. The people, your people, suffered for their freedom. So, you could represent them," Ellaria continued. But the ambassador from Kalihjan stood up and stepped in.

"How do you know what my people want?" Ambassador Sahlin asked.

Then Dunne approached the stage having seen enough.

"You mistake our courtesy here, Ms. Moonstone. We are not here to debate if we should elect a Prime Commander. We have elected one. We are here to introduce him. Now sit down!"

Ellaria left the stage, passing Edward, who sat on the waiting step. He gave her a soft smile. At her chair, she stood staring at the wall for a moment, before turning to sit down. She was struggling to compose herself and refused to let anyone see her weakened.

"The officer recognizes Confidence Knox," Ella heard Dunne say, and she looked up.

"I second Ellaria Moonstone's remarks. If you have elected a Prime, then it was without a unanimous vote. The Scholar's Guild did not vote on this, and neither did the Free Cities, I suspect. Their absence today would suggest such," Edward said, and Ellaria was proud to be his associate and simultaneously wondered why Delvette had not spoken.

"Ambassador Sahlin, you may sit unless you want to hear from Ellaria?" Dunne asked.

"No, I suppose I do not," Sahlin said, and he walked back.

"Right. Mr. Knox. We appreciate your participation. However, you know that there does not need to be a unanimous vote. Furthermore, only the Free Cities and Skyvier voted against it," Dunne said, and he flashed Ellaria a wicked grin. Ellaria looked from him to Delvette, aghast. Edward walked back and sat next to Ellaria.

"Did you know?" she whispered.

"No," Edward said.

The far side doors opened with a violent thrust. A man walked in wearing a white cloak billowing out behind him and followed by two armed guards. The guards wore red capes and had gold metal masks on. Each held long rectangular shields and pulsator guns were holstered at their sides. The man in white was tall with brown hair and dark-colored spectacles hid his eyes. He walked up beside Dunne. Both Edward and Ellaria studied the man. Edward also looked to gauge the reaction of the rest of the assembly.

"Your new Primordial Commander, Rogan Malik," Dunne announced, and the congregation stood. Ellaria reluctantly was the last to stand, and Malik picked her out immediately.

"Thank you, Lavic. The first thing I would like to do is to ask Ms. Moonstone if she would care to answer Ambassador Sahlin's question?" Malik said in a velvety voice. Ellaria felt the room's eyes all turn to her. She rose out of her seat and walked to the stage.

"Ambassador Sahlin, what I know about your people is how they struggled and fought and bled beside me in the battle of Antoree Bay. I know that under the Sagean Empire they feared their culture was being stripped away, and they had no education to speak of," Ellaria said, and she quickly turned back to exit the stage before Sahlin could come down to argue.

"Just a moment, Ms. Moonstone. I have a very important question for you," Malik said.

"Yes," Ellaria replied.

"Where is Qudin Lightweaver?"

Ellaria laughed and shook her head, "Of course. Well, I'm sorry to tell you, but I can't help you there."

"You can't or you won't? Do you know his whereabouts?" Malik asked again, more forcefully this time.

"I can't. I have not spoken to him in a long time. It's possible he's dead," she told him.

"Unlikely, very unlikely," he said to himself more than to her, "And last night. You didn't send a message to him?" he asked. The question threw her off guard. She began making a calculated assessment before answering.

"No."

"Well, as most of you already know. One of my top priorities is the apprehension of Qudin Lightweaver. I have initiated the Luminance Squadron, a specialized task force, charged with the sole purpose of hunting down the so-called Quantum Man and bringing him back before this council to answer questions. We need to know where he obtained his powers and what exactly happened to the Sagean?" Malik said.

"Qudin defeated and killed the Sagean," Ellaria interrupted, unable to help herself.

"You are sure?" Malik countered.

"Yes."

"Well, I am not. Take the beasts, for example."

"You mean the beasts the Sagean sent, under his control, to attack us?"

"Yes. Look what happened to the beasts after the Sagean's Death. Did they go away as before? No, they dispersed into our lands, killing good honest people. What did your Quantum Man do about them? The Sagean had them under control. Qudin released those beasts on us and it is possible he controls them even now," Malik said.

"That is such a twisting of the truth," Ellaria shot back.

"The truth is two men went up to the top of the Dragon Spine and only one man came back. Nobody ever saw or heard from the Sagean again. No explanation, no formal account, and certainly no trial. You may sit down now, Ms. Moonstone," He said the last part with hatred. Ellaria tipped her hat and walked back to her seat. Malik continued to rant his lies that there was never a formal account given, but she knew there had been, she was with Qudin when he gave it.

"The other major action I would like to discuss today has to deal with the New World. As you all may have noticed, Danehin has refused to come to this court today. He is no Peace King, he has decided that his nation will not be a part of this council now or in the future. To that rebuttal, I offer this: All trade to the New World will cease immediately. The land was never Danehin's to command, it is a free world, and we will colonize it. We shall try diplomacy first, but I will not hesitate to go to war with the rebels across the ocean and capture lands back that should have always been ours. It was us who found the land and we shall claim it," Malik said to some applause. There was a deep rooted hatred for the Free Cities that Ellaria was not aware of before today.

"I would also like to point out that because of my appointment as the Prime, and my connection to the Island of Kotalla, Kotalla will begin trading again with the United Coalition of Nations. Lastly, I will say this: I understand the world has changed in the last forty years, but the people deserve to have their faith in the Sagean religion and the Rule of Harmony restored. I have no special gifts; I am not a Luminary. But I am a believer in the words of the sacred Sagelight text. When a new Sagean being comes, and he will, they shall have my post. A Sagean lord should be celebrated, not feared. That is all. Thank you, brethren. May the Light guide us now and forever."

Ellaria stormed out of the room and through the Conciliates Hall. She was the first one to exit the court assembly when the meeting concluded and was desperate for fresh air. She felt like she was drowning in Marathal Lake with the great falls pumping atop her. She rushed down the main marble stairs where a giant pendulum swung in the middle of the wide winding staircase. She burst through the back doors, into the afternoon sun, and out onto the spire grounds, heading to the Arcana. The green fields were full with students. A couple of scientists walking to the Craftcore building were startled and jumped when Ellaria suddenly emerged from the Ascendancy Tower.

She wanted to get clear of there as quickly as possible, just in case the Prime meant to sequester her for more questioning. He was having her followed. Ellaria needed to clear her head and calm a bit before she confronted Delvette. How could she have voted for the Prime? At least Edward had stood up and had her back. And who was this Malik? She couldn't place where she knew him from. She was getting too old to fight these battles. Q had been right. The Coalition had harbored an obsession to find him, even after forty years. They still wanted answers, because they thought they deserved answers.

Ellaria found her way past the residence halls and up the stairs to the Scholar's Tower. There were three sections of stairs, with two round sitting platforms serving at large landings between flights held aloft by large singular columns with a built-in bench around the perimeter. They used this same design all over the Arcana complex. While some platforms were bigger than others, they all easily seated twenty people.

Ellaria stopped at the second platform, before the last flight of stairs up to the Scholar's Tower. She picked a spot on the bench beneath a lantern pole and buried her face in her hands. She sobbed uncontrollably for a moment, before regaining her resolve. She had been holding herself in check throughout the whole meeting and tried to ensure no one saw her tears. With people she trusted it was fine, but anyone in that chamber would see it as weakness, and people held weakness against you. Truth was, she wasn't weak, she wasn't even sad. Just full of boiling frustration and emotionally wrought. It was a betrayal of all she had struggled for and no one around wanted to fight.

As she looked out across the grounds from the platform, she spotted Delvette and Edward coming through the trees below. It looked like they were exchanging heated words as they walked. She heard them coming up the steps toward her. She quickly wiped her face and eyes, straightened her clothes, and got ready. She wasn't sure she would get a word out before her rage took control and she just punched Delvette square in the face. Ellaria pursed her lips and felt her fists forming at her side. The frustration, loneliness, and fear was a storm threatening to burst forth.

When Delvette stepped up onto the platform, Ellaria stomped over. Delvette lifted her face and Ellaria saw for the first time that her friend's face was bright red and splotchy. A small sob escaped her at seeing Ellaria, tears streaming down her cheeks. Ellaria's rage dissipated.

"Delvette, how could you!" she said to her friend.

"I'm sorry, Ellaria. You just don't understand," Delvette pleaded.

"Then help me understand. Why would you vote yes?"

"Because it was the only way to save the Guild."

It was not the answer Ellaria was expecting. Suddenly she felt like their conversation was too public. "Delvette, let's retire to your office and continue this there. I don't trust anyone around here, and we don't want to seem like conspirators. I remember how these things work," Ellaria said and Delvette agreed.

They moved away from the platform and up to Delvette's office, Edward trailing along. He obviously wanted to hear an explanation himself. The three of them entered her office and Edward closed the door behind them. The office was at the top of the Scholar's Tower.

Delvette's office was rounded inside on one end at the corner. Ellaria had actually never been up here. It reminded her of the rounding bay at her quarter house in the city. Delvette sat down at her desk and put her hands over her face. Ellaria had no intention of sitting in the chair opposite, or in the small sitting area adjacent. When she wasn't pacing, she stood at the window looking out at the city. From this height, she could see the raised walkways weaving above the rooftops. The exhaust pipes from the Craftcore building steamed out and dissipated in the air. People looked like ants crawling around, unaware they were hustling to appease a new ruler.

"Explain," Ellaria said turning from the window, her voice sharp.

"First Ella, I'm sorry. I'm sorry for not telling you before. I lost my nerve last night. I'm not as brave as you. I know it must have been hard to find out. But please understand, I had to," Delvette said sincerely.

"You keep saying that. Why did you *have* to?" Edward asked.

"Because they would have had the votes, anyway. They only needed ten of the thirteen votes and they had them. More than that, it was the only way to ensure our standing. They were threatening the Guild. If we didn't vote for the Prime, they were going to dismantle us. Malik was getting appointed, and anyone who opposed was going to receive retribution. Which meant they were going to dissolve the Guild, strip us of our powers and standing. I couldn't let that happen. This way we at least stay in the game, Ella," Delvette explained, and her words seemed desperate for Ellaria's understanding.

"I see," Ellaria conceded, "I'm still livid with you, but maybe you made the right decision. Certainly, I can't imagine *you* making a different one. It's not the one I would have made, but at least we can still be a voice of reason on the council. Until Malik dissolves it completely. That's another thing, where do I know him from?"

"Malik? He was Dunne's top lieutenant at the Citadel. When Dunne was still the general there, before he became the ambassador of Adalon, Malik was in charge of the Cloaked Knife."

Ellaria remembered him now. He was a kid who trained with the Ultrarians, under Kovan, many years ago. The Ultrarian company was an elite unit created by Kovan to track and hunt down the last and most zealot supporters of the Sagean Emperor. Called the consortium, they had maintained the war campaign long after their side had lost. When the consortium chose to make their final stand at the Citadel, they were defeated by the Ultrarians, following a sixty day siege. Kovan gave up fighting after that. Later, the Coalition transformed the Ultrarians into the Cloaked Knife and relocated the training grounds from the Crescent Pier to the Coalition controlled Citadel. It was worse than she thought. The Citadel, in Andal, was home to the Sagean's navy and armies. It was the power and might of the Empire, and now it was in the Prime's hands.

"So, Dunne, as an ambassador, couldn't be raised to Prime because of the rules of the pact, and he got the next best thing. How did Dunne pull this off?" Ellaria asked.

"He preyed on the Coalition's greed, of course," Edward spat.

"You're not wrong, Edward. The Coalition badly wants to colonize the New World," Delvette agreed.

"So, Dunne promised them the New World, and Malik netted them trade with Kotalla," Edward surmised.

"Something doesn't add up. Last night I was being followed. Malik confirmed for me today that he was behind it. Dunne may have manipulated the ambassadors to get Malik elected, but I get the sense he's under Malik. I don't know why. But did either of you catch Dunne's expression when Malik came in or when Malik was talking about Qudin? Dunne definitely fears him."

"Interesting observation, Ellaria," Edward said.

"Malik was wearing those spectacles, so I couldn't see his eyes, but I suspect he was telling the truth about not being a Luminary or the new Sagean, but it's almost as though someone else is controlling them," Ellaria said.

"How are the eyes different?" Delvette asked.

"Well, Qudin's eyes had an almost pulsating color to them," Ellaria replied pacing away from the window, "Danehin's absence was the most troubling. Have you heard from him Delvette?"

"No," She replied.

"What do we do now?" Edward asked.

"Well, for starters. Sign me up for the lecture, Delvette," Ellaria said.

"Really?" Delvette asked, surprised.

"Yes. Also, if I could get an office on campus that would be great. I would like to be seen at the Arcana. It will give me more protection than traveling around as a Guild agent. Accidents are harder to explain if I'm here."

"Are you willing to take over the alchemy and magical arts courses next term? It's never worked out we hoped it would. Without an actual practitioner teaching the course, I'm afraid it never will," Delvette said.

"I'm not sure the Arcana will still be open by then."

"You think the Prime will shut us down?" Edward asked.

"I don't know. I hope not, we may need the youth to save this world again. The problem is there's something bigger going. Something or someone manipulating everything. Which I intend to figure out," Ellaria said, and she rubbed the back of her neck. Her thoughts lingered to her friends, hoping they had received her messages and were on their way.

# CHAPTER SEVEN

## ESCAPE (KOVAN)

The darkness consumed time, with only a drip of water to track it. At some point, another lantern overhead had gone out. Only two of the six remained, barely producing a muted glow. Sooner or later, he expected the guards would have to relight them. A completely dark prison would be dangerous to guard. Kovan wasn't sure if he should wait for them to relight the lanterns to make his move. They would definitely need a ladder or a lamplighter's pole, meaning the door would be open for an extended period while they brought equipment inside. Even if the door closed, he could use either as a battering ram to get through. The darkness was the key to his plan. Of course, plans were always the first thing to die in battle.

Kovan's ears perked up as a bolt on the guard's door shifted, then the second. The lock clicked, and the reinforced door opened with a creak on the swing. The hinges waned under strain from carrying the extra weight of a door with fastened steel plates. Kovan sat on the damp floor, his head against the cold, stone wall, listening to the sounds. He kept his eyes closed for the moment, trying to determine if it was a full patrol or just a check-in. The check-in was quicker. One man came through the door, walked the length of the corridor and returned. A second man stood at the closed door, waiting. The full patrol had them switch positions. Wait at each end for a short period before returning. Usually, the full patrol yielded rations, by a third guard afterward. So far, they had only given him water and Kovan's stomach had grown angry and tight.

By the ease and flow of their steps in the corridor he could tell they weren't carrying anything to light the lanterns. When the second guard at the door shifted his weight, making the door give just the slightest sigh. Kovan opened his eyes. It was a full patrol, and the outer door had not been double bolted. The door to the hall had three locks. The key lock and two secure bolts. Someone inside had gotten lazy and forgotten to bolt them, only keying the lock. Kovan suspected the key was still in the lock too. It was time to go.

He quickly rocked out of his sitting position, stood, and approached the bars of his cell, careful not to make any unnecessary noise. He whispered to Thann, "Be ready, and keep your eyes closed."

The first part of his plan, the most important part, relied on the crystal doing what he hoped it would. Kovan scanned the hall. Checked on the guards. Then he knelt down to inspect the lock to his cell door. He pulled the crystal out of his pocket, which he had wrapped in a thin strip torn from his shirt. He hoped it would be thin and long enough to do what he needed.

Carefully, he slid the rolled and frayed piece of cloth into the cell door lock. The cloth caught on the locking mechanism inside on the first pass. Kovan removed it and adjusted the roll to try again. This time the cloth caught but in a deeper place. The far end barely stuck out the keyhole on the other side. Kovan reached in desperation with his fingers, trying to feel for the freed strings of the cloth. His fingers searched frantically to find them in the dark. Finally, his forefinger felt the fibers on the outside face of the cold metal plate. He rolled the strings in his fingers, pulling slightly until more and more of the cloth was through. When the piece of shirt was about half-in and half-out the other end, he stood up. He hoped he had successfully gotten the crystal inside, wedged into place. Ideally resting near the catch. With the cloth in his left hand, he called out to the guard near the door. The one closest to him.

"Hey ugly, when is dinner I'm starving?" he jabbed, getting both guards' attention.

"Get back from the bars," the guard said, moving slightly closer. *Come on, a little further*, Kovan thought.

"If we do feed you wastes of life, you're not getting . . ." the guard paused at seeing the cloth wrap at the lock, "What is that?" he asked, hustling over.

*Here we go.* Kovan thought. When the guard was at the bars, Kovan pulled down on the cloth. Nothing happened. *Oh no.* He pulled and tugged, but still nothing happened.

"Come on, damn it!" he said aloud.

The guard grabbed the cloth in his fist. "What is this, what are you doing?" Then he jerked from his side. A small, fractured crack sounded in the latch, and the guard looked down at it. Kovan smiled and closed his eyes.

The firespark inside the crystal erupted with the contact of air. Fire shot out of the keyhole in all directions, a bright blinding flare in the darkness. A caterwaul of crackling sparks followed by the guard's screams from the burns to his face and the small flames ignited on his chest and the new source of light illuminated the decrepit cells. Kovan slammed his shoulder into the bars and it gave away, more easily than he expected. The iron careened into the screaming guard, and Kovan fell through into the hallway. His momentum taking him to the floor, and against the opposite cell door. A hand reached out, grabbing Kovan at the neck from beyond.

"Let me out of here," the prisoner inside pleaded. His voice, rough and scratchy like he hadn't used it in a long time. Kovan pulled free and got up to his feet.

"Thann, help me. Grab the guard!" he barked. The second guard had his hands up in the air and waving, still slightly blinded by the flare. "Grab his arm," Kovan added. Together, they reached for the guard's arms and grabbed tight. The guard struggled, but together Kovan and Thann were easily stronger. They pulled at each arm, the three of them ran toward the exit. The guard oddly ran with them instead of resisting. They slammed him into the door like a battering ram with a loud thud and bang. It knocked the guard unconscious, but the door remained unaffected.

"Oh, that's right. The door swings the other way," Kovan muttered to himself. He had forgotten that minor detail, looking at the guard crumpled on the ground. His chest heaved in large gulps to catch his breath, a commotion stirred in the room beyond. Kovan could hear them gathering themselves to come in.

The key in the lock clicked, and the door opened. Kovan rushed and put his body against the swing to keep it from opening. "Thann, help," he yelled.

"Why, don't we want to leave?" Thann asked bewildered as he slammed into the door too.

Kovan moved over and looked around the door into the room. Three more guards were trying to barrel through. He snatched the keys from the lock.

"What are you doing sayzon?" Thann roared over the thundering calls of the guards.

Kovan ran to the other end of the block, looking for the right cell. There he was. You couldn't miss him. The man was a mountain.

"Big guy, time to go," Kovan beamed at him, and opened the gate.

The man emerged from the cell, covering the distance between them in a heartbeat. His hand slammed into Kovan's throat. Lifting him into the bars, and off the ground.

"Freedom first," Kovan choked out, "Then kill me."

The gigantic man turned to see the guards finally coming through the door. He dropped Kovan in a heap and then turned on the oncoming men. The first guard mistakenly hadn't drawn his sword yet. Gigantore grabbed him at his shoulders and flung him eight feet back, into the other two guards. A clattering ring sounded off the floor and Kovan got up and dived for a fallen sword. He made his way toward the exit as the guards recovered from the collision and attacked the Hazon man again.

In the room beyond, Kovan could see another guard had arrived. Instead of entering the riot, he turned to find the alarm bell. Bells began to sound from somewhere deeper in the building.

"Kovan, behind you!" Thann yelled out.

Kovan turned to see the guards ready to swing their swords at the big man at the dark end of the hall. His body seemed to take up the entire hallway as it pulsed with rage. In three swift motions, Kovan disarmed both of the guards. A down strike and curl disarmed the first, and a sweeping glance that sliced into the other man's hand freed the second. Satisfied, Kovan turned and ran for the door with Gigantore close behind.

In the guardroom, Thann was already wrestling with the man who had pulled the alarm bells. Kovan rushed to search for his guns. They weren't there, but he had to look. He found a long coat instead and took it. He put the coat on and looked up to see the big guy throw the guard through the wood door at the other side of the room. The oak door crashed and splintered apart. They rushed out, stepping over the moaning man. Gigantore now up ahead, rampaging like a bull. In the dark staircase, they met only one more guard, and he wisely backed out – choosing to run back the way he had come. They reached the main entrance hall. Thann started for the door to the outside courtyard, but Kovan pulled him back and into the right hallway. The giant Hovan man burst free into the outside to rampage through the courtyard.

"But?" Thann sighed.

"Shhh," Kovan murmured, pulling him back and into the dark hall that led to the pits.

In the hall, they passed a switchback stairway just as Thann described, with a single lantern on the wall at the landing. Footsteps were scrambling down. A second, larger wave of guards coming to end the rioting. Kovan still gripped the sword he had taken. He moved past the stair into the darkness on the other side. Then down a few steps on the winding stairway, where they waited for the guards to disperse. Kovan could feel the anxiety from Thann, who kept fidgeting with his hands. The idea was to wait for order to return, before sneaking out. At the top steps above the pits, Kovan could hear faint calls and cries from the depths. A chilling reality just a room away. After a short time, he heard guards coming back.

"Even with three arrows in him, that beast made it out," one guard was saying to another.

As a file of men returned to their station, Kovan decided the way was mostly clear. He moved back toward the entrance. They couldn't wait any longer. The smell wafting up from the pits was horrible. Eventually, they would send men to check on the pits, but maybe not.

Shrouded in the dark recess of the hallway, he stopped before the entrance. A guard stood just inside, Kovan dashed in and slammed the man's temple with the blunt grip end of the sword. A lone grunt emerged and Kovan caught him as he fell to the floor. He grabbed one of the two lanterns that hung on the wall in the entry vestibule and slowly opened the door to the courtyard.

It was nighttime, and there was still some chaos outside. A group of guards stood huddled just at the front talking about the breakout, the gate still ajar. On the battlements there was only one archer, looking outward to the city streets. Kovan slipped out of the door and to the side wall. The lantern under his coat. They stalked over to the stables in the side yard. Thann quickly found a horse to his liking and freed it. Kovan put his hand up, signaling him to hold. He then went and opened all the stable gates, leading each horse out a few feet. There were quite a few missing, probably riders already out to capture Gigantore. *May he live a long life and find a gigantic woman to bear his kids*, Kovan thought. Most of the horses left were pull horses. They needed something swifter and more athletic. Thann had selected a brown and white mustang horse, and Kovan found a black and brown one.

They pulled up next to each other, and Kovan nodded. Both men mounted their horses and kicked off. Kovan tossed the lantern behind and into the stables. The oil splattered up on the wood portico and in the hay, where it burst into flames. Kovan and Thann rode for the gate. The horses behind them followed to escape the fire. They passed the huddled soldiers who looked on agog at the stable fire roaring to life. They all had jumped out of the way or risked being trampled. Kovan made the gate at a gallop, fleeing into the streets.

HE WAS FORCED TO DITCH THE STOLEN HORSE WHEN HE CAME TO AN alleyway he couldn't pass. After it had narrowed down to nothing but a sliver where the building edges kissed. Cursing the haphazard city, Kovan climbed from the horse's back to the tiled eave to escape. The second tile he grabbed for leverage gave way and crashed to the gravel below. Kovan cringed at the noise and finished vaulting over. He came down into a private yard of one of the city's housing rows. A shared community space between buildings, about two hundred feet long, it was a garden with a winding, white crushed stone path. There were patches of tall grasses, blossom trees and purple flowers too. The connected homes were small, stacked high, and staggered with plunging eaves of maroon tiles. Kovan took the path to the far side, eyeing a line of clothes hanging at the end. The sagging line strung from a door to a smooth wood pole in the middle of the greenway. There wasn't much on the line of use, but he took a pair of black pants and a sort of draping shirt that he wasn't entirely positive was intended for a man. Taking the lone amber coin, a guard had been generous enough to leave in the coat pocket. He stashed his filthy garments in the corner to leave. Picking a wood lattice that leaned against a brick low wall as his exit. He grabbed a tomato growing in the lattice and climbed over the small fence. Landing in the street, he jogged for a bit before turning onto a new road with better visibility. The sight lines provided him an advantage over approaching strangers. He slowed his pace to a somber walk, bit into the tomato and tried to blend in. Anyone who passed him would know instantly that something was amiss, he looked foolish. The pants were too big, and the shirt was ridiculous and beneath it all, he still stank something awful. Though the sun had set, there were plenty of people out on the streets.

Summer was slow to arrive in Ravenvyre, as the end of spring lingered with high winds in the city. The breeze off the Brovic Ocean never let up. It was deadly beyond the Dire in the west and to the north, where the high cliff coast extended all the way to the impassable glacier filled frozen straight. Ships rarely sailed past Ravenvyre, making it a city on the edge of the world.

Because of the winds and the rough waters, the only bridge off the island was in the southeast. Thann was supposed to meet him there with a way across. Kovan wasn't sure he trusted the man, but that didn't mean much, Kovan didn't trust anyone. He wished he had a better plan to get out of the city, so he wouldn't have to consider Thann's, but he didn't. So, he headed south to the bridge.

In the distance, where the street turned downhill, Kovan could see a glow of light. The night sky was overcast, and the streets were darker than normal with the shrouded moon. It made the glow in the distance seem even brighter, and it beckoned to him. Light probably meant people, but also food. The closer he got, the more he realized it was the Amatori market with lanterns strung across the pathways and it bustled with people moving all around. A few greencoats were walking around too, but they were simply strolling along and didn't seem very alert or observant. Maybe they didn't know of the prison break yet, but with how silly Kovan looked it might not matter. Kovan walked closer into the perimeter merchant tents, trying his best to avoid attention, but the wonderful aromas of wood fired food, fresh fish and spices reminded him how hungry he was. He needed to get something to eat and preferably, something rolled up and handheld to keep moving.

Kovan moved to look at the different food stations in the middle of the market when some confusion to the crowd stirred at the entry archway. Three riders had come to a sudden halt just inside. The first rider dismounted with sweat falling from his brow; he yelled at the greencoats nearby to come over. Kovan ducked his head under a canopy and walked up to a counter to order food. Keeping his attention on the riders, he spoke to the tender.

"Can I have a lettuce monkfish wrap?" Kovan inquired.

The cook behind the counter looked at him funny. His eyebrows crinkled, and he wiped his counter with a damp white rag. Water falling to the drenched floor with the pass over the surface. Kovan presented his coin, and the man nodded with satisfaction and began preparing his order. Kovan looked back at the riders. Two turned to leave, but the third man had now gathered a group of greencoats. They stood at attention, received their orders and began to spread out. Two men each going in the three directions of the market. Kovan nervously looked around for an escape. He turned his head to the side and spotted her. Working behind a counter two tents away was the messenger. He wasn't positive at first, but the longer he studied her face, the surer he became. The cook held out the wrap for him. He paid, took the food, and started toward the young woman. He was at her counter before she recognized him.

"You!" she said, startled.

"Me," Kovan replied.

She looked him over and her eyebrows and nose scrunched up. "What are you wearing?" She asked with a chuckle.

"I don't know. Never mind this," Kovan said annoyed, tugging on his shirt. "I need your help."

"I guess. Have you seen yourself? You look ridiculous," she said, and then she looked from him to the greencoats closing in. "Errr, why Tali, why must you be so stupid," The young woman said under her breath to herself. Then she handed Kovan a black apron. "Here, put this on and get in here," she motioned.

Kovan slipped the apron over his head and stepped around a glass display of gold-scaled fish stacked on top of one another. He stood near a bowl with a pile of peeled shrimp, all resting on an ice bed that had mostly melted and he pretended to clean the area.

"You're not a murderer, are you?" she asked quietly.

"No, Flower. I'm not a murderer."

"Right," she said with a sigh.

The greencoats moved past without a look, and she rounded on Kovan. Her jaw set and eyes serious. "They're gone. Now get out," she insisted.

"Which way. The entrance is guarded?"

"Go through the other side of that merchant tent. There's a road to the south pier."

"Thank you. How far to the Sun Bridge from here?"

"You need to go past the pier and keep wrapping around to the east. It's about a ten-minute walk after you've passed the last ship. Now go before those greencoats come back."

"Can I keep the apron?"

"Please do," she said, with a nod and waved him off frantically. As he exited his pants caught on the counter and the bowl of shrimp flew to the ground. A splatter of shrimp was followed by a greencoat who called out.

"Foreigner, stop where you are!"

Kovan and Tali looked over. When the greencoat saw Kovan's face, he pulled his sword. Kovan grabbed a wet, slimy, golden fish from the board and threw it at the greencoat's face.

"Hey!" Tali exclaimed, but Kovan was breaking into a run. He stopped, reached back grabbing the black cloak he saw and sprinted out.

"That's mine," the young woman said, and ran after him.

She only got a few steps when the greencoat caught up to her and grabbed her by the wrist, pulling her around. His grip must have been hard, because she cried out in pain as she was yanked back.

"Young lady, you need to . . ." The greencoat was starting to say before Kovan's fist crashed across his cheekbone. The greencoat crumpled onto the trampled dirt, unconscious.

"Let's go, you're coming with me, come on!" Kovan instructed her, pointing to other greencoats coming for both of them. Tali looked from the greencoats and back to Kovan's hand. With a slight hesitation in her eyes, she took it, and they hurried through the crowd. The market was enlivened by the action. With most of the patrons staring at the commotion. When they were almost out, they passed an older lady with stern eyes.

"Talhaleanna!" the lady hissed out, as they rushed past.

"Don't worry I'll be back Mother," She responded loudly, but never breaking stride.

They made it to the pier and slowed to a light jog as the darkness settled in around them. Talhaleanna snagged her black cloak out of his hands and put it on as they walked. Kovan decided to take off the black apron and handed it back to her.

"You really should keep this on," she told him, refusing to take it.

"What's wrong with the shirt I have on?" he asked.

"It's a kumata smock, it's a traditional dress shirt for really old ladies. My mother is probably too young to wear it," she laughed. Kovan just scowled back. He would have to find something else he supposed, but the thing was comfortable.

They passed row after row of docked ships and fishing vessels, as they wrapped around the pier to the east, trying to get to the Sun Bridge. The young lady's calmness surprised Kovan.

"Once, you show me to the Sun Bridge. I think it should be safe for you to circle back home. Sorry for pulling you along, I didn't want the greencoats detaining you on my account."

"It's fine. Probably worth it for the look on my mother's face alone. Anyway, the bridge is just up ahead," she replied. She had a serenity about her that made Kovan think she was seldom afraid.

When they reached Reaper's Bay, the water was caked in blackness beyond the reach of the pier lanterns, but the waves pounded in at the shore. It flushed between the rocks and out again in a returning clash. The bay had constantly choppy water and jagged black rocks on both sides of the shore. Boats could easily be grounded or capsize. When they neared the end of the pier and the last of the boats, the bridge came into view up overhead.

"Kovan, over here," a voice in the darkness called out from one of the last ships in the water. He turned to see Thann stepping off the longbow drafting boat. He strode across the docking plank waving. *He had made good time and already found a boat*, Kovan thought. When he stepped out onto the main rocky pier and was closer in view, Kovan felt Tali back away.

"We need to go," she whispered urgently from behind.

"What's wrong?" Kovan asked.

"He's not who he says he is. Trust me," she muttered.

"Something wrong, sayzon? I was just leaving to look for you," Thann asked, obviously noticing Kovan's hesitation.

"Thanks for your help back there, but I think I can find my way. Good luck to you, Thann."

Thann stepped into the pier light and Kovan realized he had a short sword in his hand. He gently tapped the metal buckle on his boots with the sword tip, and two more men emerged from the boat's cabin.

"No, sayzon, you need to come with us, now," Thann insisted with a malicious tone.

Kovan measured up the newcomers, the last man off the ship was the most dangerous by far. His sword still sheathed; he crossed the gangplank in a smooth saunter, and Kovan could tell he was light on his feet.

"When they rush, don't run. Just back away so you don't get hit?" he said in a muted breath to the young women. Then he glanced to see her nod that she understood, and he spoke to Thann.

"Thann, buddy. What's going on? I'm not armed, and I won't tell anyone I saw you take this boat. Trust me," he told him, holding his hands out to prove he didn't have a weapon.

"Where's the guard's sword you took?"

"I ditched it with the horse."

"That was a mistake, Kovan," Thann said and he motioned his mates to close in, "Remember, Duraska wants him alive," Thann instructed them.

When they got close enough, the largest man of the three came first from Kovan's right. Kovan slammed his boot into the man's lead foot, toppling him out of balance. He grabbed the man's sword hand and pulled him closer and followed through with the side of his first into the man's windpipe. He ripped the sword free as the man fell, coughing and groaning to the ground. Thann paused at seeing Kovan, now with a weapon. Over Thann's shoulder, the lanky, more dangerous man finally pulled his sword.

"Don't fight us, sayzon, you will only cause yourself pain. I remember you said you weren't any good with a sword. We will cut your hands off and take you maimed if we have to," Thann threatened.

"No. No, what I said was. I'm not the best," Kovan said. He winked at them to throw them off guard and in one swift motion he spun his sword around in his hand. Until it rotated around with the point facing backwards and stepped into Thann, spinning a hard defensive blow and rotating the sword back. Now clutched in both hands now, to clash with the lanky man's blade as it swept in from above. Kovan then parried a low jab and swept up in a quick attack, cutting the man's wrist followed by a down strike across the man's face. Cleaving his ear off as blood splattered the ground, Kovan spun back and directed the point of his sword at Thann.

"Last chance. Who are you working for?" Kovan asked, catching his breath.

Thann rushed in with a primal scream that Kovan abruptly silenced. He deflected the strike, dodged, and countered with two quick cuts to Thann's throat and down his back as he went past. Kovan turned to the first man he had disarmed, still gasping for breath. The man got to his feet and ran off.

"Are you okay?" he asked the young woman who stared blankly but had never moved.

"Yes. I mean you just killed two men, and rather gruesomely, so I'm not great," she said.

"You mind explaining how you knew . . ." Kovan started to ask, but before he could finish his question, the sounds of hoofbeats thundered up from the path. "Change of plan, get in the boat, Flower," Kovan barked.

Whether by choice or fear, she did as he asked without hesitation. Kovan untied the boat, then got it moving out to sea with his feet still on the dock. He pushed the smaller vessel with all his strength until he ran out of room and jumped headfirst onto the deck. They needed to get at least three hundred feet out for the darkness of the sea to hide them. The longbow boat was a small maneuverable fishing vessel, and it took to the ocean quickly, helped by the tide pulling out and south. In the distance, Kovan could see the greencoats arrive on the scene where the two dead bodies lay slain. The riders looked out across the waters blankly. In the rolling distance they drifted away; the night's overcast sky had concealed their escape.

# CHAPTER EIGHT

## RUENOBEE SHORE (TALI)

THE SHORE DESTROYED THE SHIP WHEN THEY HIT THE JAGGED ROCKS. THE front bow of the boat crunched like crusted bread and they both lurched forward off their feet. Even prepared for the impact, Tali still nearly went into the water. Kovan insisted on crossing directly to the nearest point along the Ruenobee shore, instead of heading further south. He wasn't mean about it only hyper focused, and Tali felt she could trust him. He explained that if the greencoats put a boat in the water after them, they would close the distance in a hurry and catch up to them before they reached Cuese let alone Rylabyre. She didn't complain. She preferred they go to Ruenobee. It would be easier to find a ride back to the island from there.

The boat had crossed the bay in about two hours. Kovan was content to drift with the current until the cloud cover cleared, and the moonlight could help him see the shoreline. The boat was now lumped onto the rocks and only slightly bobbed with the waves, Kovan jumped out to a large boulder. One of the few that looked dry and clear on top. Then he turned around to help her out of the boat. It was still dark out, but she could tell the black rocks were slippery. Most were either wet or slimy with seaweed in the crevices. She jumped to the nearest and flattest rock she could safely reach, and Kovan put his arm out to help steady her landing. She navigated two more jumps before she reached the less treacherous gravel shore. They got their bearings and headed up the small cliff face. At the top, they could see lanterns in the distance. The city of Ruenobee sat withdrawn in the hills. For some reason, Kovan looked pleased with himself.

"Look at that. Landed her right near Ruenobee," Kovan said grinning.

"You mean you crashed us right next to Ruenobee?" she corrected him.

"Yes, but I did it on purpose. So, it counts," he said, trampling up the landscape.

She could tell he was intent on keeping a quick pace. One that would have them reach the city by dawn and hopefully mix right in with the early risers. As they walked in the early morning darkness, Tali found she had a lot of questions.

"So, who is the best?" she asked him.

"What?" he said, confused.

"Those guys back there, before you killed them. You said to them you weren't the best. Who is then?" she clarified.

"Well, I've been defeated a few times, but the best I ever saw was a long time ago. He doesn't use his sword anymore; I don't think. Maybe that does make me the best, but I don't usually carry a sword."

"Oh," she replied, satisfied.

"My turn. Explain to me how you knew about Thann?" he asked.

"He's a pier thug is all. I mean he's definitely somebody's dog, because he chums with the local greencoats around the pier all the time, and they never search his boats," she told him.

"Probably bribing them, then?"

"Right. I think he smuggled goods for people or *people* for people. Either way, I have never saw him in trouble with the law. He always got around the authority with a handshake. I thought something was very fishy when I saw him in your cell," she offered.

"Well, that's troubling. He was there before I got thrown in."

"Someone must have known who you were when they apprehended you. I can tell you the Whisper Chain didn't have to look long for you. Personally, I couldn't believe my delivery was to Kovan Rainer."

"Wait, you know who I am?" he asked, surprised.

"Yeah, of course, I'm not an idiot. You defeated Herradon in the battle of Zuvo," she beamed.

"Oh, you're one of those."

"One of what?"

"People who believe everything they read."

"You fought in the war, right?"

"Yes."

"And you killed Herradon?"

"Well, yes, I did do that."

"Sounds like I have the right of it. Of course, most of the accounts of the war are second hand. Only a fool would consider those the truth."

"Now that *is* the right of it. Wait, *you* gave me the crystal!"

"Shhh, I have no idea what you're talking about," she hushed him.

"But why?"

"Listen, I could get in big trouble for that. You're not even supposed to see my face, technically. But I had to see for myself, and when I saw your eyes, I knew it was you. Otherwise, I would have slipped the crystal out before giving you the letter. So, who was it from? Were they telling you to get out of the city?"

"It was a warning. Something's happening again and an old friend of mine is in trouble. I need to get to Adalon."

"Adalon? You're going to Adalon City?"

"Yes. Maybe. I need to find an airship, though. I don't want to travel the Thorn with men on my trail. There's an air station in Rylabyre I can leave from."

"How are you going to get to Rylabyre? The Kyanna Train?"

"I guess so. Though I don't have the coin for it. I might have to get a money transfer in the city, but it's risky. If they know I'm an escapee, I'm in trouble."

"You could just hop on a train, right?" she wondered.

"Dangerous, and you have to ride on the top of a car."

"Why?"

"Because the train is moving fast, Flower."

"Not why is it dangerous, why do you have to ride on top? And please stop calling me flower. My name is Tali," she insisted.

"Fair enough, Tali. Point is, there are peacekeepers on board who check tickets."

"Oh."

"So, have you ever been to Adalon?" Kovan asked.

"No, I wish."

"Are you coming with me?" he asked.

"Did Kovan Rainer just ask me to go on an adventure with him to the greatest city in the world?" she asked aloud to hear the words.

"I think I take it back."

"Well, I wish I could go, but my mother needs me. She's probably worried sick."

"Send her a message. You're in the Chain, right?"

"Maybe. Do you think the greencoats questioned her? I'm worried about her."

"They probably questioned her, but I'm sure she's fine. In Ruenobee, you can find a coach back into Ravenvyre."

She just nodded and kept the pace of Kovan's larger stride, staying next to him up the slope of tall grass. She marveled that while there was no doubt they were being pursued through the night by greencoats she had no sense of peril. Kovan seemed completely under control or very good at faking it. They traveled with a pulse of urgency, but he didn't seem hurried, just focused, and that calmed her.

Tali's shoes had gotten wet jumping from rock to rock, and her feet were starting to ache from the walk, but something about the excitement kept her mind from settling on the nuisance. Between that and the chilly morning air off the bay, she walked with stamina, glad to have her cloak to wrap up in against the colder gusts.

Tali always kept the multitude of pockets inside her cloak packed full of small, handy things and some of her most prized possessions. Some jade and bloodstone gems her mother had given her for protection, along with a couple of verium crystals with firespark, shadow dust, and one with moonstone dust which her mother gave her to ward off evil spirits. She had a small number of amber coins, two raven shaped hair clips, and the odd black and purple coin a stranger gave her once in the Bargainer's Market. It had a purple stone she thought might be amethyst, in the shape of an intricate sigil set into a shiny black coin. When light shone on it, a shimmer would always spin around the edge before settling. It took her ages to figure out it pointed north. It was the oddest compass she had ever seen. She suspected there must be some sort of magic to it, but she liked to hold it as it calmed her and helped her think clearly. The stranger had been an older man with strange eyes. She was passing through the market when she noticed he had left his satchel unattended on the ground. The Bargainer's Market was not only known for its haggling, but also the many pickpockets that were mostly perpetrated by kids. When a street urchin ran through and grabbed the man's bag, she quickly caught the little hooligan and returned the satchel. The man thanked her by giving her the coin. She thought about him every time she held the coin, because in an odd way that she couldn't explain she felt like she knew him. She only thought of him now because Kovan reminded her of that stranger.

When the sunlight started to brighten the sky it became clear that the night had deceived them. The city still sat farther away than they had originally believed. Kovan steered them to the main road, where he waved down a man driving a chart of hay toward Ruenobee.

"Sir, would you mind if we jumped in back, and rode with you the rest of the way?" Kovan asked.

"Don't see why not? Where's your horses?" the driver inquired.

"Actually, our fishing vessel grounded on the shore in the darkness, and we were just trying to get back to the city."

"The bay is not friendly during the day, at night it's perilous," the man informed them.

"We found that out sure enough," Kovan replied.

"I suppose you did. Jump on back but hold on," the driver instructed.

Tali helped herself up onto the back wooden rail of the cart, ignoring Kovan's hand to help her. She got well-positioned and clutched on to the rails with her back against a bundle of hay. Kovan got in next to her. The cart slowly got moving and Tali relished the rest for her feet and yawned an endless breath. She had to admit to herself she was in a sort of dream state, adventuring around with a war hero. She had loved reading about the war when she was in school. Kovan had always seemed like an unstoppable force. If Qudin had actually done as some books say and called on the lightning, surely Kovan was the thundercloud of the Resistance. She almost wanted to follow him to Adalon just to ask him about all the things she always wondered. Did they really come across the hidden city of the Tregoreans? How did he infiltrate the Citadel and defeat the consortium? How did they sail the Frozen Straights and live, and of course were him and Ellaria Moonstone really a thing? Those and others came to mind.

They passed through the gates of the city, where the jumbled box architecture stacked high into the morning sky. Though she had no memory of ever living here, her mother had told her she was born in Ruenobee. They lived in the city until she was six but after her father died in the skirmish of Lowtalla, they moved to Ravenvyre. The city's main road was brick laid and rumbled under her as the cart's wheels tackled the uneven surface. The buildings were wood wrapped with small, low, sloping metal roofs. The metal was more abundant in Ruenobee than Ravenvyre, because of the smelting factory, and they used the scraps all over. The overlapping roofs were discolored and rusted in random patterns of erosion. The thin wood siding was painted in various colors and together with the roofs and the people's personal decorations, the city was vibrant. At some point, Kovan tapped on the side of the cart and the driver slowed so they could jump off. He waved their appreciation, and the cart rattled on.

She followed Kovan to one of the nearest street vendors, and he motioned for her to talk with the merchant. Slightly confused, she approached the woman who was still setting up station.

"Morning, can you tell me where the train station is?" Tali inquired, looking around nervously as she had lost sight of Kovan.

"Oh, hello. Yes, it's at the western edge of the city. If you go up two blocks and take Spear Street it's a straight shot," the merchant pointed.

"Thank you," Tali said, and she walked where she was shown. At the next street, she saw Kovan coming up the side road without a shirt on and carrying something bundled in his hand. He had apparently circled around the block and stolen a shirt from the vendor as Tali distracted her. As he got close, Tali could see the jumbled array of disturbing scars across his body and the gray hair of his torso. There was a particularly nasty scar on his chest that she stared at wondering how he had survived such a wound. When they crossed over and out of sight, he put on his stolen shirt.

"You could have warned me," she insisted, slightly annoyed.

"No. It was better you didn't know what I was up to," he said undaunted.

They came to a building with marble columns and stamped metal ornamental tiles. It was the Ruenobee bank, Kovan dashed over and climbed a few steps up to a set of bronze doors.

"I'll be just a minute, don't go far," he said, and he pulled the large door open and disappeared inside.

While Kovan was in the bank, she strolled around the block. Going down one side of the street and back up, looking in shops and store windows as she went. Most places had yet to open, but the merchant window displays were as colorful as the buildings, full of small butcher hanging meats and stacked cheeses. A hat store with rounder hats, high crown hats, and women's flare and lace hats were nestled next to a spice shop with escalating sacks of unground spices. Even through the glass, there was a powerful, sharp and layered smell. When she made her way back up the street, Kovan was finally descending the steps. He wasn't running out, so that was a good sign, and he was holding two receipt slips in his hand and waving her over.

"Here," he said and handed her a slip of paper.

Tali scanned the slip. It was a train ticket, *The Kyana Train line, One way trip, from Ruenobee to Rylabyre*, and looked back at Kovan.

"You can buy them in the bank, I got two. I know you said you're going home, but the ticket is good for a week. I need you to do me a favor though."

She took the ticket reluctantly, "What do you need me to do?" she asked. He handed her two coins, "Take these to the merchant back on the main road. I owe her for the shirt. I would, but I'm not sure what she might do if she sees me in her shirt."

"What do I tell her?" Tali asked.

"I don't care as long as my debt is paid. When you're done, meet up with me at the station. I need to pick up some things before we head south, if you're coming."

Kovan turned and started down the street. She didn't know what to say to him. She wasn't sure herself how she felt. She was not used to receiving gifts. This ticket felt like a lot more, Kovan wasn't just asking her to go— he really seemed to want her to go. Which puzzled her. She wasn't sure at all what she had done to deserve that kind of faith. The firespark crystal really was done on a whim. She had it with her after leaving the alchemists that day, and when she got the details of her assignment, she felt a powerful urge to help him. Simple as that. Only now that she thought about it, she realized that she never stopped to wonder why. Of all their messengers, why was she asked to deliver a message to such an important person? It could have been Daric's attempt to conceal Thann or possibly someone higher up. The possibilities that someone she didn't know was using her preyed on her mind on her walk back to the merchant. Once there, she clumsily explained to the women that a stranger gave her some coins to bring there, because he had stolen some goods from her. The merchant looked confused but was polite and took the coins. When Tali walked away, she realized the women probably believed Tali was the one who stole from her.

She wove her way through the city and found the station bustling with lots of men in full suits and hats. She knew passenger tickets for the train were expensive and thought maybe she could sell her ticket to someone for less than the printed cost. It was a fleeting idea, though. Because while Tali knew she could, she knew she wouldn't. The crowded station limited her vision to only a few feet, and she stood overwhelmed in the throng of confusion looking for Kovan until she heard her name being called.

"Tali," Kovan said from her right. She might have missed him, anyway. He had been busy in a short time. As he was now sporting a wide-brimmed hat that partly shielded his eyes in shadow, and he had a bag over his shoulder that looked to be full of things.

"Last chance. You sure you don't want to come with me?"

"I'm not sure of anything. But no, I have to get back to my mother."

"Well, thanks for the help. I owe you one."

"Wow, Kovan Rainer owes me. That's something."

"Not really. Take care young Raven."

"Raven? Well, I like that better than flower. See you around Kovan. Try not to kill anyone."

"No promises," he said, then he tipped the front bill of his hat to her and boarded the train.

Tali moved away to leave the station platform and the crowded ramparts where she had to dodge large pull carts of luggage and another one full of chickens stacked in wire cages. The contents from the chicken cages littered the ramparts. Near the outer edge of the station, she took a last look at the train, but feeling someone approach her from the side, she stiffened.

"Hello, Rue," a deep voice said from behind her. The hair on the back of her neck stood on end. She turned slowly to see whose voice it belonged to.

"Maki!" she stammered in shock at seeing her Whisper Chain trainer, "What are you doing here?"

"You sure have a habit of bumping into the most dangerous people in this world," Maki said.

She assumed he meant Kovan and waved off the assertion. "He's a friend," she added.

"Interesting," Maki mused.

"What do you need, Maki? I know you don't seek people out to just say hello," she questioned. Tali found the coincidence improbable.

"Quite the opposite Rue, I was not seeking you out. However, I have a warning for you," he said, staring at her intensely. Tali's heart sank, and she began looking for escape routes off the station. "The Whisper Chain is looking for you Rue. It seems they suspect you of going beyond your duty."

"When, Why? The last message I delivered was to the prison. I gave my extras to my Link and told him; message delivered. I'm not sure what you or they suspect me of doing. I can tell you my Link offered me the sums as a bonus, and I refused," she said defensively.

"I'm on your side Rue. I can see you are telling the truth. Whatever part you played; I am sure it was with good intentions. For this reason, I will give my second warning. The Whisper Chain may be fracturing, and I suspect some internal corruptions. What you have told me about your

Link adds up with some of my own findings and it leads me to a frightening conclusion."

"What do I do, Maki?" she asked. Tali was unsure what to make of what he had told her, but Maki had never given her a reason not to trust him.

"When you get back home, lie low. Do not refuse new offers, but don't take many either. I will vouch for you again. If all goes well, I will sort the corruption out and I will return to you and let you know it is safe to work again. I don't believe you are a concern yet. Or . . ." he paused as the screeching scream of the train whistle blasted.

"Or what?" she implored.

"Or you can use that ticket in your hand and board the train. I believe they would overlook your absence. As I believe that the integrity of the Whisper Chain is intact outside of this region, though I'm uncertain. It's possible it will raise suspicions. Still, I don't think they will follow you. It would just be more likely that upon your return, you would be under further scrutiny if the corruption remains. However, if you leave, I could get you a message and let you know when it was safe to return. Simply open a post box anywhere under the name Rue Darkeyes and I will find you. If you choose to leave, be wary of wearing your cloak. It will give you away," Maki stopped and looked at her, judging her reaction.

He had given her a lot to think about. She was now scared to return home, and she desperately wanted to follow Kovan. Both pointed her in the direction she should go, but her mother loomed like a giant magnet with the strongest pull on her. She knew what her mother would say and she had an idea what to do. Only two questions remained. Would Maki agree and how much did she trust him? She hesitated but decided she did trust him.

"Maki, could you deliver a message to someone for me? Then I feel we could part ways until sometime down the road when we meet again," she asked him in a way she thought he would understand that she meant to leave.

"Yes," he told her.

Tali wrote a message on a slip of paper. She tried to be short but convincing for her mother. She rolled the note up, stuck a raven shaped hair beret in the middle, and neatly folded the loose corners to seal the message. She handed it to Maki, smiled and voiced thank you without the words. They turned their separate ways, and she rushed to the train. She shed her cloak on the way and held it in her hands as she ran.

Steam was filling the platform and the raucous of the engine was roaring. She reached up to the bronze grab bar of the large rumbling machine and stepped up. A porter at the door screened her ticket and let her inside. The atmosphere of the interior of the car was in stark contrast to the platform. The car's shell and glass tempered the wind and ruckus outside. She felt like she had burst in like a firework. She made her way to the back of the car, Kovan lifted the brim of his hat up, saw her, and smiled. She sat down without a word, but with the blood pumping vigorously in her veins. Kovan adjusted his hat back over his face to hide the light, as the train lurched and churned into motion.

# CHAPTER NINE

## RETURNING (LEARON)

Learon was dreaming about the moon falling into the lake, bright yellow like the sun as it fell and turning white as the glossy cracked surface touched down into the water. A small ripple spread out and grew into a tidal wave, water crashing all around. Then a man was there. His eyes were plain white and long scratches lined his face. Like a claw dragged from his forehead to his chin, and a mechanical arm with thin copper fingers was pulling at his legs. But there was a woman there too. A young woman he had never seen before. They were running with the sunlight scattered and broken on the ground into a thousand fractured points of light. Stepping from one spot of light to another, fearful of what lay in the darkness beneath. The young woman had fast hands that moved in a whirl and she caught a dart in the air. An odd-looking arrow she showed him and smiled, and blood was suddenly at her mouth and she fell. He was so afraid for her. He held her head, and the rain fell on her face, so he wiped it gently away. Her eyelids fluttered and blinked, and she opened her eyes. He was so close he could feel her breath. She was about to speak when Elias shook him awake.

"Time to go," Elias said. A light rain sprinkled down, and he had an odd grin on his face. Learon sat up. The sunlight was barely breaking into the sky, but their campsite looked clean. Elias had been up for a short time already and was prepared to leave, Learon realized.

Learon stood up, packed his bedroll, and attached it to one of his packs with rope. He gathered his gear and looked around, slightly lost. It took him a moment to realize he hadn't set the perimeter wire last night.

He was more tired than he thought. Elias looked fresh. His eyes weren't as tired, and he stood straighter on his feet today. Learon could see now he was older, but the man was in excellent condition for his age. Learon decided he had everything accounted for and led the way again.

"Here you go, kid. Thanks for the loan," Elias said as he handed him back the quartz crystal necklace.

"Sure," he said quizzically. "This is the way out of the ravine. We should be at Garner's lodge in about eight hours. I have a horse there that can get us back to town. A doctor can look at your leg and there's a coach that goes north to Atava. I'm heading there myself. If you prefer to buy a horse and travel with me, I wouldn't mind the company," he told Elias.

"I'm grateful," Elias said. He trailed behind Learon on the path, and he noticed that Elias's steps no longer included a limp, and his makeshift cane had been discarded. Learon didn't want to pry. So, he didn't ask about it. He was curious about the grin, though.

"What was so funny back there? Was I talking in my sleep?" he asked.

"No, not exactly," Elias answered.

"Then what?"

"Well, you were hard to wake up, and I got the feeling you were being visited by the Night Angel," Elias suggested.

"What or who is the Night Angel?"

"It's an old tale. Some would say an old magic. Basically, it's what philosophers used to call the person of your dreams. A person you're entwined with. Some say their visits bring with them a protection."

"There was a young woman actually. Are you saying she's real?"

"Interesting. She could be. It's similar to the philosophy of soulmates."

"So that was my soulmate, come on?" Learon said skeptically.

"Legend says every soul is split into two different people. Who's to say if that is real. I'm not sure if the Night Angel exists. However, people being intrinsically connected is most definitely real. The bond is sometimes more easily felt in the dream world. Where time and distance are unconstrained, and the barriers of existence and reality become blurred, allowing others to connect."

"And you believe in this?"

"I do."

"So, can anyone connect to you through your dreams?"

"Yes. But invading a person's dream is a unique thing. Some beings find traveling there easier than others."

"So, did she have the same dream?" Learon wondered.

"No," Elias said flatly.

"How does that work?"

"Remember, time is unconstrained, and reality blurred. You're connecting, but time is not the same."

Learon didn't know if he believed a word of what Elias was saying but he couldn't get her out of his head, and worse, he couldn't explain why he felt sad that the memory of her was fading.

They kept walking through the ravine for most of the morning. The heat gained in strength by the time they exited the woods. Elias had taken his jacket off, and it was half-spilling out of his leather satchel as they walked. The descent had been uneventful and mostly done in silence, until the lodge was in their sights. A small wisp of smoke drifted from the green stone chimney.

The lodge was a small moss stone structure with a set of stables. Old man Garner was a quiet hermit type, living out here at the mouth of the ravine, near the riverside. He charged people a small sum to stable their horse if they had the need, not much more than what was necessary to care for the horse, but he never charged Learon anything. In the winter, Learon would travel out here to check on him and bring him supplies. They weren't exactly friends, but they enjoyed the silence of each other's company. Garner was an amazing fisherman, and they would fish for trout in the local rivers together. He was also knowledgeable about a lot of things, including the Great War. Learon liked to pick his brain when he could.

At the lodge, Learon hurried around the side to check on the stables before going inside. Elias waited at the covered front porch. Oddly, Garner's horse, Dilly, was missing from the stables. It was rare he went anywhere. Learon's horse, Apple, was there. She was Learon's preferred breed of horse, a warm-blooded mare, mostly brown with white on her nose. She was getting on in age and had slowed in the last few years, but she could still pull a cart and didn't spook easily. A good warm-blooded horse was a perfect athletic mix of the cold-blooded horses that were commonly the stronger pull horses, and the hot-blooded that were fast and slim and used for racing in Eloveen.

Learon came back to the front door, knocked, and let himself in. Garner never locked his door, believing there was nothing worth stealing, anyway. Learon announced himself as he stepped inside, but the place was empty and some of the usual supplies that hung on the wall were missing. Two water cans, his sword, and a roll of rope. Maybe more.

Learon was growing concerned. He turned around and went back outside,

"Well, no one's here," He told Elias.

"You seem worried, something is wrong?" Elias asked.

"I don't know. Mr. Garner doesn't leave this place that often. Almost never, actually," Learon said, scanning the surrounding landscape.

"How many horses are around back?" Elias asked

"Just mine, why?"

"Well, there are fresh tracks of one horse coming up the trail. They arrived before the rain last night. Then there are tracks overtop of two horses leaving this morning," Elias pointed to what he'd found in the dirt. Learon mulled over the prospect of someone other than him coming out here. More troubling was trying to understand what could get Garner to leave his home.

"Well, I thought we would rest when we got here, but I'd like to keep moving and ride to town, if you don't mind?"

"I don't mind, let's get on the road," Elias said.

Learon saddled Apple and returned to pick up Elias. They rode off to the west in a slow trot. Learon still searched the area as they went, for any signs of Garner. Seeing nothing, he picked up the pace and pressed on, concern etched upon his face.

※

THE SMALL TOWN OF WEST MEADOW WAS FIFTY LEAGUES WEST OF ATAVA, right on the Tavillore border. It was a community of farmers, like most the Atava Valley. There were almost two hundred people who lived in town and twenty more just outside of it, in more secluded homesteads like Garner. There was a row in the center of town that held within it the Peacekeepers post, Rose's Restaurant and Inn, a small Sagean temple, a general store, and a merchant block. The block was a building made up of six small merchant stores with quarter houses above. All of it built out of wood and paneled cedar exteriors. Except for the inn, which was river stone and the oldest building in town.

Learon and Elias passed a few houses on the outskirts already, but only peeked at the town center. Learon was heading for his mother's house first on the east edge of town by the Pike River, they were almost there when Elias tapped him on the shoulder and told him to stop.

"What's wrong?" Learon said, "The house is just past those tall maple trees."

"Armed riders came through here."

"How can you tell?"

"The weight of their horse's hooves left deep tracks. But also, you see the pattern of them," he said pointing, "They ride in a staggered, straight filing. That way it helps them protect their flanks and avoid ambush. The tracks can look like just two riders."

"Why the staggered?" Learon asked.

"It reduces the chance more than one rider might get hit by a single bullet, but mostly it allows them to split their forces faster. For cover or coordinated attack."

"What do you think they're doing here?" Learon asked with rising worry in his voice.

"Your house is just over the hill there?" Elias asked, "I'll meet you there on foot. I can sweep around and check the area."

"Agreed," Learon agreed.

He realized he was squeezing the reins and twisting them in his palm. He stopped and smoothed the strap between his thumbs. Elias grabbed Learon's leg before walking away, "Ride up without stopping. If someone's there and they're armed, just answer their questions. If your mother is not there, don't panic. Just answer their questions. Whoever it is. The most important thing is to be on their side until they leave you no other option. Oh, and if no one's there, don't shoot me with an arrow when I come up."

Learon rode up the trail and around the maples. The large branches of one unfolded just above his head as he passed. The closer he got, the more worried he became. *Why were armored men in West Meadow?* He wondered. When he got up to the house and saw nothing, he took a deep breath. He dismounted and latched Apple onto the front porch post, and called out, "Mother, I'm back. Mother!"

One step inside, he knew something was wrong. The house was a wreck. Someone had tipped the tall cherry wood cabinet over, papers and ink spilled out to the floor. The mantle place was empty, and all the regularly displayed items were scattered to the ground. He yelled out for his mother again, but no answer. Panic rose in his chest. He stepped over the broken tall, hand-clock at the foot of the stairs and charged up; searched the two rooms aloft frenzied and found nothing but more wreckage. Hearing the door creak at the entry, he bounded back down to see Elias stepping over the threshold.

"Nobody's here!" he said, flustered.

"I noticed. Does your mother have her own horse?"

"Yes, her brother's horse. Why?"

"Does she know Mr. Garner?"

"Yes," Learon said, seeing what Elias was getting too. "You think she rode out to Garner's lodge last night?"

"Yes. Where they went from there, I can't say. Nor how she avoided the soldiers. I would think they didn't go south, considering the terrain. Do either of them know anyone in Atava?"

"Yes, my uncle lives there now."

"Do you have any idea why someone would be after your mother or you? Is your father not around?"

"No, he died when I was eight."

"What would someone be looking for in here? Does your mother have anything she shouldn't?"

"No, I can't think of anything."

"Maybe a weird object that she doesn't let you touch or an amulet she keeps around her neck that throws off a strange light or a book with odd writing in it?"

Learon stopped. The package he had just discovered in his father's cabin rested in his pack like a barking dog. But there was no way anyone could know he had found it. The only thought that occurred was that someone was simply after his father's journal. He ran back upstairs to search his desk. The journal was missing from its spot next to his drawing book and schoolbooks. He ran back down to Elias, who hadn't moved from the doorway.

"My father's journal is missing."

"What makes it significant?"

"Just that it's missing. I always keep it on my desk."

"Is there anyone in town you trust? And don't mistake my meaning. When I say trust, I mean with your life. Not trust to give you a loaf of bread."

"Just Rose. She runs the tavern and inn. She's close with my mother, but more than that she is too stubborn to intimidate."

"Well, the road to Atava takes a full day. My guess is that whoever came here, assuming they didn't find what they were looking for, would have split up. Someone will still be in town, but they would have sent someone to Atava already. Maybe someone to scout the south trails too. The bad news is that the soldier sent to Atava is ahead of your mother. They would have searched here and split up before your mother had left

Garner's lodge. We need to see if we can learn anything else about who we're facing, and I need a horse if I'm to ride with you."

"Elias, I appreciate the help, but this is my mess. You can go wherever you're needed."

"Kid, I owe you one for back there, and it looks like I'm needed here. Also, my hair is up now. I need to follow this thread until the end," Elias said stoically, and then stepped outside.

Learon returned to his room and stared around for a moment, unable to think straight. He ran his hand through his hair over and over, trying to decide what to take with him. He dumped all his supplies out on his bed and repacked. His breathing was still coming in short beats as he exchanged some of his gear out. He grabbed a bag near his door for Adalon and stuffed the contents back inside that the intruders had pulled free. He took a last look around and met Elias outside. Together, they made their way into town. Elias trusted that the two of them together might be enough to get past someone looking just for Learon, but they still took the long way around the main circle of town and came to the back entry to the inn. Learon left Elias in the rear ally as he went through the back door to find Rose.

The shadows of the alleyway partially concealed the door, but it too, was always unlocked. It connected directly to the tavern kitchen, and they used it to take trash out the back or propped open to help exhaust heat from the kitchen fires. Learon stepped inside and found the cook preparing something for the next day's meals.

"Jema, have you seen Rose?" Learon called out in a casual voice. Not too soft to seem like he was sneaking up on her, but not too loud either. It was never a good idea to sneak up on a person with a knife.

"Learon! What are you doing here?" Jema replied.

"I'm looking for Rose, have you seen her?"

"Yes, sugar, she's at the front desk, I'll go get her," Jema said. She put down her carving knife and left through the duel-hinged door. Learon's stomach growled, and he helped himself to some small pies on the table. He devoured the first one he touched, not realizing how hungry he was until the moment his hands touched the hot roast pie. Jema made these great single serving pies with roast, fried potatoes and rosemary gravy. Wrapped and baked in a dough that was soft and buttery with a hint of sweetness. He knew Jema would yell at him, but Rose wouldn't mind. He ate at the inn almost every day. When he wasn't studying for his entrance exams, he would help where he could. He took three more pies for the road and some apples for Apple, wrapping them in a thin cream-colored towel resting on the counter and placing it in his pack. A few moments later, Rose came through the door with a hurried look on her face.

"Learon!" she said excitedly and gave him a hug, which surprised him. She was like a really loving aunt, but she was not a hugger.

"Rose, what's going on? Where's my mother?"

"Honestly, I don't know. This group of soldiers, I guess they are, came into town yesterday. They stopped in the tavern and asked about your mother. I overheard them and I didn't like the look of them. So, I sent Sara out to tell your mother to go to Garner's until they left."

"Are they greencoats from Atava?"

"No, they said they were here on special orders from the Prime Commander. Learon, they were not happy when they found that both you and your mother were missing."

"What did they do when they didn't find us?"

"Well, they came back here, and they were angry, is all. Old man Garner came in, he took one look at them and left. Then three of the soldiers took off. I guess two men left heading north and one went south, I think. The fourth one is still here."

"Alright, thank you, Rose. Um, I took some pies and apples if that's ok?"

"Anything you need, Learon," she said and gave him another hug.

"Actually, I'm glad you said that. I kind of need a horse?" Learon asked with hesitation.

"A horse? What happened to Apple?"

"She's fine. I have a friend helping me, but he needs a horse so we can ride for Atava before the night."

"Well, I suppose you can take Ghost," Rose said with a cringe.

"Ghost?"

"She's a good horse, she just scares easy is all. I haven't had her very long. I got her from a traveling showman, when his troupe came through for the Awakening Festival."

"Rose, I don't know how to thank you."

"You just get out of here, would ya, and find your mother."

"Thank you."

Learon left the kitchen with a bag of food. Neither Rose nor Jema would let him leave without a bundle of whatever they could pile into a sack. When he got to the ally, he told Elias what Rose had said and handed him a pie. Elias did not look happy at hearing the words Prime Commander. They went and saddled Ghost. Elias seemed to have no problem with the mare. Elias said he would be fine, that he had a way with animals. Apparently, he wasn't lying. They strapped down their supplies and rode out of town, following the Pike river by Elias's request. They galloped in the shallow bank before finally meeting up with the road. They pulled up to the heavily trodden thoroughfare as the sun was setting. It was a full days ride to Atava, but Learon planned to push the horses as far as he could and get there as fast as possible.

# CHAPTER TEN

## THE KING'S DAUGHTER (ELLARIA)

ELLARIA SAT ON THE WOOD FLOOR OF THE TEMPORARY OFFICE INSIDE THE Mystic's Building. It had a small rectangular window that looked out at the sidewalks to the north. The view was partially obscured, but the window was operable, and she opened it to hear the noise outside. The typical chaos of campus was muted with most of the students isolated away studying for their final exams. She would have preferred a view of the elevated Arcana commons. The meandering rooftop to the student housing interconnected the entire complex of Arcana buildings and was a serene oasis.

She sat with her back against the low bookshelf, reviewing the issued alchemy textbooks. She liked the feeling of being surrounded by books. Books were sacred to Ellaria. It was an obsession born from growing up in the shadow of the Empire, a time when books were scarce. She had witnessed their power. Maybe the most important book in history, The Guardians of Illumination, helped spark the Resistance. The original text was discovered and illegally published when Ellaria was only fourteen. The thousand year old book was a collection of eyewitness accounts of the powers of the luminaries and it shed light on the history of Territhmina. The Emperor outlawed the book, and publicly executed everyone involved with the printing as warning of the consequence of treason and blasphemy.

Years later when the war ended there was a hunger to uncover more of the lost history. However, without Qudin's help, the Guild abandoned their efforts. No one could get into the same places he could. Places with powerful protections and safeguards. Ellaria wondered just how many things Qudin might have found since they last spoke nearly seventeen years ago. She was positive his thirst for knowledge would have only increased over time. The oldest books Ellaria and Qudin had found were written in a dead language no scholar could decipher. Their shared devotion to the past boarded on obsession and Kovan never understood it. What was discovered had rejuvenated the practice of alchemy. However, it was still considered to be a heretical field of study by some.

Delvette was confident Ellaria would change that, but Ellaria knew that ignorance would never be convinced with the truth, especially when the truth was inconvenient. Ellaria didn't have any such delusions about her lecture. Maybe she would reach the students, and maybe she wouldn't. Realistically, all she wanted to accomplish was to buy time until Kovan arrived. *If he was coming?* She thought, a doubt creeping in, but she pushed it back. Of course since she was going to speak, she figured she couldn't help but try to shake the pillars that be. Part of her wanted to escape this entanglement for the New World, if her window for retreat hadn't already closed.

Ellaria continued to look over her things, when a messenger came through her open door. She watched as he checked the door number twice, before finally asking, "Ms. Moonstone?"

"Yes, you're in the right place, dear," she motioned him to come across the room to where she sat on the floor. The messenger was dressed in the typical tight gray jacket with yellow trim at the shirt collar. He wore a flat cap, embroidered with the post emblem in the center, and he walked a few steps further inside her office and held out a handful of letters.

"If you're expecting me to get up and take them from your hand, you're going to be waiting awhile. I'm old. I'm down here. I'm not getting up just for you," she said.

"Sorry," he said, taking the few extra steps and handing her the letters.

"There's a coin there on my desk for your efforts. Thank you."

"Thank you," the young man said and left.

Ellaria turned in place on the floor, leaned her back against the bookshelf, and started to look through the bundle of mail and messages. The majority of it were red envelopes that indicated magnotype messages. When her office location was finalized, she went and set up a forwarding service to deliver all her posts here. Most of the messages were congratulatory and from her colleagues. Apparently, the word was out that she had resigned from her special emissary position in the Guild and it was assumed she had retired. There was one from Kalihjan, which was curious. She opened it last.

*Bonemen in Kalihjan. Stay vigilant.*
*I fear the shadow's quest to grow stronger again, unseen, has emerged from the darkness. No longer hiding away inside the long cold forgotten night.*
*Your friend 1&5*

She thought for only a split second before understanding what the code one and five meant. It was from Qudin. His name, written in the first letter of every fifth word. He was alive and was recently in Kalihjan. Something scared him enough to send her this. If the Prime's legion of men were screening her mail, they missed one. The only way they would have missed the code was if they were far less capable than she suspected. The other possibility was they had intercepted this and wanted the communications to continue. Something about Qudin's observation made her rethink the armored soldiers that had accompanied the Prime. They had also reminded her of the Sagean's private army, called the bonemen, named because they were bound to protect the Sagean's spirit longer than anything living or dead. After the body had died and the flesh decayed, the bones would remain. What Ellaria didn't understand was if Malik and Dunne were working with a new Sagean luminary, why hasn't someone claimed the Emperor's throne?

She finished reading her mail, she stood and stared out the window at the grass field and the stone path. When a knock on the door sounded, she turned around to see Wade Duval standing at the threshold. He stood in the doorway with an odd expression on his face. Ellaria noticed a bandage wrapped around his forearm, where it disappeared under his rolled-up sleeve. She had heard about the street fight, but no one had any details except that someone lost their life and it was Wade that took it.

"Hello Wade," she said, surprised to see him. "What are you doing here?"

"Ms. Moonstone, or can I still call you Ella? You're a professor here now, so I don't know," he asked with a smile. Ellaria's face grew flush. She had forgotten she had told him to call her Ella, and now she had a feeling he might never let her live it down. He had such a charming way about himself, it was disarming.

"I'm not a professor. You can call me Ellaria. Now, what can I help you with, Wade?"

"I wanted to talk to you about my altercation in the streets a few days ago," he said.

"Oh? Have a seat," she motioned for him to take the chair opposite of her desk.

Wade moved across the room and sat in the leather reading chair in the corner. He put his elbows on his knees and looked back at her innocently, but intensely. He seemed to be waiting for her to sit as well, so she sat down behind her desk.

"You might have heard that I had a fight in the streets near campus that resulted in my attacker's death. You may have also heard the attacker's identity has yet to be figured out. Well, what nobody knows is the reason he attacked me. The greencoats think he was just trying to rob Ander and I, but the truth is he was after you," he said, and he paused, "You're not surprised?"

She was surprised, but she was good at hiding her feelings when she wanted too. "I'm confused," she told him. "What made you think he was after me?" she asked.

"He must have seen you and I talking outside the coffee bar that evening. He was convinced you had given me something. He kept demanding I hand it to him. I can tell you he wasn't in his right mind and he was a far deadlier fighter then I am. I only bested him with help and by accident really," he admitted.

She could see the incident still shook him. If the assailant had seen them talking, then it was likely the same man who was following her, but she wanted to make sure there weren't two men that night. "Did the man have a mustache and a rounder hat?" she asked.

"Yes, and sideburns. Did you know him?" he confirmed and sat up straighter.

"No. When I was leaving the bar, I thought I saw someone like that spying on me. He was smoking a cigar, and I had smelled cigar smoke earlier that day. He started to chase me but I lost him in the city."

"After he lost you, he circled back and found me. Did you report the man to the greencoats?"

"No," she said.

"I guess it doesn't matter now. I had enough witnesses to clear me of any wrongdoing. Do you know why he was after you?"

"I couldn't say. Though it's not the first time I've been in danger, Wade," she told him. "But I am terribly sorry you were put in danger because of me."

"Right. Well, I just wanted to warn you that someone is after you. I was definitely under the impression he was working for someone. Also, it seems connected to recent events."

"What events?" she asked.

"Well, a new Prime Commander was announced, and the next day I hear you have resigned?"

"How perceptive of you. What can I tell you Wade, is it's a dangerous world and it is more dangerous today than it was yesterday."

"Is that why I have the feeling I've got myself involved in something?" he asked with worry in his voice.

Ellaria shared his concern and didn't know what to tell him. She assumed the Prime was having her followed. Whoever it was, they would now be under the impression that Wade was with her. He *was* involved now, for better or worse.

"Wade, listen, you may be in further danger. I don't know, but things are happening that have me worried."

"Like someone willing to kill to get information about you or what about all the people going missing?" he asked with a rise of tension in his tone.

"Wait, who's gone missing?" she asked, confused. This was news to her.

"I received a letter from my mother that they haven't heard from my older sister, Tara. My mother was worried she might have been taken. She said there have been reports in the south of people going missing," he explained.

"I was just in the south. They're going missing from the cities now?" she said.

"Well, I guess they thought it was just a rise in activity from the beasts coming in from the forests to feed, but there hasn't been any blood or signs of struggle," he said.

"What part of the south?" she asked.

"My mother says it's happening in all of the major cities. My sister Tara was working in Aquom. She was an apprentice at the Liberty Printing Company."

"I know them well. I will reach out to my contacts there and see what I can find out for you."

"Thank you, Ellaria," he said.

"In the meantime. All I can say is keep your eyes open for anything suspicious. If you see someone watching you or following you, come tell me. Don't handle it on your own," she cautioned.

"If there's something going on. I want to know," he countered.

"Honestly, I don't know. Yes. Something is happening, but I don't know what just yet. If I knew more, I would say more," she said.

"Sure," he said acceptingly and stood up to leave. She followed to walk him out. He stopped two steps into the hall just outside the door.

"Oh, I wanted to say that I'm excited for your lecture. Everyone I know on campus is as well. There are a lot of us who are hoping you teach a class next year. Most people dropped the magical arts classes because last year's course was kind of a joke. If you don't mind me saying."

"Why would I mind I wasn't teaching those? I should tell you and you can relay this to whomever you like: If I do decide to teach, my classes will not be a joke. I'm sure some of them think alchemy is something out of a joybird's troupe or showman's spectacle."

"Some do. I guess I'll see you around. Thanks for hearing me out," he said, and he was about to walk away when a young woman rushed toward them in the hallway.

She had dark skin and her dark purple dress was elegant with a bodice designed with firm lines in a military like styling. The shoulders flared out in points, and a sheer black cape flowed from beneath and out, trimmed with gold edging. Her hair was pulled back by a scarf of gray lace with gold stitching. She was younger than Wade and around her neck was a polished silver and red bloodstone. Ellaria's first impression was that she must be from the Free Cities, and someone of importance. Wade had hung back by Ellaria's side, too curious to leave, and by the look on his face interested in meeting the beautiful young woman.

"Are you Ellaria Moonstone?" the young woman said, slightly out of breath.

"Yes, child. How can I help you?" she asked.

"I'm Dalliana. I'm Danehin's daughter, my father said to come find you if anything happened," she said.

"What's going on, what's happened?" Ellaria asked.

"He's missing!"

"Come in, come in," she said and pulled the young woman into her office, she directed her to the chair Wade had just occupied.

"Have a seat and tell me what's happened," she said. Then she turned to Wade, "Wade. In or out. But shut the door."

"In," Wade said. He closed the door and stood near the wall. Ellaria noticed the young woman was hesitating. She had her hands folded in her lap and glanced at Wade.

"Oh, Wade, would you sit down? You're scaring her," she ordered him, "It's safe dear, I trust him. Go ahead, you're with friends. When did your father go missing?"

"Well, that's just it. I'm not sure. I received a magnotype from him over a month ago. In it he said he was traveling from Adalon to the Citadel to look into something. Nobody has seen nor heard from him since," she stammered.

"Over a month ago? Why was Danehin was in Adalon?"

"He received an invitation to come and speak with someone named Dunne. He had received many letters the week prior to his departure, but I'm not sure what any of it was about, only that my father was angry and worried. I've never seen him so worried. He doubled my guards and doubled the patrols throughout Illumeen. He also ordered army recruitments to increase and had the treasurer plead with the trustees to finance something called the High Tide Program. I'm not sure what that is, I'm not completely involved in all the affairs of state yet. My father was just bringing me in. The plan was for me to get accustomed this year while I finished basics. Then he wanted me to go off to the new university on Ioka, before he would allow me a seat."

Ellaria thought for a moment and no one spoke, awaiting her to react. It sounded like someone had tipped Danehin off to the appointment of the Prime. Maybe Dunne brought him here to convince him and when he couldn't, he threw him in a jail cell somewhere.

"How many times did he contact you while he was here in Adalon City?" Ellaria asked.

"Three times. Once to say he had arrived, a second time to check in on the progress of the Illumeen battlements, and then the last time to say he was traveling to Andal. He said he wanted to put his eyes on the Citadel before returning. The three messages were a day apart from each other."

"So, he was only in the city for a short time. Where's the squadron he arrived with?" she asked.

"He didn't really bring one. Just two soldiers and Ragor, his personal bodyguard. They're all missing," she blurted out, obviously getting more upset the more they talked.

"Where are your guards now, dear?"

"Outside the entrances to this building. I only let four men disembark with me into the city. I have another ten on our ship in the harbor. Believe me, I wanted to bring the entire garrison here, but I only left word that they should send warships to Adalon if something happens to me."

"I get it. The first thing we need to do is get you back on that ship and back home. Now that I know your father is missing, I will search for him. I don't want you to go missing and a war started just yet. Though I fear that is where we are heading. We need to set up a relay post and codes so we can communicate. When you get back home, please have someone set up a post under the name Burke Hill. Have someone you trust pick up the messages and deliver them to you. Our point of the relay will be Azlo Hill. This way we can try to communicate without fear of our messages being intercepted . . ." Ellaria paused and grabbed a book off the shelf. She tore out a page in it, circled a word inside, and wrote on the top of the page the name of the book. Then she handed the page to Dalliana, "This will be our code word and code book. When you receive our messages and there are numbers in the message, you must use this book to unscramble the message. The page number sentence and word. You'll know it's from me because the first coded word will be this one every time. Got it?" she asked. She knew she was speaking fast, but she wanted Dalliana out of the city as quickly as possible.

"Got it. One condition. One of my guards will stay behind with you," Dalliana said.

"Why, what am I supposed to do with him?" Ellaria asked.

"His name is Semo, he is Ragor's brother. I don't know what you should do with him, but I want him to stay. If you are my country's only ally here I want to see that you are protected," she said, Ellaria thought that while she may be young, she had her father's fire in her.

"Fine," Ellaria agreed, "Maybe he can be my assistant or something. I'll make up a story."

"I don't know how good he will be at that. He is a Darkhawk warrior," Dalliana told her.

"A Darkhawk!" Wade exclaimed. Ellaria and Dalliana both shot him a look. "Sorry."

"Well, he'll just have to figure out how to be someones assistant. Now the real question is how to get you back to your ship without incident," Ellaria wondered.

"I can help," Wade chimed in. "I can lead her through the fish market and across their shipment bridges. I have a friend who works the docks on the north end," he said. It wasn't the worst idea. The markets were crowded enough they could get through without much notice.

"Fine, but you need to go now, before the sun sets," Ellaria stipulated.

She walked them both through the halls and out the doors, where Dalliana's guards were waiting and obviously on edge. Dalliana introduced Semo, who was a lean and muscular man with serious eyes.

"Thank you Ellaria. My father always said you were the only person he still trusted on this side of the Anamic," Dalliana said.

"Please be safe, and wait until you hear from me before you or your people do anything we can't comeback from," Ellaria told her, and they all turned to go. Before Wade could walk away Ellaria tugged on his sleeve, pulling him back.

"Wade, I'm trusting you to get her on that ship."

"I know."

"Get her there and get back. And Wade keep in mind, she's the Princess of the New World. Don't charm her. She has people that would do whatever she asked of them, do you understand?"

"Wouldn't dream of it, Professor."

From behind him, Ellaria watched as Dalliana kept her face down, but she thought a smile crested her lips at the sounds of their conversation.

They all departed to the north, and Ellaria only watched for a short time before returning to the office. *Where are you Kovan?* She thought as she walked back down the marbled floors. If she had wanted to keep Wade out of harm, she had done a terrible job of it. Things were escalating faster than she would have liked. She needed help; she needed her friends, wherever they were.

# CHAPTER ELEVEN

## GREAT DISTANCES (TALI)

THE TRAIN ROLLED ACROSS THE VALLEY ALL DAY AND INTO THE EVENING, veering further inland to the east than Tali had realized. She always imagined the train line followed the coastline the whole way. Living on an island, she loved the ocean. Staring out at the Brovic was one of her favorite diversions. But finally seeing the mountains up close and the empty countryside was intoxicating. The wide and distant fields of grass and rolling hills were a different kind of serenity, than the endless waves of the ocean. Truth be told, both she and Kovan slept most of the trip and she had missed most of it. At first, she was too excited to sleep. Her gaze fixated beyond the window out at the land moving past. Eventually, her eyes got heavy, and she reached that place where every other breath was jarring her back in and out of consciousness. She finally succumbed to the rumbled rocking of the train car two hours after leaving Ruenobee.

She awoke after the sun had come out of the blue, about three hours past midday. Her cloak mounded against Kovan as her pillow. He was already awake, but he hadn't bothered to move her off his shoulder yet. Embarrassed, she apologized, sat up and began staring out the window again. He handed her a half loaf of bread and a paper wrapping of meat and cheese. She ate vigorously like she hadn't had a meal in days. She glanced back at Kovan. He must have sensed her staring at him because he turned his head.

"What?"

"Just trying to figure you out," she told him.

"If you do, let me know."

"I'm still trying to figure out if you're a bad guy," she said.

"I don't feel like the bad guy."

"That's comforting."

"It is actually. It's how I sleep at night."

"You don't worry about what you've done?" she asked.

"Not really. I worry a lot more about what I haven't done."

"You don't feel bad about killing those men?"

"On the pier? No. I mean I did share a water filled cell with one, but no."

"Could you teach me?"

"What?"

"How to fight."

"No," he said flatly, "Nothing good comes from me teaching people how to kill. Just more death."

"How about, just to defend myself?" she asked.

"I'll think about it," he said, and she left it at that.

The train was pulling into the station and Tali realized this was the farthest she had ever been off the island, not counting a few fishing trips in the Brovic. They were still in Rodaire, but she was having trouble believing it.

The train station in Rylabyre was like the one in Ruenobee in set up and size, but it was constructed of cut limestone. There were three large archways leading to the inside of the station center and trainmen here wore a uniform of maroon instead of brown. The noise of the train grew louder when it neared its stop. Finally, it came to a stuttering halt with a swirling exhaled hiss, and the platform outside was instantly enveloped in a fog of steam.

Kovan bumped her with his elbow — "Let's go. I want to exit before the steam dissipates away."

They shuffled off the train, having to dodge multiple people getting handbags from the cargo nets above their seats. Stepping off the train was a small drop, her feet hit the brick pavers further down than she expected, and it was definitely less graceful than she intended. Not quite the first step to her adventure she had envisioned, but she recovered well, and the steam hid the look of horror on her face.

Kovan hurried her away from the platform and through the station at a brisk walk. At first, she was so enamored with being somewhere new she had forgotten she was escaping with a fugitive. Seeing a group of greencoats jogged her memory, as Kovan steered her into the flow of the crowd and out of the station. The evening air was warmer and drier than she was used to. They walked up the first main street from the station and into the city above.

"If you're coming with me and you want me to teach you how to fight, you first need to start tracking and calculating with your eyes. I can tell you have a good sense for your surroundings, but you have to track everything and gauge its meaning constantly. Understand?" Kovan asked, still rushing up the sidewalk.

"I think so."

"It's not something you master right away, but everything matters. Take for instance how fast we're walking. It's just a notch above the others and purposely rushed but not hurried. Any faster would be noticeable."

"Got it."

"At the station how many greencoats did you see?"

"umm…"

"Quicker."

"Three."

"Good, there were four, but good."

"Where was the fourth?"

"He was at the tip of the platform when we came in. Putting him near the very back of the train when we stepped off."

"You're right I never saw him."

"No big deal, but if you want to learn how to fight, the first thing you need to learn is how to track everything you're sensing. This becomes important in combat and you will be able to pick up the slightest shifts in weight, weaknesses or intentions of your enemy."

"Everything matters?"

"Yes."

"Like the pile of horse manure, you're about to step in," Tali said and pulled Kovan slightly off course. He skipped around it and continued.

"Yes, like that. Unless I meant to step in it."

"Did you?" Tali asked and Kovan scowled back and started to slow when the city grew larger around them.

Rylabyre was a city of massive stone structures, some had to be nine or ten levels tall. Buildings were rarely that tall on the island, each stone facade had intricate bands of colored stone reliefs. One building looked like a thousand stone relief blocks piled together. The intricate cubes had detailed geometric patterns. The smooth stone pediment with jade lettering that read 'Imperium of Rodaire' interrupted the patterns. Eventually Kovan slowed their pace when the street they were on widened to triple its size and turned into a long tree-lined park with merchant shops on either side of a long pavilion.

"Sorry about rushing back there. I didn't want to linger at the station. I don't think the greencoats will be too intent on finding us, but I can't be sure. I sent two men to the house of death, but I slew both according to rules of the honor code and neither of the men were angels. We need to get to the air station and it's on the other side of the city in the flatlands," he explained.

"Do they take off at night?" she asked. Realizing she knew almost nothing about airships, since they didn't fly to Ravenvyre.

"Sometimes. The real problem is, I would prefer to take a winddrifter instead of those huge metal cloudparters. They can take us somewhere, no questions asked. But we need to catch one before they're gone. They don't keep a schedule like the cloudparters," he said.

It took them a few hours to traverse the city. Eventually the road turned from brick pavers to dirt and then faded into the land all together. The roads ended at what Kovan had called the flatlands. They reached the west edge of the landing fields with the sunlight waining. Kovan went to talk to someone manning a small wood tent. She stood trying to see the ships in the distance. When he finished, he motioned for Tali to follow him past the short wood fence and out into the field. The airships were exciting, and it was all she could do not to launch question after question at Kovan.

"The porter says the cloudparter leaves tomorrow for Eloveen and one of the winddrifters is already under contract. He doesn't know about the other as the aeronaut landed this morning but has not checked in yet," he explained.

"Why not?" she asked.

"The porter told me they've been doing repairs all day."

"Um, that's not good," she said.

"Let's see what his rate is. He may be just what we're looking for."

"So, death? Death is that what we're looking for?" she said.

"Don't worry so much, these things fly themselves," Kovan said.

They walked along the patch of trampled ground out to the winddrifter where an aeronaut was working on his ship. The land was a flat field of grass for as far as she could. There were three ships in the field and beyond them was a short stone storage building with wood carriage doors. There was a steady stream of a cloud-like vapor trickling into the air beyond that. The Cloudparter was impossible to mistake next to the two winddrifters. From a distance the winddrifters didn't look that big, but she knew they were, because the man working outside of his looked tiny compared to the balloon that towered way above him like a six-story building.

The cloudparter by comparison was so enormous it dwarfed the other two ships. It was easily three times their size. Rows and rows of vertical metal rivets made up the structure. In between the rivets were a thousand smooth, bronze metal panels that held the tubular air balloon inside. Each panel reflected the glow of the fading sunlight, pink hues shimmered over a bronzed sheen. Thick rope lines strung from the hull to the ground to stabilize the ship. There was a bulky, four-directional tailfin with cables at the back and a rear bay door. Workers were wheeling carts full of cargo aboard, up a ramp and into the ships belly. The steam engine exhaust tubes extended out near the bottom of the craft. The lower passenger car nestled the ground with clawed feet, and the front caged window looked like the driver's station. Smaller windows punctured the underside of the shell and went up the side. Tali guessed that the ship was three hundred feet long and a hundred and fifty feet tall and she understood Kovan's reluctance to fly in one.

When they walked to the winddrifters, Tali was equally in awe. They were an amazing collage of ropes and silk, wood and sails. The closer she got, the less she understood how they flew at all, the airships classes couldn't be more different. The cloudparter was a giant engineered metal contraption– shiny, rigid, and mechanical. The winddrifters looked handcrafted and rugged. One in the distance looked like the main hull was an interior cabin and the sails were on the sideboards. It was also longer than the one they were approaching.

They walked up to the airship and Kovan climbed the wooden ladder that hung down from the ship's side door to talk with the man working on the engine. Tali waited below and walked around gawking at the wondrous size of the balloon floating high above and the confusion of ropes stringing all around. It was like a beautiful, golden cedar sailing boat for the sky, with front and back sails. The aeronaut had placed lanterns on a few of the rocks in the field around the ship. Tali tried to take it in before the light disappeared and the darkness concealed the details. The elongated balloon was wrapped in a cream-colored silk cloth and bound by large ropes from the bottom over the top. A stitched center point lined around the balloon and had twelve large ropes attached that strung down to the two booms at the front and back sails that crossed the hull. The back sail was small, and a faded orange color. Both the main sail and head sail at the front were maroon. Just below the balloon was a wide, flat platform of wood, with what looked like fifty ropes around it and tied back to the balloon's underside. The frame looked just like a boat. There were twenty bags of sand hanging off the edge, all attached to a rope that strung through attached side rings. At the very bottom, below the hull she could see the lower half of the steam engine and the exhaust port. She moved closer to hear Kovan's conversation.

"Impossible. I can't get you to Eloveen or Jenovee. The farthest she goes without a refuel is a thousand leagues or fifty hours. I've pushed her to sixty hours, but it's a scary ride coming down," the aeronaut said.

"Atava will have to do. How long before you're air worthy?"

"Oh, I'm just tinkering now. It's ready. You want to take off tonight?" the man asked surprised by the urgency.

"If we can, yes. You tell us," Kovan said.

"We'll it's more about the weather than the light. We can fly tonight. I wanted to head into town to get some things and some food, then I have to check in and pay my fees. What say we meet back in an hour?"

"It's a deal, we'll be here," Kovan said, stepping down from the ladder, and leading the way back toward the city.

"Do you trust him?" Tali asked Kovan when they were outside of the landing field.

"No, but he needs the money. I trust that."

"Where are we going now?"

"We need to get some supplies ourselves. We'll be in the air for almost two days."

"Two days. What do we do when nature calls?" she asked in a mild panic.

"You really don't want to know. You're not going to like it," he said with a slight laugh to himself, and when he saw the concern on her face he laughed even harder.

AFTER RAMBLING AROUND THE CITY, THEY ENTERED THE AIRFIELD AGAIN with new supplies. They had gone back to the merchant pavilion, ate a quick meal and picked up some necessities. Kovan insisted on getting Tali a wool-lined patchwork blanket for the trip. He told her the cold up in the sky was brutal. They picked up some food stores and Kovan spent a long time at a crafters store looking at small gears and electron tubes. They left and were back to the field within the hour, figuring they could get whatever additional supplies they needed in Atava.

At the ship, Tali stepped up to the first couple of rungs and the aeronaut helped her the rest of the way in.

"Thank you and good evening, my name's Tali," she said clutching the wood side rail to steady herself.

"Hello miss Tali, name's Bazlyn Idara. Welcome aboard the Ragallia-Savona. I'm the captain and this is my ship," the aeronaut said, taking his hat off in greeting.

He was around the same age as Kovan. Maybe younger, but in far worse shape if that was possible. He was a thin man with a month's stubble on his face. He had a plain shirt with two pockets and dirty brown pants. As soon as Tali was three steps onto the ship, she heard something scratching and scrambling around. A small white and beige terrier dog, with spotted black hair on its face and paws, was rushing to greet her. His ears were large and pointing up, he had an exuberant smile and a small set of goggles around his neck as a collar.

"Be careful of little Zephyr, there. He thinks he is the captain of this vessel and I'm his hand," Bazlyn told her.

The small dog yipped and barked, but it wasn't menacing at all. The barks were more of a conversational hello, and at least he didn't jump up on her. He simply bounced around her feet and ran in and out from under her cloak. If Zephyr treated her like a long-lost friend, he was almost the opposite with Kovan. When Kovan stepped aboard the dog backed away and barked, back-stepping until it ran into the side of the hull. Kovan didn't pay it any mind and found a spot near the stern to put his stuff down.

Bazlyn jumped to the ground and pulled the staked ropes out, and the ship lifted ever so slightly as he detached each anchor. He returned to the ship and closed the small swinging side door that came to about waist high.

"Tali, you think you want to help us lift off?" Bazlyn asked her kindly.

"Sure, how can I help, what do I do?" she asked, jumping up to help.

"Go around the hull and dump some sandbags. Start with two at the back then two at the front. I'll let you know how much more when you're done," he directed.

The interior of the hull had a built-in wood seat around the sides and stern. She set her rolled blanket on the seat and kneeled on it. Tilting her body over the side slightly with the side wall at her waist she reached over the edge, grabbed the nearest bag she found. The sack cloth was coarse and heavier than she expected. She dumped out the contents to the ground below. She tied the sack back on the line where she found it and crossed the hull. Then did the same on the other side. When she had released the two at the front of the ship, she noticed it was slowly rising. She turned to get further instructions.

"I think another four more should do it, dear," Bazlyn told her.

She went around and did it a second time, this time in reverse. When she poured the last bits out, she noticed some of the dust drifting in the air behind them and she finally realized how high up they were already. Her breath caught, and she stumbled back from the edge in a moment of panic, and she froze. She gazed out at the city of Rylabyre, transfixed at the world shrinking below. The dark shapes of buildings and the scattered pinpoints of light growing fainter as they drifted away. She exhaled and realized she was still holding the last empty sack. She tied it off and turned to find a seat close to Kovan, finding him staring at her with a smile as she sat down.

"Are you afraid of heights?" he asked.

"No I'm fine, I'm just lost for words," Tali admitted.

The night air was getting colder, and she decided it was safe to pull out her cloak from the blanket roll. As soon as she put it on, Zephyr came bounding from where he was lying near the captain at the controls station. He jumped up onto the seat next to her and laid his head on her lap. She ruffled the fur on top of his head. Kovan shifted in his seat and Zephyr perked up, scowled at him, and laid back again in a tiny huff.

"I think Zephyr may have a crush on you," Bazlyn told her. "I've never seen him so taken with a passenger before."

"He's nice, and an excellent judge of character," she said looking at Kovan to see if he caught her jest. He must have, as he seemed to huff just as the dog had.

Bazlyn sat down on a wood box in the middle of the ship and sipped something warm out of a squat, tin cup. There was only one lantern on the ship that was lit. It cast just enough light to see where you were walking but not enough to read by and not enough to dampen the brightness of the night sky. From this high up, the night encircled them, and the sky seemed bigger than on the ground. The stars were a swarm she wished to swim in. It stretched all around and cradled the world. The moon was half full and more alive in its clarity than she had ever seen. Tali stretched her hand out pretending she could touch it. The movement of the ship reminded her of being on sea with calm water and nothing but the wind and breeze to push and pull against you. She liked not having to feel the constant rolling and dipping of waves and could see how someone could fall in love with flying.

"Are there women aeronauts?" Tali asked Bazlyn.

"Oh yes one of the best I know is a woman named Margo Adree. She flies in the south of Tavillore mostly, and in a much fancier ship then this, with dark purple sails."

"How long have you had your ship, Mr. Idara?" Tali asked.

"Well, my partner, and I, may he have risen above, finished building the sweet Savona about eight years ago. We started out building a boat, but when people started adapting the deep well pump to aeronautics. We shifted our design and built this. She's not as fancy as some but she's fast and can take a storm," he told her.

"I was curious about that. How do those massive cloudparters have bronze paneling and not get struck by lightning?" she asked.

"It's not bronze, actually. It's quandinium with a patina coloring. But it does get struck by lightning, only the metal cage protects the integrity, and their gas cells are lined inside with another layer of protection," he explained.

"This ship doesn't have a cage. What happens if we get struck by lightning?" she asked worried.

"Well, it's no good. I can tell you that. As I explained to your . . ." he paused for a moment, realizing that Kovan was definitely not her father. "Friend. If I see signs of a storm, I set the ship down as fast as I can. Though we can fit into some smaller spaces than you might think."

"Has it ever happened?" she asked, and from the corner of her eye she could see Kovan shaking his head not to ask. Too late.

"Lighting? Yes, it hit the front mast once. We were flying down south by Lowtalla. Myzer was at the helm," Bazlyn motioned toward the steering wheel at the bow and continued. "The wood mast exploded, and the front sails caught fire. Myzer was killed," he said with eyes glossy and far away.

"Oh, I'm so sorry," she said.

"Yeah, it was a horrible thing. Myzer was the love of my life. I was up on the ladder trying to bypass the descent valve and manually release gas from the balloon to get us down in a hurry. The blast knocked me into the back sail. I don't know how I didn't fly out. With the front sail on fire and the master lines burnt up. I picked myself up, ran over and chopped off what was left of the boom to save the hull. Somehow I survived with only a few bruises and some nasty burns on my forearms."

"I really am sorry," she said.

"Thank you, miss. I rebuilt and kept flying. Also, I got a storm glass barometer over there. The crystals inside it change when the weather is about to change. Rest easy, miss we'll be safe."

Bazlyn's story was discomforting, and a small claustrophobic anxiety itched at the back of her neck with the confines of the small boat shrinking the more she thought about it. She made peace with the fact that Bazlyn was still living in the sky, so maybe they would be safe. Unless he was only continuing to fly because he wished for death, but she tried to block that idea out. Tali unrolled her blanket and put it over her legs which she propped up on the seat. Zephyr came back to lay down with her. He circled and circled before plopping down with a sense of finality. Tali smiled at the happy dog and turned her attention to admiring the ship, the balloon above and the rope wrapped wooden plank.

"Bazlyn, what's that wood plank do?" she said, interrupting him while he was checking on his instruments.

"That's the ballast mass, it stabilizes the entire ship. You can go sleep up there, if you want. There are enough ropes around the edges, you won't fall, I promise. When stationed, I do it myself, me and little Zephyr here. I drag him up there for the night. It's like a crow's nest on sea vessel," he explained.

"I think I'm comfortable here thanks. Besides Zephyr is already sleeping," she told him, and he just laughed.

She rested her head down and eventually fell asleep.

About eight hours into the air, the clouds became thick, and the air was cold and wet. She awoke with a chill and the slight blindness of a cloud startled her. The sunlight was trickling through giving the cloud a glow. The combination of silence and mist was eerie. She got up, too enticed to go back to sleep. She wrapped the blanket around herself and stood. Kovan was standing close to the bow looking out into the mists of nothing. Bazlyn was busy managing his instruments, rotating a metal wheel and wiping condensation from a valve readout. She walked over to him.

"Good morning," she said, half-yawning.

"You too. How did you sleep?" Bazlyn asked.

"Well, thank you," she replied.

"Tali I'm glad you woke up. Pretty soon I'm going to lift us above this cloud cover and you're going to see the greatest sight in the world. It was Myzer's favorite thing about flying," he told her. Then he continued to tinker with his devices. There were valves and metal wheels and a pipe that continuously made a clacking sound. Most of the mechanisms were in the middle of the ship, and Bazlyn would fiddle with them, then turn around to face the stern and steer. The wood ship wheel was ordinary and similar to any she had seen on a boat before with eight round spokes and an outer circle. There were no metal embellishments or center emblem. The only thing unique about it was that it was the only part of the ship stained a dark color. She wasn't sure how it worked. It maneuvered the booms somehow through the exposed pulley systems. She watched as he would take a reading and then slowly rotate a valve. Then take another reading.

"What's that you're doing?" she asked him.

"Well, I'm adding heated air to the balloon to get us to rise. This valve controls the relay of heat, and you see that pipe there? The pipe that follows the ladder up. That's the supply line. Matter fact I forgot to mention if you get too cold just come sleep near the engine it will definitely keep you warm. Zephyr and I have to do it when we travel north," he said.

Feeling she should leave him to it, she walked over near Kovan. He was silently brooding and clutching onto the sidewall.

"Are you alright, Van?" she asked. Not intentionally shorting his name, but there it was.

"Ha, you know only my close friends call me Van?" he said.

"Sorry, I mean Kovan," she said.

"No, go for it. It sounded right," he smirked.

"What's going on?" she asked again, not meaning to pry but something was obviously bothering him.

"Nothing. I'm just not a fan of being trapped. It makes me restless. That and I wish we were moving faster."

"Nothing's faster than air travel," she said.

"True, but even when we land in Atava it's still a long way to Adalon," he said.

"Well, all we can do is keep moving, right?"

"That's right," he said

"Kovan, I don't mean to pry, but were you and Ellaria ever married?"

"Yes," Kovan answered flatly, and didn't seem interested in offering anything further.

"I'm sorry I was only curious. The history books said you two were inseparable."

"We were," he said.

"And Qudin?"

"I haven't seen Qudin in many years," Kovan said. It didn't seem like a line of questioning Kovan was amenable to, and Tali chose not to press any further.

Kovan tapped her on the shoulder and nodded his head sharply for her to turn around. The airship was emerging out of the clouds. When she turned, the most immaculate sight she had ever seen in her life was before her. A glorious sunrise freely stretched and flooded the skies with violent color. An expanding light turning the darkness into shades of purple and blue, as the bright red sun pierced the horizon and the world awakened. The clouds spread out below them like a soft sea of pillows glowing pink. The shadowed sides revealed dimensions of depth. Below them, snippets of mountain peaks were visible in the open pockets of mist. It was vast and immesuearable, and Tali breathed it in like she was starving for it.

# CHAPTER TWELVE

### ATAVA (ELIAS)

THEY GALLOPED LONG INTO THE NIGHT BEFORE STOPPING TO SLEEP. THEY had reached the halfway point to Atava before calling it. Learon took convincing, but the strains on both horses was reason enough to break their pace. Another league would have exhausted their horses to the point of crippling them and the coming day's travel would be under the sun and they all would tire faster from the heat.

They set up camp quickly. Elias made a fire with anthracite while Learon scouted the area. He came back, broke a pie in half and split it with Elias. He was grateful to have something to eat before they slept. They laid down without saying a word. Elias fell asleep at the close of his eyes.

It wasn't long before they were on the move again. Elias awoke as soon as the sun started to rise and found Learon sitting up already. Elias questioned whether Learon had slept at all. They smothered their fire, mounted up, and were off again.

The kid weighed on his mind. Elias could tell the kid was hiding something, but he understood that trust came slow between strangers, so he didn't push. Learon's quick actions on the mountain revealed him to be sharp and steady, but finding his home in wreckage had shaken him. Elias could see Learon had become singularly fixated on finding his mother. That narrowed focus would propel him beyond his usual limits, but it would also blind him to simple dangers.

Elias was especially curious how Learon had made the shot that killed the first beast. A wolverack's mane was thick and tough to penetrate. Elias had fought and killed many in his lifetime and seen many more killed during the war. He had never seen anyone get a heart kill in one shot, they typically required at least two. The beasts were genetically modified to be so ravenous. They would keep going even after being mortally wounded, seemingly beyond the point of death. Learon had saved his life back on the mountain and now Elias was determined to help him anyway he could. Life debts were sacred, not easily repaid and impossible to walk away from.

As they traveled north on the road to Atava, Elias contemplated his next actions. He was going to help this kid find his mother, because he owed him that much. Yet the situation had a high probability of getting messy and Elias preferred to avoid any entanglements with the authority. News of a Prime Commander was troubling. Combined with the bonemen soldiers he saw on his travels through Merinde, he knew something was happening. It was probably time to stop his hiding. Whatever the situation was, he knew someone who was bound to be in the middle of it.

They rode for half a day, before Atava came into view. The central road gathered additional travelers the closer they got. Farmers and riders from other outskirt towns converging on the south gate. They hurtled past a field cart and then a passenger carriage, kicking up clumps of dirt high and far in their wake. Eventually, Elias reached out and grabbed the reins of Learon's horse, forcing him to slow down. Riding in at that speed brought attention and made them look like panicked men. They reached the city gates sometime just after the blue. They passed stationed greencoat wall guards who didn't pay them any special attention, traveling along at a slow trot. Learon veered them to the west and to a stabling house.

The City of Atava was almost as big as Adalon City in sheer size, but not population. It was encased behind a guarded stone battlement. A double layered wall with a fifty-foot-tall outside layer backed by a taller fortification, an archer walkway spanned the top. Something had scared the original builders. At some point someone decided that fifty feet wasn't tall enough to protect the people inside. There were two gates into the city, and both were heavily protected. The gates were flanked by stone towers with marksman windows overlooking the entrances. As the major western city of Tavillore, it probably had a history as the first defense from threats beyond the mountains, but like most things the truth had been lost. It was a shame the Sagean Empire had stripped the people of their pasts, but it was a bigger shame that the people hadn't handed down their own histories to their children. Some legends survived, but each generation was more and more self-involved and less interested in the past. His generation had fought and changed the world to have control over their future, and the new generation took that freedom for granted. He had trouble understanding their apathy.

The architecture of Atava was similar to the mountain city where he most often resided. The buildings were wood crafted with heavy timber posts. Stone foundations was typically large cut and mud-packed. The wood was mostly weathered cedar that had turned gray. Some had kept their golden hue, but even those were weathering after years of driving snow from the west. Exposed rafter tails that ended in tapered points gave the buildings an aggressive feel.

In the southwest quad, they found a place to stable their horses. Learon removed the saddles, secured his pack across his shoulder, and stood running his hands through his hair waiting for Elias. Elias lingered with Ghost, the mare he was given in West Meadow. She was definitely skittish, but Elias had figured out that she was lonely and edgy. She was a unique hot-blood breed from the coasts of Lowtalla called a Nyrogen. How she came to be on the other side of the mountains was a story he would like to hear one day. The Nyrogen breed was known for their speed and agility. She needed to be taken out and ran– not kept stabled. The Nyrogen were a proud breed and the mare's agitation with being confined had manifested into an aggression her owners mistook for skittishness. When they rode out for Atava yesterday, Elias could feel how her spirit lift once they hit the open road. With the wind racing by and her muscles working in unison; at a certain point he slowed her at the risk of leaving Learon far behind. The mare had an energy Elias could relate to. That force can turn wild if repressed or pushed to extremes. Like the fiend mentality, it's a powerful substance, but it's also the lineage of madness.

Elias could see that madness burning like a small flame in Learon's eyes. Untethered and unfulfilled, it would consume him. Learon stalked the streets stone-faced and ruffled. Elias followed him through side streets where overarching framework bridged across and created caves of wood. They rounded a corner and the sidewalk below their feet changed from hardened clay to a wood plank walkway. This area of the city was shabby, and less maintained. The drainage was stagnant, and the light disregarded by the towers that shielded it out. They shuffled under a series of cantilevered wood awnings. Learon turned to speak for the first time all day.

"My uncle's quarters are above a small chomp' house up ahead. I think I'll look inside there first," he declared.

"I'll go with you, but let's stagger our entrance," Elias replied.

Learon nodded his agreement. A few paces down they came to an arching double door with flanking high rectangle windows. Each had crisscrossed dividers proud of the panes of glass in the window frame. The door had a sign that read Carrow's Chomp' House. Learon swung the door aside and trampled in. Elias waited a minute, observed the surrounding layout of streets and buildings and scrutinized the meandering locals, before he took a breath of light, pulled the door open, and slipped in after Learon.

A whiff of charred meats and tobacco smoke hit his senses instantly as he strode past the front seating and advanced to the bar at the center of the room. Hanging tin lanterns provided most of the ambient lighting for the space. The crowd noise was oddly raucous for a cave-like atmosphere. Surveying the occupants, he found an animated Learon in the back talking with three other people. The cramped place was half-full and dim with only muted glows from table candles to see others by. The remaining shrouded corners concealed questionable clientele. The beverage selection was impressively diverse and abundant, stacked tall on rows of wood shelves with a rolling ladder to reach the highest stock. In the gloom, Learon finally located Elias and waved him over, his relief evident from afar. Elias swept past the bar toward Learon and his companions. A lovely woman with partially gray hair pulled back in a green ribbon, sat motionless and eyeing him. The two gentlemen across from her were busy in conversation. When he reached their table, Learon began to introduce Elias. One of the older men sitting with them looked up to see the new arrival. He glared at Elias, his eyebrows wrinkled a moment before his eyes popped open wide and he staggered backwards out of his stool. The stool clanging to the ground and sliding away. Elias grew stiff, the man had obviously recognized him, but Elias couldn't identify the stranger yet.

"Garner, what's wrong, did you see a ghost?" Learon asked in jest.

The man didn't retreat, he stayed on the ground where he fell. His knees on the floor and his head bent down chin to chest. It struck Elias who the face belonged to.

"Let me help him up," Elias said, moving around the table to aid the old man that Elias knew so long ago. Elias knelt down to one knee near him.

"General Graves, sir, please get up," Elias whispered to him. Then he helped the man they called Garner to his feet. The General had led many battles during the Great War and worked closely with Ellaria on strategy throughout the liberation campaign in Tavillore.

"Sorry if I startled you, sir," Elias said aloud.

"Well, it's too blood-dead dark in here. You can't sneak up on an old man like that," Garner exclaimed.

Learon snatched a spare stool from a nearby table and brought it over for Elias to sit at. Elias thanked him.

"Elias, this is my mother, Cara, my uncle Jaimen and Mr. Garner," Learon said, introducing him around. Elias thought he recognized Cara as well, but he simply nodded and sat down. Jaimen was drinking something with a froth to it and Cara had a finished cup of tea. There were coins on the table suggesting they had been ready to leave when Learon arrived.

"My mother has already yelled at me for not being on the road to Adalon," Learon said to Elias with the tightness of his shoulders now washed away.

"Adalon?" Elias asked.

"Yes. The Arcana doesn't accept a lot of kids from the west lands and have never taken one from West Meadow," Cara fumed, "You need to leave Learon, session starts soon. I'm fine. I've got company. I can manage. It's the Arcana son, you need to go. You're smart like your father," she scolded him with a slight flustering stammer that made Elias think she could have wanderer's mind. A disease that put your mind into a small frenzy and made it difficult to express your thoughts. It caused a state of confusion and sometimes paranoia.

"Mother, summer hasn't even started yet. I haven't missed anything," Learon said.

"I know you *could* wait, but I don't want you too. Plus, the paper! The paper, Learon."

"What about the paper, mother?" Learon asked gently.

"Ellaria Moonstone is going to be a professor there, that's the rumor. That's the news. You need to go, the first days are important," she told him. Elias's breath caught at the sound of his friend's name.

"Truly. You read that Ellaria Moonstone is teaching there?" Elias asked.

"Yes, yes of course, it was in the newspaper. Today's paper . . . Yesterdays? I read it. Please help me convince this kid," she said.

"Mother, we have other pressing issues. Like Mr. Garner, weren't you just about to tell me of the soldiers in West Meadow? Without Elias there, I would have walked right into them," Learon said.

"Right, well there were four of them that I saw. Three looked like typical greencoats. Except the cut of their coat was shorter and it bore an insignia I've never seen. The leader wore a red cape and a face plate. Have you ever seen anything like that?" Garner asked looking directly at Elias.

"I have actually. I saw three just like it in Kalihjan not too long ago. All with red capes," Elias said.

"Kalihjan!" Learon said astonished.

"That far south, huh?" Garner said.

"Yes. Did the one in West Meadow carry an eruptor rifle?" Elias asked.

"He did, and his entire squad had their own pulsator," Garner said.

"We heard two of them came north. How did you manage to get past them?" Elias asked.

"We rode in with a caravan of folks. We never saw them," Garner said.

The other three looked from Elias to Garner and back, afraid to interrupt.

"But you don't know if they saw you?" Elias asked.

"What I don't get, is what this mix up is all about?" Jaimen asked.

Elias clocked Cara and Learon as they shared a look. He would get to the bottom of that later.

"What are you thinking?" Garner asked Elias.

"Well, there's a lot to consider. How knowledgeable are they and how smart? How willing are they to work with local greencoats and how afraid of their captain are they?

"Wait, who are you?" Cara asked Elias. A motherly tone kicking in.

"One man in his time plays many people, and I've played my share. I played as a general in a war once. Which has me thinking, if they're smart, they spotted you two arriving and followed you here. I would assume they are knowledgeable enough to know Jaimen lives in Atava. Something easily learned by asking a few questions around West Meadow. If they're afraid of their captain, then they won't involve other greencoats because they're desperate for approval, and would wait to make a move until Learon showed up. Honestly, I'm afraid they're most likely waiting in one of the buildings outside to ambush us the instant we walk out of here."

"Blood and thorns," Garner said, with his eyes beginning to dart around the room.

"What? Wait, you think someone's waiting for us outside?" Learon asked in disbelief.

"Yes, but the good news is they're looking for something. They're not going to just kill us outright," Elias said.

"Kill us!" Learon exclaimed.

"Look at it this way, if they were really smart, son, they would have got help and apprehended your mother and I already. Then just waited in Jaimen's quarters for you to arrive," Garner said.

Elias started moving his head to scan around the room again. Fearing he had missed someone, but it was too dark in the corners to be sure. Movements were as masked as faces in the shadowed recesses. An idea struck him. To try something he had never done before. He closed his eyes and tried searching for the faintest sense of energy that would be emanating from the pulsator guns. Everything in the room pulsed with a unique signature vibration. Every spirit in the room, the small flames in the lanterns, the kitchen fires, and the faint sunlight from the front windows, but filtering energies was extremely difficult. His eyes shot open. He found it opposite the bar, in a side booth, there was a humming tinge of a power cell at rest. But if one was waiting inside at the front, then where was the other one?

"Is there a back way out of here?" Elias asked Jaimen.

"Um. I'm not sure. Through the kitchen I would guess," Jaimen answered.

"Learon. Do you trust me?" he asked earnestly. Learon looked at him confused.

"What's going on Elias?" Learon asked.

"Just search your mind. Do you trust me?" he asked again.

"I think I do, yes. Why?" Learon replied.

Hearing the answer, he was looking for, he turned to the old general. "Mr. Garner, in ten seconds I'm going to walk over to the bar and sit down. Once I'm there, please escort Learon, Cara, and Jaimen out the front door. I think I miscalculated, and they have already closed in. I believe one of the soldiers is inside near the front waiting. When he sees you, he will signal his partner who is most likely waiting in the kitchen. When they both emerge, I'll distract them, and then you get everyone out of the door. Got it?" he said.

"Yes, sir," Garner said.

Elias slowly stood up to leave and Learon yanked at his coat.

"Distract them? Elias, wait," Learon urged.

Elias looked down at his young friend and placed his hand on his shoulder, "Trust me. Follow Garner out the door."

With Jaimen and Cara gawking at him. He left Learon's grasp and glare and strode away. He slid onto an empty stool at the bar. Garner rose from his seat and ushered the others to follow, including Learon who sparked and argued but reluctantly submitted. The four together began to shuffle toward the front. When they passed behind Elias, he could see Learon searching for any signs of disturbance. They got to within fifteen feet from the entry when Elias saw movement from the side booth. A man rose out, his gun drawn but huddled against his stomach with his other hand shielding over top. A second man came cantering from the back.

Elias inhaled deeply and waited for the partner to get closer. He looked to the lanterns above. For Elias, the thought behind the enacting use of energy was important. He exhaled his breath through pursed lips, like he was blowing out the candles. Releasing some of the energy he had been holding since he walked inside. He put the emanation to work, extinguishing all the flames in the room that he could sense. The chomp' house descended into darkness and a caterwaul of complaints erupted from the patrons.

The two soldiers were momentarily stunned but began to run for the door after their escaping prey. Elias bounded atop the bar then surged himself across the room, discharging energy to propel himself the distance. The entry door flew open, and light briefly flooded into the room as Elias was in the air. He landed between the soldiers with a detonating impact that concussed the air into a shockwave. The expanding ripple knocked the men off their feet and slammed them into the side walls. Their guns rattled to the hardwood. In a single sweeping motion, he threw aside his coat and drew his Elum blade, but both men stayed crumpled where they fell. He replaced his sword and then reached out with the trickle of energy he had left, pulling the weapons from the floor to his hands. Then darted for the exit.

Elias stepped outside into the fading sunlight. Garner and Learon rushed to his side. Elias nodded toward the old general on his way to assure him it was done. Learon registered the latest exchange between them with a wrinkled brow. His eyes grew wide when he realized what Elias carried in his hands. He unlatched the straps to his satchel and placed the guns inside.

"Time to go," Elias told them. "Where are your horses being cared for?" he asked.

"Just up the road," Garner said.

"Alright, lead the way," Elias said, and they began walking up the street. Cara and Jaimen fell in beside them.

"Do you two know each other?" Learon asked.

"Yes, I'll explain later. We need to leave the city. I only knocked them out."

"Learon, please go to Adalon, we can get ourselves out," Cara pleaded with her son.

"Mother, I don't have enough yet. I didn't bring a buck out of the mountain, only Elias," Learon said.

"Learon, I'm going to Adalon myself. If you need money because you helped me in the mountains, then I can compensate you for what you would have received," Elias told him.

"That settles it Learon, you go with Elias to Adalon and we'll go the opposite direction. It's good, it's the good thing to do. You go, you go," Cara said.

"There is no way am I agreeing to that, Mother," Learon argued.

"Learon we should all ride out north to Jenovee together. There we can take the east road to Adalon and they can continue north. I have a friend that could meet them in Thelmaria. We'll linger awhile at the crossroad to watch their trail and look out for any followers," Elias said.

"I don't know, Elias," Learon replied weakly.

Elias halted Learon on the sidewalk. They were similar in height and Elias stared him in the eyes. "Listen, Mr. Garner was a general in the war. That's how we know each other. I know you trust him and so do I. If we protect their trail, they'll make it to Thelmaria and be far away from this mess," Elias said.

"I agree, but only because I don't have a better idea," Learon grunted, he exhaled audibly, "Stay with them," he said, turning to walk away.

"Where are you going?" Elias asked.

"To get our horses, I'll meet you at their stables," Learon waved and jogged away.

They continued walking and made it to the stables. Learon met up with them a short time later. Ghost sounded a soft neigh at Elias when he approached. She was excited and shuffled in place restlessly wanting to gallop. With everything packed and everyone mounted they departed for the north gate with the night sky overhead, pursued by soldiers for reasons still unknown to Elias.

# CHAPTER THIRTEEN

## ROUGH LANDING (TALI)

THE BALLAST PLANK WAS STRANGELY SERENE AND TERRIFYING. TALI SPENT the last part of the afternoon and the last hours of their trip in the high lofted space. The wood was heavy timber, cross braced on the bottom side but the top of the platform was smooth and wide as a large bed. The headroom provided enough clearance for Tali to stand with a slight stoop. Stiff rope entwined the plank around the outside completely, creating the enclosure, with lines strung back to the balloon's underside. A single gap allowed her to sneak through from the fixed ladder. Bazlyn said it was safe to lean against the ropes, but she couldn't bring herself to do it. While the rope prevented her from tumbling out, it did not block the wind. Without a wind barrier, it was freezing compared to the main craft where you sat sunken behind cedar sidewalls. The first time she got the courage to climb up, she had to scramble right back down and drag up her blanket. Scaling the ladder was the horrific part, a powerful gust would send her into the clouds.

Tali sat cross-legged and staring out behind the winddrifter to the west. For most of the trip, she spent her time staring out to the east to see what was next. But they had just come through the Warhawk Mountains and they were too majestic to turn away from.

The captain said that they had made incredible time. Going with the wind was always faster, and the weather had been perfect. Next to the ship's wheel, Bazlyn had a tilted table slab with an amazing map of the mainland of Rodaire and Tavillore. He carefully charted their positions as they went. Constantly checking his compass. There were other markings on the same map from previous voyages, and she was unsure how he kept it all straight. Based on his readings, he expected them to touch down at the Atava airfield in a few hours. The airfield was just northeast of the city. Bazlyn said she could see the entire city when they were landing.

Spending the day in the sky was beautiful but unnerving. Trapped in a small area was getting to her. Tali was eager to get her feet on the ground. Kovan seemed to do worse than her. He had said he hated being trapped, and she was witnessing it play out. He paced around the ship, examined and re-examined parts he had picked up in Ruenobee and Rylabyre. She had no clue what he used them for. His stash looked like a tinker's table of fragmented machinery waiting for assembly into an absurd device. They ate what little food they had brought, and Bazlyn shared a spiced cider of his own. She was careful not to indulge too much; she didn't even want to think about the lavatory situation ever again. It had been so embarrassing she couldn't stop laughing. Her fit of laughter extended for so long Kovan thought she had cracked.

Sitting in the ballast, she saw they had cleared the last peaks. In font of them, forests and green plains stretched out as far as she could see. Down below her, Kovan and the captain were conversing, but she couldn't make out what they were saying. Tali could see Kovan was pointing to something the captain had stashed on the floor by the steering wheel. Bazlyn had his sleeping compartment there built into the side of the wall. She watched as Bazlyn walked over and grabbed what looked like a steel walking stick, she thought it must be an old rifle. Curiosity got the best of her, and she climbed down the ladder to join them, clutching tightly to every rung.

"It's still functional but not in as good of shape as this," Bazlyn said, handing Kovan a small pistol.

"You still carry a silver six! These are great. I carried two just like this during the war. The bone handle and everything. I miss these. It's too bad they don't make the ammunition for them anymore. They're terribly inaccurate, but there's nothing faster to draw," Kovan said.

"Yeah, the bullets are tough to find. Even harder to find for the small box rife. But I just never could commit to the electrified blasters," Bazlyn said.

"I know what you mean. I like my pulsator guns but they're heavy and it's all about the modifications and the quality of parts used to complete them. The right electron tube can make all the difference. I lost my last set and now I'm itching to get a new one in Atava, cause of course you can't find one anywhere in Rodaire," Kovan said.

Tali found their conversation odd. Since guns were outlawed in Rodaire, her exposure to them was almost non-existent. She'd seen them on ships docked at the southport pier, but the two in front of her were the closest she had ever been to them.

She moved away from them and back over to the seating at the stern of the ship, Zephyr scampering after her. They sat curled up with each other with the blanket over her legs and Zephyr atop the blanket coiled into a ball with his head placed to watch the guys talking. Tali scratched the black fur atop his head and rubbed his pointy fox-like ears. Bazlyn moved back to his commanding station, checked some gauges and his map.

"Not long now," he called out. "I'm starting our descent now. We had some leeway, but the cross winds have died out and we should see Atava once these clouds pass."

Tali stretched her neck to see, but it was no good she couldn't see anything yet and she didn't want to leave Zephyr. Then a cool mist flooded the cabin space and Tali breathed deep and sighed. The wind picked up inside the cloud and chilled the already cold, moist air around them. A few minutes later everything cleared away, like a curtain being drawn, and she heard Bazlyn curse.

"Thorns! We are already over the field. I'm going to swing us around. Stay seated," he ordered.

Tali could see the city below them as the ship dropped quickly. Her stomach catapulted into her throat. The city was in full view, but she had to turn her head away. The falling sensation coupled with watching the land was nauseating. She held on tight to Zephyr, while Bazlyn rotated valve after valve and then spun the main steering wheel. The sails rippled and whipped loudly. The entire craft spun, and the city quickly whirled from behind her to in front of them. Then the severe falling slowed and she could see they were drifting down to the field below.

She looked around and at the wilderness behind them and Atava in front. It was an immense city, and the battlement wall was one of the most impressive man-made things she had ever seen. Equally magnificent as the cloudparter. The air smelled more fragrant from the pine grove below and she could hear a faint beat on the wind just over the hum of the steam propellant engine dying down.

Suddenly, she thought she saw something large pass by in her peripheral vision. It was a large dark shape, but when she turned, it was gone. She could see some birds faintly in the distance, but this thing had been bigger. With the engine completely silent, she could make out a faint scratching sound. She looked down at Zephyr, and his ears perked up somehow higher than normal. He could hear something too and was searching for the source.

"Does anyone else hear that?" she called out to two of them.

"Hear what?" Kovan said.

Zephyr jumped from her lap and started barking, and his tail stopped wagging. A giant winged animal circled and cried out in a terrible high-pitched screeching caw. A shiver ran up Tali's arms and shoulders from the sheer size of it, and she yelled out for Kovan. A large beast landed on the edge board with its clawed feet scratching into the polished lacquer. Tali screamed.

The menacing, featherless, beast smelled like rotten fish, with a wingspan almost eight feet wide. It had hands, a neck, and a menacing tooth-filled grin. Zephyr's barks turned to a nasty growl.

Kovan ran over and snagged the rifle they were looking at earlier. A second beast vaulted on deck behind him, making an unintelligible sound. Kovan pivoted and shot three successive blasts into its face. The beast cried out, flopped back and careened over the edge with the force of the gunfire strikes. Then Kovan yelled out, "Get down!"

Tali dove to the ship floor as the dark green-skinned monster slowly crept forward on its feet toward her. Tali was paralyzed, her breaths came short and fast. Kovan stood above her and pulled the trigger, but the gun failed to fire. Without pause, he darted over and slammed the rife into the second thing's face. It reeled back, saliva droplets fell as it bared its teeth and suddenly snapped its neck forward where Kovan stood. A second slower, and the beast's jaw would have snared him, but Kovan dove backward to the ground avoiding the attack.

The thing then went wild as Zephyr attacked its clawed feet. Shots blazed from the stern of the ship, where Bazlyn unloaded his pistol into the creature's bulging chest bone. Black blood oozed from the wounds, but the thing was only staggered. Not killed. It contorted its neck to bite Zephyr.

Tali shoved her trembling hand into her cloak and threw the first varium crystal her fingers touched. The crystal shattered against the monster's eyes and it screeched. A black puff of shadow dust burst free and entombed the craft in darkness. She heard a rolling click and blasts of orangish-red flashes from the ground near the beast. They heard it wail, and she saw the thing falling out as the shadow cloud drifted away into the atmosphere. Tali lurched up and forward, looking for Zephyr, but she couldn't find him. She almost didn't dare to look, but she leaned over the edge of the craft to see if the dog had fallen out with the beast. Zephyr barked at her from the side. She reached down and picked him up to inspect for any injuries. The beautiful thing was astonishingly unharmed. Tali was breathing hard and Kovan's gasps were audible too.

Bazlyn hollered out, "Hold on to something!"

They hit the solid ground with a brutal crash and a loud crack. Tali fell hard into the wall but held tight to Zephyr. Groans sprang from the stern, and she looked to see Bazlyn stumbling, his head bleeding from a gash taken in the crash.

"Sagean's butthole!" he exclaimed, and he woozily looked over the side at the damage, muttering more curses. Kovan reached over to Tali and lifted her to her feet.

"You hurt? Anything broken—you weren't bit were you?" he asked her.

"I'm fine. What the under-death were those things?" she asked.

"Bonelarks. Though I've rarely ever seen two together, let alone a coordinated attack," Kovan said.

"Yeah, that was a sack of thorns," Bazlyn said, still cursing from the stern of the ship.

"Yeah, I don't think I care for them," Tali said.

Bazlyn opened the half door, and they all climbed out. Amazingly, they had landed in the airfield. The only damage she could see to the Ragallia-Savona was to the landing ski. Both lay cracked in half. Bazlyn still fumed and scurried about inspecting every inch of the hull.

"Well, I won't know if the exhaust engine was damaged until I get under there. Which could be difficult with the landing ski completely torqued. Sorry about the wild landing. I abandoned the descent control during the fight and lost track of our altitude in the shadow cloud," Bazlyn said.

"Sorry about that," Tali said, cringing.

"No, don't apologize, I can't thank you enough for saving Zephyr. I found him the day I fixed up the ship after Myzer's death. He's really the only thing I got," he said.

"Of course," she said.

"Besides the last thousand feet, it was a pleasure," Bazlyn said, standing upright and placing a smile on his face. He reached out and shook Kovan's forearm.

"For us too, thank you. Sorry about your winddrifter," Kovan said.

"I'm used to fixing it. Safe travels," Bazlyn said.

They gathered their things and Tali said her goodbyes to Zephyr. She had trouble walking away from him. Kovan waited behind her. She kissed the top of the Zephyr's head, straightened his tiny goggles and ruffled behind his ears. She signaled she was ready, and they left the airfield and the teetering winddrifter behind them.

# CHAPTER FOURTEEN

## THE STORM (LEARON)

TWO DAYS WITHOUT A SIGN OF SOLDIERS ON THEIR TRAIL. TWO DAYS' TIME lingering around the city of Jenovee camped out by the Fork. The Fork was at a clearing halfway in the hills, where the main road split into two directions. A flat area with rising buttes of grass in each of the trisections split around the road, with forests creeping in all around the knolls. There was an outpost building at the Fork that stood alone. With nothing else around for leagues, it was the last stop for supplies before long journeys to the north or east. Learon was sure it saw its share of travelers. At the converging vertex of the forked road was a tall fire basin on a tripod of wood poles, tied together by thick rope. The stone bowl rested atop the knot, while the poles still extended a few feet beyond. At night, the outpost keeper lit the basin full of blue pine for protection from whatever monsters lived in the surrounding forests. The outpost itself was triangular with a roof that went from the ridge all the way to the ground. There were a few rooms for guests, the proprietor's quarters, a resting area with a vaulted hearth room and the supply depot.

Learon had said his goodbyes to his mother and watched her, his uncle and Mr. Garner, ride north at dawn the previous morning. Afterward, Elias and he split up for the day. Learon watched the roads at the Fork and Elias returned to scout inside the city. Elias was confident that if they had seen no sign of the soldiers over the next day and a half, they could leave for Adalon knowing that Learon's mother was safe. Learon wasn't so sure.

The daylight had disappeared, and Learon's fire pit was just coming alive when Elias rode in. He had to admit the white mare was an elegant horse, and Elias looked regal on it. The mystery of the man had escalated with his exploits at the chomp' house two days ago. Learon had seen a glimpse of what Elias had done, and he was dying for an explanation.

Their camp was on the east mound, cradled by large, wild oak trees at the dividing line of grass and forest. In the distance, Learon could see small, glowing blue dots of three other campsites in the surrounding hills. He sat on the dirt carving tree branches with his knife, preparing pieces for a quick lean shelter. He had gathered the materials earlier in the day, but never set about to build it. The gathering cloud cover suggested a rainstorm was coming, and he wanted to sleep under some cover for the night. He slowly spun the branch as he scrapped a clean point to the end. Elias dismounted, tended to Ghost, and joined Learon near the blue fire.

"Anything?" Learon asked.

"No. I sent a message to my friend in Thelmaria to expect your mother. Then I traversed the entire city all day. There was no sign of them. How about you?"

"Nothing. I only saw nine different travelers all day and most headed east. None fitting your description. During the blue, I took a quick ride up the high hill, just north of the fork, to look around from the higher vantage point. There is an amazing view of the Dragon's Spine up there. You can see how tall the ridge line is, and just how far it stretches. Is it true that the war ended there, in a lightning storm?" Learon asked.

"That's where the Sagean died," Elias said.

"How old were you during the war?" Learon asked.

"I was sixteen when it started and nineteen when the Sagean died."

"I'm nineteen, soon to be twenty. That's hard for me to comprehend," Learon said.

"Life is hard, you adapt and learn to survive," Elias said.

Learon paused and since he had Elias talking he pressed froward with more important questions, "Elias, How did your leg heal so fast? Was it the crystal?"

"Yes."

Even though he knew what the answer would be, Learon tried to wrap his mind around the admission, confused by it.

"How could that be? I've had that stone around my neck most of my life. It has never helped heal me, not that I can remember."

"Crystals are a living thing. They contain intrinsic energies unique to each one. The white quartz is a healing stone. If you know how to access that energy you can borrow it, but like most things the first step begins with belief."

"What? It only works if you believe it works?"

"Sort of. Let me ask you. Did you learn to shoot that bow of yours, or did you always know how to?"

"I was horrible at first, but I practiced for years to improve my skill with it."

"Why?"

"Because my father said I had a knack for it and I wanted to be good at it."

"What was the first thing you needed to commit yourself to practicing?"

"I don't know, a reason to want to be good at it?"

"No, before that even. What you needed was to believe you could be good. You needed to believe that the practice, the hard work, would yield the skill you sought. It is the same principle with all things. Your soul, your mind, and the nature of life are displaced elements. Belief is the first action of alignment. It is your soul, convincing your mind, to enable an empowering of your spirit through the strength of will."

"What?"

"Simply put, it's called willpower. You see, willpower is the act of channeling the force of belief. Belief, young man, is power."

"So, if I just believe in something, I can make it happen?"

"No, don't be ridiculous. Belief is not so easy, and I'm not talking about defying the fundamental truths of existence. I'm talking about the path to achievement, and it begins with belief. It's the reverse of your question. You cannot make anything happen if you don't first believe it possible. Belief is not a shortcut, it's a starting point. If you want to build that shelter you're messing with, you have to first believe you can do it, before you can learn to do it."

"I think I understand what you're saying," Learon said, though he was unsure.

"I know my words sound like an old man's ranting but take them to heart. It will serve you well at the Arcana. Much of alchemy and the mystic arts are about believing," Elias told him.

"Do all crystals have special properties? Like rose quartz? Is it actually a love stone?" Learon mused.

"They're real, but they function differently then you're imagining. There's a tribe of people called the Ordona in the far east in the New World that uses them. The crystal needs to absorb the energy of love and then you retrieve the energy when needed. However, the belief involved is intense. The Ordona use them in their bonding ceremonies. The slightest falter and the crystal breaks. The ceremony ends and the two who were to join must abandon their pursuit. When young men leave on their warriors' journey to live in the cold north for a year, they are given a necklace with a rose quartz crystal in the shape of a small teardrop by their mother as a protection."

"Wow, I always thought people's belief in gems and crystals was just superstition. Is that how you could blow out the candles back at the chomp' house? I also saw you hurtling through the air farther than any old man I've ever seen jump," Learon asked.

"I'll tell you how that was all done, if you first tell me what these soldiers are after?" Elias asked.

"My father's journal," Learon said flatly.

"You said that before. Why, who was your father?" Elias implored.

"Rylan Everwyn, he worked for the Coalition on . . ." Learon began, but Elias interrupted him

"I know who your father was. He worked on the Field of Ashes excavation. What is in his journal?" Elias asked.

"Nothing really, he just talked about some of the research and the artifacts they found. Wait, you knew my father?"

"Artifacts? They didn't recover any artifacts," Elias asked, his eyes piercing and attentive.

"They definitely did. They sequestered him for a year, working with the things they found. He talks about it in his journal. What is so important about this excavation? Is it the reason my father's dead?"

"The only thing I know of your father's death, was what I read. A shipwreck was found in the Mainsolis, having killed four members of the Guild and ten in total. As for the excavation, it was thought to be the lost city of Ashalon. Ellaria and I believed for years that the Field of Ashes outside of Adalon was the remnants of the ancient city and there were further ruins below. We hoped it was the hidden location of the Sagean's Tomb. About twelve years ago, Ellaria sent me word that the excavation was underway. Sometime after, she sent me a message, that the team found ruins but nothing else, and the site was not as extensive as we thought. Subsequently they defunded the project and considered it completed. If your father's journal says that artifacts were recovered, that would be news to the Scholar's Guild. You have the journal, I assume? When you were saying goodbye to your mother, I thought she handed you something."

"Yes," Learon said, not sure where this was going. Elias was obviously interested in its contents as well.

"Relax, kid, I'm not going to take it from you. It's good to know what they're after, though; and to be clear I didn't know your father, but I did meet him a long time ago. A man named Brugo introduced us. Can you tell me what he said they found?"

"Innocuous things mostly. Clay pots, mosaics, small stone statues. The most important thing sounded like it was a broken amulet and some of his journal suggests they were under some serious scrutiny and intimidation."

"Interesting, did it say by who?"

"No, but one of the men scared my father, and he sent the journal on to my mother shortly before his death. Apparently going through great trouble to have it delivered. Are you a historian or explorer too? You said you were in Kalihjan not too long ago," Learon asked, trying to gauge his interest.

"Something like that. Mostly I've searched out anything from the Ancients. The Eckwyn age fascinates me, but I've been looking for the tomb of the Sagean's my entire life."

"Just you, by yourself?"

"Yes, mostly."

"Isn't that lonely?"

"It can be."

"They said he died on that ship, but I don't think that's the whole story."

"Why don't you believe it?"

"It's just that the open water terrified him. I don't believe he ever would have boarded the ship. He refused to sail ships on the Uhanni River, I don't see him sailing on the Mainsolis sea. This journal is really all I have left of him," Learon said, patting the pocket of his coat.

"As long as you have it and they don't, they will be after it. I wish Ellaria was here. She knows a spell that could hide the journal in plain sight. Someone would read it and not see the truth of it."

"Ellaria, do you mean Ellaria Moonstone?" Learon asked.

"Yes."

"Who are you, Elias?" Learon asked, but at the same moment their attentions were diverted to the sound of movement and rustling leaves in the surrounding forest. They both got to their feet. Elias drew his sword in a flash of light, the shining blade reflected the fire. Learon crept within the camp. Slightly crouched and ambling to retrieve his bow that rested lightly atop his pack of supplies. He slid the bow off and up, notched an arrow, then paused in place to listen for more movement out in the forest. Whatever it was, it was moving lightly in the underbrush. He looked over toward Elias to signal that he couldn't see anything stirring. Elias gestured back with his hands he was going to go out and come around from the back. Learon cringed at the idea but nodded his agreement. Elias slowly stalked away and out of sight on the far side of their camp. Learon softly stepped back to the fire and positioned himself with the fire to his back.

The light wind was picking up as the night went on, and the wisps of wind flung the flames close to scorching his clothes. Sweat ran down the side of his face and down his chin. He tried to focus on his breathing, tension and nerves would do nothing but compromise his accuracy.

Suddenly a small black shape hurtled into the clearing. Learon's fingers twitched, but he held the arrow. A black cat trotted toward him, it was small, almost kitten size, with large paws and long ears. Sleek and slender with a white tufted fur at its chest that stretched around his neck like a raised collar. The cat came right up to Learon's legs and began brushing against him. Learon eased off the tension in his bow and lowered it. Then lifted it again to aim as Elias came into view.

His eyes went wide at the site of the black cat, but something also seemed to drain from him. His posture lumped a bit, and the creases at his eyes looked darker and more defined.

"Just the cat, then?" Learon asked him.

"Must be, I saw nothing and there were no tracks in the bog either," Elias said.

They went back to their previous spots around the fire. Learon looked over to Elias to finish their conversation but he was already sound asleep. His head propped up on his piled up long coat. He would get his answers, but not tonight, it appeared. Learon finished his leaning shelter. He placed some leaf-filled branches overtop. Then he laid underneath, watching the peculiar cat as it climbed above them into the low-hanging limb of the wild oak tree. It sprawled out with its paws hanging down over the bark and settled in to watch over them.

THEY WERE SLEEPING NESTLED IN THE GRASS BENEATH THE DARK, CLOUD-filled sky. The rain came soon after Learon had gone to sleep and had been coming in waves of varying strength ever since. Learon was restless and struggling through a weary-filled slumber. His mind reeled and was unable to teeter into a deeper state. His thoughts oscillated from calculating ideas to nonsensical connections. He could have sworn that he hadn't slept at all when the black cat shocked him awake by vaulting onto his chest and off again.

Learon's eyes were slow to adjust. He pried them open long enough to assess the fire and see it still burned despite the rain and wind. He mumbled something at the cat to leave him be and rolled back over to sleep.

"Ow!" pain shot through Learon's arm and he bellowed out.

"What's going on?" Elias asked, sitting up.

"The cat just bit my arm while I was sleeping," Learon cursed, and saw Elias jump to his feet.

"Get up!" he said, "Get your bow, something's wrong."

"What?" Learon asked. He gathered to his feet, and grabbed his bow from next to him on the grass and gazed out over the landscape. They both scanned around until Elias found it.

"The basin's flame is out at the fork!" Elias said.

"From the rain?" Learon questioned.

"Maybe," Elias replied, "How many campfires around us before you went to sleep, three others?" he asked.

"Yes," Learon answered, but they could see only one still burning. "What do we do?" Learon asked.

"We need to get down there and see what's happening. Get the basin relit. Otherwise, this place will swarm with beasts," Elias said.

Learon made quick torches with blue pine bundled in. Elias grabbed the guns he swiped from the soldiers two days ago and offered one to Learon.

"I'll stick with my bow," Learon said, declining, but Elias thrusted the thing in his hand, anyway.

"Take it. I know, I don't like them either, but you might need it," Elias said, turning the pre-charge switch of his own gun, on.

They threw more wood on their own fire and started down the slope on foot. They were three hundred feet from the outpost when they heard screaming. It was a woman's voice, a loud chilling scream of terror and desperation from the opposite hill. They turned their attention to the uproar and could make out the shape of a person running down the slope to the fork. A wolverack on her tail. Learon and Elias launched into a full run to her aid, but before they could reach her the wolverack struck in a leaping attack. Long claws sunk into the woman's back, followed by a ripping bite to her neck, the blood splattered to the ground.

"No!" Learon called out, stopping in his tracks at the sight.

Elias sprinted forward unrelenting while shooting two charged tungsten bolts into the wolveracks head.

The shots rang out with a distinctive piercing electrical resonance. A buzz that hummed in a slight echoing wave. Both the woman and the wolverack crumpled in dead heaps in the wet grass.

"Help!" someone screamed out from the outpost. The yells were followed by a cracking shatter of broken glass. Learon's heart was hammering. He ran his shaking hand through his hair, looking all around.

"Learon! Light the basin!" Elias yelled over to him.

"Right," he said, and darted to the basin, he tossed his torch in when he was close enough to make the throw. Then he reached down to add more fuel from the piled brushwood prepped at the base of the poles. He threw in the full stack that was there. The flames grew larger and life bloomed, illuminating blood splattered up the side of a pole. A small bit of vomit curdled up his throat as he looked.

"Learon, come on," Elias waved him to follow.

The rain was picking up again and thoroughly drenched his hair now. They ran to the building entrance. Elias attempted to kick at the door, but the oak was sturdy and thick, and it didn't budge. A succession of loud blasts bellowed into the night–gunshots followed by thunder cracking overhead. They abandoned the front entry and looped around the building toward the shrieks.

There were two dormer windows protruding from the pitched roof, both with broken glass. Blood marked the outside of the upper window frame and streamed down the side. More blasts from inside and shouts.

"Here," Elias said, handing Learon his torch. Raindrops speckled over his face and eyelids. Together they entered the building through the broken window. The room smelled of iron and wet wood. The torch light flickered off the surrounding surfaces and revealed a gruesome sight at the doorway. The body of a man ripped to shreds. Then came a clatter of scattering claws on the wood floor scratching above them.

Elias looked up at the ceiling to the sound, then a large mass dove through the doorway. The wolverack knocked Elias to the ground and charged at Learon, undaunted and despite the torch in his hand, that the beast didn't seem to care about. Learon retreated backwards, stumbling on something unseen in the dark, he fell to the floor, spilling everything he held. The wolverack sneered with its mouth of jagged teeth bared and ravenous.

Learon searched frantically for the gun, but his hand couldn't find it. At the moment it struck, Elias blasted it three or four times. The charged rounds found the beast. It barreled to the floor next to Learon. He scrambled back up to his feet to get away from it as fast as he could manage.

"You good?" Elias asked.

"Yes, thank you."

Learon grabbed what he could find of his things off the floor. Though he felt like he had missed something, he was breathing too hard to focus. Blood pounding in his head. He found his bow, and the gun. At the moment, that's all that mattered.

Trying to catch his breath, they entered the hallway, stepping with care. It was still partly lit by a lantern at the hall's end, but the light extended only so far. They stepped over a pool of blood and scanned in either direction, the wood floor creaked with each step. The patter of rain being thrown against the roof by the gusting wind could be heard, but no more sounds of movement above. Then Elias swiftly dashed toward the end of the hall and to the vaulted room beyond, rushing to the location were the last shouts carried from. Elias paused at the wall where the hall ended. Both of them were still breathing hard as water dripped from their clothes.

The large room beyond was completely dark except for the light of the basin fire glowing outside the top band of windows. There was a terrible wet sloping sound of something eating. Elias lurched out, pointing the pulsator at the sound, found his target and blasted five times. Learon followed, angling in the torch to expand their field of vision. A large wolverack was twitching on the ground near the expired hearth. A decimated body sprawled near– mangled and unrecognizable.

Knock, knock, knock… three thudding whacks resounded against the entry door across the room. Learon and Elias both jerked their heads to the sudden intrusion.

"Hello!" a voice yelled out from the outside stoop.

"Open the door!" Elias told Learon. He bounded over and pulled the barge lock free. Undid the latch and pushed the door open. The door yanking free of his grasp, it swung out wide as a man and young woman barreled in. The man helped his friend inside before him and then pulled the door back shut and locked it afterward in a hurry.

"What in the Sagean's beard is happening out there?" the man shouted while entering. The young woman straightened herself on her feet, she held a pulsator in her hand and her black cloak had rolling drops of water spilling to the floor, but Learon couldn't see her face. The man spun around, water spilling off his hat as he did, and he pointed a wicked looking pulsator at Learon. It had emblems on the side that were difficult to make out with the thing up his nose. The man holding it had shrewd and serious eyes that made Learon recoil almost as much as the gun.

"What's going on here kid?" the man demanded at gunpoint.

"Drop it!" Elias yelled from near the hearth. His form obscured in shadow.

"I don't think so, pal. The world's gone berserk out there," the man said, but kept his eyes on Learon.

"In here too," Learon said.

"I said lower your weapon, sir," Elias said again, moving closer. His face now more visible in the flames' reflected glow. The woman seemed startled by him and moved closer to her friend, muttering quietly to him.

"Kovan, lower your weapon. They're not enemies," she whispered.

The man grumbled and lowered the gun to his side. His friend nudged him in the arm. He turned to inspect Elias. Evidently, he discovered something that annoyed him, as he shook his head and let out another grumble. The intensity in Elias's eyes, like a swirling storm moments ago, flooded away.

"Yep, this seems about right. Crazed beasts beneath the Dragon's Spine and you," the man said.

"I'm charmed, what can I say?" Elias replied.

Crash! They all spun on the raucous sound of falling pans from the kitchen. Two wolveracks sprung on top of the counter, hissing out their low, guttural growls.

The man named Kovan shot, but the beasts dived and jumped back. Then another smash; and a third and fourth wolverack barreled through a door in the hall that led to the upper floor. Smoke wafted through at the top of the frame and collected. The second floor was on fire.

They all scrambled back to the entrance to leave. Kovan, threw the lock board away and opened the door.

"Be ready, there's more out here," he said as he pushed free to the outside. They spilled out and into the rain. Their shoes trampled into mud and pools of water forming on the road. Shapes still lurked on the hill behind the outpost like phantoms.

"God's beard, Q, why don't you just light these things up?" the man said—evidently talking to Elias.

"It's not as easy as you always make it, Van," Elias said with a grunt.

They kept retreating to the far hill while the stranger kept shooting blasts into the building and dark hillside beyond. The flames at the rear portion of the outpost where rising high, fighting against the downpour. The glowing embers crackled and hissed.

"Q, use that pulsator or better yet pull your blade. You're a horrible shot anyway," the man said. "Tali, cover our backs," he said, addressing the young woman. She pulled her hood back and with a steady hand, aimed a gun into the woods they were backing into. Wolveracks started to pour out of the building and from around the sides. There were now seven or more approaching them, and their yellow eyes glowed with intensity. The ones from the hill skirted around the protection basin, staying twenty feet clear but otherwise were unfazed by it.

"Van, they're behind us too!" Tali said. They were creeping in from all sides now and surrounding them. Their numbers, swelling to double digits.

"Q, if you're going to do something, now's the time!" the man called out.

The growls of the beasts hummed in unison, and drool dripped from their gritted teeth and blood-coated muzzles.

When the sounds of the growling grew so loud in Learon's ears it drowned out the rain's persistent patter, Elias stepped in front of them and into the middle of the road. Learon made a move to grab him, but Kovan put his arm against his chest to halt him in place.

Crack! Boom!

Thunder overhead roared out and rumbled, the territh shook at their feet. Learon's eyes blinked away rain droplets, waiting for the wolveracks to strike; but a new hum resonated, this one coming from Elias. The air vibrated and Elias burst into a blinding white light that enveloped him completely. A glaring flash casted against everything that surrounded them. Then a white light shimmered and thrust into the sky above, where it lingered for a breath. The surrounding rain slowed in midair like it was being frozen in place. The moment ceased and lighting cascaded down into twelve bolts blaring out simultaneously all around them. It struck every wolverack that was near and killed them all. The air reverberated with energy and then dissipated in a blink.

Learon finally let out the breath he held and looked at the newcomers. The young woman's eyes were about to pop out of her head. They both were having trouble believing what they just saw.

"Show off," Kovan said.

Elias slumped to his hands and knees in the road, and they rushed to his side. His pulsator fell to the gravel and the young woman picked it up while Learon and Kovan helped Elias. The outpost was full ablaze now and the lightning show would draw a squad of men from the city soon, they needed to get out of the area.

"Elias, you alright?" Learon asked.

"Q, can you walk?" the man asked.

"Yes," Elias answered them both in a hoarse voice. Then he stood up, his face depleted, and his breathing labored.

"We need to get out of here," Learon said.

"Definitely. Where are your horses?" the man asked.

"Up there a short way," Elias answered, pointing to the hill behind them.

"We left ours at our camp on the other hill. We'll get them and meet up on the east road to Adalon," the man said.

Elias nodded his agreement and rubbed the bridge of his nose. They moved to depart, but the man turned back. He grabbed Elias and hugged him close. They both smiled and laughed out loud. Learon looked to the young women and they shared a look of equal confusion.

# CHAPTER FIFTEEN

## THE RIDE AWAY (TALI / LEARON)

THE RAIN CEASED HALFWAY UP THE HILL WHILE THEY RAMBLED THROUGH the drenched grass to retrieve their horses. Precarious mud holes hidden in the slope kept them from advancing at the hurried pace that they wanted to. Tali's nerves were still buzzing, and she had yet to slow her breathing to a normal rhythm. She should have been exhausted, but something about the night's ordeal had strengthened her. She wasn't sure how long the entire nightmare had lasted, but her hands were wrinkled from the rain. She stuffed them under her arms to keep them warm, but to little effect. Kovan was in good spirits, but also still on edge. He trudged ahead of her with his gun still drawn. She had placed the gun Kovan bought her back in her holster, and the gun she had picked up she stowed inside one of the largest pockets of her cloak. It was imperative that she find out what it was about the cloak that Maki had warned her about. *How did it give her away as an agent in the chain?* She wondered. She had grown fond of this thing. The pockets were advantageous, but having it tonight in the rain proved how useful it was at wicking the water away before it settled and soaked in. Hours in the rain and she was still relatively dry. Her shoes were another matter, each step squished. They somehow let water in with ease and then trapped it within her shoe. She made a note to get a new pair more adequate for traveling.

The blue flames of their fire were still burning when they arrived at the grounds. Their horses were agitated, but still tied, and Kovan went to work saddling them. Earlier when Kovan woke her because of the shouting near them, they ran out of there so quickly she never threw any more wood on. It gave her a sinking feeling the entire walk back that something might have happened to the horses. She had never had a horse before, and almost zero experience riding them. Most of the people in Ravenvyre walked or rode bicycles to get around. The horses she was used to seeing on the island were all pulling carriages. It took her most of the day to get used to the horse, and she was happy they stopped when they did, so she could rest her aching legs.

Tali picked her blanket up off the ground, and it was soaked and twice as heavy as normal. She twisted and wrung out whatever water she could, starting at one end and progressing through, and threw the freshly squeezed sections over her shoulder as she went. When she finished, she rolled it up and tied it to her horse Bronn, who neighed and shuffled slightly. Tomorrow the blanket would need to dry properly in the sun. Bronn was a light, golden brown mustang with a black mane and tail. Fairly indistinguishable except for a bright white patch on his muzzle that ended in a point on his forehead. Kovan told her he was a cold-blooded horse best used for pulling carts and long rides. Tali mounted up onto Bronn and fixed her cloak. She looked over to Kovan, who was finishing the tie-offs to the supplies rig on the back of his horse. She was puzzling something out and needed to ask before she could reconsider.

"Kovan, you called that man Q. Does that mean what I think it means?" she asked, biting her tongue. He shifted his gaze to her and exhausted a breath audibly.

"What do you think? You think there are a lot of people running around with the ability to pull lightning out of the sky?" he said with a laugh.

"I know. I just . . ." she didn't know what to say.

"You can't believe what you just saw with your own eyes," he said more as a statement than question, while buckling the last strap.

"Exactly. How do you get used to it?" she asked.

"If you figure that out, tell me, because I never could," he said as he pulled himself up onto his horse, and then he turned to trot next to her.

"Let's get down to the road. I'm eager to talk with my old friend. Honestly, it's been years since we've seen each other. If we're going to be riding with him, you should know he is a complicated person," Kovan said.

"How so?"

"Well, he's lived a very solitary existence for one. I can tell you, the night he killed the Sagean, he changed. One man went up to that ridge and a different man returned," Kovan said with shuddered breath, and he pointed to the west where the faint outline of the Dragon's Spine loomed beyond. The sharp ridge lines could barely be seen. Kovan reeled his horse to a trot and began descending the hill. She did the same, trying to remember his instructions. Tali patted the horse's side in encouragement when she saw it followed Kovan's lead. She pulled her hood over her head and tried to focus on navigating the horse down the hill without falling off. When Tali got closer to Kovan, she continued their conversation against her better judgement.

"Different how?" She wondered.

"I knew you would ask that," he mused. "Well, he acted like he had been the one defeated. He was weak and unsure of himself. That was understandable, but he also seemed lost and certain that evil was lurking behind every corner. For me and Ellaria, it was shocking. Q was always the most optimistic of the group. To see that destroyed was painful. The person he was disappeared and, in its place, a desire to find truths about the past and his powers, an obsession really," he said with a weariness to his tone.

"Do you know if he found what he was looking for?"

"I hope so, he's spent his life crawling through dust and bones."

"The Ancients?"

"Yes, they became his fascination. Ellaria used to call it a quest for phantoms."

"For forty years?" she asked, astounded.

"He gave it up once. He found someone, and they lived for a time peacefully in the New World. But his affliction had him seeing things in the shadows, and he drifted back. He sent his loved one into hiding and showed up at my door in the middle of the night. Gave me a way to find him if we needed him, and a cryptic warning. I hadn't seen him again until tonight."

"How long ago was that?"

"Eighteen years ago."

"Did you try to stop him?"

"Of course. Ellaria and I both tried. But we were dealing with a tragedy of our own at the same time. Our daughter had died."

"Oh, Kovan, I'm sorry. I didn't know," she said.

"Nobody knows, but it was a long time ago," he said, his voice gruff and strained.

"What was the warning about?" she asked.

"It was something he called the Wrythen."

"Like the Wraith demon?" she asked. It was a mythical creature of the dark spirits. That captured the dead souls that don't rise, to bring them to Ovardyn the demon god of death and into the Nothing. These were creatures from some of the oldest myths from Rodairean culture.

"I don't know. He was never clear about any of it," Kovan said.

Then he turned them off the slope and onto the road. Where Qudin and the young man he traveled with were waiting. She didn't know what to make of the young man. He was around her age and by the look on his face he was equally astonished by what had happened. He sat tall on his horse with his broad shoulders and muscular build. High atop his horse, he was taller and more forbidding than she had realized before. As they got closer, Qudin stared at them with those odd eyes, and his white horse starting to spin in excitement. She placed her hand on the black coin she liked to hold to help her think, wondering if Qudin had recognized her.

LEARON MEANDERED IN A DAZE FOR MOST OF THEIR ASSENT BACK UP TO their spot beneath the wild oaks. He didn't even notice when the rain had stopped, his jumbled thoughts prevented him from regaining control of his wits. The beasts were terrifying and what Elias just did was equally so. He ran his hands through his wet hair, moving it out and off of his eyes. The climb up had been in silence. Learon wasn't avoiding Elias, so much as he didn't want to ask the wrong questions.

Learon felt himself holding his breath, his brain too preoccupied to exhale. If he could somehow wrap his mind around the truth, he could breathe normally again. The fact was this stranger he had been riding around with for the last seven days, just pulled lighting out of the air and manipulated it through the force of his will. When Learon blinked, his vision still held a silhouetted apparition from the brightness of the blinding white light. There were only two people he ever heard about that could control lightning. One was the Sagean, and the other was Qudin Lightweaver. Most people thought Qudin was a myth and that the Sagean simply died trying to harness too much power. Learon never knew what to believe. Old man Garner told him once that Qudin was real, he now he understood Garner's insistence. Learon always trusted Garner. He seldom spoke, but when he did, it was the truth. Though he never believed the stories of a battle of lightning, and yet here he was walking next to a legend.

The flames of their fire were still strong, and the anthracite still burned as they reached their campsite. He wondered why the blue pine hadn't worked at the basin and made a mental note to ask Elias later about it. The horses looked unharmed, except the white mare became erratic as soon as it recognized Elias, making noises like she was talking to him. Elias crossed the grounds and approached her first. Placing his hand on the mare's side and then looking back at Learon to speak.

"I know you have a lot of questions Learon and I owe you answers to some. If you can wait until we're settled and safe from here that would be better. We should get packed up as quickly as possible and meet the other two. You were right, we need to get moving. Greencoats will be here soon," he said.

"Agreed," Learon replied, and secured his pack atop his horse and his bow atop that, pausing out of uncertainty.

"Elias, how fast are we riding out, should I keep my bow or strap it down?" he asked, because he honestly didn't know. Elias looked over from his horse. He was already mounted up. Though he only carried a satchel with him and a second bag he gained in Jenovee for food storage. After a week of traveling together, Learon understood how lightly Elias packed and how quickly he moved once a decision was made.

"Fast. Strap your bow, and here," he tossed two pieces of brown leather and strappings at Learon. One made it to Learon's hand, but the second fell short. Learon bent down to pick the other up. They were holsters for the pulsator guns. He looked back to Elias. "I got those in Jenovee yesterday. Give one to the young lady when we meet up with them. Van was right, I'm a terrible shot. Plus, I have no need for a gun, the young woman can keep it. I got the extra strap length so you can attach it wherever you feel comfortable, but you should be able to draw it on horseback."

"Thank you," Learon said, and he meant it. Learon always wanted a pulsator gun, and now he held one of his own. The holsters had different designs in the leather. Learon chose the one with the burn indentation of a crescent moon. While he held the holster admiring it, he felt a quick tug on the dangling strap. The black cat was still at their campsite and swiped at the thin ends as they swung about. Learon smiled; then the cat climbed up his pant leg.

Ow!

The cat's sharp claws pierced through the pant, to his skin.

"Stop that, what are you doing, cat?" Learon said.

But the skimpy cat moved swiftly from his leg to his coat and up his back. It stopped at his shoulders, precariously balancing there. Then it licked water off Learon's neck below his ear with its tiny, rough tongue. Learon chuckled and pulled the cat off. When its paws got to the ground, it bounced away to investigate something else. Learon shook his head at the curious thing. He had never had an animal take to him before. He continued what he was doing, removed his hip sword and packed it away, happy to be rid of the thing. He strapped the new holster in the sword's place and slid the gun in for a smooth fit. All packed up, he clutched the saddle and lifted himself up. Elias waited at the edge of the tree line for Learon to catch up.

"I noticed you never drew your sword tonight. You don't know how to use it?" Elias asked when Learon got close.

"Not really. Not with any skill," he admitted.

"If you would like to learn, let me know," Elias offered.

They started down the hill to the road. The horses slowly plodded their way from the sodden north slope. In the distance, they could see the outpost blaze was raging. The entire building was in flames, with large sections already collapsing. The black cat was trailing behind them.

"Elias, have you ever seen a cat act like that?" Learon asked as they neared the road.

"I have, but they're very rare," Elias said.

When his mare stepped onto the gravel road, it galloped a few feet and Elias had to rein it in to a stop. He turned in place and the horse huffed. Learon trotted over to them to wait for the others.

"Do you think more soldiers will be sent after my mother now?" Learon asked.

"No, I think they'll believe you died back there, but I don't know. We'll just have to keep watching our back as we go. Either way it should take some time to sort out what's happened tonight."

"So, who is this guy we're waiting for? I think the woman called him Van or Kovan?" Learon asked, resting his hands and weight on the pommel.

"Kovan Rainer," Elias said.

"Kovan the war general and leader of the Ultrarians?" Learon asked, bewildered.

"That's the one. I should warn you he's easily agitated and not a very trusting person," Elias said.

"Great, then there's two of you now," Learon said.

Off the north hill, two riders approached. The firelight from the outpost flickered off the land and at their backs. Kovan with his wide-brimmed hat and long brown coat, one side of which he tucked back behind his leg, revealing the gun he had holstered at his right hip. He rode a black horse out in front of the young woman.

She had the hood of her cloak back up, shrouding her face in shadow. When they got closer, Learon could sense Elias's mare wanting to bolt. She spun in circles in anticipation.

"Q, this is Tali. Tali this is Qudin and . . ." Kovan paused, looking at Learon then to Elias for a prompt.

"This is Learon. Nice to meet you, Tali. You can call me Elias, if you'd like," Elias said. They nodded to one another and Learon meandered over to Tali and held out the second holster for her.

"What's this?" she asked softly.

"It's a holster," Learon said.

"Yes, I understand that, why are you giving it to me?"

"Elias said to give you it for the pulsator," he told her. She looked from him to Elias. Then she took the holster and examined it. Her eyes grew wide and brightened when she saw the emblem in the leather. She reached inside to a pocket on the left of her cloak. Removed the gun, placed it in the holster and back into the same pocket.

"You're giving me your gun? Are you sure? Kovan bought me one in Atava, you can have it back."

"I don't need it. Kovan was right. I'm terrible with them. You can sell it if you want."

"Thank you," she said to Elias. Then the black cat maneuvered below, weaving in between the legs of Learon's horse. The young woman seemed surprised at the sight of it. "Hey, that's my cat," she said.

"Your cat?" Elias said before Learon could get the words out.

"Yes, he came to us two nights ago in Atava. He's been hanging around ever since," She explained.

"He came to our camp last night. Actually, he's the reason we woke up and noticed something was wrong," Learon told them. He noticed Kovan and Elias share a look.

"Well, I hope you didn't name him, because I kind of already did," She said sheepishly. She pulled her cloak back, revealing her face, and called for the cat. She had delicately soft features and bright big brown eyes.

"Remi. Come here, Remi," she said, her voice soft and pleasant. The cat immediately looked up and pranced over to her. She leaned back and patted her thigh. The cat leaped up onto her, and she wrapped her cloak around it. Learon could see it turning and moving under the cloth a moment, then its head peaked out the top, near her neck.

"You're going to ride with him like that?" Kovan asked her, amused.

"Sure, he's fine, he's sitting in my top pocket," she said confidently.

"Well, like I told you before. He's your responsibility Raven," Kovan said.

"Let's get moving. We can catch up later, but I want to put a couple hours between us and this place," Elias told them.

"You want to stop at the Maiden's crossing?" Kovan asked him.

"Yes. Though it might be light out by the time we get there," Elias said.

"Lead the way. It looks like we're all going to struggle to keep up with that white mare of yours," Kovan suggested.

Elias nodded, then looked at Learon and Tali and kicked his horse into a gallop to the east. They shot out like lighting in the night, and set a pace the rest of them would struggle to keep.

# CHAPTER SIXTEEN

## SEARCHING THE NORTH (ELLARIA)

THE PLATFORM RUMBLED, AND A CLOUD OF STEAM ENVELOPED THE walkway. The Mancovi Train Station in Andal was a series of barrel arched domes, formed above red brick arches that each stemmed from black stone columns arranged equally throughout the space. Across the cavernous expanse, people bustled all around like flies.

Ellaria wished she could sit in the station spectating the eclectic disorder. With every passerby, their own personalities so evidently on display. Men are less brave and thus less effective at expressing themselves; a fact that doesn't end with their fashion sense, but they are no less interesting to analyze. The ones shuffling around her wore suits and hats, filigree vests beneath long coats, capes and cloaks. Some carried canes and had the gold chains of their pocket watches swinging at their sides. Since they were in Andal, most also carried a weapon of some sort. Steambursters, b-series pulsator guns or a fine intricately crafted sword, too fine to use in a real fight. Men seemed to find one look that fit their needs and they all copied the same styling.

Women's choice of clothes varied from one individual to another. Lots of divergent factors in play: body type, affluence, personal style, but seldom personal comfort. Only strength, confidence, and overconfidence. Subconsciously probably all adhered to a look when someone first showed interest or maybe the most opposite thing from what Mother suggested. It was an endless struggle constantly adapting that established look to your age and evolving figure. The result, women wore dresses of all kinds, or trousers with blouses, or bodices, stylized hair or fancy hats. Men's hats were muted, but strongly shaped, and all fairly similar. By contrast woman's hats were small or dazzling, floppy or delicate. No matter a woman's status in Tavillore, her hat could always elicit praise by a discerning eye. Ellaria stared at all the hats with envy, she had left hers in Adalon to avoid the possibility of being recognized.

Semo, Wade and Ellaria negotiated the congestion of travelers careening in all directions and emerged out to the city streets. Rows of carriages and stagecoaches awaited there to take passengers anywhere in the city. Their destination was not actually in the city proper, but the massive compound in the outskirts. Ellaria and her new cohorts needed to find a discrete way across the south of the city and back. The best they were going to do was hire a coach to take them to a field and leave them stranded, and then walk back when the time came. Semo and Wade split to talk with the various coach masters to find the most willing driver. Ellaria stood on the curb, wondering why she had agreed to this. Knowing something was a bad idea and still going through with it, surely was a sign of her own fading mental capacity.

Three days ago, Semo and Wade escorted Dalliana to the docks and began cooking up this scheme on their walk back. They burst into her office the next morning with energy and a plan to go investigate the Citadel for themselves. They acted like they were old pals. Wade seemed to have that way about him. They reasoned that if Danehin went there, then maybe he found something that the Prime was hiding and was imprisoned in the Black Spire. They could find him and get him out. Wade laid out the plan like it was a sure thing. She was coming to realize that he liked to make everything out to be far easier than it truly was.

The real problem was Semo. She could tell they would not talk him out of finding his brother Ragor. It was his only thought and Wade had provided a thread to pull on. She didn't have the heart to tell him that Ragor was mostly likely dead. The most probable scenario was that he died protecting Danehin from capture. She suspected Semo knew this deep down, but it didn't diminish his drive.

She rubbed her old hands together, massaged each palm, and tapped her foot restlessly on the mudstone sidewalk. She found old age had given her less patience in equal quantities as wisdom. Finally, she saw Semo stalking back to her, his expression unreadable. His physical appearance was tough to disguise. He was tall and more muscular than most civilians. She had forced him to wear baggy clothes to downplay how imposing he was. It worked, but not to a significant effect. His sharp jawline was a giveaway, almost as much as his stiff movements and close-cut hair. His dark skin color already signaled that he wasn't from the northern cities. Ellaria looked around but still couldn't find Wade. How long could it possibly take? She wondered.

"Sir, I mean Miss. Moonstone, the man in the red coach will take us for a talon each," Semo had a habit of calling her sir. She liked it. It was better than ma'am, which made her want to poke someone in the eye. Nothing made her feel older.

"Thank you, Semo," she said and looked around for Wade. He was bounding back with a smile that went ear to ear. He did not project an imposing figure at all. He came up to them slightly out of breath.

"Follow me, I found a guy that will drop us and pick us up," Wade said, and he immediately turned back down the sidewalk without waiting for their reaction.

"Wait, what?" Ellaria asked, scampering to his side. He was impossibly frustrating. "Wade, slow down. How did you manage that?" she asked. He slowed his gait slightly and looked over to her.

"I was talking with this guy, Pullson. He said he'll drop us up the road from the Citadel and pick us up at the same spot later," he said.

"How much is that costing us?" she asked in disbelief.

"Just a couple of talons, and a favor," he beamed.

"What favor?" She demanded.

"Well, it turns out he's always wanted to visit Adalon. I offered to put him up for the night if he's ever in the city," he said dismissively.

"How. Err. Never mind," she groaned and threw her hands up.

They reached the coach with the man named Pullson holding the cabin door open for her. She climbed up and crossed the corner to sit. The worn interior leather showed splotches of distressed coloring and scratches. Semo followed her in and sat next to her, while Wade stood chatting with Pullson. He patted him on the back, laughed, then climbed in too.

"I told him to pick us up at four in the morning," Wade said smiling.

She scowled, before reluctantly smiling back, struggling to sustain her anger with him. He was such an infuriatingly innocent overachiever. He reminded her of Kovan in his youth. For a fleeting moment, she thought she should try to protect him and kick him out of the coach. Force him to return to Adalon. It was an old ache she never got right. It surfaced when she got close to caring about anyone. She knew his grin would retreat from his face as soon as he saw the fortress that awaited them. The idea that they could somehow infiltrate the most protected building in the world was foolish.

The Citadel was more than just a building. It was a small contained city of its own, built as a fortified military complex that protruded out from the cliffs. The lowest level was warehouses and shipyards. Right on the sea, there were three water gates to allow naval vessels to dock. The second level housed the training deck for the special fighters' academy, the Cloaked Knife and the army. The third level was the stone base for a giant tower that rose high into the sky. A bundled mass of rectangular prisms gradually oscillating in height like a black crystal shard. The main military compound was imposing, jagged and monolithic.

The carriage took them along the sea road, through Andal's coastal landscape rising high off the Mainsolis Sea. Much of the shoreline was a just a colossal wall of sheared cliff face, one hundred feet above the surface of the water. The tide collided into the rocks in violent clashes of exploding mist.

"Let's go over this again," she said. "Remember, we don't need to unearth all the secrets in one night. We simply want to see if anything looks amiss. We just need to get to the pier and get a closer look at the warehouses."

"How do we do this?" Semo asked.

"There are a series of caves to the west. They're treacherous to navigate, but one of them opens out to a walkable edge. We have to use handholds in the cliff face to balance ourselves. As long as we don't fall to our deaths, it leads to the small jumble of boulders we can use to crawl up to the top of the fortress wall. Over that and we're in," she explained.

"If you, did it, we can do it no problem," Wade said.

"No, I've never done it," she clarified ardently.

"Then how do you know about it?" he asked.

"Kovan Rainer told me how he slipped in undetected during the siege," she said.

"Well, this should be interesting. What if the access has been demolished or broken away with the sea?" Wade asked.

"Then we will be waiting in the middle of the road for Pullson to come back for us," Ellaria answered.

As the coach rattled along, the Black Spire stood in the distance like a nightmare. A hundred tiny windows of light glowed from it in the night. From the road, the land disguised most of the complex from the field of view. The coach passed by the area and pushed on to the west.

"Here," Ellaria said, and Wade rapped on the coach side for the man to stop. They all got out of the cabin, stepping onto crushed gravel that shifted and crunched under her feet. Wade thanked the driver, who Ellaria saw was shaking his head as he pulled away. The darkness of the area was overwhelming. The moon could only illuminate so much of the rolling landscape. They crossed over to the edge where the land dropped off, to peer down into a spray of the sea below.

"We're going down there. Are you sure?" Wade asked, checking her sanity.

"Um," she hesitated. Now that she put eyes on it. She wasn't sure. She could see the caves Kovan mentioned, but not a simple way down to them.

"Over here!" Semo called out to them from beyond the edge. His head just above the ground. He had found a crooked path down the cliff. They started the descent, and she noticed her hands were shaking. Not from the sneaking around, but from their precarious position high above the sea. The closer they got to the surface of the water, the more the spray of the crashing sea hit them. She wore a cloak over her clothes for the concealment of her identity, and it was also the only thing keeping her dry. It had quickly soaked Wade, but Semo seemed to have perfect timing and move at the right moments to avoid getting wet. At the bottom of the slope, three caves punctured the cliff wall in front of them. Kovan never said exactly which one he had taken. One was obviously too small and collapsed and not an option. She hoped it wasn't the one they needed. Leaving two to choose from.

"Ok, so which one is it?" Wade asked.

"I don't know. How lucky are you, Wade?"

"Depends on who you ask."

"Well, Kovan would have taken the easiest and fastest route first," she thought aloud. "So that one," she pointed to the first cave that looked like it led them back and deeper underground. Semo climbed in and turned around to help her. The bottom edge of the cave entrance was just about at her neck. She placed her hands on the cold rock, feeling around for a dry patch to grip, but there wasn't any. He reached down further and grasped her forearms. She clutched on to him and he heaved her up. She tried to use her feet against the rock face to help. Semo essentially picked her up and placed her down with barely a trace amount of effort on her part. He made sure she had her footing and then reached back to help Wade.

The cave was pitch black, and the wind howled within. The sound rebounded and echoed on. Semo pulled his pack off and the torch he carried inside free. He handed it to Ellaria. She reached into her cloak and grabbed a vial and a flaking flint stone and steel. She poured a few drops from the vial on the torch, then sparked it to life in a bright flare. She picked it up off the rock floor and handed it back to Semo. She turned and got her first good look at the cave. It was both vast and cramped at the same time. The rock all around jutted in at them and there was standing water in small puddles at random low points. Confirming what she already feared; a high tide would flood the cave and drown them if they didn't hurry.

They climbed a half wall and continued deeper into the underground. At one point, the cave opened up into a wide and tall room. Hanging rocks like spear points loomed twenty feet above their head. They continued, and the cave turned them back, but exactly what direction they were heading was tough to determine. The cave ended at a wall with a small horizontal crevasse ten feet above. The sound of the ocean crashing outside was audible again.

"Up there, you think?" Wade asked.

"Maybe, though I'm not sure a person can fit up there. Can you hear that? It sounds like the ocean on the other side," she said.

"Alright, Semo, hop on," Wade said, and he knelt down patting his own shoulder. Semo looked at Ellaria and then followed Wade's direction, stepping up on to Wade's shoulders. Wade lifted him up along the rock wall. He was just tall enough with his outstretched arms to grab above. He pulled himself up and just barely fit. He crawled in and disappeared. Moments later, his head appeared out of the crack.

"There's a way out. Just like you said. Here," he said, lowering a rope from his pack. Wade again let Ellaria go next. She grabbed the coarse rope and climbed up, but fell back to the ground. Wade breaking her fall.

"Bloody thorns!" she cursed. Spelunking at her age was exhausting. She could feel the eyes of both the young men staring holes through her. She cracked her knuckles and rubbed her hands. Then reached inside her pocket and took out a hair tie, pulled her hair back, and shook her hands. She grabbed the rope again and pulled and walked the wall jointly until she got close to Semo. Near the top, he reached out and snatched her cloak, then pulled her fast to him. Her feet slipped, but Semo's arms were there to clutch to. She pulled and crawled over his back into the dark crevasse.

There wasn't much room for two people, let alone three people in the low flat space. She crawled in deeper into the dark, reaching out in front of her as she went. She noticed the space between floor and ceiling rose and fell but was never taller than three feet. The rock below her stomach was not smooth, it dipped and mounded as she moved over it. Her cloak caught on the rough surface as she slinked along, and she could feel her heart pounding and being stiffled by the rock pressing against her. The jumbled sound of the ocean waves became louder and the salty air stronger as she went, but try as she might, she couldn't shift her head enough to see ahead. Sweat beaded on her forehead as she continued crawling blindly. Eventually, her hand reached a point where she couldn't feel stone any more, just the breeze of the night air cool on her damp fingers. She placed her hands in panic over the outside face, fearing it dropped to the sea. Once her arm was mostly out she could feel cold rock below and she pulled herself out completely.

The Citadel pier was now only feet away, stark and imposing. Just like Kovan had described, there was a pile of boulders mounding up to the pier wall, but the way across looked impossible. Outside the crevasse, she stood on a small ledge before a drop off into the water below. The gap from the ledge to the boulders on the Citadel side was probably only ten feet; however in the night, with the sea assaulting the cliff side below, it looked three times as far. Besides, she couldn't jump ten feet anyway. She got closer to examine the smooth side wall they needed to scale. There was a shelf that ran the full length of the wall, to the other side, where they could put their feet and various horizontal cracks where they could put their hands, but one slip and they would fall. Kovan made it sound like a walkway. She cursed him under her breath. The guys joined her and stared at the same daunting task.

"This just gets better and better," Wade huffed.

"Next time stay home Wade," she said, and she attached herself to the wall. Wade's obstinance propelled Ellaria beyond her terrible fear of height. She slid her boot into the foothold first and clutched the cracks she could in a death grip with her tired hands. She started out slowly to get the feel of sliding her feet along and picked up speed as she went. She made it across faster than she thought she could. She wanted to jump up and scream in excitement when she had made it. She was breathing fast, and her blood was pumping. Instead, she lifted her hand up to Wade, flashing him an obscene gesture. He smiled and followed her over. Semo followed, and all three stepped from boulder to boulder up the side of the fortress battlement.

Semo was out in front and at one point he stopped them because he heard voices. It took a moment to locate the sound on the ramparts beyond, before they continued. When they were on the stone wall, the drop to the other side was substantial, but there was a small box crate below that they could more easily reach. From the fortress sea wall, she had a view of the entire pier level. The interior bay laid out in three sections according to the water gates and it was full of navy ships. Most of the soldiers awake and on patrol were on the docks or manning the fortress wall near the gates, where large lanterns perched high and shining out to the sea with movable mirrors. The middle level training grounds were more active than she expected at this time of night. It was best to avoid the whole level.

Semo tied the rope off and climbed down. He stepped lightly to the roof of the crate and then climbed down the metal side wall. Ellaria's turn. She tried to do just as she had seen Semo, but she was not a tenth as graceful. Her feet slipped on the fortress wall and her body slammed back into it. "Drop, I'll catch you," Semo whispered up to her. She looked down. Contemplated her options, took a deep breath, and dropped. He caught her with a small grunt that she irrationally took offense to. He put her on her feet again. *Was it always this hard?* When they were all down, they huddled behind the crate, all three of them breathing hard.

"Now what?" Wade asked softly.

"See all the warehouses and the factories spewing smoke into the air. I only came here once before, but those factories were not here then. On the wall, I saw they had glass skylights. I want to get a look in at those," she said, and she could see Semo shaking his head. "Semo, I know you want to go sneaking about the place to find your brother. You'll never make it. If they're here, they would be in the black spire somewhere. That spire is too hard to reach from here. You have to cross the academy and ten thousand soldiers, even if you could get there. The building is a maze and there's no telling where he's located. It took us almost two hours to get here. Two hours back. That means we got just over an hour to search the pier level and get back to this crate. Otherwise, we miss our ride and are stranded on the road with the sun rising," she said, trying to reason with him, but his gaze was distant.

"Please, Semo. We can get them back, but not tonight. Trust me. I have sent for help. When my friends come, we can get your brother out. Please, I can't make it out without your help," she pleaded. He let out a sigh and by the look in his eyes she could see the last part had convinced him.

"Alright. I'm going to search this pier for any signs of them. I will meet you both back here," Semo told them, and then he slipped away.

"I guess that leaves you and me, darling," Wade said with a wink. Ellaria rolled her eyes and walked away, pulling Wade by the shirt over to the nearest warehouse. They walked around the outside as quietly as they could manage. There were roughly twenty buildings scattered throughout the pier. Only a few had guards stationed at the doors. Those were definitely the ones they needed to look in, and if they stayed clear of the docks, they might avoid detection. Scrutinizing the buildings, they found a lot of them had ladders affixed to the outside up to the flat roofs.

They creeped around the first guarded warehouse and found a ladder on the side. Following a quick silent argument with their eyes, they both scaled the ladder to the roof and lightly stepped over the parapet and onto the gravel rooftop. Their boots crunched lightly with every step. The building was a large rectangle, with gable ends emerging at the side as flat walls above the roofline. They snuck over to the long skylight in the middle of the roof with black square grids in the windowpanes. Some sections of glass were movable, and Wade pulled up one. It emitted a low squeak as he angled it up. Ellaria tensed at the noise, but it was over quickly. They stuck their heads inside and looked below to see rows and rows of tables with scattered parts. One table had high stacks of wires. Another just an endless number of gears. There were bronze colored face masks laid out on a lot of the tables and large shield-like plates on others. An odd arrangement of materials, but nothing terribly strange.

The next building, they checked was essentially the same, except for the piles of small red orbs in baskets and stacks of tubes in various lengths. She wanted to get her eyes on the foundry to see what they were making. Another building had an extensive collection of weapons she had never seen. The handheld guns looked similar to pulsators, but it housed all the components in the gun's metal shell. They also looked to have large exhaust ports. The larger guns looked like war machines for ships. They had a similar style to harpoon cables. Another weapon looked like a large spear.

More lights in the Spire winked out and Ellaria and Wade both found themselves staring at the dark tower.

"What's in there?" Wade asked.

"It's full of offices, a prison, the alchemist reliquaries and laboratories for the Citadel's scientists."

"The Citadel employs alchemists?" Wade asked.

"Some. Let's keep moving," Ellaria said and slipped back to the ladder.

They finally made it atop a factory to look inside. The steam and heat rising off the roof was unbearably hot even in the night air. Between the haze of smoke, she could see a line of odd metal parts being molded, cast and duplicated. The factory floor illuminated in pulses as the fires billowed and the smoke came in wave after wave of heat. Her eyes blinked and started to water due to the chemicals in the air. They were busy manufacturing something, but what she couldn't say. *Maybe Semo was having better luck.* As she pulled her head out, a set of sunken eyes in a face below momentarily startled her. She blinked, and they were gone. Then Wade grabbed her wrist and tapped his finger on the face of her watch. Their time was up. They needed to get back to their exit point.

They climbed down and snuck back through the way they came. They could only check a third of the warehouses. Trying to maintain their stealth had crippled their time. They made it back to the crate, but no Semo. They heard footsteps behind them and a sound of someone unconcerned with making noise. Her heart started pumping fast, and she reached for her vial of shadow dust. Then a tall figure dropped from above them. A muffled tumble of two people hit the ground. They looked and found Semo had knocked a soldier unconscious. He waved frantically for them to climb atop the crate and leave.

This time Wade helped her scale the wall while Semo kept a lookout. They passed the cliff face walkway and back into the twisting hollow. The cave seemed easier to navigate the second time through. At the mouth of the cavity, the rock floor had a lot more water than before. The tide was rising and in the final room the seawater came up to Ellaria's waist. They trudged out and rushed up the path back to the coastline plateau. In the distance, they could see a coach rolling away. They had missed their ride. Wade ran to the road, waving his arms. The coach halted and Pullson got down from his driver's seat to see them. They bolted inside and Pullson got them up to a gallop again.

Ellaria took off one of her boots, apologized, and rubbed her foot. Her body sagged with her old aching bones and her arms felt heavy. She looked at the other two and they seemed tired, but not as bad as her. Then she noticed Semo was brooding and upset.

"Semo, what's going on? Did you find something?" she asked, and he handed her a leatherbound book without saying a word. She opened it and read. It was a logbook from a ship named the Illasuava. She looked at the log entries. Its port of origin was the Illumeen.

"The Illasuava, that's Danehin's ship, isn't it?"

"Yes," he said.

"Was it in the bay?"

"Yes."

"You searched the docks?" she asked, astounded. He nodded yes. "Did you find anything else?" she asked. His head was down and when he lifted it, he had a faraway look in his eyes.

"Bones. Piles of human bones."

# CHAPTER SEVENTEEN

## PATH TO ADALON (TALI)

THE RIVER FLOWED PAST, FREE AND UNCONSTRAINED AND OFFERED reflections of light and life, without memories or measure of time. The churning water in the upstream ripples folded around the bridge supports and rolled on into the distance, undaunted by the stones she threw into its current. Tali gazed out at the sunrise glistening off the surface of the river, her eyes melting into the serenity, amazed that she had made it to the banks of the Uhanni River. The others were still asleep in the grove behind her, all of them exhausted from the night before. They arrived at Maiden's Crossing two hours before dawn and decided to wait until midmorning before getting a room at the inn and making their presence known. She was equally exhausted, but something had awakened her. Her blanket wasn't dry and getting comfortable on the cold ground was impossible. Eventually she gave up and walked to the riverside, where she sat alone for a time before a rustling behind her signaled that someone was coming to join her.

She turned, and to her surprise it was Elias. He sat next to her on the bank, his brown boot heels slightly digging into the damp soil as he settled down. They were nearly shoulder to shoulder, and he picked up two small stones and spoke to her in a calm voice.

"Do you mind if I sit with you?" he asked, handing her a rock.

"I don't mind," she told him. She took the rock from between his thumb and forefinger.

"Couldn't sleep?" he asked.

"No, but that's fine, I like to watch the sunrise," she said.

"Me too," he said, "I never miss it."

"Have you ever seen it from the sky?" she asked.

"No. I've seen it from a lot of places in this world, but not up there," he told her.

"We saw it over the mountains. In the drifter, glowing over a blanket of clouds. It was breathtaking."

"I imagine it must have been," he said, and he threw his rock to the middle of the river.

"Not bad, I've almost gotten one all the way to the other bank," she said, and she threw her rock to the middle where the sun shone brightest. There was a long silence as they both sat gazing at the horizon.

Elias loaded up another stone in his hand.

"Elias, how did you control the lighting?" she asked.

"Ha, I see why you and Kovan get along so well," he responded, shaking his head.

"Does that mean you're not going to tell me?"

"Well, ask me again when the others are awake. So, I only have to answer the same question one time for the two of you. Sound good?"

"I think so. Can you tell me what's going on then? I - I feel like this country is an unwatched pot, turning up the worst monsters of the world as it sits boiling out. Men in Ravenvyre attacked us, then bonelarks on the winddrifter, and wolveracks last night," she confided.

"I don't know. I can tell you, that of the three: men are the scariest monster of them all. They all have their weaknesses, but men are the cruelest and most easily influenced. We're the only creature manipulated by time itself and so easily turned into the worst parts of our nature by perception. We become too busy, too preoccupied, too stressed, and too angry to breathe properly. In the process, we lose the ability to feel the energy of the living world around us, and the energy of the natural world is essential to our humanity. For we are of the depths of light and bound to the tempest of life. Like this spot you found this morning. You sat down here because you felt the energy, right?"

"Um, I guess so," she said, unsure how to answer.

"You wouldn't have moved over here otherwise. Even if you were feeling depressed, worried, or scared. You came to this spot, on the bank of the river, because something in your mind knew it would be a soothing place to rest," he explained, and she thought she understood his point, but he was exaggerating a simple decision.

"I guess I did feel better once I came over here. You're saying there's an energy here?"

"There's energy everywhere," he said, and he flashed the rock he held in his hand out for both of them to look at. "What I'm trying to figure out is how much you can feel of it. How about a simple test?" he asked.

"I… I'm not sure what you're asking. Do you want me to do something to the rock? Or talk to it?" she asked, feeling uncomfortable.

"No," he said with a laugh. He was about to explain when Learon interrupted them.

"Morning," Learon said to the two of them.

"Perfect timing, Learon," Elias said, and he motioned for him to sit, "I was just about to do a test with Tali. Why don't you sit and take the test with her?"

"What, what test?" Learon asked and sat on the other side of Tali, curious and looking at Elias with confusion. Shifting his eyes quickly to Tali, Learon searched her face for a moment looking for an explanation. She wasn't used to people staring at her in the eyes and it should have been uneasy, but it wasn't. She felt an unexplainable comfort with Learon like they were old friends.

"Don't look at me, all I asked was why the monsters attacked us," she grumbled.

"It's simple," Elias continued, "I'm going to throw this rock into the river and after it hits the water. I want you two to tell me what you felt. But I should warn you. When it hits the water, we might get wet," he said and held out the small stone again to show them how impossible it would be for the tiny rock to create a splash large enough to reach them.

"Concentrate on the rock and the surface of the water. Ready?" Elias said, his voice low and serious.

Tali wrapped her cloak tight around herself and nodded the go ahead. Her pulse quickened in anticipation as she stared at the volume of flowing water and thought about the moment of collision. Elias turned toward the river and threw the stone out into the wake.

Tali and Learon's heads followed the arc of the stone through the air. She concentrated on the stone, trying to sense what Elias was going to do, but also worried about what was going to happen.

The stone hurdled down to impact and stopped. Frozen in air, inches from the surface, she felt a vibration from the tension as it waited to hit. The vibration dissipated, and the rock slipped into the stream undisturbed, like it was a drop of rain.

Tali looked at Learon whose eyes were wide and they both seemed to exhale together. They were equally stunned by the oddity they just witnessed. She shivered at the thought of it and turned to Elias, who put his fingers to his chin and mouth. He seemed to think for a moment, then rubbed his fingers as though a thought he pondered had solidified. Elias got up and walked back to Kovan, who was watching them from behind. She noticed Elias shake his head up and down slightly as he passed, and Kovan's eyes did a double take like Elias had said something strange to him.

"Wait, aren't you going to ask us if we felt something?" she called out over to him.

"Maybe later," Elias said, and he sat on a large rock near the dying campfire. Kovan sat on a nearby rock handing his friend a cup of something and they raised their cups and drank.

Learon and Tali got up off the dirt and quickly joined them. They almost ran over, not wanting to miss out on the moment. She took a seat at Kovan's side.

"What message?" Elias was asking, and his posture and face intensified.

"From Ellaria. She said she needs help. She's in Adalon and someone's following her. Where were you headed then?" Kovan asked.

"We got mixed up with some bonemen and I was helping the kid get to the Arcana."

"Bonemen, are you sure?"

"Yeah."

"Bonemen and beasts attacking, does that mean a new Sagean has come?" Kovan asked.

"It must, but so far they've chosen to stay in the shadow and let a Prime Commander take the initial lead," Elias said.

Both Tali and Learon moved their attention back and forth between the veterans. The implications of their conversation and the underlying tone was terrifying, and yet they spoke in such a matter-of-fact way.

"If everything is falling apart, we need to get to Ellaria, like yesterday. You know how she is," Kovan said.

"Impulsive?" Tali asked, chiming in.

"Fearless!" Kovan and Elias said in unison.

"I'm going to take my horse and go see about getting us a room to get cleaned up before we head out again. You three pack up and meet me down there," Kovan said, standing and striding over to his horse.

"Tali, do you still have the coin I gave you?" Elias asked. She stared at him, her body going rigid.

"Yes. I thought maybe you hadn't recognized me, our meeting was so fleeting," she said. She reached inside her pocket to fish the coin out.

"Wait, you two met before?" Learon asked, dumbfounded.

"Only in passing, I like to wander the markets in Ravenvyre," Elias said in answer to Learon. Then waved her off. "I don't want it back. The reason I asked is that it may be the reason you couldn't sleep this morning if you were holding it," he suggested.

"I wasn't, but why would that be?" she asked.

"The sigil inlay is amethyst, but I made the coin of obsidian. Obsidian is a protection stone, and it gives you clarity of mind. However, it can also wreak havoc on your dreams," Elias explained.

"I'll remember that. Thank you for the coin. It's amazing. Is the sigil what makes it act like a compass?"

"That's right," he confirmed.

"Elias used my quartz crystal to heal himself too," Learon added, and she looked at him curiously.

"Really! What about blood stone or heart stone, what do they do?" she asked excitedly.

"That's what I asked. Well, not about the blood stone, but about the love stone or heart stone," he stammered. She got the impression he was nervous around her.

"They all contain energies. They're broken into categories: power stones, protection stones, and healing stones," Elias told them. Then he stood and grabbed his satchel, "We should meet up with Kovan before he has to come back and get us," he suggested, and they all got their things and walked out to the inn.

Kovan met them at the stables.

"The innkeeper gave us two rooms to use since we're not staying. Providing we hurry. We'll get cleaned up and eat in shifts and get back on the road. Youngsters first. The rooms are just off the stairs opposite the hall from one another. They should have baths ready," Kovan said and waved them to hurry.

The inn had a center tower with a high mounted clock face on it where you entered. Learon opened the main wood doors and let Tali go ahead of him. Inside was one long room with a series of doors on the opposite wall that opened up to a stone porch on the riverfront. The staircase to the second floor wrapped over their heads above the entry. Two small groups of people were in the main sitting areas. Learon and Tali took the stairs and avoided any interactions. The stairs creaked as they wound around the tower to the second floor. In the hall they found their separate rooms. The room was furnished with few embellishments. The vaulted ceiling was wood, and the slope started off at the sidewalls lower than Tali's head. There was a door on the far side and simple drapes covering a single window next to it. Tali crossed the room and peeked out. She pulled the drapes aside to reveal a view of the river undulating through the landscape from the north. There was a small deck outside, and she wished she could go out there and drink tea and watch the river flow. The caretaker had pushed the two beds against the wall to fit the bathtub inside. The tub looked inviting with a slight steam rising from the surface and an assortment of bathing accompaniments lay on the floor next to it. She took off her clothes and slipped into the hot bath. The water singed her slightly and got to work instantly on relieving her aches from the horse ride early that morning. The water was soothing, and the silence threatened to lull her to sleep. She felt her eyes fading.

SOON AFTER FALLING ASLEEP IN THE TUB, A BLARE OF LOUD CHIMES FROM the clock signaling the blue rang out, and it quickly brought her back awake. She hurriedly got out, got dressed and let the quartermaster know the water needed changing. Then bounded down the stairs and into Kovan, coming to see what the holdup was. She cringed and shrank away from his gaze, hoping her natural charm kept his anger at bay. She stepped to the main floor and found Learon at a small table near the back wall and fireplace. He had a plate of food in front of him that he seemed to be enjoying. Her stomach growled at the sight. She figured by the amount of food left on his plate she couldn't be running that late.

"I'm not running way behind, am I?" she asked. Taking the chair opposite from him. He looked up, smiled, and covered his mouth as he finished his bite of food.

"No, only ten minutes after me. Kovan already paid for the food. Just go up to the kitchen and let the tender know. They have a few things to choose from," he told her.

"Was he mad?" she asked, squinting her eyes and nose, bracing herself for the truth.

"No, Kovan and Elias were deep in conversation when I got down here."

She let go the breath she was holding and turned her eyes to Learon's plate of food again. "What's that you're eating?" she asked. It looked like a slice of white meat with a charred crust. Next to some grilled orange vegetables she didn't recognize.

"This is fire grilled boar steak and bright karodash," he said, pointing to the meat and vegetable with his fork. "I already ate the redvine fruit."

She went to the kitchen and came back with a plate. She had chosen the white fish and it was light and buttery, with an herb topping that mellowed the flavor nicely. The orange vegetable Learon had called karodash tasted like a sweet squash. The redvine fruit was perfectly ripened and bursting with juice. She ate ravenously and finished her plate in no time. When she finally emerged from the trance her meal had put her in, she looked up to see Learon laughing at her.

"What?" she said, wiping her face over a few times, "You know it's not polite to watch someone eat?" she said, but she couldn't help but smile back even if his smile was infuriating. Learon did actually clean up rather good. His light brown hair, when not matted down by rain and sweat, was slightly reddish. He had clear blue eyes and a hard jaw line, but though she knew they were the same age, Learon had a youthful almost pristine quality to him. She supposed they all had been slumming around in weeks' worth of worn clothes, with dirt, smoke, and more on themselves. She actually only had two outfits. The one she left Ravenvyre with and one she picked up in Atava when they landed. Today was the new outfit: tight green pants and small fitting thin leather vest over a long-sleeved shirt that flared past her waist. As they waited for Kovan and Elias, she fidgeted with her new double strapped leather belt pack she got at the Fork outpost before it burnt to the ground. With three compartments, it worked well but cut her storage by a third from the cloak. She had reluctantly decided to store the Chain's cloak away in her roll pack. She knew she needed a new cloak, hat or hood for the ride they were about to embark on, but her amber was down to almost nothing.

"You got accepted into the Arcana," she asked Learon, who sat stoically. "I've wanted to go there since forever. It is supposed to have the best archives out of all the universities."

"I passed their entrance exams about three weeks ago. I'm definitely hoping their archives are as good as I've heard."

"What are you planning on studying?" she inquired.

"Honestly, I don't know. Something with machines? Maybe alchemy. Though, I'm not sure what it even is," he admitted.

"Oh my god it's amazing," she blurted and could feel her face lighting up, "It's spells and sigils and the history of elements and magic," she rambled.

"Magic, like what Elias does?" he asked.

"No, not like that. But there are some amazing things you can do. Since it was only rediscovered during the war there are a lot more shodders out there then true crafters, but I've seen some potions work before. An alchemist in Ravenvyre let me craft some stuff in his shop."

"Like what?"

"Shadow dust and firespark mostly. I've never been allowed to see their sigil spells though. They guard those from outsiders. Don't you have any alchemists where you're from?" she asked him.

"No, West Meadow is small. Kind of hidden away."

"Where about is that?"

"It's west of Atava. Right at the foot of the mountains," he said.

"Oh, I think we flew over it, maybe."

"Could be, we see winddrifters sometimes. So, you flew on one, what was that like?" he asked, his eyes lighting up.

"Scary, beautiful, and cold. Without a proper blanket you'd freeze solid up there," she said and paused because she felt like she was bragging, "Sorry if it sounds like I'm bragging, I'm not. I've just never been anywhere is all."

"I wasn't thinking that," he said, and she smiled at his ease.

"This morning, at the river, did you feel anything?" she asked.

"I don't know. It looked so wrong suspended in midair above the surface that I think it made me feel weird," he offered, but she thought maybe he was holding back. His eyes had darted to the left when he talked. "How about you?" he asked.

"Same," she said. They looked up from their conversation to the old men coming toward them. They left the inn and got to their horses to ride out. Remi sat bathing in the stable next to Bronn. Somehow, she knew he would wait for her. She picked him up, and he squeaked at her as she positioned him to ride with her.

"Which way Q? The east road gets us to the Imperial Road and Midway, or north to Anchor's Point?" Kovan asked.

"Anchor's Point is faster, but we will have to buy passage on the river."

"Anchor's Point it is. I have the coin," Kovan said.

They trotted out, crossing the nearby stone bridge that arched over the river with green vines growing on the side walls. After they all had crossed, Elias's horse kicked up to an uncatchable pace, and they were off. Riding rapidly through the countryside on a road that almost followed in unison with the river.

They reached the port city of Anchor's Point at sunset. The Uhanni river had steadily grown so vast that the opposite shore was hard to see. Their side of the shoreline was mostly small tower shacks and large warehouses. There were blue flamed basins scattered all around, which was reassuring, but for a major port, the apparent poverty surprised Tali. As they approached the point where the Uhanni river converged with the Frayne river, they could hear a small clattering and shouts and she noticed a few suspicious groups of people lingering on the streets. One group of four or five men stared at them the whole way. The men had nasty expressions and wore torn, baggy clothes. Their pants were rolled up to their knees and the bottom of their legs were caked in mud. One man seemed especially irate by their presence.

"You two listen to up," Kovan said to her and Learon. "This place may look unassuming and simple, but Anchor's Point is full of the worst sort. While it is a major exchange and shipping center for the Uhanni river, it attracts all kinds of trouble from all over. The river is the main transport of goods throughout Tavillore, and this is a place of questionable character."

"Say nothing to nobody, got it," Learon said.

"No, don't even look at anyone. It's called the 'cutthroat city' for a reason," Kovan said.

"And we chose to come this way?" Tali asked.

"The Free Trade Guild maintains order inside the primary port of Fort Verdict," Elias said in an attempt to calm them.

"He's right, the really dangerous criminals are civilized and shrewd, and most of the bounty hunters moved on to Amera years ago. Plus, to answer your question, the river cuts a day and a half out of the trip. A day and a half of riding on horseback," Kovan said.

"Totally worth it then," Tali said.

They continued deeper into the city and at first she thought the ruckus she heard might be a festival. Since the New Year and the the Day of Light were so near, but sadly, she was mistaken.

A mass of people had gathered outside the fort, in a rally for the return of the Sagean. It was a protest but the temperament of the crowd suggested it was edging toward a riot. A bonfire burned brightly and beyond stood a man shouting from a makeshift stage of crates and wood planks.

Skirting the crowd, they arrived at the gates of Fort Verdict and dismounted from their horses. Tali's legs ached when her feet hit the dirt. Remi, apparently afraid of the fire, remained tucked inside Tali's saddle bag. At this distance, they could hear the man's ranting more clearly. He was barking and raving about injustice, and the lost rights of the people. His rhetoric was agitating and venomous.

"We have lost our culture! Our civilized purity! The sacred unification of men was abandoned, and for what? For a life of struggle and torment? They promised freedom, but we got poverty. The Light guided us before, and it shall guide us all again. The Sagean shall return, and he will put the demon Qudin to death. The people will once again be in harmony as one nation, working toward the shared good of all– shepherded by the messenger of Light," the speaker paused as someone approached his feet. It was one of the men they had passed coming in. The speaker looked up and over toward where they waited to enter the gate.

"Look there!" he called out to the crowd and pointed at Tali, "More foreigners coming for your jobs. There at the gate, there's a Rodairean girl. We know they are born with the unfair edge to succeed. She will take your job and leave you begging for scraps," the speaker announced.

A few people closed in on them. Learon puffed up and his hands went to fists. Elias actually paid it no attention at all. Like it was a breeze of something foul in the air and nothing more. Kovan's eyes darted in constant motion, scanning every movement. The throng of people began shouting at them. Two men advanced on them as Elias bartered their passage through the gate and lead the horses through.

A stranger, with a full beard, pushed Learon into the wall and the second went right for Tali. His hand reached out to grab her when Kovan kicked him in the knee, with a loud crack. Then he whipped his gun up in a blink as the bearded man made the slightest turn. The crowd pulsed with rage and anger. With his pulsator aimed a mere foot away from the bearded man's face, Kovan spoke in a deadly serious rasp.

"I promise you, if you touch this young woman, I will kill you and anyone who helps you. Before you're able to lay a finger on her I will have blasted the light from your eyes. I have bathed in more blood than that river, and your death wouldn't make a ripple. Look in my eyes, I don't lie, and I never miss. Now, grab your friend and move back."

The spite and anger previously in the man's eyes evaporated to terror the longer Kovan stared at him. He grabbed his friend from the ground, and they limped away. The gatemen ushered them inside. Kovan backed his way in, apologized to the gatemen, and holstered his weapon only when the doors had shut.

"What's going on here?" Kovan asked the gatekeeper.

"The news of the new Prime Commander has the Lionized excited."

"Who are the Lionized?"

"They're zealots like the Legion of Light, but more radical."

"And big mouth up on the stage?"

"The speaker? Some man named Aramus. He arrived about a week ago, he's not a local. He showed up around the same time they appointed the Prime Commander."

Kovan thanked the man, and they proceeded across the square. Inside the walls of the fort, the shouts and calls continued but the volume was greatly muted. It sounded like it was bordering on losing control, and Tali hoped it faded as the crowd tired. The river actually had its own roar at the apex point, and she caught glimpses of it through pockets in between buildings. The river collided and rolled off to the south and east. Barges and sailboats of all kinds were in the water. Most moving in and out of view through the gaps.

There was a large open square with a fountain in the middle. Surrounding that were large wood buildings, clustered together and lining the river. They walked around to the riverside and the long boardwalk that wrapped around the entire headland. It was brightly lit every ten feet by lanterns along the outside steps that led down to the piers. The harbor was full of vessels, either anchored or moving in the water. It was the apex point where the Uhanni river joined the Frayne River. Centuries prior, a grand canal had connected the two.

Learon and Elias took the horses and went to secure their passage to Adalon on one of the larger barges that could carry them all. Kovan and Tali decided to continue down the walk, Tali holding Remi in her arms. The entire area was like a completely different world than the one just outside the gates. Out there, the crowd was fueled with anger and hatred over some misconception. Here the boardwalk was vibrant. There was music, open air restaurants, and watering holes. A vast assortment of merchant tents were erected all along the boardwalk, and people were in good spirits and moving around from tent to tent. The open tables were full with people drinking and eating and watching ships pass on the river. Kovan was eyeing one of the outdoor eateries with a large grilling pit.

"I'm going to find us a table. Don't linger too long and don't get swindled," Kovan said, recognizing how enticed she was by all the merchants. He shuffled away to find a table and Tali went to inspect the bartering tents. She looked at everything everyone offered, relishing the variety of goods. She found lots of things she couldn't afford but stopped to negotiate with one merchant for some clothes.

The lady's tent was propped up on poles off a small cart. Her young daughter helping with sales was also tending a young boy. Tali purchased a new outfit, the merchant assured her was more in the Adalon style, and a new dark green overcoat cloak. The cloak was stylized to fall in waves, it only had four pockets, but it was fine and soft, and it draped nicely over her belt pack. She was excited to find that her amber coins fetched far more from this riverside tent than they had in Atava. She also purchased a new bag. It was lightly tanned like her belt and similar to Elias's satchel. She thanked the proprietor and jogged over to meet the others at their table. She made her way back along the boardwalk and found everyone waiting with food already. The brief euphoria of new things suddenly faded as the reality set in that she didn't know what she was going to do for amber when they finally arrived in Adalon. She moved around the table to sit down and Remi jumped out of her hands and snuck away. She started to chase after him, but Elias stopped her.

"Don't worry, he won't go far, eat," he said, and sure enough Remi slipped away and was back again before they had left. They ate and were on their way to the ship in short order.

Down the boardwalk they heard a commotion in the fort square but didn't pay it much attention. They walked by crates along the pier and began boarding the large flat barge docked at the very end. It had giant wood wheels at the back and steam stacks in the middle. A simple rope lined the sides of the ship and Tali gripped on to them as she stepped aboard. Elias took them to the back, and they stood at the bow of the ship as it slowly headed out into the river. Noises from the ship pulling out and the sounds of the night blurred with shouting in the distance.

Suddenly, an enormous explosion decimated part of the boardwalk. A ball of fire bloomed and blasted apart a building and part of the walk. Wood and debris flew far and out into the river. By instinct, Tali dropped to the deck. They were far enough out that only a slight wind of air passed over them, but very little heat. They heard screams carrying over the water to them. Horrorstruck, she looked to Kovan and Elias for what to do.

"What's happened?" she gasped.

"The extremist's rioting breached the fort," Kovan said.

"They've attacked their own people?" Learon asked, bewildered.

"What can we do?" Tali asked. Kovan looked at Elias like he was waiting for orders. But Elias just shook his head slowly. Kovan turned back to her.

"Nothing," he said, but after traveling with him for a week she could tell he was mad.

The fire raged on and all they could do was stand on the back of the ship and drift away. They watched the flames and chaos, until it disappeared, into a glow on the night's horizon.

❧

THE NEXT DAY, LEARON AND TALI SAT WITH THEIR LEGS OFF THE SIDE OF the barge. The rolling water turned and rushed by below. Tali couldn't shake the scene from the night before out of her memory.

Eventually, Learon talked her into fishing off the side as they sat there, but her heart wasn't in it. Learon was a good fisherman, much better than Tali. The ship's captain was happy for the catch and said Kovan could use their fires for cooking later that evening.

To further pass the time, Kovan sat with Tali and Learon and gave them a lesson on handling their guns. He explained the workings of the pulsators to them. Between the current dispatcher, the electron tube, and the flux inductor, it was a finicky machine.

"Keep your fingers off the exhaust ports, adjust the charge with the amp controls only if needed and if the reaction chamber gets dented— don't fire the weapon," he explained.

While she looked at hers, Kovan took it from her. He set the controls for it and told her not to mess with them. She gave Learon, who was watching them, an exacerbated look, and he snickered. Kovan could sometimes be overprotective of her, and she was not familiar with that kind of interaction from anyone. Not that she disliked it, but it was odd to get used to.

As the day wore on, it was becoming more obvious that Kovan and Elias were fighting. Tali had seen them arguing on two separate occasions. Once in the morning, when she thought Elias was coming to talk to her, and another time after lunch. She knew Kovan was mad about last night. Maybe Elias was right? *What could they do?* Though, she didn't have a full understanding of what Elias was capable of, so maybe Kovan was right; either way. They had done nothing and doing nothing while people got hurt was eating at her. Kovan's brooding suggested he felt the same.

When the night came, it was cool and welcoming. The sun had bounced off the river all day making it a sneaky sort of hot. Her weariness had faded, and she found her excitement to reach Adalon was sustaining her. That, and watching Remi hunt around the barge all day. He was living his best life. The captain even offered Elias money for him, not just for the mice hunting, but because he felt the cat was good luck, an old sailor's superstition.

Learon and Tali again found themselves sitting on the side of the ship with her feet dangling off. They talked about their hometowns and their mothers. Learon was very self-reliant, strong, and kind of quiet. But what she probably liked best about him was his respect and love for his mother. It was a powerful thing that instilled in him a reverence for all women which was rare. While they talked, Remi came pouncing back to her from the dark and rubbed endlessly against her back. He finally sat in the small fold of her shirt that draped behind her on the deck. An amusingly tiny amount of fabric, even for the tiny cat.

"He sure is a funny cat," Learon said.

"I'm guessing neither of you have seen a cat like him before?" Elias asked from behind them. She hadn't thought much about it, but no, she hadn't. He had a unique way of winking at her with his ears.

"Um, I guess not. Why, what kind of cat is he?" she asked.

"He's a mystcat," Elias said.

"What's a mystcat, are they mystical?" she asked.

"Yes, kind of, they're special. They're very rare. They search out and attach themselves to certain kinds of people."

"What kind of people?" she asked wearily, pulling the cat into her lap as she spun around to talk.

"Elias, don't," Kovan interrupted, and she watched as they shared a look.

"I'm sorry, Van. She has to know," Elias said. Tali held Remi closer. She didn't want them to take the cat away. He was her friend. She saw how annoyed they were when they had to stop for Remi on the ride to Anchor's Point.

"Are you sure? You said it might be either of them?" Kovan asked.

"It could be both, but I am sure about Tali," Elias said.

Now she was confused, and she spoke up, "I'm sitting right here. Just tell me," she said staring at Elias. Her eyes challenged. Elias turned from his conversation with Kovan and met her glare with his own intensity.

"It's time to talk about the test the other morning," Elias said.

She saw Learon sit up straighter, with a worried expression on his face to match her own. Her resolute confidence a second ago wiped away. Elias turned his head from Tali, his eyes lingering a bit, and directed them at Learon. Somehow wordlessly expressing to them both to pay attention.

"Yesterday, when I threw the rock into the river. Did either of you figure out what I did to make it stop in the air?" he asked, studying their eyes.

Tali and Learon shared a look, and both shook their heads no. Tali's pulse raced, and she held her breath in anticipation of the answer.

"Nothing," Elias said flatly.

She recoiled and inhaled deeply at his declaration. "What?" she asked, confused.

"What do you mean you did nothing?" Learon added.

"I mean, I just threw the stone and watched how you two reacted. One of you, or both of you, stopped the stone before it could hit the water."

The implications of Elias's words hung in the air like a fog. Tali felt herself shaking nervously, as if a bucket of ice water washed over her. She refused to say anything. Afraid to sound defiant or obtuse. The silence was excruciating as Elias let his words sink in.

"Mystcats," He finally continued, "Attach themselves to luminaries, people like me."

As hard as she tried not to, she could feel herself shaking her head no, in disbelief. Learon looked stunned. Kovan was rubbing his forehead with his right hand. She tried to keep breathing.

"Tali, I'm positive you have the gift," Elias declared.

"Why, because of Remi? Couldn't he just be here for you?" she asked.

"No. I have a mystcat at home. She came to me years ago. Eventually, they don't have to follow you around everywhere, because the connection gets strong enough for them to be apart. It's not just the cat. It's the stone, it's not being able to sleep once the sun rises, and it's the coin. The sigil in the coin is not what makes it work like a compass. You did that. The sigil is simply the conductor, you supplied the energy."

"But how? I wasn't trying to. Even with the stone, I didn't try to keep it from hitting the river. I was afraid of what was going to happen when it did is all," she protested.

"In the beginning that's just how it works, effortlessly."

"Are you still suspicious I have it?" Learon asked.

"Honestly, I am. You could have easily been the one who stopped the stone this morning. I know Tali channeled energy because I was sitting right next to her and could feel the draw. You also made an incredible kill shot to the wolverack in the mountains. Which made me think somehow you attuned to its heartbeat. The same way I could target and kill fourteen of them with lightning. I'm not sure yet."

"So, what now?" Tali asked, oddly devoid of emotion.

"Believe me, I know how tough this is to listen to. I had a similar conversation with my master when I was sixteen. The important thing is that I found you Tali, because now I can guide you."

"What if I don't want a guide?"

"The truth?"

"Yes."

"You'll die," he said flatly.

"What?" Tali gulped.

"It's called the illumination surge. Essentially, you have to learn to channel the energy you take in. See, in the beginning you draw in the energy without meaning to, but you don't transfer it. Eventually, you'll draw too much. You will either burn up from the inside or your body will explode with light, killing you in the process."

"Delightful," she said looking at the ground. She was upset, but she honestly didn't know why. She wasn't afraid, just overwhelmed.

"Thorns, Elias," Learon cursed.

"Come on, Q," Kovan admonished.

Tali smiled at their support, shook off her anxiousness and looked up at Elias, "What's the first lesson?" she asked.

Elias walked over to her. He sat down cross-legged like she was and spoke softly.

"I know it's overwhelming," he said, almost like he had picked the word out of her mind, "Don't worry, you'll be fine. The first thing you need to know is that learning to control other energies begins with learning to control your own energy."

"How?" she asked wearily.

"I'll teach you," he said. Then Kovan came walking over and handed her a bowl of stew. She hadn't even noticed that he had been cooking on the open flame.

"Eat. You'll feel better with something warm in your stomach," he said, and she beamed at him as he returned to the barrel he was sitting on. She sipped the stew and found he was right. Relief flooded through her with each bite. After she finished, she didn't feel like watching the land move on shore anymore and decided all she wanted to do was curl up in her blanket. She lay down and looked at the black coin a moment before shoving it back in her belt. Remi barged his way inside her blanket and settled down atop her chest, purring. She rubbed under his chin absentmindedly until she fell asleep.

# CHAPTER EIGHTEEN

## REUNIONS (ELLARIA)

THE MANCOVI TRAIN LURCHED AND SWUNG ALONG THE COAST OF THE Mainsolis Sea, skirting the tree line as the metal machine spun along the elevated rails. The tall suspended cabin swayed on the turns, while the open underside swept past the uneven ground. The steel hangway frames rhythmically repeated in the window and Ellaria watched in trance. Calming Semo had not been an effortless task. He was willing and determined to kill himself, to storm the Black Spire. What Semo had described to her and Wade sounded horrific; a cargo hold full of bones. Somehow, it was his description of the crates of clothing that disturbed her more.

She hadn't even bothered to look at the logbook again. It simply rested in her arms as proof of a betrayal, proof of something sinister going on.

Ellaria was also steaming from the news she picked up at the station. Rotha Durrone, the Queen of Andal, had submitted Alden Vic for the position at the Citadel, vacated by the new Prime. Vic was a well known Sagelight radical and a former member of the Sagean's Consortium.

If the Peace King was meeting at the Citadel, it was possibly through an invitation from Queen Rotha. Of all the nations in the Coalition, Andal and Merinde were the only two with long held monarchies. Under the Sagean Empire it allowed them to keep their positions of rule, but it was strictly territorial, and they had no actual power. Under the Coalition they were brought in as monarch ambassadors, equally in control of their regions as the other appointed ambassadors of the other nations. The difference being they both had years of perceived authority in their homelands. Which allowed them to attain a slightly higher station among the Coalition simply because they had a foothold of control over their lands that the other ambassadors sought.

Rotha was a nasty woman, and they had mutually avoided each other for years. She was a few years older than Ellaria and was a princess when they first met as teenagers. Rotha spent her summers in Adalon, and they would run around the Crescent Pier together. Rotha was a devout believer in the light. Despite their differences, they were close for a few summers before Ellaria felt the pull of the Resistance and their differences in views became insurmountable. In the second year of the war, Rotha's parents were killed, and she was never the same. At the time, and apparently it was still true, Andal was staunchly in the Sagean's corner. Centuries of military funding financing your city, creates loyalty.

She flipped through the logbook absentmindedly, feeling the leather binding in her fingertips and listening to the pages flutter when she flipped them with her thumb. She scanned the ledger again and read the ports of call. Her eyes fluttered as she stared at the last written line. Someone had scribbled 'Aquom' in as the last port after Andal, and a minor note of a name was next to it, 'Meroha Uvari'. Ellaria didn't know what that meant. It was a name, possibly of the boat, but she didn't know.

She kicked Wade's foot, who was asleep with his head against the glass. He stirred but didn't wake. She kicked him again, and Semo's head whipped around to see the disturbance. Wade opened one eye, blinked, and looked at her suspiciously.

"Wake up Wade, I found something," she said. He finally sat up and rubbed his eyes.

"Look," she said, showing both Semo and Wade.

"Why is it after the stop in Andal?" Wade asked

"It's good to see you know how to ask the obvious question, Wade," she quipped. "I can think of two possibilities."

"They left the Citadel and sailed to Aquom, where they were captured?" Semo asked.

"Maybe. That still implicates the Citadel in their disappearance, since the ship is in their possession. But why let them leave, only to seize them in another city? No, the second possibility, and the more likely one, is that they planned to go to Aquom next. See the name scribbled below," she said, placing her finger just beneath the name as she held it up for them to look, "Does that name mean anything to either of you?" she asked, but they both shook their heads no.

"Another ship?" Wade wondered.

"Maybe? Probably worth looking into," she said and thought about the probability of traveling. "Thorns! I have to give that seminar in two days," she cursed.

Ellaria knew, any further investigations would have to wait. They spent the rest of the train ride in silence, in a collective disappointment over their failure. Realistically, they had come away with more than she expected. But it was hard not to feel like they had made the trip for nothing – two more mysteries were not what they were hoping for.

The train reached Adalon in the early evening. They filed out of the station and took a quick coach ride up to the core. During which she talked Wade into sending a coded message to Dalliana. They went to her office to code one out and she handed Wade the message on a scrap of paper. Semo left for the small room she had secured for him, and Wade took off for the magnotype post.

Ellaria strolled around the city and decided to hit the coffee bar before going home. She waited behind a young couple getting through the door. The Twines Knot was crowded from open to close, and this night was no different. She placed an order and found a table near the front where she could keep her eyes on the entrance, an old habit of Kovan's she picked up along the way. A server delivered her hot coffee and sweet bread when a man's voice spoke to her from nearby.

"Miss. Moonstone? Pleasant evening?" Edward Knox said, putting the copy of the Independence paper he was reading down. He was two tables away against the wall. She hadn't spoken with him since the day at court and was surprised she hadn't noticed him before she sat down.

"It is, thank you. Are you enjoying your drink?" she asked.

"Yes, their green tea is excellent," he said, but she was more interested in the cover of the newspaper flat on his table. She pointed at it.

"Are you finished with that?" she inquired.

"Sure, allow me," he stood and brought her the paper.

"Please join me if you would like?" she offered.

"Thank you I will, but only until I finish my tea."

Edward got his tea and returned. He sat with tall posture and watched others in the bar from behind his silver-framed spectacles. The glass in the silver frame reflected the surrounding lights. He had a gentle disposition and looked like a mathematician, meticulously dressed but with a preoccupied glaze to his eyes. Ellaria turned the paper over to look at the cover that had sparked her interest. Malik was pictured on a stage with a squad of bonemen behind him.

## 'THE PRIME VOWS,
### A return to Light and harmony!'

She read on and was made more and more upset with every sentence. The Prime had been holding speeches for the press every other day since his appointment. Spouting equality and harmony for the people and freedom of faith. Though the people have never had more freedom to believe in whatever faith they choose in a thousand years. His repeated reframing of the truth or blatant lies were sparking anger over perceived discrimination against long time Sagean believers. Still no word yet on trade negotiations with the New World. They saved the more disturbing news until the end, that the Prime was financing a new weekly publication to compete with the Independence, calling it the Veritas Journal. He was determined to control the truth. The Independence paper had begun during the Resistance and was the main source of news throughout the world. The existing paper before that was just a weekly Harold that was a propaganda pamphlet. After the magnotype came into use, The Independence began collecting all the news from around the world.

"What do you think, disturbing, isn't it?" Edward asked. She swatted the paper down on the table and Malik's cold eyes faced down with it. The greed of leaders determined to see their amber chests overflowing at the expense of their own beliefs astounded her. The people just went along with it. Some persuaded, some pulled and a lot too uninformed and too busy in their personal lives to raise alarm.

"He's reigniting the old divide," she said, referring to the Resistance movement that divided the world.

Edward nodded. "I can't say you were wrong to leave the Guild when you did. The court sessions have been maddening."

"Not sure I had much choice. Is Delvette still rolling over or is she biting back?"

"There's little we can do. Delvette and I have been trying to talk with the ambassadors, but most are behind the Prime, and all of them for their own reasons. Most want to secure power over their own nations, with the goal to leave the Coalition."

"Is that what's driving the Rodaireans? They want to separate from the others?" she asked.

"Rodaire and Merinde. Yes. They're tired of the Coalition. Both are very prideful people. Nahadon will support whoever will help them temper the escalating wars down there. Apparently, the fighting between the Viper Lords has become worse. They fear sooner or later the coastal cities will anger the Tregoreans. Skyvier knows that they straddle the line between Rodaire and Tavillore, so they try to remain neutral and simply oppose change."

"They also know that no one is going up north to claim their lands. Even the Sagean Empire stayed out of there. They have nothing to gain from the expansion into the New World either," she added.

Edward nodded and sipped his tea. Looking up from his cup, his eyebrows raised slightly, "Where's your hat?" he inquired.

"I left it at home for the day," she said.

"Oh, it's such a beautiful hat."

"Yeah, I don't feel quite like myself without it," she said, but inwardly she beamed from the compliment.

"Is it the source of your powers?" he asked in jest.

"It is actually," she said.

He leaned in closer, like they were sharing a secret, and he smelled clean. "I won't tell anyone," he said and leaned back. "Besides, you look good without it."

"Thank you."

"Are you ready for your seminar?"

"I think so."

"I think you're going to do great. Not just the seminar, but as a professor," he said.

"If I accept a position?"

"You should. I think you would enjoy being around people eager to learn. Instead of wasting your energy fighting 'the encumbrance'. It would be good for the Arcana to have proper alchemy studies."

"I didn't take you for a supporter of mystical arts?"

"Very much so. When I traveled to Kotalla, I saw firsthand how powerful it is."

"I forgot. You actually went behind the Kotalla wall. What was that like?"

"Depressing and magnificent. Contrary to popular belief, the people there are doing well. As well as anywhere else, but the brainwashing is deeply ingrained. We stayed in our assigned tents outside the mines. The crystal cavern was breathtaking," he said, checking his pocket watch, and he stood up from his chair. "I'll tell you more about it sometime. For now, I'm going to call it a night. It was a pleasure talking with you again, Miss. Moonstone."

"Thank you for the company, Edward," she said. He took his empty teacup and plate to the dishwasher and left. He was actually very pleasant. She had definitely misjudged him originally. He was far more capable of dealing with the ambassadors than Delvette was, which gave her hope that the Guild was in excellent hands. He was intellectual and agreeable without being arrogant, a rarity around university folk. Ellaria stayed a fraction longer to finish her bread and another cup of coffee before heading out as well.

The lights glowed orange in the night. Steam floated around the streets stagnant with a gentle breeze off the sea tonight. She took a long meandering route home as she always did. Careful to track others on the street. She carried her small knife with her now at all times, hidden under her wrist. The streets were busy, but there was no one following her.

She reached her building and for a second– she swore she saw someone moving in the window of her quarters. She went around to the side door and into the lobby, smiled at the quarter's master, still on duty, and walked around to the stairs and up. When she reached her door, she finally realized how exhausted she was. She opened it and stepped into the room. She closed the door, turned around, and instantly realized she was not alone.

THE LANTERNS INSIDE HAD ALMOST ALL COMPLETELY BURNT OUT, BUT SHE felt the presence of someone in the darkness without having to see them. Turning from the door as she locked it closed, Ellaria slipped the small knife from her wrist wrap.

Blade in hand, she spun on the intruders to throw it– almost flinging the knife at a doe eyed Rodairean girl. She stood staring at her with the whites of her eyes showing. Ellaria paused. Someone near her shuffled close and grabbed her arm.

"Ellaria," the man called out in their struggle, but she threw her elbow back into his nose, hearing a rewarding crunch and a yelp of pain.

"Ellaria," called another voice she couldn't believe was there. She gazed up and a familiar man she knew so long ago was lifting a freshly lit lantern back up on the hanging chain. Qudin stood beneath, his face illuminated by the candlelight growing stronger. He was standing in front of a young woman and a tall young man with long hair. From behind her, another man was groaning and holding his nose. She knew who it must be, and she didn't feel the least bit bad for socking his nose. She reached for a towel nearby and handed it to Kovan, then stomped on his foot for good measure.

"Ow! What was that for?" Kovan asked, he took the towel from her and pressed it to his nose.

"The elbow was for sneaking up on me, and the kick was just because. What are you two doing here?"

"You sent me a message you needed help. We're here to help," Kovan mumbled through the towel.

"You can't send a note. You're lucky I didn't stab you," she said.

"We're not sure who to trust in the city?" Qudin said.

"Just use the Whisper Chain," she said.

"We have reason to be wary of them too," Qudin said. Her eyebrows drew together in a look of confusion. She took a deep breath seeing Qudin brought a tremendous relief she didn't know she needed. She crossed the room, threw her arms around him and hugged him tight. It had been a very long time since she had seen him.

"He gets a hug and I get kicked. That sounds about right," Kovan complained.

"Where have you been Q? I'm so glad you both are here. Things are getting too big for me. I have so much to tell you," she said with her head on his shoulder and eyeing the youngsters in the room she pulled away, "Who are they? Did you finally graduate from shadow cats to humans that follow you around?"

"Ellaria, this is Tali Alari and Learon Everwyn," Qudin said, pointing out each as he introduced them. Ellaria looked at them and thought they made an odd pair, but both seemed to have a manner that fit in with Qudin's nature. A mix of resiliency, awareness, and a kindness in their eyes, though the weariness of their travels was obvious on their clothes and face.

"Hello youngsters, I hope you know you've stepped into the whirlwind?"

"We know," Tali said.

"They know, Ellaria. We ran into some obstacles getting here: zealots, beasts and bonemen," Kovan said, walking closer and standing near the round bay window. He looked out on the streets below just like the man she had always known, constantly restless and watching. Ellaria truly was happy to see him. It had been tough for a long time for them to be together. Their combined memories had weight that neither could bare for very long. Yet, seeing him provided an instant comfort she had been missing. She never could stop loving him no matter how much he infuriated her. A power only the people you love the most contain. She watched him a moment and turned back to Qudin.

"Were you chased by the Luminance Squad?" she asked him.

"Um, I don't think so, what is that?" he asked.

"The Prime, you heard about the Prime, right?" she asked. When they nodded, she went on, "He ordered a special squad to track you down, Q. He seems more determined than the Coalition ever was, and he has an army of these new bonemen to do it," she noticed he cringed slightly at his own name. Kovan noticed it too.

"Oh yeah, he goes by Elias again, though I'm still calling him Q to irritate him," Kovan said to her.

"Again?" the young man Learon asked.

"My name is Elias Qudin, but my first week with the Darkhawks everyone just called me Qudin or Q," Elias told the youngster.

"You trained with the Darkhawks? I've never read that before. Though that doesn't mean much since there's not much written about you and what is, I would say is wrong," the young woman said.

Ellaria grinned at her assessment

"I never officially attained their symbol. I left after one year to train with a man named Zaus and learn how to control my powers. When I returned to help the Resistance. There were only a handful of people who knew who I was. Still, everyone continued to call me Qudin," Elias explained.

"So, what's going on? Are you still being followed?" Kovan asked Ellaria.

"I'm sure I'm being watched, but the guy who was following me was killed," she explained.

"Your work?" Kovan followed up. His eyebrow raised, wondering if she had killed the man.

"No. It was a friend of mine, a young man at the Arcana that I met."

"A young man who was willing to kill for you, what's his name?" Kovan asked.

"Oh, stop, Kovan, His name's Wade. He's beautiful, but he's way too young for me. Anyway, this world we helped free is falling apart. The Coalition transferred their power to a Prime with the intention of claiming the lands in the New World. It seems greed and power are the two evils we never defeated, and with the Peace King missing, I fear war is on the horizon. The Prime meanwhile is positioning for a return of a new Sagean, but I can't figure out the delay."

"They're being told to delay," Elias spoke up.

"Interesting. I thought they might be waiting for the Day of Light to announce it. Why do you think they're waiting?" Ellaria said.

"To ensure the Sagean has less opposition. That's why the Prime's principal objective is to capture me. It also explains why the beasts are more active. You can bet there's probably a lot more going on that we haven't pieced together yet," Elias said.

"I can't believe they nominated Malik for Prime. This new Sagean must have forced Dunne's hand. There's no way Dunne would have picked Malik. He's uncontrollable. Malik turned that band of thugs he calls the Cloaked Knife into mercenaries. Who do they have heading the Luminance squad?" Kovan asked.

"Someone named Duraska, I think," she said.

"Say that name again?" the Rodairean girl asked.

"Duraska, why?"

"Kovan, that's the name Thann said on the pier, remember?"

"Yeah, I think you're right."

"Did I say how glad I am that you're both here? I needed someone to share this nightmare with, but I don't know where I'm going to hide all four of you," she admitted.

"Learon is enrolled at the Arcana, and we were hoping you could get Tali enrolled as well?" Kovan asked.

"What?" Tali blurted out.

"Shouldn't be a problem, though a dorm room could prove difficult, but I have to say, it may not matter. I'm not sure the Prime won't shut down the Arcana given the chance."

"Miss Moonstone, Kovan, thank you, but it's not necessary . . ." Tali paused and shook her head as if she didn't believe what she was saying, "A few days ago, I would have done anything to go to the Arcana. But I think my path lies elsewhere now, I feel like there's a storm coming and I can't run from it."

"Where did you find this one?" Ellaria asked, and Elias pointed to Kovan.

"She, sort of, helped me escape out of a prison in Ravenvyre. Then she came with me to Adalon. She's how we know something is going on with the Chain."

"What's wrong with the Whisper Chain?" Ellaria asked.

"I don't know, my trainer said he was worried it was corrupted, but he thought it was only in the west," Tali said.

"Trainer? You were working with the Chain? If it's true that the Whisper Chain is compromised, then that's scary. If the Prime gained control of the Chain, his grip would tighten rather quickly," Ellaria commented and moved her attention to the young man in the corner.

"Then what's his story? Wait, maybe we should all start from the beginning," She suggested before Kovan could answer.

They spent much of the night telling their stories and catching one another up. Elias stood stoically in the corner. Kovan, unable to sit still, got up and paced around. At some point the young woman, Tali, as curious as a cat it seemed to Ellaria, wandered around the room looking at all of Ellaria's things. Their tale was worrying, between news of people going missing, the beasts coordinating attacks and zealots rioting, it was enough to see things had progressed faster and farther then she realized, a storm indeed. Equally interesting was the boy's journal. That excavation was supposed to have yielded nothing. It suggested that Malik and Dunne may have been positioning for a takeover as far back as ten years ago. When it was her turn talk, Ellaria told them about the last few days and her recent trip to the Citadel to dig up dirt. Kovan was furious.

"You hard-headed woman. See what I mean, Q. Ellaria you could have been killed!" he stormed.

"You said it was a simple way in," Ellaria protested.

"No, I said it was the *only* way in. I think I said that they never watched it because it was too crazy to try," Kovan spouted.

"I don't remember that. It is crazy though," she agreed, looking at Elias she could see he was distant, "You're going to run off again, aren't you? You're still obsessed with your hunt for the stone?" she asked.

"I am, and I'm closer than ever. With these recent developments, a Prime Commander, a new Sagean. It's more important than ever that I find it."

"What stone?" Tali asked.

"The Tempest Stone. It's a myth. It's supposedly a stone that contains all the Ancients' knowledge," Ellaria said.

"It's no myth. It's real. I know it's real," Elias countered.

"So, where is it?" Tali asked.

"Ha, if he knew that he would have it," Kovan answered for him.

"I think it's in the lost Tomb of the Sagean's."

"Now, ask him where that is. Elias, it's lost for a reason," Kovan said.

"You say you're close, do you have a place to start?" Ellaria asked.

"I think so."

"Fine, just give me a few days, Elias. I have a seminar to give and then I will go with you to find your stone."

"A seminar? No, I'm getting you out of here," Kovan argued.

"It's only a couple of days away, and I can't back out now," Ellaria said.

"But you'll help me find the stone?" Elias asked.

"Yes, but I'm not giving up on finding out what happened to Danehin. Without the Peace King, and the might of the New World, the Prime will go unchallenged."

Her offer to help Elias agitated Kovan, but she didn't understand why. She thought it was best that Elias got out of the city before they captured him. Whatever accomplished that goal, she was all for it.

"What I don't understand is why is a Sagean inherently bad?" Learon asked.

"They're not. They don't have to be, they are just luminaries like Elias," Ellaria said.

"Not exactly," Elias said staring out the window.

"Explain," Ellaria urged him.

"I believe that all Luminaries have different strengths. The texts I've found lead me to believe these strengths are passed down. The line of Sageans comes from an Order of Luminaries highly skilled in the manipulation of the energies of humans. I don't know if this makes them inherently evil. However, their line has inherited unopposed absolute power for ages."

"Based on the attacking beasts, your pile of bones Ellaria, and the flood of bonemen. I would say this new one is no different than the last," Kovan said.

"But being a luminary does not corrupt you, does it?" Tali asked with a look of concern.

Elias didn't seem to want to answer the question, so Ellaria did, "No child it does not."

Ellaria was slowly realizing she was dead on her feet. "We will not solve everything in one night. Kovan, why don't you take the boy to an inn and Elias, you and Tali stay here. Elias takes the couch and Tali that big comfy chair in the window. You're small enough it will work. I have had some of my best night's sleep in that thing. You guys hang out in the city for a few days, I'll give my seminar and we'll go searching for the stone," she said, laying out a plan.

"Great. I think I'm going to go see the Field of Ashes tomorrow. I'm curious to see the site for myself," Elias said.

"I'll go with. We'll meet up in the morning on the pier," Kovan said.

She wasn't surprised that they both were only half a day in the city and already itching to get out again. It was just the way they were.

"I want you here and staying put, but fine. What we really need is a way to communicate. Did you ever figure out how to get the book-to-book sigil connection to work Elias?"

"No, paper doesn't have any inherent properties to sustain a connection," he answered her.

"What about a crystal? Like the coin you gave me. It moves the sunlight to show where north is. Could it do other things like shine words on the wall or something?" Tali asked, sitting in a chair near the kitchen.

"Maybe," Elias said, putting his hand to his chin. "Yes. Not light, but something similar. It would be limited between maybe three coins at the max, and every coin would activate when someone sent a message. I need to think about what crystal we would need, but that's creative. I wouldn't have thought of that. I'll come up with what I need and leave you a list before I go in the morning."

"We will meet again, and this time Ellaria, I'll leave a note," Kovan said, and he reached for the door, "Come on, let's go," he said to Learon.

"Van," Tali got out of her chair and walked over to him. She paused before him, smiled and hugged him. "Thank you for bringing me to Adalon. I'll never understand why you asked, and I can't ever repay you. I just wanted to tell you I'm so grateful I went with you," she said, and her eyes started to fill with tears. Kovan stared at her, taken back a moment and about to make a quick remark, but watched as a tear rolled down her lifted cheek.

"I'm glad you came with me, Talhaleanna. Thank you for helping me. Whatever happens, I'll always be there for you, young Raven," Kovan said in a gruff voice and hugged her again. Ellaria could feel the tension of a lump in her throat and her own eyes welling up, for her, it was a startling revelation to witness. Kovan opened the door and a small black and white cat who had been curled against the door tumbled inside. It was stretching after being awoken and thrown off balance. It cried softly and pranced right to Tali, and she picked it up and talked to it. Ellaria saw its ears bend a few times at Tali, and she flashed Elias a look with her hands on her hips. He had definitely left one story out. He squirmed under her glare and swallowed.

"We may have forgotten one detail about our trip," Elias said as innocently as he could manage.

# CHAPTER NINETEEN

### ERRAND (WADE)

WADE JOGGED THROUGH THE STREETS TO REACH THE NEAREST MAGNOTYPE station before it closed. Ellaria was adamant that he sent a message to Dalliana tonight. Wade reminded himself over and over on the way there that he was Azlo and he was sending a message to Burke.

His stomach was rumbling, and he could feel his weakened legs. He really needed more than the two hours of sleep he had on the train ride in. It was surprising how willing Ellaria was to go through with the infiltration. It wasn't easy climbing around the cave and up and down all the ladders in the dead of the night. She was one of the most impressive people he had ever met, easily living up to her reputation. Stasia was going to be so jealous that he got to go on a secret mission with Ellaria Moonstone. The thought of her stomped foot and scrunched nose made him laugh.

He reached the magnotype station as they were about to lock up. Wade shoved his hand into the closing door.

"Time for one more?" Wade asked desperately.

"Can't it wait, sir?" the porter asked, annoyed.

"It really can't. I'm trying to send my brother an urgent message in the New World. Come on, I ran all the way here. It won't take long," he pleaded.

"Er. Alright. Come in," the porter said, locking the door behind Wade.

"Where to?" the porter asked, moving around to the back of the counter.

"Illumeen," Wade said and handed him the coded message to send.

The man looked at the numbers with a questionable scowl but submitted it, anyway.

When the message was sent, Wade handed the man an extra amber coin. He left the station with the porter locking up as he thanked him again. He went to the Arcana dining hall first to get food before heading back to his room. There was an unusual amount of people swarming the dining area for this time of night. Most new students didn't arrive until after the Day of Light. While he waited in line to get his food, he noticed a small troop of people were gathered in the corner, clamoring over something.

"Do you know what's going on?" Wade asked the kid in front of him.

"Some Andal royalty is going to school here this year," the guy said.

"The Prince of Andal?" Wade wondered.

"I guess," the guy said, throwing his hands up.

Wade grabbed a bowl of steaming food and returned to his room. He passed the east park fountain and under the stone walkway with hanging lanterns to his wing of the dorms. He stepped through the outer hall opening and at his door he found Stasia sitting on the floor, waiting for him. She had a light blanket over her legs and a book in her hand.

"Mims," he said, smiling to find her.

"Where have you been?" Stasia barked and stood up.

He handed her the key and she let them both in. His roommate was out, which was always nice to have the entire quarters to yourself. He had grown used to it over the summer and somewhat possessive. He crossed to his small desk and sat down to eat.

"Do you want some?" he offered Stasia. She was a notoriously picky eater, and she took a glance at what he had, scrunched her nose and shook her head no in disgust. Then she stood over him with her arms on her hips.

"So?" she huffed.

"So, what?" he garbled with his mouth full of potatoes.

"Where were you? We were supposed to study together for our final exams, remember?" she fumed. A sudden pit in his stomach opened up. He had totally forgotten, in the excitement of going to the Citadel.

"I'm so sorry, Stasia, I forgot," he said, placing his fork down.

"What do you mean you forgot? I waited outside your door all day. I'm worried about you. What's going on?"

"You waited outside my door? How sweet."

"I'm not in the mood, Wade. I know you're slow, but this is me, angry with you," she said crossing her arms.

"I was helping Ms. Moonstone with something."

"Why, what with?" Stasia said, with her eyebrows crunched.

Wade hesitated not wanting to lie to his friend, but he also wanted to protect her, "Ms. Moonstone has a new assistant, and I was helping him get moved into his place."

"All day?"

"Yes."

"You're such a horrible liar, Wade. Are you involved in something?" she asked.

"I'm not lying. His name's Semo, and I'm not involved in anything," He assured her, but paused slightly at the end.

"But… I can tell you're not saying something. What is it?"

"Well, I've been talking with Ms. Moonstone and this Prime Commander business is bad."

"Well, of course it is. The Coalition has relinquished its power. What does Ms. Moonstone think?"

"She thinks a Sagean has returned, and all our freedoms are going to be taken away."

"Did she say that?"

"Not exactly, but she doesn't believe the Arcana will be open next year."

"Is that why she resigned?"

"Yes. She mentioned possibly teaching at the new university in Ioka instead."

"Ioka, really? Well, if she did, I would consider transferring."

"You would?"

"Of course, Ellaria Moonstone is the foremost expert in alchemy and while it's unpopular to say, the New World is the real epicenter for scientific advancement, or they will be."

"Interesting, I hadn't thought of that. It may not matter because she believes we're headed for war. The Prime and the New World."

"Why?"

"Danehin, the Peace King, is missing."

"That is troubling. Well, whatever you're wrapped up in, I want in."

"I'm not wrapped up in anything."

"Oh, you're not? This is the most politics I have ever heard you talk. You're blowing off your studies and you killed someone only a couple of nights ago, or did you forget?"

"It's not as nefarious as you make it sound. I was only helping Ms. Moonstone out, that's all. Honestly, she said she would look into Tara's disappearance for me, and I believe she may be the only person who can find out what happened to her."

"I understand that, but if you go missing, I swear I will kill you. Now hand over the bowl of food, I'm starving," she said and Wade handed her what was left. Her hunger obviously overwhelming her typical tastes. Wade was just relieved to move on from the interrogation. Stasia was his best friend and there was no way he would drag her into whatever this was. But protecting her in the long run may mean involving her. It was a balance he had to consider as things continued to develop, and based on last night, things were escalating.

# CHAPTER TWENTY

## MORNING LIGHT (TALI)

SHE DIDN'T HAVE TO OPEN HER EYES TO KNOW THE SUN WAS BREAKING ON the horizon. There was no great surge of energy, she simply felt rejuvenated and alert, like it was the middle of the day. The lingering exhaustion that typically accompanied the first moments of waking wasn't there. She hadn't always felt this way. She may not have even noticed if Elias hadn't pointed it out. She used to enjoy sleeping in. There was a time when her mother had to drag her out of bed, argue with her to get up and stop wasting the morning light in the dreamworld.

She heard Elias packing his satchel and relented. She opened her eyes to the dim light flooding in from the rounded end windows. She found Remi lying above her head. He kneaded her hair the instant he sensed her stir. His claws prickled against her scalp. She quickly and gently shooed him away and rose up from her slumped position in the big chair. Startled by Elias's presence standing next to her, she flinched slightly.

"I didn't want to go away without at least one lesson. Follow me when you're ready," he said in a soft whisper to not wake Ellaria in the other room. Tali felt a sudden pit in her stomach and a quickening to her breath. She got up, grabbed her new, short cloak, and followed Elias out the door to the main stairs. They went one flight up and through another door at the top. Elias held it open for her.

They emerged onto the roof of Ellaria's dwelling quarters. The air was crisp and cold and had a freshness that didn't exist during the day. It was darker than she had expected, with very little sunlight actually in the sky yet. A lot of the electric lamp lights had died down to the faintest whisper of a glow. The clear skyline only harbored a few drifts of clouds stretched thin in the atmosphere.

"Come on," Elias said as he walked past her and sat down flat on the roof facing himself toward the rising sun. She followed and sat next to him, shoulder to shoulder, like back on the bank of the Uhani River. The roof had gray gravel and it crunched as she settled down. As close as they were, she could hear his deep, slow breathing. She didn't know if she should follow and start breathing like that too or not. She wanted to ask but didn't. Instead, when he opened his eyes, he found her staring at him from the side. Her head tilted awkwardly while she tried to analyze his face. Her eyes popped, she turned away and inhaled deeply from being caught.

"Relax, I just wanted to talk with you. I wanted to explain the luminance and talk about the next steps," Elias said.

"Yes, I would like that," she said, nodding yes and returning her breathing to normal.

"What do you think the luminance is? What do you think it is I can do?" he asked.

"I don't know, magic, I guess?"

"Some people call it that, but that always sounded too abstract for me. Magic is a term for something unbound and created from nothing– that doesn't fit the definition of what we can do. So, I don't think of it that way and you shouldn't either. It's not a power to create what doesn't exist, it's an ability to harness the surrounding forces."

"That sounds daunting, impossible, and restricting."

"It is, and it isn't. Most of the constraints are self-imposed. Your mind is the conductor. Ultimately, it comes down to the individual's capacity and creativity. I sense that for you, binding will be the hardest thing, not emanating."

"What are those?"

"Emanating is what we call it when we emit the energy we've borrowed. Binding is coercing the forces around us and fusing it with our own energy."

"Great, now it sounds impossible," Tali said, taking a deep breath.

"Don't fall into the trap of your own making. Belief is essential. You must believe you have this inside you in order to expand the ability further. Only then can you work toward mastering the ability. Take that small inkling you have in the back of your mind and let it free. The first step is controlling your own mind and spirit, once you learn to recognize it in yourself, you learn how to go beyond yourself."

"Right, and how is this possible?"

"You understand that different animals in this world have different senses, right? A hawk can see clearly for a great distance, and a bear can smell blood from five leagues away. Some birds like the hummingbird see light completely different and can see colors on a spectrum we can't. You must develop your ability of perception. We don't see and hear clearly from the day you're born. Naturally, we grow to use our senses. Our senses when taken for granted can dull with age like a worn knife or they can be taken from you. This is no different, it is a perception, and it is one not easily learned."

"How do I sense it?"

"There's a feel to it. The same way that water has a consistency, and solids have textures, energy has a vibration. You will find it first through meditation. You need to relax your mind and body, push out the external distractions and influences. Everyone is different. I found that dawn was the best time for me to do this. I was up already and nobody else was. The more I practiced meditation, the more I sensed the energy I picked up on from the sun as it rose in the morning."

"The sun gives off a lot of energy, but not the moon?" she asked.

"The moon reflects light. It's difficult to harness," he corrected her, and she felt a sudden shame for such a dumb question. Still, the moon held a certain pull for her.

"There's a gravitational force with the moon, but I've never been able to feel that vibration," he continued.

"Is that a thing? Feeling gravity?"

"I believe luminaries of old could."

"Is it alive, this vibration, these forces?"

"What is life but energy and light. There's an energy to all things and to all energy there is a light – a signature. We can absorb it, store it, and put it to work in different ways, but we cannot destroy it. You will feel the light as a vibration, even if you can't see it. They are all distinct, and the way I feel them may or may not be like how you will sense them. The thermal energy of the territh feels different from electrical, which differs from magnetic energy and those differ vastly from the energy of living things."

"Living things?"

"The energy of the soul," he clarified.

"Wait, can you manipulate people's souls like you can lightning?" she was both astonished and terrified about the prospects of that.

"It's possible, yes, but I never have. It is a law of Luminaries. It's wrong. The same way murder is wrong."

"That's not comforting," She said.

"No, it's not, and it should worry you. Remember, we aren't the only two people who have this power. That's what I was talking about last night."

"The Sagean?"

"Yes, but there are others still. The Sagean used his ability to manipulate people's will. All the Sageans throughout the reign of their empire did this."

"How is that possible?"

"Look at it this way. People change their mind all the time. A skilled orator can incite a crowd, and a friend can convince you of trying something you wouldn't normally do. When you understand your own energy, you will learn to recognize the same layers in others. The same way your mind can decipher facial expressions and body language to know if someone is angry. Then, you can influence a change to their state of mind, through your own will and belief. Affecting their actions and thoughts, but it's a very delicate manipulation. Try not to worry about the complicated stuff, just focus on yourself. I want you to get up early every morning and meditate. Kovan and I will be back in a few days and we can meet again. In the meantime, focus your mind during the day on tasks that keep you calm," he said.

"Why? What happens if I get angry?"

"It's not anger I'm worried about, but control. If you lose your grip on the energy you are unintentionally pulling on you could bring on the illumination surge before you're ready. You could be a danger to yourself and others," he said.

He stopped when he noticed the look she was giving him. Her eyes darted around, and her eyebrows turned up. She didn't want to frustrate him, but this was all too confusing and crazy. If she hadn't seen him call lightning from the sky and throw it back, she would think he was cracked. But looking into his eyes, she could see the honesty in his words. She bit the inside of her cheek and wondered why all of it couldn't be easier. She wanted to just be able to snap her fingers. She knew he understood, from the worry blanketing her face, that she wasn't getting it and feared she never would.

"Don't worry, it will come to you. At first, it's only the sensation of a presence. More akin to the emotional response that accompanies you're senses then the actual physicality of them."

"And you can do all this?" she asked.

"Yes, and you will too. The more you practice directing your focus inward, eventually you will come to understand the nuances of your own energy. With that awareness you will learn to control your bloodstream and your heartbeat. Then you'll see how the energy around you affects you and how you can control it. Ultimately, it will be like snapping your fingers," he said, and her eyes opened wide at the tiny sparks of lightning in his palm. She was getting annoyed at that little trick of his.

"Lastly, there is one essential principal to master. It's called the Luminaries Edict, and when you can come to terms with its meaning, you will have grasped the eternal nature of light and the forces that surround us. It is this: Your mind is the state of your being, but you're being is also a state of mind."

Elias stood up and said goodbye with promises to meet again and left her alone on the roof with the sun blazing in the east.

# CHAPTER TWENTY-ONE

## TOURISTS (LEARON)

LEARON CHECKED THE PAVILION FIRST AND TO HIS SURPRISE, FOUND TALI already waiting by the fountain. They decided to meet on the Arcana campus in the morning to explore the city. She sat on the steps looking out at the water splashing down the tumbling tiers of marble. Her dark hair gently moved in the breeze and stray strands settled across her face. She looked up at him, clearing her tousled hair away with her fingers, and smiled. A pair of jade symbols and small black stone feather earrings flashed in the sun.

"Can you believe this place?" she asked, standing up. Learon put his hand out to help her, but quickly pulled it back when she didn't take it. *Maybe she didn't see it.*

"I can stand up on my own, thank you, Learon," she said. *Nope, she saw it.* Tali rolled her eyes in contention. "Honestly Learon, it must take you forever to do anything since you're constantly trying to aid us poor helpless girls," she jabbed.

"You don't think I see it that way, do you?" he asked, slightly offended.

"No, I'm just making a point," she said, waving her hand as if she was blocking his question away. "What do you want to do?" she asked.

"I don't know, walk around. Knowing you, I'm sure you'll want to eat soon," he said.

She pouted her lips and hit him on the arm with the back of her hand, "Watch it. Elias said I'm not supposed to get angry."

Learon felt his stomach drop, "I–I didn't know. I'm sorry."

"I'm only kidding. Kind of. Well, I am hungry actually. Let's go, we can find something to eat anywhere."

"Yeah," he agreed, and they started across campus.

"There's not as many students as I imagined, and they're not terribly friendly," Learon observed.

"Well, they're going through end of the year exams. I met this incredibly pretty woman up on my way here. I asked her for directions, and she was really nice. She said we should go walk around the green belt."

They wandered for some time to the west and the greenbelt. The sunlight gleamed off the vertical surfaces of metal and glass. The multitude of people, shops, carriages, and signs swirled with the surges of noise and endless clattering around them. The magnitude of the metropolis was almost too much to take in. Massive, imposing, buildings rose high above in all directions and caused an instant disorientation Learon wasn't used to. Elias recommended they traverse across the city on one of the high promenades, called the rooftop walkways, in order to get the best view. After a few blocks on the ground, away from the Arcana they heeded his advice. Their necks were straining so much from looking up, they were liable to run into something or someone on the ground as they gawked.

When they found a way up to the nearest bridge, at first, they didn't know what they were looking at. It was a large crafter's automation of metal wheels, gears, and stone. Tali watched the giant bronze wheel revolve, as Learon looked in the window of a nearby shop. She called him over after only a few seconds.

"Learon, come here! It's a moving stairway up to the bridges," She hollered out to him.

Learon turned at her call and shuffled over. The rotating stair lift had ten-foot-tall bronze wheels and stair steps that revolved around a ringed metal pole. It operated through a system of gears and pulleys. The stone steps locked in place with tungsten pins, escalated up to the bridge above and rotated back to the ground. Tali didn't hesitate, stepping on a stair as the wheel reset to re-spool. Learon followed her lead, and the contraption lurched into motion again. They held onto a moving rope and rode the lifting stairs to the top.

It was more than just an upper level of the same city. The air and light were different. Stepping to the walkways was like entering another world. The bridge was brightly lit by the sun. The noises tapered off from below, and the city almost looked peaceful from this vantage point.

With the city on full display, the massive amount of material it contained stunned Learon. The combination of metal, glass, and stone woven together and gleaming, gave the city a defiant strength. Yet gazing out across the rooftops, it surprised him to realize that he preferred the soft tactile grittiness of Atava. Both cities were equally shadowed on the sidewalks. While Adalon was far more impressive in its scale, Atava felt older and handcrafted.

"These walkways are amazing. They are like walking through a dream," Tali said as they wandered along.

"You mean you dreamt of this place?" he asked.

"No, but there's something familiar about it," she clarified.

They continued walking across the bridge back toward the spires. Passing under large archways of stone at random intervals. The bridge elevated higher as they neared the heart of the city where they started the day. Seeing it from this vantage was completely different. At the highest point they could see all the way to the east and the Mainsolis Sea.

"How similar is this to Ravenvyre?" he asked.

"Not at all. Ravenvyre is a lot more chopped up. A lot shorter. There's an endless number of tiled roofs and they slope in long swoops. It's really quite stunning. These buildings are enormous. I can't believe them. This place feels almost unnatural, like it's one interconnected machine."

From the walkways you could see how the architecture reflected the higher orders of society in correlation to the distance from the center of the city. The buildings were pristine, but the people were different too. Less rowdy or alive and more suspicious and intense. When their gaze hit you, you felt their judgment. They wore more vibrant clothing of finer quality in a wider range of styles. It seemed to Learon that every other person wore shaded spectacles, and everyone wore a hat. The outlier of it all was the influx of youth amongst the swell. Like a chaotic, energizing, heartbeat amongst the preoccupied swarm.

They stopped on the bridge and found a flat bench of polished marble to sit at that overlooked the spire grounds and all three complexes. The campus now buzzed below them in the splinters of shadows and light cast by the carefully crafted angles of each magnificent structure, foreboding and strong.

"Wow, I can't believe I'm here right now. I've dreamt about seeing Adalon and the Arcana forever it feels like," Tali said.

"Why didn't you try to enroll before?" Learon asked.

"Honestly, I never thought I would get in they're very selective, and I couldn't afford the trip here or the books. How hard were the exams?"

"They weren't easy, but the hardest thing for me was finding the books to study from. It took a few trips to Atava to find them and then again to take the exam. I think I got lucky because my father worked for the Guild," he admitted. "You can't go to the university in Ravenvyre?"

"No, they only accept boys really. There are very few women that attend and they're all from high order families," she said and shrugged.

"What are you going to do now?"

"I guess, I'll go off with Elias. I mean, I have no choice, right? Honestly, I'm fine with that, maybe excited actually."

"Are you . . ." he paused, not knowing how to ask if she was afraid.

"Terrified? Yes, that too," Tali said and pulled her legs up to sit cross-legged. "You heard him. I will die if I don't learn control. No better yet, I'll explode with light."

"You'll master it."

"How can you say that so confidently?"

"I've only known you for four days, but I get a sense you can handle anything," he said honestly. She turned and smiled at him.

"I'll admit I'm excited too, but my first lesson with Elias was more confusing than helpful."

"I think that's his way. I rode with him for six days before we met up with you and Kovan, and I don't really know any more about him then you. What about Kovan?"

"Oh, he's not exactly chatty either, but he is straightforward, and shaper-edged than Elias," she said and Learon understood her meaning.

"Hungry?"

"Yes," Tali admitted.

They continued on the walkway as it angled them to the east, eventually deciding on a small restaurant that overlooked the sea.

"Where's your cat?" Learon asked her as they sat down to eat.

"Remi took off this morning. Elias told me he would find his way back to me wherever I was. So, I'm not worried. He'll find me," Tali said. She reached into her side bag and pulled out a scroll of paper. "I wanted to show you this. Elias left it for me this morning. He must have designed it last night."

"I don't think he sleeps," Learon said, unrolling the scroll. Elias had sketched a schematic drawing of the communicators they talked about the night before, with notations and detailed instructions on materials needed. It was interesting, but Learon had no experience with this sort of thing. "Do you understand any of it?" he asked.

"I think so. Yes."

"Can you build it?"

"Yes, but we would need access to a crafters workshop, and I don't know where to get the materials."

"We will have to ask Ellaria. She'll know how to help us."

"So, I have to ask you a serious question," she said, and his heart started racing, trying to anticipate where she was going.

"Go ahead, I can be serious."

"How committed are you?"

"To what?" he asked and tilted his head.

"I mean, you're here now. You made it to Adalon. Are you going to keep hanging out with the crazy bunch?"

"Oh, them, that. Yes and no. I'll be honest with you, Tali, the journey here was wild, and part of me wants to get as far away from those people as I can," he said, and he watched her shoulders slump slightly.

"I get it," she said, her fork hitting the plate.

"Let me finish. There's another part of me that knows that just because I can stay clear of them doesn't mean I can run away from what's coming. None of us can. You were right when you said it was a storm, and if we don't stand against it who will? I'll tell you what. As long as you're in, then I'm in."

"Really?"

"Yeah, I can't leave you stuck with them by yourself. You'll go crazy."

"Deal," she said smiling.

"My turn to tell you something. Why I actually came to Adalon."

"Why?"

"I'm here hunting for my father's killer."

"What? You didn't say he was murdered."

"Officially, according to the Guild, he wasn't murdered. But I have a lot of reasons to believe he was, and I intend to prove it."

"How?"

"I'm going to start at the archives. You said yourself that it's the most extensive. They have to have journals and travel logs. If I have to, I will search the 's personal records."

"You're hoping one of the others might help you?"

"No. I hope that my association with them will help me. I'm not looking for anyone's help in this. It's just something I have to do."

"Well, too bad, I'm helping you however I can."

"Thank you, Tali. You know I've never had a really good friend."

"Me neither," she said with her mouth full.

# CHAPTER TWENTY-TWO

## RUINS (ELIAS)

Kᴏᴠᴀɴ ᴀɴᴅ Eʟɪᴀs ᴀʀʀɪᴠᴇᴅ ᴀᴛ ᴛʜᴇ ᴅᴏᴄᴋs ɪɴ ᴛʜᴇ ᴇᴀʀʟʏ ᴍᴏʀɴɪɴɢ ᴀɴᴅ convinced a small fishing vessel, called the Aberden, to take them to the south shores, beneath the ruins of Ash Field. The ship was grimy and smelled with years of fish guts baked into the decks, but it was fast. When they arrived, they had to anchor offshore from their destination. The old pier was too dangerous to get close to, having long ago crumbled into the sea. In it's place remained a jagged wreckage of large, splintered wood sticking out of the surface of the waves like thorns on a bush. They were now death spikes for ships that ventured near.

As the green sails of the Aberden dropped to the boom and were being tied off, they drifted to the land in a small white boat, rowed by one of the crew members. Gentle waves propelled them in, while the craft took in small laps of sea water on its course to the sandy shore. The odd rust colored beach stretched for roughly a league along the coast. The color, another mystery from the past. Forgotten, like so many other things in the world. There were several legends about the area, but any truth they contained couldn't be substantiated. Depending on who you asked, either the Light's wrath destroyed the city of sin or sunfire engulfed the city to defeat a plague of the walking dead. It existed now as a lingering shadow of the past. A barren wasteland of blackened territh and dead trees.

The wind was breezy, but Elias pulled the hood off his head to feel the air. His eyes fixated on the rising hill above the sands where the sun blasted off pillars of stone. Some were free standing still, but most toppled over and interlaced with others. The old world's pierced heart stretched out before them. While they knew very little, Ash Field was undoubtedly the location for an ancient city destroyed in a forgotten war.

"What are you hoping to find?" Kovan asked from his side.

"I want to see how extensive the dig was," Elias answered.

"Didn't you find the entrance originally? I figured you searched the place a long time ago?"

"No, I thought I sensed a chamber below the ruins. Lavaren and I told Ellaria about it. The Guild quickly seized the opportunity to bring a team in. They didn't want me to have the first chance at it, after the escapade at the Sagean's Palace. They didn't trust me."

"Was it Lavaren or Ellaria who went behind you?"

"At the time I believed it was Ellaria, but it was Lavaren. He trusted too many people in the Guild. As their Regent, he believed they all fell in line with what he wanted. They pressured him to go forward with the excavation. More and more I became wary of him and our partnership disintegrated. I stopped working with the Guild altogether and would simply send things I found to Ellaria directly."

"So, they were right to keep you out then?"

"Yes, they were right, I would never let them have anything I found. Mind you, we never found much. Old versions of texts we already had and lots of archeological pieces like pottery or pieces of cloth, but rarely anything significant. A few times we found large crystal blocks, usually cracked from falling to the ground, which I kept. I was never very interested in digging up the dead, only their secrets."

Moments later they were ashore and climbed up amongst the ruins, looking for the underground access point. The small boat they came in on was now staked to the land, and its navigator wandering the water's edge, biding his time until their return. They had a few hours before the fishing vessel wanted to move out and their ride back to the Crescent Pier would be gone. With the field of blackened ruins stretched out before him, Elias's thoughts strayed to another time, and the looks on the Guild member's faces when he walked away. He had walked away from a lot more in the years that followed. Somehow, from then to now had passed in a blur. A lot had changed in the last forty years, even though Elias felt he was the same man, he knew better. Years of searching ruins in vain, looking for every scrap he could find about the Ancients. *As much as you want to believe you're the chef of your own life– choosing the ingredients and cultivating a perfect stew. Over time, you eventually realize you are the soup, being stirred by unknown hands.*

He had forty years to find the knowledge and weapons to defeat the darkness he knew was waiting to descend on the world. Now the time was up, and he still had found nothing to explain what he had witnessed that fateful night. He was sure that something beyond the vileness of man was gathering against them now. Eventually, he would have to tell the others. While the Prime was a puppet of the Sagean, the Sagean was a puppet of a greater darkness they had no means of defeating.

From a distance, Kovan waved and called out to him from a point further in near the center. Elias found Kovan, with his boots resting on the sloped side of a large stone that tipped into and met another at a point above their heads. It created a triangular shaped entrance.

"Is this what we're looking for?" Kovan asked with a half grin, clearly impressed with himself.

"Yes," Elias answered and retrieved the lanterns from his pack. Two cylinders of glass that worked like the electric glass lamps in the city. Not as effective as his orbs, but the best he could do. Elias channeled a trickle of electricity into each, and the gas trapped inside glowed orange. Kovan stared at them reluctantly, but took the one Elias held out, "Let's go," he said.

They plunged down below the rubble on a steep slope of soil that eventually led to a cascading stairway. It disappeared into the depths of the dark ground. The lantern glow bounced off the walls with each step down. The air was growing more stagnant, and dust layered everything the deeper they traveled. They eventually emerged into a large rectangular shaped chamber, with the side walls broken up by a rhythm of protruding square columns.

"Are we safe in here, Q? It won't collapse on us, will it?" Kovan asked. His voice projected into the entombed space.

"It shouldn't. The Guild would have had engineers clear the area. I'm sure we'll be fine," Elias said, and he continued on to the far side. At the end of the room, it split into three directions. Three doorways, each leading off into corridors. All evidence from the excavation team was long gone, but footprints in the layers of dirt on the floor suggested that they did the bulk of work in the center hall. Elias followed that hall, while Kovan went to check the side routes. Through the center doorway, Elias came to another chamber. This one extended into an octagon shape with an altar cove on every angle. The center of the room held a dirt filled fountain, where large boulders of stone from the ceiling had crashed down, destroying the pool's edge.

Elias tracked around the perimeter, inspecting each cove for anything the team might have missed. There was an outside possibility he might sense the humming well of power from a wave gate in a hidden chamber nearby. If this was the ancient city of Ashalon, then it followed that there would be a gate here, but nothing stirred from anywhere. Kovan entered, his face illuminated as he stalked inside. Elias cast him a quizzical expression.

"Nothing," he said. "Both routes look like simple sleeping chambers. There are two empty rooms in each hall. Anything in them was picked clean. Find anything in here?"

"Nothing."

"What's behind the wall?"

"Where?" Elias said, missing something. Kovan walked up to the far wall and to one of the flanking columns. He disappeared behind it.

"This wall," he called out.

Elias followed. His feet crunched on a shattered mess of mosaic tiles that had crumbled from the wall. It wasn't a hidden chamber, but in the darkness, it was hard to see. Elias shook his head. He focused on the wrong things.

The chamber beyond was small and only one mural remained unshattered by time. Kovan stood staring at it.

Elias approached. The wall was stepped back to create a deep shelf like an altar. Elias put his lantern down. There were markings in the dust, like something that once rested there was missing. Kovan shone his lantern against the mural.

"What am I looking at?"

Elias stepped back to look. It was a faded painting on the wall. Some parts were completely faded away, making the entire right side impossible to make out. The left side showed a man pictured with lines rising up, and at the top was a depiction of the sun being eclipsed by the moon. The center image was the clearest one. It was a red pyramid with rays of light extending from the surface. Some writing at the bottom caught his eye, and Elias pulled out his journal to copy down what he was looking at.

"Kovan, I need more light," Elias said, and Kovan moved his lantern in. It was definitely an ancient script, four symbols that were interconnected as one.

"What's that?" Kovan asked to point to the pyramid.

"That is the Tempest Stone."

"Was it here, did they find it?" Kovan said, alarmed.

"I don't know. This does not look like an altar where the stone sat. I think it's a depiction of something the stone does."

"What?"

"I don't know. With the right side missing it's hard to say."

"Whatever it is. The eclipse makes me think it's not good."

"Probably not," Elias said, and he moved away, "What's at the end here?" he walked over and found more rubble on the floor surrounding a crashed plinth. It was in several pieces, but it looked familiar to one he had found before. The sidewall opposite of the stone mural was another painting, but it was lost to time.

"Well, there's not much here. Just ground stone, dirt and a few murals," Kovan said.

"A few? Did you see another one?"

"There's the symbol in the main hall. Didn't you see it?"

Kovan led him back into the first room and sure enough there above the entrance carved into the stone was the Sagean symbol, the rough outline of the sun with an eye inside it and rays of light extending out.

"We can go," Elias said.

"Great, you don't have to tell me twice. I'm not a fan of being trapped below ground. Especially in a creepy old crypt."

"It's not a crypt. I think it was a Sagean Temple or the lower level of one. From what I've seen, I don't think this is the ancient city of Ashalon. I'm surprised the original team found anything."

"Why?"

"Ashalon was a city of the ancients. Through my research, I've determined that the Sageans were not in power during the Eckwyn age. They were one of four major religions. From what I can tell around sixteen hundred years ago, they somehow stole power from the rest and became the dominant force in the world."

"Sounds about right, so what?" Kovan asked.

Elias could tell he wasn't interested in a history lesson, "Point is this site isn't old enough. If it was there would be more than one temple."

"What are you looking for if not evidence of the stone?"

"Evidence is one thing I have. I'll explain later, when we meet up with Ellaria again."

"Fine, let's get back to the Crescent. Ale and crisps await."

# CHAPTER TWENTY-THREE

## ALCHEMY (ELLARIA)

SHE WALKED THE TUMBLED STONE FLOOR WINDING AROUND THE decorated walls. They displayed fabrics of faded patterns discovered in the old world. All of them were encased in thick slabs of glass and inset into the plaster. There was a tension to her seminar that she didn't anticipate, born out of elements beyond her control, and now an exaggeration of expectations. Ellaria could feel it, trying to navigate the crowded corridor that hummed with students waiting to find a seat.

She had given seminars to her peers before, and students didn't scare her, but something about today had her unsettled. The stakes seemed raised in light of recent events and a plan for her seminar had been slow to materialize. Escalating her trepidation was the angry mob she suspected was lying in wait for her. The admissions officers had reported to her requests for her class next year, that didn't exist, were getting out of hand and that she needed to announce her intentions to join the Arcana already. Which was a problem, because she had no such intentions. Ellaria hadn't exactly made a lot of friends over the years and she suspected her presence on campus was making more enemies amongst the staff. She neared the doors to her classroom and found a familiar face coming toward her.

"Edward, hello," she said. He was dressed expertly in a nice, slim fitting dark blue suit and his silver spectacles reflecting the light. He held a cup of water in his hands and smiled widely at her.

"Ellaria, I thought you might need water while you were speaking today," he said as he handed her the cup, "I also wanted to wish you luck."

"Thank you, Edward. That is kind of you," she said, taking the plain gray ceramic cup that looked like it was from the campus kitchens. She sipped it immediately and peered inside the room to see it packing up already, with students and faculty alike.

"There are professors in there?" she said to Edward.

"Of course. Everyone on campus wanted to hear what you had to say today. We had to start limiting seats."

"Well, I better get in there. Thanks again," she smiled and entered the fray.

The collision of hundreds of insignificant sounds, movement, and voices bursting disjointedly inside was agitating. It contributed to her anxiety and she felt herself breathing short quick breaths of air. It was a foreign feeling for her to be nervous. She had never felt anything similar with her peers. For some reason she was valuing the opinions of the youngsters more. The sheer surprise of that was hard to come to terms with. She took a moment to take in the scene, but only a moment. She remembered her long standing motto: *never allow friend nor foe to see her weak.*

The room inside had a cathedral ceiling shaped into a pointed barrel vault, with a sequence of smooth stone ribs meeting at a keystone beam from the entrance to the back of the room. High lofted windows with diamond patterned dividers punctuated the left relief wall, and the light from them was perfectly controlled and cast across the tables inside. Small dust particles floated in the glowing sheets of sun rays and she found the peace she was looking for.

As she walked down the main aisle, past rows of students packed into the many seats and tables, she felt herself hardening like stone, and her strength and focus returned to her amongst the chaos. It was a beautiful room and her anticipation and nerves turned into clear determination. Her steps transitioned from a slow stride, to a deliberate cascading stomp. She was here for the youth and open minded, not the stagnant fools or skeptics. Any professor in attendance that fit the description of the latter could get torqued. She wasn't interested in swimming against the tide of expectations. This was a battle for the minds and passions of the youth. A new resistance would need brave souls. She didn't have time to coddle weakness.

She reached the front of the room where a large desk and shelves packed with various devices, bottles and small storage boxes were positioned as a backdrop. Semo was there too, waiting at the front for her. He stood tall and rigid, and casted a suspicious gaze over the entire proceedings. He somehow straightened even more at seeing her and nodded a hello. Ever the sentinel, she appreciated his disciplined nature. She checked the clock on the desk to verify the time. Just a few more minutes left, and she would start. She turned around and saw the room was filling up, and some chaos was resulting from the lack of seats.

"Come in and find a spot along the walls if you can please. Feel free to sit on the floor if you think you can see, but don't block anyone else," she called out. The room's commotion died away with her voice as it echoed into the tall ceiling. She checked the clock once more and saw it was time. She waved Semo to come with her, and they strode back toward the entry. She seized the large bronze ring of the arched wood door and pulled the two together. A few late stragglers hurried in at the sight of her. She paused for the three of them and shut the doors after they were through with a loud crash.

The room hushed. It had the intended effect of coercing silence from the gathering and eliciting their full attention. She looked to Semo, who watched her with his hands clasped together. "Please let anyone running late into the room. Thank you, Semo," She said in a muted voice. On her way back to the front, she spotted Wade sitting off to the right. An idea for an equally persuasive effect blossomed in her mind. An inspiration for a proper introduction of alchemy and a way to end her lecture sprang into place.

"Welcome, everyone. I am Ellaria Moonstone. I apologize for the unusual circumstances of this lecture. There are about four times as many of you than what we initially planned for," she said. She heard some low murmurs chime around the room. "I'm fully aware that in the past, the Scholar's 's efforts to teach Alchemy and the mystic arts has been floundering and met with ingrained skepticism. This is not by accident or negligence, but as part of a purposeful reluctance to share the knowledge of such a powerful art. Alchemy is not a speculative, theoretical study of nature, intended solely to enrich your mind like philosophy. It is a craft and art form with practical applications," she paused to see if their attention had waned. So far so good.

"Before I begin, I need a volunteer," she said, and a throng of hands raised. "I'm sorry, I should warn you first that I need a drop of your blood."

Most of the hands faltered and dropped save a few. The hand she suspected would still be raised, was, and she called on Wade to come up. He approached and they retreated to her desk.

"Thank you Wade, nothing to worry about, just a demonstration for later," she said to him.

"Sure, I trust you," he said carelessly.

She found what she needed in her bag. Taking the small needle out, she pricked his finger, and a small grunt of pain escaped his lips. She thanked him and waved him back to his seat. Then she took the needle, a piece of parchment and a fountain pen to the small podium up front that she had no real intention of standing behind. Holding up the needle with Wade's blood high for the class to see. She placed it all on the podium and readdressed her audience.

"Alchemy is a quest to understand and control the furies of the unknown nature. What we know about the craft has tripled since the end of the war, when a lot of knowledge that had been kept from the people was returned. The books that surfaced, the ones we have been able to translate, have served to expand upon and explain the once obscure practice of alchemy."

"But it existed before the war, right?" A young man's voice chimed out from along the wall.

"It did, but practitioners were shamed or outright outlawed under the Sagean Empire. A broader interest was then reignited by the war and the discoveries that followed. What we now know is that alchemy comes from the spiritual traditions of altruistic intentions for both improving our lives and searching for precious metals. That's right, a lot of this knowledge comes from people experimenting in order to get rich."

She heard some light laughter in the room trickling out, but most of it was the nervous kind. She continued, beginning to move around as she spoke. "Their pursuits, however, led them to experiment and in turn they began to decipher the properties of crystals and the intricacies of how elements of nature interact. Please be mindful there are both serious artisans and pretenders working in this craft. The deceitful tricksters, the shodders, will sell you spells and elixirs of seaweed and wine and tell you it will cure your back aches, help you sleep, or make a woman fall in love with you. Be most wary of the ones who seem outgoing and verbose. This is a craft that requires years of working in dark rooms and poring over riddles of language. A real alchemist will have tired eyes, be preoccupied and have no idea or interest in selling you anything," Ellaria paused to take a drink of water and saw a hand raised from a pretty blonde woman sitting next to Wade.

"Yes?"

"What's the difference between alchemy and territhamy?" the young woman asked.

"Territhamy is the science of elements and the study of the calculable properties of geological and biological particles. Alchemy is the science of studying the deeper interconnections of nature. Alchemists discover, territhmists or chemists as they sometimes call themselves, explain. They are concerned with the chemical composition, not mystical connections. They see the chemical compounds like a mathematician. It's similar to the difference between architecture and engineering. Though they are both problem solvers of the built environment, they have very different skill sets. An engineer can tell you if the building will structurally work without falling down, but they have no skill for designing. They don't have the mind for it, and neither does the architect have the patience to calculate forces of weight and wind. An architect is an artist and a crafter, an engineer is a calculist. Territhmists, they don't understand the power of symbols and elements. They don't see how incantations work, how words spoken in the correct order matter. They don't believe and don't concern themselves with the energies or essences that flow and bind. These are the furies alchemists are most familiar with. They include both negative and positive intentions. The world is a collection of elements and forces: light, gravity, spirit. All of it in constant tension. The Alchemist's Codex, by Xand Zosmos, explains these relationships and their interactions. In previous classes this book has not been made available. I have written to headmasters of all the universities on your behalf, demanding that copies be commissioned for all the students in the higher-level classes. If my request is denied, then the efforts to keep you in the dark will be obvious," she said, and a good amount of clapping ensued, along with sparks of more side chatter.

Ellaria looked around at the faculty. Some she knew as longtime supports of alchemy smiled and seemed pleased. The others who weren't supporters, did not. The same ones, incidentally, who had come out already supporting the appointment of the Prime. At the very back of the room, standing in the shadows, she could see Haden Mathis scowling. He was probably infuriated by every word she had to say. The sight of him made her want to hammer home her message.

"These books, these texts are sacred. If the war taught us anything it was that we should never ever let anyone take the freedom of knowledge away from us. See, we thought the empire had saved our histories. Protected them and locked them away in a secret archive. But the truth was that they truly burned anything that went against their teachings or version of history," Ellaria said, she saw a hand raised next to Wade, "Yes?"

"I thought that the secret archive of the Sagean had yet to be found?"

"Possibly. The vault that was found inside the Sagean's Palace did yield a lot of unknown things. But an extensive collection of books it was not. Some believed the archives could be in a different location. However, no location has ever come to light. After forty years, it's unlikely that there is a secret Sagean archive. However, there could be other vaults out there, older vaults."

"Do you think there are?'

"I don't know child, but I hope there are."

Another hand raised. A really tall boy off to the side.

"Yes," she called on him.

"I have two questions actually. Do you know if we will ever actually be experimenting in class and will you be teaching next year?" he asked, and his last question was met with a loud clattering of voices and shouts, both for and against her teaching.

"Good question. If you are not experimenting in the higher-level course, then the Arcana is not teaching it correctly and I will do my best to solve that. As far as me teaching here at the Arcana, I do not know what the future holds, but I have not committed to a teaching position. How . . ." her words were cut off by a boiling roar of caterwauls and cries from the audience of 'trader' and 'charlatan'.

"However," she projected loudly over the shouting, "I will help the Arcana, as I help all of the universities throughout Territhmina. This will include a new outline for the entire studies path, leading to real apprenticeships. The person who teaches is irrelevant, what matters is what they are teaching you and it must be real truth. Let me be clear: alchemy is magic, and don't let the outside world convince you otherwise. Much of our society has been trained to despise the practice. Disregard them. It is an engrained reaction fostered over centuries and rooted in ignorance and fear, like all horrible prejudices are. You should be studying the complexities of symbols, rules of families of ingredients, techniques, incantations, and potions. This scares some people, because anything that threatens their way of life is a defiance of what they hold dear. They see magic as the practice of manipulating the natural world through supernatural means and that it defies the teaching of the Light. Magic is simply the act of bringing about change through the manipulation of forces empowered by your will. Do not mistake it to be through simpler means without effort! You will fail. There are no shortcuts even in magic."

She could see some restlessness and checked the time. Though she still had plenty of time left, the room was quickly getting too hot to breathe with this many bodies inside, so she shifted to her closing. "A few scheduling notes and I'll finish out our session for the day. The gentlemen standing in the back is my assistant, His name is Semo," she looked at him and put her finger up and twirled it like she was stirring the air. Semo saw the signal and began handing out small pieces of paper to everyone.

"Semo is handing you a slip of paper. Please fill this out and return it to my office. I would like to know who is interested in alchemy and what your current skill level and knowledge base is. This will help me make determinations and suggestions to the Guild as how best to ratify the curriculum going forward."

There it was again, the young woman's hand raised high. Her arm stiffly locked at the elbow. At least she had manners. She stopped her pacing shuffle to call on her. "What's your question, dear?" Ellaria asked.

"Can you explain what is the real truth, what's different about the curriculum that you believe needs to be changed?" the young woman asked confidently.

"I can definitely address that," she said and moved to the podium. "This class was taught in the past by analytic minded scholars, but never by a practitioner. So rather than explaining theory I can show you," she told them and could tell by the limited rustling that they wanted to see what she could show them. "What I want to show you is the significance of synchronized systems. By this I mean elements and furies attuned by your will. Does anyone know how a sigil works? I would hope some of you could answer this much," she said and saw a few brave souls willing to speak. One belonged to Tali standing near the front, so she called on her. "Go ahead."

"A sigil is a symbol meant to channel an energy. It's written for a specific purpose and you can do things like wards or spells," Tali said.

Ellaria shook her head in general agreement then clarified. "More or less, that is all true. Specifically, the symbol is crafted with precise lines that combine like an equation to produce a desired outcome. The power comes from the sequence of marks in the correct order and alignment. Along with the drafters will, and usually an additional element is required for a connection or as a charge. It is a synchronized system. I asked for a volunteer at the beginning of class so I can demonstrate this. Please, come to the front, Wade," she said, motioning to him with her hand. "Wade was brave enough to give me a drop of his blood," she said, raising the needle again for all to see. Then she looked down at the parchment and drew out the sigil she thought would have the biggest impact on the classroom. She looked back up and showed the class what she had drawn.

"This is the sigil," she said, waving the drawing around, "And this is the charging element," she waved the needle and then made it obvious she was smearing his blood over the symbol. She looked over to Wade whose eyes were blinking rapidly. She could see his chest thumping, and almost felt bad. She looked back over the spectators and put her open hand in the air. "This is the force of my will," she said loudly and slammed her palm onto the paper. A thudded smack sounded as it hit hard on the wood podium and Wade standing forward, with his head looking sideways at her, suddenly collapsed, crumpling to the ground in a huff. Loud gasps erupted from the room.

"Wade!" the pretty blonde with all the questions screamed out and came running forward.

"Please leave the paper with Semo on the way out," she said loudly to be heard over the ruckus. "Thank you for coming."

Semo opened the doors, and she noticed a rare smile on his face as he walked back to her. She turned and hurried over to Wade's side.

"Wade! Wade. What did you do to him?" the young woman asked Ellaria in a venomous hiss. This young woman just witnessed something powerful and threatening, yet her voice held no fear of Ellaria. She showed promise already.

"He'll be alright. It's just a sleeping spell," Ellaria assured her, "What's your name, dear one?"

"Stasia."

"Stasia, he will be fine, I promise you," she said and watched as Stasia was now holding Wade's head and running her hands through his hair. She looked up at Ellaria with desperate eyes.

"Can't you wake him?" she pleaded.

"He's fine, just give him a slap, he'll wake," she told Stasia.

"Just smack him?" she stammered,

"Should work," Ellaria confirmed.

Stasia looked at Wade and swiped her hand quickly across Wade's face. Wade's eyes fluttered open just as hand was about to connect. "What's —"

Slap.

"Ow! I guess you're still mad at me?" Wade said to Stasia and she apologized and backed away to give him space to get up. Wade moved his eyes off her and glared at Ellaria, "What did you do to me?" he said grimacing as he tried to stand. Semo went to his side and helped him up.

"I am very sorry, Wade. It was a simple sleeping spell. Maybe I could have warned you. How do you feel?" Ellaria asked.

"Maybe you could have? You're cracked. Do you treat all your friends this way?"

"See, he's fine, Stasia. Semo, please walk with Wade and help him get wherever he's going next," She grabbed her things to leave. The other three started to make their way out. "Wade," Ellaria called after him, "Thank you."

"Sure, anytime."

♣

AFTER THE LECTURE ELLARIA RETURNED TO THE OFFICE TO GET A FEW things before heading home. The plan was to meet up the following evening after Elias and Kovan had returned from Ash Field. They needed to come up with a plan of action that somehow prevented the takeover by a new Sagean and averted the destruction of everything that they had ever worked for. Seeds for the inevitable dark empire seemed to already be sown. The roots of mayhem were deep and wide, they just needed to be awakened. She feared that war would be upon them before winter and it might be a war that they couldn't win this time. Most of her old contacts, the prominent members of the Resistance had aged beyond their fighting years. Others had gone silent, afraid to make any notice of their movements. With the reliability of overseas communications questionable and dangerous, no-one was talking. If feathers were being ruffled elsewhere she had yet to hear and the silence scared her.

On the whole, she thought her end-of-the-year lecture had gone well. She could have dug deeper into the politics of the takeover and the hypocrisy of the Sagean faith, but that would not have accomplished her main goal: to excite a new generation about alchemy. If she went to Ioka maybe some of the students would follow her there.

The only thing keeping her from leaving Tavillore was the many promises she had made in the recent weeks. Promises first to Dalliana, then to Wade. Now to Elias, to search for an artifact she was skeptical even existed. At the same time there was a disturbing number of people that had gone missing, and that number had risen by some accounts to upward of a few thousand people. When asked about it in the press, the Prime blamed the Quantum Man, continuing his attacks and attempts to discredit Elias with the public. More than discredit, he had outright made Elias a criminal of the Coalition.

Ellaria grabbed the books she came for and locked up, leaving the halls for her apartment. She crossed through the core grounds outside of

218

the Craftcore building and noticed there were fewer scientists than normal roaming around. As the year had come to an end and the weather provided for easier travel, more and more of the professors had already taken their leave. Yet she didn't expect so many of the crafters to have already taken off. In other years, they would have stayed for the New Year festivities before leaving. But the Prime and his upheaval of the Coalition left many believing the Scholar's Guild would be the next to fall.

Ellaria paused at the road a moment and thought about waiting for Semo to return from helping Wade to his room, but decided to walk without him shadowing her. She scampered over the road and around some colorful dollop cars parked at the street side.

A few blocks away from the spires she began to notice that her steps were being echoed in sync from someone not far behind. She could run, but she hated running. When the right opportunity presented itself, she dashed to an alley and slid her concealed wrist knife free. Standing with her cheek against the white stone, she waited for her pursuer to show themselves.

A person closed in on her position at a slower pace than they should have. Their shadow emerged on the cobbled walk and it paused, shifted and tapped its foot, looking around for her no doubt. With the advantage hers, she sprung on them.

"What do you want!" She yelled out from the side.

The person flinched drastically and toppled to the ground. He was young and looked completely out of his element. His head shook slightly with his eyes fixed on her knife.

She slipped it back into the wrist pocket realizing her mistake.

"I'm sorry I thought you were following me," Ellaria said, and she reached down and helped the kid to his feet. He brushed off his pants and looked back at her.

"Are you Ellaria Moonstone? I mean Azlo?" the kid asked. Ellaria crooked her eyebrows and shook her head in slow confirmation.

"I have a message from Burke," he said.

The kid pulled a small scroll free and gave it to her. The paper was thin and felt like the same type, the Whisper Chain used, that disintegrated in water. Though there was no way this kid was part of the Chain. Ellaria tucked the note away and placed her hands on her hips. So much for subterfuge, Ellaria thought. In less than a week, princess Dalliana had already broken from their communication system. She looked back to interview the kid but movement at the top of the street caught her attention. A small squad of bonemen were coming toward her.

It did not seem like a mere coincidence and Ellaria prepared for the worst.

"Kid, you should run. Now," she urged him, and the messenger looked to see what had her attention and ran without hesitation. Ellaria remained motionless hoping the bonemen wouldn't pursue the kid further. It looked to have worked, but she now had three armed bonemen bearing down on her. Her mind raced to what she could throw at them to escape. She could throw a vial of shadow dust, but the evening breeze would clear it quickly and one of the three would catch her, and firespark seemed drastic.

Then from the side alley footsteps clacked toward her, she turned as a bonemen grabbed her wrist.

"Hand over the message, Ms. Moonstone," the soldier ordered.

The shock of being grabbed caught her wordless and she pulled back to no avail.

"Let her go!" A familiar voice called out.

Ellaria turned to see Edward rushing over from the opposite sidewalk.

Edward, go away you fool. She thought, but only shook her head to signal and warn him not to interfere. But either he didn't see it or didn't care.

"I said remove your hands from the lady," Edward demanded.

"Stay out of this and move along. I'm only going to warn you once," the solider said in a strong challenging voice.

"Please Edward I'll be fine," she told him, but he ignored her.

"I am the Headmaster at the Arcana, and I demand you let her go."

The soldier's grip loosened, and he peered at Edward.

"I can see you're struggling to make the necessary calculations here young man, but that makes me a colleague of the Prime and whatever your orders are I am telling you to stand down. Please report back to your superiors that Edward Knox stopped you from accosting a lady on the street. I have no fear of your Prime, and if he has an issue, he can take it up with me. Am I clear?"

Ellaria struggled to keep a smile from blooming on her face as she watched the panic in the soldier's eyes grow. Edward's words had him doubting himself. She supposed the mere act of someone standing up to them and the way Edward spat the word Prime with such venom and zero reverence, was enough to throw him off. Finally, the soldier stepped away.

"I promise you, I will be telling my superiors; Mr. Knox, was it?"

"Yes. That's Kay, en, oh, ex. The Kay is silent."

The soldiers smirked and turned toward his squad and they followed his direction and retreated back the way they came.

Ellaria's first thought was that she couldn't tell Semo or else he might handcuff himself to her. Then she looked at Edward. He continued to surprise her. His face broke into a grin and he pushed up his spectacles on his nose slightly.

"Thank you, Edward."

"Don't mention it. I can't believe these thugs. This is getting out of control."

"I know they seem to be everywhere now."

"Yes, and the greencoats have almost disappeared. I'm not sure if that's by order or necessity."

"I'm sure they've been directed to limit patrols."

"Where are you headed, I can escort you?"

"You know I was just turning to go back to my office when they stopped me," She lied, but she wasn't about to let Edward walk her home.

"Would you like some company?"

"Sure," she replied. He was so formal in his manners sometimes she didn't know what to make of it, but she thought she liked it. They walked slowly and instinctively she continued to scan for bonemen or anyone else following them. However, the roads were clear and oddly empty.

Edward walked with a mixture of perfect posture and ease. He wasn't exactly jovial, but he wasn't a somber person either. Her moments with him were beginning to feel rich in a thoughtful way that she hadn't experienced with another man before. Ellaria had never fallen for someone so serious but could sense herself liking him more and more. He had a strength to him that was similar to Elias and an easy comfort was starting to build between them.

"Your lecture went very well," he complimented her.

"Oh, well, Thank you. It's kind of you for saying so. I guess I was happy with it."

"You don't seem sure."

"Don't I? That's because the audience had so many unfamiliar faces I think."

"I thought it was a powerful statement on the power of alchemy. How is the young man doing?"

"He's fine. It was a simple spell, really."

"You say simple, but I have read through the alchemy books and the sigils and the spell work is far from simple. If anything, you downplay the willpower needed to make such spells work successfully. I've only heard of a very few accomplished practitioners. The Arcana was lucky to showcase your talents."

"You're starting to sound like Delvette. Trying to talk me into teaching here?"

"Would that be so bad?"

"That's assuming the Prime and the Sagean don't dismantle the Arcana."

"They won't. If they wanted to, they probably would have attacked it already somehow. Yet I have heard nothing. I don't think they could bring it down if they tried anyway. You should be proud. You built that."

"Well, they do seem far more preoccupied with the New World or finding Qudin."

"That reminds me. I heard that the Luminance squad will be here in full force by the New Year. The Elite soldiers have been terrorizing the southwest as far as I know, but the leader Duraska is supposed to be meeting with the Prime."

She wasn't sure how he came by it but this was useful news, "Where did you hear this?" she asked.

I overheard Dunne telling some Soldiers they needed to straighten up before the arrival of the elite squad. Then they would see what the best of the best really looked like."

"Interesting. It sounds like the squad is made up of the Prime's former unit the Cloaked Knife."

"Could be."

They stopped outside of her building entrance and sat on the steps a while finishing their conversation. When a light rain began, Edward excused himself to see to something, and Ellaria thanked him for his timely aid again and went inside to find Semo pacing outside her door.

"Semo, there you are."

"Where have you been? I came here and you were missing, I went to your apartment and you're not there."

"Wait, you went all the way out to the greenbelt and back already?"

"Yes. Of course. My job is to protect you. Did anything happen?"

"No, well, yes, actually. Dalliana sent a note. Come inside, let's find out what she needs."

They walked in and closed the door. Ellaria pulled the note free and unfurled the fine parchment.

*Dear Azlo,*

*The Trustees are clamoring to break the brigade by any means necessary. Without my father, I fear it won't be long before war is again consuming the world. They believe my father was killed by the Prime and want retribution. So far, they are recognizing me as their princess and as their leader, so long as I don't make a mistake and show weakness. I require someone of your abilities and leadership. You once helped my father, and he has always praised you above all others. If you would be willing, then I urge you to please join me as my advisor, to defeat this new foe that threatens our peaceful and thriving world. With your guidance by my side, together we can swiftly win this war. I now see no other alternative. I need you. I will stall the Trustees for as long as I can, but the Prime's brigade is destroying trade and our economy and hurting my people. Once the line presses across the Anamic I will be forced to act.*

*-Burke*

ELLARIA SAT BACK IN HER CHAIR AND PUT HER FINGERS TO THE BRIDGE OF her nose. With the rain picking up outside and starting to patter against the glass. Semo read the letter and handed it back to her. Ellaria stood up and walked to the window. She opened it, and the fresh rain filled air rushed in. Ellaria placed the letter out on the windowsill and held it while the rain reduced it to nothing but a chemical swirl on the stone lintel.

# CHAPTER TWENTY-FOUR

## COMING TOGETHER (WADE)

WADE DROWNED A MOUTH FULL OF HIS ALE AND STROKED HIS ARM WHERE it still ached from collapsing to the floor. He looked over at Stasia, who was surveying the crowd piling into the Frog's Leg Tavern since the afternoon.

"So, you are mad at me still, or you're not?" he asked her.

"I'm still mad when you bring it up and I remember how you ditched me. If you would leave it alone, I might forget how much you drive me crazy, Wade," Stasia said, snapping off the last few words.

"You're just so much nicer when you're not mad at me."

"Fine, I'm not mad at you. Is that what you want to hear?"

"Yes. Thank you."

Stasia raised her hand and waved toward the door. Their friend, Lyka had made her way through the entrance. "I'm surprised Lyka came out without Vargas tonight," he observed.

"I'm not, they're always at each other's throats," Stasia said as their friend walked over and sat next to Wade.

"Thanks for saving me a seat, it's a madhouse in here tonight. How was the seminar?" Lyka asked them.

"Not bad, Miss Moonstone tried to kill me, but other than that, it was good," Wade said.

"Oh Wade, she did not," Stasia corrected him.

"I know, but it's a better story."

"I heard there are already rumors floating around that she is testing spells on everyone to see how they work," Lyka informed them.

"I can tell you; they work. She doesn't need to test," Wade said.

Lyka ordered a drink from the server making rounds and turned back to their conversation. Stasia kicked Wade under the table and nodded her head up so he would look where she wanted. A group of three young women were at a stand-up table, staring at him. "You have a fan club," Stasia said.

"Yes, I always wanted to be popular."

"How do you like the middle one Wade?" Stasia asked, continuing their game of dating dares. Wade looked again to see the middle one. He turned back, cringed and shook his head an emphatic no. Lyka looked at the person they were discussing, squinted her eyes.

"So, you're still mad at him, huh?" Lyka said to Stasia.

"No," Stasia said, in denial.

"See, she says she's not, but . . ." Wade said, throwing his hand out, gesturing at the women behind him as evidence to the contrary.

"Well, maybe just a little," Stasia admitted.

"How about him, Mims?" Wade said to Stasia, pointing out a guy at the bar, who was rats and unable to sit on his stool. "He looks fun."

"No, not my type. How about . . ." she paused and searched the room, "Him?" Stasia said, with a rare spark in her eye, while pointing to the front. Wade turned to look, and glimpsed the man, but had to look again. Coming through the front crowd of people was a petite young woman with black hair followed by an obviously strong young man. He carried himself with an ease and nimbleness that projected confidence that his face didn't actually reflect. There was nothing overtly intimidating about him. He wasn't the biggest or tallest, but his movements made him look like someone you didn't want to mess with. Even though his longer hair made him look too pretty to be good in a fight, his posture said otherwise. Standing with his sleeves rolled up and his forearms crossed, he looked like a coiled snake. His companion was equally fierce.

"Oh, I was wrong. She is livid with you, Wade," Lyka said spotting the guy they were discussing and laughing.

"That's not funny, why is that funny?" Wade bristled.

"Oh, I think I know her actually, I should ask her who her friend is," Stasia said when the two were closer. They stopped about fifteen feet from them and faced the stage. The guy called the server over to order drinks.

"I think they're a couple, Stasia, don't bother them," Wade told her.

"You think? What was her name?" she wondered aloud, "It was something funny like Dotty or Tilly no, I remember. Tali, over here!" she called out to the young woman.

She whirled around at the sound of her name and waved. Her friend turned to see who she was responding to. They said something to each other as the server brought them their drinks. The guy took both and paid. Handing one to the girl Stasia had called Tali. Tali took a sip and tapped her friend's arm and pulled his sleeve to follow her.

"Hi," Tali said and pointed to the fourth chair that was unoccupied.

"Please," Wade said. She went to pull it from under the table, but her friend beat her to it and pulled the chair out for her. She sat and gave him an annoyed grimace.

"Hi, it's Stasia, right?" Tali asked.

"Yes, did you find the statues in the greenbelt?" Stasia asked.

"We did. Thank you for the directions this city can be overwhelming."

"Definitely," Stasia said, and she turned to Lyka. "Tali, this is my friend Lyka, and Wade. Well, you know him, you were at Miss Moonstone's lecture."

"Yes, we saw that. It's nice to meet you. This is Learon," she said, slapping the guy standing next to her in the gut. He stood over her like a bodyguard. "He's shy," she said.

"I'm not shy," Learon corrected her.

"Well, he's not talkative. Better?"

"Better. Nice to meet you," Learon said to all of them, but Wade noticed his eyes lingered on Stasia when he spoke.

"So, what's that you're drinking?" Wade asked.

"Something called emberbroth? It's great, but my throat is on fire from it," Tali said swirling her auburn-colored drink.

"Yeah, that stuffs no joke," Wade told her.

"How about you, Learon?" Stasia asked.

"Me? I'm just drinking the house ale. It's good. It's not watered down at all."

"Best in the city if you ask me," Wade agreed before he could think otherwise. For some reason, he liked these two.

"Are you both enrolling for next year?" Stasia asked.

"I am," Learon said, "But Tali's not."

"No? But you both attended the seminar; how did you get tickets?" Stasia followed up. Wade was sensing a pattern of her directing all of her questions at Learon.

"We're friends with Ellaria," Tali said.

"Oh, you know Ellaria Moonstone?" Stasia asked.

"Through a mutual friend. So, what's your settled area of studies?" Learon asked

"I declared for mechanics," Wade answered.

"Really, I didn't know you had decided," Stasia said, surprised.

"Only so I could work on my project all summer."

"How about you Stasia?" Learon asked.

"I'm a pupil in physics. When you pick your classes, I recommend the intro to energies class. There's a whole segment on electric currents. It's fascinating," Stasia said, continuing a level of sweetness even for her.

Hours passed while they sat together, drinking and watching unique acts go up on stage. They told stories about where they were from and discussed Adalon and the Arcana. Where the best places to eat or shop were and what spots were best to study and get your work done. To Wade's mind, Stasia was flirting all night with Learon, but he was too dense to notice or polite to flirt back. Wade suspected both, but he found that despite himself, he liked them. They were not the usual green first years that even he himself was last year. At some point, Lyka left, and it was just the four of them. The bar maintained a rowdy atmosphere, with lots of people blowing off steam.

"Wade, you're in the mechanics field, does that mean you have access to a crafters shop?" Tali asked him.

"Yes. That's what I was saying before."

"So, you have access, even after hours?" Learon asked again.

"Yes, pupils get keys to the crafter shop that's partly why I settled. I was always in there anyway, and I wanted more time to work on my new gadget."

"I would love to see what you're working on, what is it?" Tali asked, interested.

"Come by, I'll show you sometime. Are you a crafter? Is that why you need access?"

"Yes, I have an idea for a device, but I didn't know where to get the materials or where I could build it at," Tali said.

"Let me know, I can get you in. Where did you learn to craft?" Wade asked.

Stasia stood up, interrupting the conversation, "Excuse me everyone, I'm going to see if Harlow is working tonight, I haven't seen her yet," she said, excusing herself from the table. They watched her walk away to the back of the room and Tali and Learon shared a look between them before they both turned back on Wade and leaned in closer to the center of the table.

"You're Wade, right?" Tali said.

Confused by the question, Wade gave her an odd look. So, she clarified, "Wade Duval, you're friends with Ellaria. You went with her to the Citadel?"

"How do you know about that?" he asked, surprised.

"Like we said, we're friends with her too. We're helping her. I wasn't sure if Stasia knew anything about it or I would have said something earlier."

"Thank the Light you didn't. She doesn't know anything about it, and I would like to keep it that way. She would have attacked both of us until we spilled everything. She may look meek and mild, but she's feisty," Wade told them.

"This thing I want to build it's for Ellaria. It's a communicator device. She wants us to build it before the New Year festival. Actually, we need a few of them."

"Do you have drawings to work from, a materials list?"

"We have those. I'm not comfortable pulling it out of my side belt in here, but yes."

"I understand. Tinker schematics for new devices are becoming sought after more and more and by the wrong sort of people. Why don't we meet up in a few days to work on it?"

"Great, where?"

"Let's meet at the archives. From there we can walk to the east end of the core beltway. There are fantastic shops for parts and the best place to find obscure items."

"Perfect. When?"

"Tomorrow. Let's say, two hours after the blue."

"Perfect."

Wade sat back in his chair, reshaping his thoughts about the two of them. They were such an odd pairing. The two of them together and further still, them and Ellaria. He was missing something that explained their connections. Their earlier clipped off stories about traveling to Adalon made more sense now. They had been omitting parts. He looked up to see Stasia coming back alone.

"Is Harlow here?" he asked as she returned to her seat.

"No, she's not working tonight. I was hoping to have her meet Tali and Learon," Stasia said.

They all turned as another poet took the stage.

"Do you enjoy poetry, Learon?" Stasia asked.

"I don't believe I've ever listened to one before tonight. I mean, I've seen a showman's troupe do readings and plays, but never a poet. West

Meadow only has one bar and its part of the inn. I don't think Rose would let one in."

"I'll take it over the horrible flute player," Tali suggested.

"I'll agree with that," Stasia said.

"Have any of you seen Lamdryn perform?" Tali asked.

"Yes, he came in once last year. It was amazing. Where did you see him?" Wade asked.

"He came to Ravenvyre last summer. It was life changing, I swear," Tali said.

"Who is Lamdryn?" Learon asked.

"Thorns. Learon," Tali said, slamming her glass down. "He's a traveling minstrel, and he's amazing. He travels throughout the world and stops in places. No one ever knows when or where. Not like a showman's band that sends word of their route and dates. He just shows up. He puts the poetry of these shodders to shame," Tali said.

"He pops up in Adalon, but when he does– drop everything to get there. It's usually a small venue that gets super crowded," Stasia said.

"Can you believe there's people who just don't get him?" Tali asked.

"That's because people are stupid," Wade submitted.

"Agreed!" They all cheered together and the froth from the tops of Wade and Learon's ale spilt to the table below, and covered their hands. Wade set the tin-tank down and flapped the excess off his hand to the floor.

"Is that a Reckoner deck?" Learon asked, pointing at the action turner.

"Yes, do you play?" Wade said.

"No, I've heard of it, but I've never played it."

"It's a city game for sure. Want to learn?" Wade asked.

"Don't play with him, Learon," Stasia warned.

"Oh, she's just mad cause I always win. Here," Wade grabbed the cards out and started dealing a quick demonstration hand on the table, "It's simple we each get nine cards. You pick one as the head card. It goes face down and five for the field, go face up. The rest you keep as your reserves and then we battle. Unwanted card goes to the graveyard. We take turns, it's fun. You battle, or swap ranks, but when the two swords come up on the turner that's called the reckoning and the games over. We flip our leader over and the best squad wins. The idea is to end up with the best field paired with the top head card. There are other games too, but that's the gist of Reckoner. Of course, there're strategies about what teams are the hardest to defeat. Synergies between squads and the best head cards and when to change your guards."

"And all the cards are legends?" Learon asked, examining a Tregorean archer card.

"Yeah. This is an Empire era deck, so it includes Sagean lords. Some people prefer the original series."

"Oh, so each card has its own strengths and weaknesses," Learon said.

"Right," Wade said as he gathered the rest of the cards and passed them over to Learon to look at, "Tali, do you play?"

"No. I have played it, but I'm not any good at it."

"The cards are fascinating. Is every deck the same?" Learon asked.

"Now that's where the actual game gets competitive. Sometimes you play people with their own sets and the game gets crazy because they have a different luminary with a ruby amulet instead of obsidian. Anyway, there are some real collectors out there with big pockets. Games with serious people playing for high stakes and timed matches. We must play sometime."

As the night wore on, Wade seemed to drink more than usual, and he talked in random batches. The scene felt more like a blur of choppy exaggerated moments and he was struggling to keep up with Learon, drink for drink.

"Hey guys, did I show you, my gauntlet?" he asked and couldn't remember.

"Yes!" they all said in unison.

"Right," He remembered now. He almost accidentally triggered the catch pin release on the sword right at the table when Learon didn't believe him. Which might have been bad. He was proud of the recent improvements he had made to it since the fight with his attacker. The entire thing was smaller and sprang out much faster. The lighter weight allowed for an easier movement, but it was still funny looking on his arm.

"It's funny looking!" he announced.

"What is Wade?" Stasia asked, and he sensed a tone of annoyance.

"My arm sword. Where's your sword?" he examined Learon and realized he didn't have one.

"I don't carry one," Learon said. *What was this crazy talk? A mountain kid not carrying a sword. Didn't he say he hunted?*

"What? Why not? You should. If you're friends with Ellaria, you really should," Wade said, shaking his head up and down to emphasize his point. They looked at him funny, but Wade shrugged it off. He had to concede that the others didn't understand Ellaria Moonstone was dangerous. It had surprised him to realize who she was and his admiration for her had only increased since. *Hard to believe an attractive older woman like that and death followed her,* Wade thought.

"Wade, doll, maybe you should go back to your room," Stasia said in a gentle voice that seemed off somehow. Was she sad?

"No, no, no, I'm fine, Mims. Plus, I'm talking with my new friend, our new friend Learon," he said and turned back to Learon, "So, why?"

"I don't know how to use one. I'm good with a bow, but people don't carry bows anymore."

"No bows. But you have a point. I wish I was better too. We should get lessons!" he said.

"I would love some lessons."

"It's settled, we'll get lessons at the Trainer's Yard on the Pier."

"Who's Mims?" he heard Learon ask.

"Me, I'm Mims. Wade calls me that to annoy me. My last name in Mimnark," Stasia replied.

"I like it," Learon said, and Wade reeled from the obvious flirtation, but was equally struck that Stasia appeared to blush. He looked over to Tali, who was observing the exchange as well. At least she looked as aggravated as he felt.

"What a mudfoot you are," Wade slurred.

"What?" Learon asked.

"Oh, don't mind him he's drunk, but maybe you should take him to the dormitories," Stasia suggested.

"I can do that. How will you two get back?" Learon asked.

"With our feet, dad," Tali said.

"It's dark outside there has to be a bunch of crazies out this late. Are you sure?"

"We'll be fine. Take him before he falls down," Tali said, and Learon got up and helped Wade to his feet. Wade struggled to watch the continued conversation.

"Tali, I'll see you tomorrow, and Stasia it was nice to meet you. Anyone know what passage and number he's at?"

"He's in Daraveer's passage, number three, it's near the commons."

Moments later Wade was stumbling out of the bar. He punched the peacekeeper Enric on the arm, joking about blades through the neck. But Enric gave him a funny, menacing look.

"Enric. What's wrong with you?" Wade asked.

"I don't think his name's Enric Wade," Learon said.

The rest of the walk back to Wade's room was fuzzy until he felt his face up against some stone and recognized the interior vestibule to his room, followed by loud knocking.

"I like you, Learon. You're not nearly good enough for Stasia, but I like you," Wade said staring at his new friend.

"Thanks, Wade."

"I think she likes you. She's my best friend in the entire world and if you hurt her, I will kill you."

"It's alright, Wade. I'm not trying to make a move on Stasia."

"Sure, Learon, sure."

The door opened and Wade jerked in his stance. He heard his roommate Geff's voice and then Learon was dragging him into his bed. He tried to say thank you but was unsure his muffled voice escaped the pillow. The room spun, and he pulled and tugged until one of his feet came free. He placed it on the ground, hoping the land would stop spinning long enough for him to fall asleep.

# CHAPTER TWENTY-FIVE

## OPPORTUNISTS (KOVAN)

Somewhere into his sixth tank of ale, Kovan chatted up everyone in the dockside bar, because that was his way. Elias had left him alone for the evening and he was amongst his favorite sort of people: seadogs and wave lifers. The tavern was a large, elongated shack with a bar and a canopy extending out from the front. The blue tinted wood held firm as the evening winds kicked hard against the outside. It was the last gasp of spring calling out through the gusting swale.

About twenty paces down and across the crushed gravel, the waves of the Mainsolis Sea were rolling and the ships in the harbor tipped and swayed endlessly. Kovan sat at the bar near the door and watched as a tender ran out to the canopy poles and re-fastened the strap downs to secure it from the uplift. The sea air smell was pungent as the door flapped back to a close with a smack.

"They'll be tough water out there tonight, mark my words, friend," The gruff old man in layers of tattered cheap clothes, announced. His face was nothing but wrinkles and frizzled gray hair. The stocky old man had the sleeves of his shirt and jacket rolled up and Kovan could see he had strong swollen forearms and sunbaked skin, a lifer for sure.

"How can you tell?" Kovan asked. The gusts didn't seem like a storm yet, just wind kicking up as the awakening season gave way to the zenithal.

"Been liv'n on the roll my whole life, when the wind drives hard in gusts like that, it's like that front rider run'n at the head of the cavalry. Something worse is to follow."

Kovan downed the legs of his ale and placed the empty tank on the counter. Almost immediately a tender was dropping off another.

"I didn't order this," he called back, and the tender pointed with two fingers to the far end where a lady in black sat with both hands clasped around her cup. Her cloak hood obscured her face.

"From the woman at the end of the bar," he told Kovan.

Kovan rose off the stool and patted the old seadog on the back as he passed behind him. The closer he got he finally recognized the woman under the hood.

"Many thanks, is this seat taken, flower?" he asked. She peeled a few fingers off her tank to motion him to sit, but she didn't speak or look up. Kovan slipped into the seat and stared into the green eyes of Myra Dolan, an old revolutionary friend he fought with in the southern plains of Lowtalla.

"Myra, it's been a long time. What brings you to Adalon?" Kovan asked, happy to see an old friend.

"Opportunity," Myra said in a soft voice.

"Are you running cargo for a cause again, or for profit this time?" Kovan asked.

"Neither. You think I would resort to working with the Supremacists of Adalon?"

"I don't know, you always were opportunistic."

"That's true, but they've gone quiet lately."

"Have they now? Why is that?"

"A squad of bonemen put down two ships and their crews the other day. Proclaimed them conspirators and wiped them out. Now the syndicates are afraid to stick their necks out. Afraid they might be mistaken for enemies of the Prime. The bonemen put the fear of the Light into them, that's the sums," she explained.

"Yes, they do that," Kovan said, but he was slightly shocked to hear of the escalation of force by the Prime.

"What are you doing in the city, Kovan Rainer?"

"Oh, just sightseeing. It's a big city, there's lots to see."

"Are you looking for any added power, I see you still refuse to carry a blade?"

"You know, I might be. You can never have enough, especially these days," he replied, and an image of Q evaporating wolveracks sparked in his mind. He probably had all the power he needed, he covered a smile and continued, "Anyway, I don't plan on sticking around long."

"You never do."

"What I do need is a nice and shady spot for the festival tomorrow. One with a lot of cover."

"I might know a place. There's a restaurant called the Skyline, in the east end of the merchant belt. It's under construction, so it's vacant. I can get you in for a short time. Would that work?" she asked.

"It would," he said and eyed her closely.

"What's it worth to you?" she said. There it was, Kovan thought. That's the Myra he knew.

"Wouldn't be much. My amber is low as it is."

"Well seeing as I owe you for that skirmish in Amera, how about just some information?"

"What are you looking for?"

"I have a few questions and you always seem to know more than you should."

"Ask away."

Myra leaned over the table and spoke in a soft voice, "Have you heard of a group called the Court of Dragons?" she asked. It was not a name Kovan was familiar with, and he gave her a quizzical look.

"Can't say that I have, why?" he said, and her posture sagged slightly.

"Maybe nothing, I heard the supremacists are afraid of them and I thought maybe they were a new player."

"Sorry. Anything else?"

"What do you know about the missing king of the east?"

He took her meaning to be referring to Danehin—"The Peace King, not much," he told her.

"Here I thought you were on your seventh ale. I was hoping you would be more open to talking and possibly other more exhausting activities," she said with a sly grin. Kovan shrugged, so she moved on. "Can you find out why trade has ceased across the ocean?" she asked.

"I didn't know it had, but I'll look into it," Kovan said.

"It's not been openly stated, but that's the bottom fact of it. I hear there's an uncrossable blockade lining the Anamic."

"Let's say we meet again, at this Skyline place. You let me in, and I'll tell you what I find out, deal?"

"That could work," she said, and she stood up to leave. "Kovan, it's good to see you again, but I always feel the need to remind you, if you keep fighting for the underdog, eventually the odds are, you will lose. You know that right?" Myra said, tugging gloves over her hands that covered most of her arm and the small blades she kept there.

Kovan put his open palms out and shrugged. "What can I say, I like the action," he said.

She left him at the table watching her stride away with her high laced boots softly pattering the wood floor as she disappeared off along the docks. The night's wind rippled the folds of her cloak until the darkness swallowed her silhouette.

# CHAPTER TWENTY-SIX

## FRAGMENTS (LEARON)

"Learon, what do you think? Do you like the poets? Oh, Learon, you're so nice," Tali teased in an overly sweetened voice to which Learon could only shake his head.

"It wasn't like that," Learon said passively, doing his best not to give Tali's assertion any sort of purchase.

His steps quickened as they made their way through the raised gardens toward the Arcana Archives. They were there to meet up with Wade, who had promised them access to a crafters shop. But they both wanted to arrive early to look around. Neither of them had ever been there before. Learon saw it as his first genuine opportunity to research whatever he could find on his father and the Ash Field excavation and the capsized boat he perished on.

The archives were housed at the center of the Scholar's Tower. The building soared high into the sky with a gleaming white stone facade that twirled upward adorned with columns. Gradually the columns ended and the cylindrical glass center rose higher. Free of the stone and gleaming in the sun, it looked like a crystal held in a roll of parchment. The connecting side towers had large expanses of glass with distinct metal mullions swirling in from the edges.

They approached the entrance under a large balcony held up by an array of ornamental round columns. Each with twelve bands of stone and large symbols carved into the bands.

"Learon. Don't be evasive it was obvious she fancied you," Tali continued her observations of Stasia from the previous night.

"Fancied!" he repeated in amusement.

"Yes. Why don't they use that word where you're from?" Tali asked.

"Did Wade say where he would meet us?" Learon asked.

"You're changing the subject."

"Am I?"

"Yes. We're talking about Stasia."

"What about her?"

"How you like her, you don't, do you? Of course, you do. 'Oh, I've never heard the name Stasia before'," she mocked.

"I hadn't."

"Well, do you like her?" Tali asked, frustrated.

"I like her fine. But I'm fairly sure Wade and her are a thing."

"They're friends, but I'll ask, and no, he didn't say where."

He acknowledged her statement with a nod and reached for the handle to the entrance. With the scale of the building, his eyebrows pinched when they walked into a low-ceilinged space. The room opened up with decorated marble floor to a center desk inset into the wall. On Either side were staircases rounding up and out of sight. A third wide set of stairs, off to the side, arched down to a lower level. Passing beneath glowing orbs inset into the ceiling, they approached the steward's counter, to speak with the attendant. A young woman with pale skin and wildly untamed red hair sat behind the counter reading. She looked up from her book and eyed the two of them suspiciously, but with a pleasant sliver of a grin.

"First time?" the steward asked.

"Yes, how did you know?" Learon asked.

"You looked lost, that's all."

"I guess we sort of are."

"No problem. Here," she said, handing Learon a slip of paper that read Archives Rules and Procedures. There was a small drawing on it of a cylinder broken into segments and each segment labeled with the books in that ring.

"Look that over. It will tell you how to find what you're looking for and all the rules you have to adhere to. Break anyone and you're banned for a month. Break either of the three listed on the bottom there and you're banned for the year and have to petition to get re-admittance. You'll see it says there's no fire or lanterns or candlelight allowed. There are light sources available, so don't worry about that. Check in here with me upon arrival and sign up for a reading room. You're not allowed to remove books so don't ask me, ask a professor and they can usually get you what you need. It's daunting to find what you're looking for, so in most cases you'll want to come here first, and we'll go through the stacks to narrow your search," the steward explained and pointed behind her.

A huge wood compartmented casement cabinetry filled the wall. It was pristinely finished and lacquered in a dark brown color. Learon estimated that the casement held a thousand small drawers, each no bigger than a hand, "Oh, and downstairs is the restricted section. There's a much meaner steward down there. Don't even go down there without the correctly signed permission form and even then, they usually turn you away unless you're accompanied by a Guild member," the steward warned.

"Is there a room available today?" Learon asked.

"Yes, there are two left. You're lucky most of the exams have finished, otherwise the spots fill up fast at the end of the year. You can check it out for one hour time blocks. Most of the rooms accommodate four people, but there are a few bigger rooms at the top that accommodate six or eight."

"We just need a four-person room for an hour, thank you."

She took down their names, including Wade's, and led them up a spiral stairway. At the top landing there was a rounded top door. To the right was another stair that switched back up against them, and to the left there was a tunneled opening in the side wall where a golden glow filtered out. The steward took them through the short tunnel to the left. It ended at a balcony with a gold bar railing, overlooking the archives vast collection. Learon audibly heard Tali's breath catch when her eyes took in the sight.

It was a massive cylindrical room, roughly seventy feet wide, with bookshelves that towered from the floor up a hundred feet above them, to a glass ceiling. The fragrance of the room was overwhelming and intoxicating. A smell of parchment and leather mixed with glue arose from the volumes of books. Suspended in the middle of the room was an immaculate glass and mirror contraption that extended nearly the full length and served as a light source throughout. It gently spun at a very slow tick and the collection of brass framed mirrors, in a multitude of shapes and sizes, tilted and reflected the sunlight from above through elongated slabs of amber-colored glass and illuminated the room in a soft gold glow. The rounded wall of books contained a system of ladders attached onto metal lines that allowed you to roll around the perimeter. But amongst the rail lines were thin walkways and stairways navigating the perimeter. These led to octagon shaped breaks in the shelving that looked to be hallways to rooms beyond.

"Through those hallways are the reading nooks and rooms," the steward whispered, "There are plaques every so often to label different subjects and studies. You'll find that the verified truth texts or profession manuals are this level and below and the unsubstantiated books and any fictional works are in the higher rings," She said and then motioned for them to follow her back out and up more stairways. She took them to their assigned reading room and left.

The room was simple and cozy. Wood lined walls draped in thick dark red fabrics at the corners. A second door to the side led to the archive stacks, and the room was lit by a circular hole in the ceiling with a large glass disc. Above which Learon could see a shaft where the tiny windows he saw from the outside let the sunlight in. A single table rested in the middle with four seats around it. There was also a big comfy chair that Tali immediately scampered to and plopped down into.

"Oh, this is so soft. I might check out a room every day to get some sleep," she said.

"You're still not getting along with your roommates?"

"No, I'm just not sleeping well, but Stasia and I have a plan. We are going to talk one of her roommates into switching with me," Tali said.

Learon nodded his understanding and ducked out the side door. This door opened to a short hall that barely allowed for the door to open. He walked to the end, took a long look at the rows and rows of books and realized he had no idea where to start. He turned back to the reading room and Tali was closing her eyes. Learon left to get help from the steward. When he hit the bottom step into the main lobby, the steward looked up from her desk and smiled.

"Sorry, I think I need help to find something," Learon told her.

"That's why I'm here. What can I help you with?" she asked.

"I am looking for anything I can find on the Ash Field excavation. I'm not sure if there's any field journals or reports. Also, a book on shipwrecks in the Mainsolis Sea."

"Alright," she said and turned around to search the drawers. She pulled a drawer from the top left and two others. Then returned to the desk. And started leafing through the small cards inside.

"What's your name?" Learon asked.

"Fiona," she answered, still searching the cards.

"Thank you, Fiona," Learon said earnestly, and she looked up at him through the stay hairs partially covering her face.

"You're welcome," she said and returned to her search. Learon was realizing that his research was going to take longer than he thought.

"Do you work here by yourself?" Learon asked.

"Typically, no, but we're shorthanded during summer."

"You're a student, right? Does the Arcana pay you?"

"Yes, not much, but every bit of amber helps."

"Who do I ask about working here?"

She reached over her desk and grabbed a small slip of paper, handing it to Learon. "Fill this out and someone from the Guild will let you know in a couple of days," she said. Then shortly into the second set of cards she found something and pulled it out. "Here's something. It's a field log for the excavation," she said and stood up to show him the card. Pointing out the ring location he could find it at. He thanked her again and went to find the book.

A short time later, after he had navigated the sliding ladder and retrieved the book, he slipped back through the tunnel to their nook. When he placed the thin leather logbook on the table, Wade came into the room with a sly grin on his face. Tali peeked one eye open and sat up. Maybe she hadn't been asleep after all.

"Ready?" Wade asked

"Yes. Are you coming, Learon?" Tali asked, seeing his hands resting on the book.

"Can I meet you both at the shop, after you've gone to the stores?" he asked.

"Sure," Tali said, understanding.

Wade explained where he could find them later, and then the two of them departed. Learon dove into the logbook for any insights into the dig and possible findings.

It was there on the first page, a description of the field team and his father's name in the middle of the page. Something about seeing it in published print made his heart sink. Instantly there was a gap placed between him and his father. A distance filled with a reality of events and moments of his father's life he didn't know. The field notes continued to describe the delicate effort to enter the subterranean temple. It noted that they had received an anonymous tip of its existence. It was clear from the description that the tip was a leak from someone spying on Elias's movements. It described the inside chambers and some more mundane items they found. One passage about the main chamber with a fountain had lines blacked out and redacted from the record. Learon could only assume this was where descriptions of some more interesting artifacts were previously detailed. He perked up anytime his father was mentioned, but nothing was really said about him or the sequestered study afterwards. There was a timeline of events that didn't add up.

Learon pulled free an empty journal he had purchased and made his own detailed notes from what he read. Coping down all the names listed and anything he found pertinent. When he finished, he packed up and left the room. He dropped his books with Fiona at the front and thanked her again.

He crossed the campus, heading to the mechanics building in the north. About halfway there, he ran into Tali and Wade cutting across the lawn. Tali had a wide smile on her face, and Learon waited on the walk for them to catch up.

"Did you find everything?" Learon asked.

"Everything but the nickel pellets. They didn't sell them as small as we need. Those we are going to have to make on our own. We'll need access to a metallurgy room, but Wade knows someone who can do it," Tali assured him, "How about you, did you find anything interesting?"

"Not sure yet."

They followed Wade into the crafting shop and over to his station. Wade was excited to show them what he had been working on. There was a wire stand near his table that looked like a good place to hang your jacket, and on top of the table was a gray tattered canvas covered over something that bulged from underneath. Wade removed the tarp to show his new creation.

Before them was a set of four larger bronze wheels stacking on top of each other with gray metal poles sticking out of each and rippled cloth piled up and folded over itself in a heap. Somehow the wheels and poles were attached to a set of straps. At first glance, Learon believed it was meant to be worn on your back, whatever it was.

Wade looked at their confused looks and jerked like he had forgotten something. He reached down and rotated the interlocking wheels. Smaller gears, Learon didn't see before, began to spin and the wheels unfurled multiple poles out in an array. The cloth grew taut and arranged out before them on the table as a set of wings that extended nearly ten feet wide.

"Does it work?" Tali blurted out, clearly enthralled by the creation. Learon found himself unconcerned that it was wings and far more fascinated in the design and construction of it.

"No, this is just a prototype, so to speak. I'm not sure it will ever work with this fabric, it's far too heavy right now. But I have some ideas on how to change out the materials," Wade said.

"What would be great is to have some sort of compressor injection that extracts them all at once," Learon said thinking out loud.

"Right. Do you have experience in mechanics or crafting?" Wade asked him.

"Not really, I fix a lot of things around town. My father died when I was young, so I had to fix a lot of things on our small farm. The last few years I have been helping a friend I know fix things around his property too and doing some carpenter work for the town inn for food and coin," Learon explained.

"I can relate. I helped all the time at home. Something about the mechanics classes spoke to that instinct in me," Wade said.

"Myself, I'm not very creative, but I am good at problem solving. My father used to say all the time to me that the world needs problem solvers. Anyway, that mentality stuck."

"So, let's see this design you guys want to create," Wade said, and Tali retrieved the scroll, unrolled it and pinned the end to the table. Wade's eyes grew wide. "This is either brilliant or crazy. Ellaria thinks this will work?" Wade asked.

"Not Ellaria exactly. I mean it's not her design," Tali corrected him.

"You said it was a coin and I can see that, but that doesn't seem like the right form for this. I would be afraid I might lose it."

Learon stared at the design for the first time, having only glimpsed the drawing previously. "You're right, Wade. What if it's a watch instead?" he offered.

"That's brilliant," Tali said. "That way it's strapped to us."

"That would work, it might be suspicious looking. While the size is right, it doesn't look like a clock face."

"Then let's stack it behind a clock face that hinges to the side and reveals this below?" Learon suggested.

"Yes! I love it," Tali said.

They spent the rest of the night sorting the materials for their communicators and going through the details of the design. Wade made a list of additional materials they would need, and Tali sat down at the tinker's table and pieced some elements together. With the shared excitement between them, they worked long into the night together.

# CHAPTER TWENTY-SEVEN

## SPARKS (TALI)

Tali worked on the communicators throughout the night, with help from Wade and Learon, she had almost completed them. Assembling the parts for all three was difficult when each contained so many easily lost tiny pieces, repurposing existing watches helped.

Tali worked at the tinker's bench and her eyes were heavy from working through the night without sleep. Learon slipped out to get them something fresh and rejuvenating to drink. The new day slowly filled her with an energy that conflicted with how tired her mind told her she was. Wade was still asleep, his head and arms slumped atop his crafting station. He had been that way for most of the night while Tali worked. Learon had slept against the wall, like the watchdog he was.

She was trying to fasten the swiveling top when it happened. She pinched the mechanism together and precariously held the pieces into position. But she needed the soldering iron to join it on to the bronze ring. The iron still sat on the cooling plate near the burning coal stack. As she stared at it across the room, annoyed that she had forgotten to grab the coppering, an odd sensation built up inside her. Tali focused on it like a single candle in a dark room. Every detail of the iron rod became completely succinct in her mind. The twisted rod and bulbous end were suddenly vibrant and coarse, as if she was touching it from across the room. The heat of the iron rod, solid and hot, and the copper tip smoldering. She took a breath and then suddenly; it was flying at her. It peeled off the resting plate and into her hand in a flash. The burning copper tip hit her hand in her fumbled attempt to catch it, searing into the fatty skin between her thumb and first finger. She screamed out in pain and dropped it to the stone floor with a ringing clatter.

Wade jumped awake and stared at her. She quickly lied about accidentally grabbing it wrong. She wasn't sure why her first instinct was to lie about it, except that the truth was unbelievable. A truth she wasn't ready to share with more people.

With Wade awake, they continued to piece everything together more efficiently. It was a tedious process of soldering bit by bit. But eventually they built all three. Each watch was thick, and the final weight was substantial enough to warrant the stiff leather cuff they used. The communicator dial itself comprised a pool of viscous liquid in a sandwich of glass and metal, with thousands of tiny balls floating inside. They divided the circle face in half. With the lower part shielded by a brass plate and the upper portion open to reveal the crystal pool that sparkled in the light. The balls rested behind the plate, magnetically pulled there by the inner construction of the ring.

By the time they completed the devices, they looked up at the one clock in the room to set the time. They were running late. Leaving a mess of scrap parts all over Wade's station, they burst from the shop doors into the buttress enclosed colonnade path. Nearly knocking over Headmaster Knox, who simply implored them to be mindful of running around the crafter's shops.

They ran to the raised walkways and scrambled through the crowd.

# CHAPTER TWENTY-EIGHT

## THE WAY FORWARD (ELLARIA)

ELLARIA AND KOVAN WALKED HIGH ABOVE THE CITY ALONG THE ELEVATED walkways. The setting sun on the horizon bathed the hills in a vibrant orange. The sun itself an eerie bright red. She remembered seeing it that way once before, when the city of Adavan burned for a month during the Great War. Whatever horror was producing this evening's red glow, she feared the worst.

Ellaria blinked hard against the sight and rubbed her eyes gently with her finger and thumb. She hadn't slept much, Dalliana's request kept her staring at the ceiling all night. She was never good a resting her mind while the details of a task were still unsettled.

They continued east toward the hideaway that Kovan had secured for their meeting. Ellaria noticed the walkways were already getting crowded with people. All of them gathering to celebrate the New Year's Eve fireworks, best seen from the rooftop walkways. The people were joyful and drinking and merry. The following festival filled Day of Light, would see the same people flood the lower streets. Ellaria saw young children playing with aurora spinners. She laughed inwardly at the contrast of their mirth and how she would fulfill her own obligations that night.

When they passed a small squad of bonemen patrolling the high walks, she couldn't help but worry. Their armored presence had steadily thickened in the last few weeks. The Prime was tightening his grip on the city. A reminder of the albatross they faced. If the bonemen got word of Elias's movements, she was certain they would do anything to apprehend him. Kovan had eyed the bonemen as they passed, but had done so far more covertly than she had. A simple glance and he could probably tell her what weapons each man carried, what their strong hand was, and which was the biggest threat. He had always been talented in that way. For as long as she had known him, which was a long time.

To be next to him after being separated for so long was like the tide coming to shore. It was unexplainable how safe and comfortable she felt with him, and like the sand, she wanted to cling to the wave before it retreated back into the ocean. It was strange how years apart, vanished into nothing. As if the rhythms of their beings seamlessly aligned without effort.

"Kovan, you're sure this place is safe?" she asked him and fixed her eyes on his face for the lie.

"I hope so."

"You hope so! Do you trust this Myra or not?"

"Myra looks out for herself; She wouldn't work for the Prime directly. Anyhow, we're not setting up a headquarters. It's just a safe spot for the night. We should be fine."

"Still, it's conspiring against the Prime."

"I know, feels good, doesn't it?" he said with that small half-lifted grin of his.

"I don't know. It feels different. Don't get me wrong, it feels good to be in the same room as you and Elias again. Like coming home to family. But things have changed," she admitted.

"You're right it feels different. I suppose it should. Last time we were so young, and we were attacking, now we're defending," Kovan said.

"Yes, but it's more than that. It feels like some unknown force is binding us together."

"That's defense. You're always playing catch up, but I know what you mean. Imagine how shocked I was to find Elias on the road. After not seeing him in twenty years."

"You've spent some time with him getting here. Is he . . ." she trailed off not knowing how to ask.

"Crazy?" Kovan finished for her, and Ellaria reluctantly shook her head in agreement. "No. At least I don't think so. He still doesn't say much, but I get a greater sense of calm from him than before," Kovan admitted.

"I sensed that too. He really believes Tali has his power?" she asked and saw how Kovan's entire body sagged slightly.

"Positive," he said, and she noticed his eyes grimace, "In a weird way, I think I must have known it too. Something drew me to her. Sagean's

Light! I should have left her in that market. What was I thinking asking her to come with me?" he said with a tinge of despair.

"She helped you first, right? She trusted you and you trusted her. It's obvious you two have a connection. She is a grown woman Kovan. She's capable of making her own decisions," Ellaria said.

"You're right, she trusted me. She looked me in the eye and helped me, and I dragged her across the world, nearly getting her killed," Kovan said.

"Kovan, stop," she urged him, but she could tell he was closing his ears off to her words. "It's good to care for someone," she finished.

Immediately she saw the muscles in his jaw flex and knew she had struck a nerve. She reached out and clasped his arm. He pivoted and stared at her with such hatred that part of her cowered away. He was the love of her life and they couldn't stand to talk with each other for more than a long walk. Still, she needed to reach him.

"Kovan, I'm not judging you. I know you have spent your life trying to fill the hole," she said, pressing her hand gently over his heart. "That hole that lives in both of us. You have looked in every crevasse and dug through every grain of dust finding people in strife to help. Trying to fill it. I know, because I spent my life trying to build up universities and helping the Guild. It works. The distraction of helping and the feeling of being needed. But it only works for a short time. It's fleeting, because you don't stick around long enough to get hurt. Then the pain returns, and you have to search for something new. Since our daughter died, you have spent your life trying to save others, but you never get close to anyone. You make sure not to let anyone in. Even me. But Tali is different, Tali saved you. You've convinced yourself, so vehemently, that you're not worth anything. This young woman saw you and saved you."

"And I've dragged her into a war!" Kovan burst out.

"Van, I've met her. She is special. Maybe you brought her into danger, but maybe you were meant to. You connected her to Elias, the one person she needed to find."

"Only the most dangerous man in the world."

"Kovan, she saved you and you have saved her. Without Elias's intervention, the power inside her will kill her."

"I'm . . . I'm afraid I might not be able to protect her when she needs me the most. I'm just not the man I was."

"None of us are the people we were. I don't know if you can protect her or not, but I will be there to help you," Ellaria implored.

Kovan lifted his head. For a moment she thought he would keep fighting her, but he put his arms around her and pulled her into his chest instead. He embraced her tightly, and the heat from his neck radiated against her temple. Slowly he pulled back and placed his hands to the sides of her face to cradle her head, just as she remembered him doing long ago. Ellaria rested her own hands over Kovan's. The touch of his skin was soft and strong. Gently, he tilted her chin up and her eyes locked onto his own penetrating gaze. He stared at her deeply and in the silence. Her eyes blinked rapidly. She tried to concentrate on the bright flare of gold at the edges of his dark eyes. Her heart pounded, a remembrance bloomed inside her chest. It was a feeling she had locked away and it tugged at her wall and will. Suddenly, she couldn't breathe as the weight of the last sixteen years stretched before them in a singular moment. Then Kovan blinked, his eyes relaxed and his face broke into a soft grin, as he slipped his hands away from her face.

"I'm sorry Ellaria," he said.

"Me too," was all she could muster.

Kovan took a deep breath and returned to motion, "What I don't get is why are you hanging around the Arcana, playing this role?"

"What role?"

"At being a professor? What's the point?"

Finding her voice again, she said, "I'm going to build an army, stupid."

"Ha, that sounds more like it."

When they got to the Skyline restaurant, the entrance was under a long overhang that was part roof awning and part unfinished deck. The canopy was like a solid slab of stone that floated out over the walkway and ended in an angled point. They walked beneath it and something about the weight of the floor, stagnant above her, incited a reflex to flee. She shivered and shifted her feet restlessly as they waited for Myra to show.

The youngsters were coming up the road and Tali's face beamed brightly, she was obviously excited about something. Ellaria turned to greet them. Kovan turned in the opposite direction. Peering over, she saw the door was opening and Kovan waved them to follow. He talked to the woman holding the door with his face intimately close to hers. Myra had a sharp-angled appearance, with long gloves, and a fine black cloak. Her hood was down, and her eyes were focused on Kovan. Ellaria scrutinized her from afar. She didn't trust her, regardless of what Kovan had said. Once inside, she heard Kovan shut the door and the sound of the bolt locking into place. His confidant swiftly disappeared down the walkways, her hood back up. He remained by the door. Scanning out and waiting to let in Semo and Elias when they arrived. Semo would only be a moment behind them. He hung back to make sure no one had followed. Ellaria turned back to the youngsters who all stood staring at her for direction. Ellaria took a quick estimation of the space and pointed to the middle mezzanine floor in the back. The restaurant had three seating areas on different platforms. An entry level, a middle level in the back and a third floor that switched back to the front. The place looked nearly ready to open, and she suspected someone was probably angry they had missed an opportunity for a grand opening during the New Year celebration.

"Let's go up there. Maybe the crowds outside won't see us," she directed them.

# CHAPTER TWENTY-NINE

## ROGUES OF THE APPARATUS (TALI)

A RESTLESSNESS WAS EATING AT THEIR NERVES. EACH OF THEM SAT fidgeting with their hands, clothes, or in Tali's case the straps to her bag. They waited for everyone to arrive and to hear what Elias had found. Tali was just excited for everyone to be together again. She had never been part of anything before, even if she was unsure what this was. Tali's family's order in Ravenvyre meant that only a certain class of people would associate with her, and among her peers her interests diverged. They would tell her she was straying from her position, from her place in the world. She didn't feel out of place here. She felt she had found what her mother said she was searching for amongst these legends.

Elias finally came through the door, looking disheveled. An intensity to his eyes overtook his typically stoic expression. Kovan locked the door, and they scampered up the steps. Elias took the steps two at a time and his long coat unfurled at his urgent pace. A glimpse of steel at his side. Wade shifted in his seat uncomfortably, and Ellaria stepped in to meet him.

"Elias and Kovan, this is Semo and Wade," Ellaria said, introducing everyone who had yet to meet. Elias put his hand up in a short wave and pulled Ellaria over and whispered something to her and Kovan. Wades eyes blinked in comprehension, he paused from rocking his chair on its back legs.

"Kovan Rainer!" Wade said and slapped Learon on the shoulder.

A single lantern flickered from atop the small table between them and Tali watched as the quiet conversation continued. Growing irritated she looked to her side, and could tell both Learon and Wade were as annoyed as she was. Finally, she spoke up.

"Does the entire group get to take part tonight?" she asked. They turned in unison, recognized the dejected faces of their audience, and dispersed to sit down around the light. They now looked across from one another in a haphazard circle.

"Sorry, Tali, we were discussing the oddity of the red sun. Elias was just telling us that Anchor's Point is consumed in flames," Ellaria said.

"Oh. Oh no, still?" Tali asked.

"Yes, it's the same blaze we witnessed. It has been raging for four days. They lost most of the city. I fear the hour has come to choose our paths," Elias said.

"What do you mean?" Learon asked.

"I mean, now is the time to walk away. No one here will think any less of you. I must leave tonight. My path ends with the Sagean and his men. Are you staying or going?" Elias said.

"Wait, who are you exactly?" Wade asked, looking at the others for information.

"Wade, this is not the time," Ellaria said.

"What about me?" Tali asked.

"I have promised to train you Tali, and I mean to keep that promise. You must come with me until you have gotten past the surge, then you can choose the best path for you. It could be a year from now or it could be a day. I can't be sure. Have you seen any signs."

"This morning. I made something happen," she admitted.

"I'm confused, what is going on?" Wade asked.

"Wade, this is Elias Qudin," Tali said.

"Qudin as in - wait, He's Qudin?" Wade said, in disbelief.

"Yes," Learon and Tali said together.

"The Quantum Man, this guy?" Wade said pointing at Elias while leaning back in his chair, "Sure."

"Yes," Ellaria said annoyed.

Wade looked around at everyone in doubt until a spark of lightning ruptured between Elias's eyes, crossing the bridge of his nose before setting into his irises and disappearing. Wade fell back, stumbling to the ground. Semo recoiled like he'd seen a venomous snake.

"Now that, that is settled, back to the question at hand. Elias is right, the time of pretending you're safe is over. If you want out now is the time. I just learned that the squad hunting Qudin will be returning to Adalon tonight," Ellaria looked pointedly at Learon and Wade awaiting their decision. Both of them nodded yes. Ellaria took it as their intention to stay. "Right let's move on," she continued, and turned to

Elias, "I get you want to find the stone. Did you find anything at the excavation?"

"We found a mural depicting the Tempest Stone, and there were also some sigils or ancient text that I copied down to translate."

"Why would you think you could translate the Elegan Language?" Ellaria asked.

"Because of this," Elias said, pulling an old, tattered book from his bag, "I found this journal about a year ago and have been able to decipher some of it."

Ellaria's eyes lit up. She took the journal from him delicately with both hands.

"You're saying you have translated this journal. You have cracked a cypher to the Elegan language? No one has done that in two thousand years. How sure are you about the translation?" she asked, flipping through the journal.

"It led me to a discovery. I don't pretend to have a gift for code breaking. Most of the passages are confusing. The nuance in the language is not in the words but the many meanings behind any one symbol."

"And you have found something with this?" Ellaria said, her eyes growing wide.

"Yes. I have found two Acuber's Wave Gates. They are traveling gates and I have reason to believe there are more, and that one of them will lead me to the stone," Elias told them.

"Acuber's Wave Gates?" Kovan asked.

"Where are they?" Ellaria asked in a desperate and penetrating tone, clearly determined to know everything Elias knew.

"I found the first one partially buried amongst decaying ruins, near the Cracked Lands on Merinde. Once I activated it, I traveled to a mountain peak just beyond Hawks Perch," Elias explained.

"So that's how you got up there?" Learon said, as intrigued as the rest of them.

"Yes."

"And you thought you might find one at Ash Field?" Ellaria speculated.

"I did, but that city – it's not old enough. Both gates I found were inside very old sites, ruins that were crumbling and near dust. I don't think Ash Field is the lost city of Ashalon. Just an old city that was destroyed when the Sagean Order took over," Elias explained.

"Where is Ashalon then? Text's say it lies at the heart of the great bay. If not Ash Field, then where?" Ellaria asked.

"I think it's here."

"Here in Adalon?" Tali asked. Trying to get a handle on what Elias was telling them.

"Below the city," Elias confirmed, shaking his head yes. "Being back here again, seeing how high they stack the buildings. I started thinking it was a possibility. That's what we do. We build on top of the past. I know there are catacombs under Ravenvyre. I've been inside them. Maybe the same exists here?"

"These gates, how fast did you travel through them?" Tali asked.

"It was instantaneous."

"How is that possible?" Learon asked, amazed.

"I don't know," Elias admitted, and they all sat frozen, stewing on the revelation of Elias's gates for a moment.

"Elias, I was here twenty years ago and saw the foundation dig for the spires. Those treadwheel cranes went deep into the ground. I'm not saying you're wrong, but where would we start?" Ellaria asked.

"We can start by looking in the oldest buildings in the city. Maybe the Arena," Learon offered.

"That won't work," Kovan said, "The Prime is keeping a close watch on Ellaria."

"I can hide my movements from those bonemen," she said, exhaling in annoyance.

"There's no time, we need a way out of this city tonight. Whether the Sagean choses tomorrow or tonight or next month to make his appearance doesn't matter. If the Luminance Squad that has been hunting me is back in Adalon, I can only assume that they know I'm in the city. I need to leave. I have some ideas where other gates might be. Which is why I need to get back to my home in Polestis. I need to translate these new symbols I found. I have other books there and extensive maps," Elias submitted.

"What do the symbols look like that you found in the temple?" Ellaria asked. Elias pulled a rolled-up piece of parchment out of his bag and handed it to her. She looked them over while the rest watched her.

"I recognize these!" Ellaria said.

"You do?" Elias asked.

"Yes, they look like the symbols in the Alchemist's Codex."

"There are no symbols like this in the codex."

"Yes, there are, and they look like this."

"How come I've never seen them?"

"They're only on the original. Any sigil the Guild did not understand, they had redacted from the publication."

"What? The entire book is about sigils and forces," Kovan asked.

"Right, but these were different. Their art and design was without explanation."

"We need that book," Kovan said.

"Where is it?" Elias said.

"The archives restricted section, but I can't check it out without raising an alarm," Ellaria said.

"What if we stole it?" Wade said.

"I like this one," Kovan said, pacing behind them.

"I thought you might," Ellaria said, and she turned back to Elias, "It would be difficult, but not impossible. The security is fairly minimal, and I know it well. But it is essential we also find out what happened to Danehin. Somehow everything is tied to that. I've made promises and now his daughter Dalliana is requesting I sail across the Anamic Ocean to be help her."

"Are you going?" Kovan asked, frozen in his steps.

"After I have found the Tempest Stone and searched for Danehin."

"Then Elias, Tali and I, will leave tonight for Aquom and see what we can find out about this Meroha Uvari from the log you found. You four figure out how to get this codex from the archives. Then we will all meet in Polestis," Kovan said.

"I'm going too," Semo blurted out.

"No," Ellaria said sharply.

"Why?" Semo asked eyeing her defiantly.

"Dalliana's orders were for you to stay by my side," Ellaria said.

Semo looked ready to argue, but Ellaria stared him down– meeting his deadly scowl with her own resolute gaze.

"Fine!" Semo relented. He crossed his arms and stood away from the circle, brooding. If he wasn't so intimidating, Tali would swear he was pouting.

"Aquom is a jumbled and complicated city. To find one boat in a city of boats might be impossible. If only we knew someone who could help," Elias said, punctuating the last part toward Kovan's direction. Ellaria locked eyes with him too, and Kovan withered under her gaze.

"Fine, I'll talk to him," he huffed out. "He will not be happy to see me though," He remarked and sat back into his chair.

"Do you owe him money?" Elias asked.

"Money? No. At least I don't think so," Kovan replied.

"A woman, then?" Ellaria suggested.

"No," Kovan answered quickly.

"Then, what's the issue?" Ellaria followed.

"He's been holding a favor over my head for years. He wants me to help him find a blue fulgurite crystal," Kovan explained.

Tali, tired of looking back and forth, interrupted them, "Wait, who are you three talking about, and what's a fulgurite crystal?" she asked.

"My brother Tavish," Kovan said.

"You have a brother?" Tali said, surprised.

"He's not blood, but as good as. We grew up together, running around the sunken roads of Aquom. As for fulgurite crystals, they are crystals that form from lightning hitting the territh," he told her.

"Can't Elias just, you know. Make one?" Learon suggested.

"Hey that's a great idea," Kovan said smiling and looking to Elias to gauge his willingness.

"No," Elias said flatly.

"Come on," Kovan pleaded.

"I can't, I could spend a month trying and not see a crystal form. Also, they're usually white or gold. A blue one would only occur from lightning hitting the sandstone in the south of Nahadon, near the black shore," Elias said.

"Yeah, that's the one he wants," Kovan said.

"So dragon glass. You owe him a piece of dragon glass!" Elias said flabbergasted.

"Yeah, blue fulgurite," Kovan confirmed.

"No one travels to the black shore," Elias said.

"Maybe, we'll get lucky when we find him. Knowing him, he will be in some sort of trouble he'll need our help with," Kovan offered.

"So let me get this straight. To find the missing King, we need help from a man who may or not be your brother, to find a boat, that may or may not be a boat. But we first need to locate a piece of lightning glass that a luminary, who can create lightning, says is impossible to get. While we also have to steal an ancient text you may or may not be able to translate, so we can find a magic gate that will enable us to instantly travel around the world. All in order to find a stone, only half of you believe exists. Because we need it to stop an evil Sagean Lord with an endless army of Bonemen to prevent a war, and save a princess, across the ocean?" Wade said half-jokingly.

"We might not *need* the glass," Kovan said.

"Also, I never said it was a *magic* gate," Elias corrected.

"I'm sorry. Not magic, a *wave* gate," Wade said.

"So, in or out kid?" Elias asked.

"I'm in. I'm just trying to keep up."

"Right," Ellaria said refocussing the group. "After you find out what there is to discover in Aquom, get word to us and we will meet you in Polestis."

"Get word to you how?" Kovan asked.

"I know how," Tali said excitedly. She had almost forgotten, "Three communicators, just like you designed," she said and held them up. Then, she got up and handed the three out to Ellaria, Elias, and Kovan. Elias looked at them quizzically, "Well, not exactly like you designed. We thought they would work better as a sort of double-faced wristwatch," She clarified.

Each one of them manipulated the watches as soon as their hands got a hold of them. Kovan's suspicion had him holding it like it might catch fire. Elias swiveled the skeletal top watch face out to the side to reveal the metal communicator beneath. His eyes flickered and a calculating grin spread across his face. Ellaria seemed to judge it on aesthetics.

"These are . . ." Elias stammered.

"Amazing," Ellaria concluded Elias's sentence, "Will they work?" she asked Elias skeptically.

Elias turned the watch over and about in his hands. Inspecting the finer details of the construction. "You inscribed the underside like I dictated?" he asked Tali, looking up to her where she stood.

"Yes, everything you asked. All to your exact specifications. Even the crystal infused liquid pool that the pellets sit in," she confirmed for him.

"Perfect," he said, and he pulled three fountain pens from an inside pocket and placed them on the table in front of them. The pens were silver with copper bands equally spaced and intricate symbols carved into the sides. He motioned for Kovan and Ellaria to hand him the other two watches. Then he kneeled near the table and organized everything into a circle. From the corner of her eye, she could see Wade and Learon getting out of their seats to see what Elias was doing. They all watched while he put his hand out over the arrangement of trinkets. Tali's eyes opened wide before the others as she saw the air vibrate and ripple out in waves from his fingers. A soft glow emerged from all the individual pieces at once. She heard Wade's breath catch when the clock faces spun. The glow disappeared. Elias reached for the pieces on the table and handed a watch and pen to Tali. A second set he handed to Ellaria; whose eyes were wide with anticipation.

"Anyone have a piece of parchment?" Elias asked, and Ellaria fetched one out of her bag. He took it gratefully and placed it on the table. Then looked up at Tali.

"Write a message on here," he instructed her.

She leaned over and wrote a few words. The instant she lifted the pen, a blue glow emitted from all three of the devices through the watch face at the same time. She stepped back unintentionally startled and then swiveled the top face out to see the communicator work below.

Unlike the exposed thin calibrated gears and flutters of the clock, the communicators were stagnant most of the time. Now it glowed blue and slowly the tiny pellets inside tracked through the liquid, before settling into place. Gradually they formed the words she had just written. They held in place briefly, before they fell away like grains of sand beneath the plate at the bottom of the dial. It was an astonishing sight. No one had ever seen anything like these devices, and Tali had a swelling sense of pride for what she had helped create.

"Wow!" both Learon and Wade remarked in a hushed tone.

"These are perfect," Ellaria said, impressed.

"They helped too," Tali said, pointing to the boys.

"Well done," Elias said to them.

Kovan rose from his seat and walked over to the nearly finished bar at the front. He searched for a moment and returned with his hands full. He had found something in a box nearby that pleased him. He placed a collection of cups on the table and uncorked an amber tinted bottle. He poured the dark liquid out and handed a cup to everyone. The pungency of spice and a fermented alcohol smell attacked Tali's nose. When everyone had a cup, he raised his own, "To the future, and to the stand and let the Light be damned." he said proudly. Tali looked at them all in reverence. Forty years was a long time and had allowed the people to forget and to dismiss these war veterans as faded warriors, simply myths whose time had passed. Only in their most tired moments had Tali glimpsed the toll of life on any of them. They stood before her energized and powerful, and Tali smiled, her awe of them had yet to subside.

They all drank, and the warm liquid, full of spices of clove and cinnamon, attacked her tongue instantly. It was sweet and slightly thick, and it burned going down her throat. Tali started coughing from the strength of it, and her eyes instantly watered. The others laughed at her flailing and she tried to smile but couldn't stop coughing long enough to do so. When she could finally speak again, she looked to Kovan next to her.

"Is this what it was like in the Resistance?" She asked.

"No," Kovan answered. "There was a clear enemy before the last war. You either supported the Sagean Empire and the collective way or you didn't."

"If things get worse . . ." Tali started to say.

"When," Kovan corrected her.

"When things get worse, are you afraid there won't be anyone to fight?"

"No. According to what Ellaria has told me, the first Sagean's took over through bloodshed and destruction. We have burnt ruins and a lost history to prove that. I think this time they are taking a different strategy. I'm afraid the new Sagean will strip this world of all it has gained so slowly that people won't know there is a war to fight."

"But they can't just steal our freedom away right from under us."

"Can't they?" Elias chimed in, "Look around, how quickly this world has taken its freedom for granted. For the past forty years this has been a world lost in the mist. Under the Sagean, the people worked and were beaten down. For centuries, a frustration of individual expression built up. The war was that frustration coming to a head. Now the insecurity and inequity of this new reality has quickly created a deep mistrust. The Prime Commander will unite this world through fear and hatred," Elias said.

"But aren't the people happy, safe, and thriving? Why would they follow a new Sagean?" Wade asked.

"People's first instinct is to protect themselves. We all live insecure in the reality of our own mortality. It's an ever-present fear that lives inside all of us. Some can control it, but for others it can dominate their actions. This is why fear is the first poison. All the Prime has to do is make the people believe they are going to lose what they have, and their own fear will lead them to hand everything over willingly to the new Sagean."

"Then don't we need to contact everyone we know and warn them?" Learon asked.

"At the very least we should start contacting old allies. In order to do that, we would need to know if the Whisper Chain is working," Ellaria said.

"I could go to the Adalon office tonight?" Tali offered.

They looked at each other for a moment, debating the merits of her suggestion wordlessly between them.

"Tali, we don't want to put you in more danger than you already are," Ellaria said.

"I'll be fine. I have the cloak I can . . ." she paused before finishing her thought. Her eyes ballooned to nearly bursting from her head. An image of the woman that had let them inside the restaurant surfaced in her mind. Her cloak wasn't just unique, it was a Whisper Chain's black.

"What is it? What's wrong?" Kovan asked.

"Nothing. I don't know. That lady that let us inside and rushed out of here, did you know she was in the Whisper Chain?"

"No, no way," Kovan said.

"She didn't tell you?" Ellaria asked agitated.

"No," Kovan said.

"Is she trustworthy?" Elias asked.

"More than some, less than others," Kovan said, "Are you sure?" he asked Tali.

"Yes. My trainer warned me not to wear mine because it would give me away. Before, I didn't understand how. It's just a black cloak. I just figured it out. There is a small symbol sewn into the back of the cloak behind the hood. I never noticed it before but I'm positive that the woman's cloak had the symbol," she said.

Elias stood quickly and bounded up the third flight of steps to overlook the bridge walkway out front. Kovan looked to Ellaria, who simply rolled her eyes. Semo, alerted by Elias dashing away, moved in closer. "What's happening?" he asked.

"Kovan's *friend* sold us out," Ellaria said.

Kovan grunted and went to check out the front entrance. Tali shared a worried look with Wade and Learon. They had been double-crossed and now sat in the trap. Tali lightly grasped to the hope that she was wrong.

# CHAPTER THIRTY

## ESCAPE FROM ADALON (ELIAS)

ELIAS SCANNED OUT INTO THE DARK NIGHT. THE SKYLINE WAS FULL OF steam stacks across the scattered rooftops, puffing away. The wisps of drifting smoke rose, under lit by the soft orange glow from the electric lights. At first glance, the bridge looked deserted, but then as his eyes adjusted, he could see the small shifts in layered shadows. He expelled a trickle of energy. Using it to search out to get an idea of how many people surrounded the building. Like before, he tried to sense the circulating charge of their guns. Two groups of three men squads stood motionless across the bridge, followed by a four-man squad to the south, awaiting a signal he presumed. There was something odd about them. Elias couldn't sense the men's energy and he thought he should be able to, and they were carrying some sort of larger capacity charged weapon. He searched further. Shuffling above the building was a set of bonemen crossing over from a nearby rooftop. Elias's mind snapped back, and he scrambled down the stairs to the others. Their heads popping up in attention to his reappearance. Kovan came bounding back from the front door.

"I can't see anything, you?" Kovan asked Elias. His pulsator already gripped in his right hand.

"They're out there," Elias said and then explained what he had sensed.

"Is there a back way out?" Ellaria asked.

"Not a back way, but a down way. The ventilation shaft room connects all the floors. From the ground to the roof," Kovan suggested and looked to Semo, "Semo, you can lead the others out that way. Elias and I will, well, we will do what we do," Kovan concluded.

"Kovan," Ellaria said in a desperate voice.

"We will be fine. We can handle some bonemen. Besides, there's only eight."

"More like twelve," Elias corrected.

"Twelve," —he corrected himself—"Wait, twelve?" he double-checked, looking over to Elias.

"Yes. Four bonemen are waiting to move in from the south and don't forget Kovan, we need to protect Tali at the same time," Elias said.

"You can handle so many?" Semo asked Kovan skeptically

"By myself?" Kovan clarified. "Maybe. With Elias? Definitely."

"Once you get out. Contact us on these," Ellaria said, tapping her watch. Elias and Ellaria each got one, and Kovan gave Tali the third. Still, Ellaria was reluctant to leave, "And please keep Tali safe. If I recall you both like to charge into danger without thinking. On second thought, Tali keep these two from doing anything stupid."

"I will," Tali assured her.

They found the internal air shaft for the building. As with most of the gigantic buildings, the shaft was a small room with a metal stairway snaking around various pipes and venting crisscrossing in and out. Semo led them down and with Learon and Wade close behind. Ellaria lingered to say goodbye.

"We just found each other again, and you're both leaving. There is something so familiar about you both leaving me to go off on an adventure, but I don't recall it feeling like this. Like we're being torn from something," Ellaria said.

"It won't be long, and you'll be rummaging through my vault in Polestis," Elias said. He hugged her and moved back to the room. Through the still slightly ajar door he could see Kovan and Ellaria talking intensely. He was so close to both of them he never felt awkwardly out of place. Even though they had a relationship, in a lot of ways he had a friendship with each that the other didn't. Like he was the front wheel of a barrel cart. When their goodbyes were over, Kovan closed the door and came back looking stone faced as usual.

"All right, Quantum Man. How do you want to do this?" Kovan asked, and Elias reiterated his plan and the three of them moved into position.

Elias and Tali slid out onto the raised patio above the entrance. Slowly creeping out in the darkness. There was a larger crowd gathered on the raised walkways, all of them trying to find a spot to see the New Year's fireworks.

The door clanged and rattled slightly from below. Elias listened to the soft crunch of the key in the lock and Kovan stepped away from the door. After only two steps, the bonemen squads from across the bridge scrambled in through a small group of people. Elias heard the clapping stomps of the various sets of boots slapping the stone ground in a rush. Then a roar of yelling burst from multiple sources.

"Stop where you are!"

"Throw your weapons down!"

Elias moved swiftly to the edge of the roof with Tali following behind. Hoping the yells and chaos masked the sound of his own footfalls. He could faintly hear Kovan replying to them, antagonizing them from the sounds of it. The six soldiers were surrounding Kovan, but they hadn't signaled the south squad yet. What Elias was planning next would bring them running.

"I said drop your weapon to the ground, now!"

That seemed like his cue. Elias jumped from the roof overhang, turned in the air to face the surrounding bonemen and landed behind them with a concussion of force. A blasting shock wave threw all seven men high and hurdling out like leaves in a gust of wind. The ones that were closest to Elias flew into and through the front glass of the restaurant, with a shattering crash and cascade of shards spraying wide. Kovan had braced for it but was still sprawled out near the building facade, groaning. Elias's body momentarily reverberated, and his bones ached from being rattled. The crowd that had backed away when the authority came, but now they were all hollering and talking, unsure what they had just seen was real. The closer ones to the scene were picking themselves off the ground.

"It's Qudin!"

"It's Qudin Lightweaver, look!"

Elias recovered, caught his breath the best he could, and stepped from the cracked crater he found himself in. The onlookers continued to call out to him.

"Tali," Elias hollered up. She looked down from the patio platform above.

"Ready?" She asked.

"Jump."

Tali jumped and Elias helped her safely land, then they rushed to check on Kovan. The south squad would have heard the collision by now and be on their way. Elias depleted a lot of his energy in the expelling wave and was sucking air.

"Kovan," Elias said, reaching his friend and helping lift him to his feet. Kovan's eyes squeezed tightly, and he groaned again, "Can you walk?" Elias asked while inspecting him.

"Where's my gun?" Kovan grunted. Elias spotted it a short distance away and retrieved it for Kovan. When he returned, Kovan was standing more secure on his own feet and handed the weapon over. Somewhere close, a slight hum droned to life. Both of them jerked their heads to the sound. Elias's hand clutched onto Kovan's sleeve and he pulled him off his feet just as a screaming red glowing bolt hit the wall where Kovan previously stood.

The four-man squad from the south had arrived. They approached shoulder to shoulder, with the distance between them spreading out as they got closer. The crowd scattered further away. The bonemen seemed to hold their assault. The site of the scattered soldiers on the ground had them reassessing the situation. The lead soldier raised his eruptor rifle and fired again. This time Elias anticipated the shot. As the charged tungsten bolt hurdled through the air, time slowed for Elias. He could feel the energy of the bullet and raising his hand up, he caught it. Recoiling in the momentum and absorbing the energy at the same instant. The thermal energy, electric energy, and even the kinetic energy of the bullet's propulsion was all now his. The slug still pierced the skin of his palm, partly imbedding itself there, and he cursed that he wasn't as fast as he used to be.

From the group of soldiers, he heard one exclaim, "It's him!"

Kovan and Elias shared a look and watched as the squad of soldiers raised their guns. Kovan moved in front of Tali. One of the soldier's weapons was larger than even the blast rifles. The heft of the thing was clear, as the man holding it slumped slightly in a wide stance, with the gun at his waist. Elias didn't wait to find out what it could do. He channeled his replenished energy into the supporting beams above that held the cantilever floor. First, as a heat energy to weaken the metal and then a kinetic surge ruptured the beam in half with a loud crack that echoed out. The entire framework was compromised and sagged immediately. As it came down, Elias saw Kovan's face break into an odd smile. With the building collapsing, they turned to retreat. A bloom of bright light flooded the area, as the guns from the squad erupted a firestorm of charged bolts at them. With the floor crashing behind them like a shield, they ran as fast as possible to the north. They moved swiftly along the bridge and onto an adjoining roof. They scaled the fire escape stairs down to the street level. The gunfire and crashing building had created enough ruckus to cloak the others' escape but also raised an alarm in the city. Greencoats would flood the area any minute. In order to escape the city, they would need to circle back to the south and find a ship off the Crescent Pier before dawn. The bonemen now knew they were hunting Qudin Lightweaver and would probably move to close the pier by first light.

At the street level, the people gathered there on the sidewalks were all staring up to see what the source of calamity had been. Elias and Kovan slowed to a more natural, but still quick pace. They weaved around onlookers pointing up to the area of the bridge they had just descended from. Then the fireworks of the New Year exploded in the sky all around.

None of them bothered to look back. They had to keep moving. The unmistakable clap and clomp of greencoats galloping up the road made them pause for a moment, but the greencoats passed them by.

Somehow, they slipped through the city undeterred. The fireworks eventually died away. The trek had taken most of the night and they crossed from the mainland over to the Crescent on one of the merchant bridges instead of the main road. Kovan scrambled down the docks ahead to work his magic and find them a ship out of Adalon. Elias slowly crept around the outer banks, looking for the soldiers he knew would be patrolling. The harbor was starting to come alive with activity as the sky was brightening with the morning. Kovan headed toward the smaller marina, while Elias and Tali searched the wharf and the larger cargo ships. Elias climbed the large river rock breakwater mole to cross over to the wharf, when he saw the two teams of soldiers dimly lit and moving on the pier in the distance. The hanging lanterns of the walk were nearly all burned out, but the gleam of the metal mesh armor the bonemen wore was unmistakable, as was their uniform patrol movements. Elias crouched back on the stone bank, he pulled Tali down and out of sight. Together they drifted back. A crunch of small gravel under boots nearby reached his ear just over the sound of lapping waves, and Elias saw a patrol on the top of the mound. These were unmistakably greencoats on patrol. Elias slunk away from the breakwater mound and quickly hid low in the first slipway ramp he found. Tali followed every movement exactly. The seawater slowly rose to their feet and fell away.

After the patrol passed by, they started back toward the marina, hoping Kovan had more success. At the second jetty, he heard Kovan whisper out to them.

"Elias, Elias over here," Kovan breathed.

Elias stalked closer to the sound and found Kovan crouching near a fishing vessel. "Any luck?" he asked

"I found a ship heading to Aquom. But they're still loading up. The captain said he would take us."

"How long till they sail?" Elias asked.

"Within the hour, why?"

"We may not have long. The wharf is crawling with snakes."

"Then let's see if we can get them moving faster."

Kovan led Elias and Tali to the ship and aboard to speak with the captain. The captain was busy scanning a ledger and accounting supplies when they came upon him. He had a single billed cap that ended in a forward point and a set of goggles around his neck with emerald green lenses.

"Captain Morales," Kovan said.

"Have you decided to come aboard the I'Varrin then?" the captain asked. His gravel filled voice matching his gruff appearance.

"Yes. My friends and I would also like to help if we can," Kovan said, and the captain finally looked up from his work. He had streaks of age lines like cracked territh unfolding from his eyes and beard covered full cheeks. He took a moment scrutinizing Elias and Tali. He scratched his beard and pointed to a man stacking cargo.

"Barton can put you to work," the captain said and dismissed them.

The captain's man escorted them to the dock side shanty where crates of bait, tackle, and passenger provisions were stacked high in four off kilter piles. They got after it quickly and without complaint. Both grateful to have passage, but also an authentic disguise to any quick observation while they waited to ship out. When the sun broke on the horizon line, the ship floated out to sea. They stood on deck watching the smaller boats being moored into the marina. Instead of heading directly south, the ship turned up toward the wharf warehouses.

"What's going on? Why are we heading to the wharfs?" Elias asked Kovan. Kovan hissed under his breath and charged up to the second deck to ask the captain. He returned and by his ashen face Elias could tell it was bad news.

"They have orders to check in at the Sea Tower before they can head out."

"Is that normal?" Elias asked.

"Normal as of a few weeks ago. Still, it's troublesome," Kovan admitted.

"Ideas?"

"Nothing that would pass inspection. He agreed to say we're new hands if he's asked."

"Let's hope they don't ask?"

"Exactly."

The ship slowed as it reached the lands' end tidal point of sea swept rocks. A series of staggered masses of rock swells, portions of which were submerged in the morning's high tide, formed the pier's northern tip. The spearhead shaped Sea Tower lighthouse stood tall there, like it had grown unnaturally out of the sharp rock chiseled land. They spotted the bonemen immediately. There were five stalking around the yard. One with a face shield that brightly reflected the sunlight, stood beside the port inspector at the dock head. Elias took him to be a commander. Both men were impatiently waiting to come aboard once the ship stopped.

Captain Morales was there to greet the inspectors as they stepped onto the deck. Elias scanned the shoreline, contemplating strategies to escape. Tali spotted a cargo pile of confiscated goods and pointed it out to Elias. He liked the idea and nudged Kovan. After a few seconds, Kovan spotted what Elias was trying to show him and exhaled an agitated moan, confirming what they all suspected was in the crates.

The inspector and the captain spoke briefly, before he submitted his ledger and manifest for review. The inspector scanned the decks and seemed satisfied. He stepped to the gangway to leave and the bonemen commander followed. They breathed a sigh of relief. The ship had passed its inspection and was pulling away from the dock when the inspector and the bonemen commander got into a heated exchange. The commander reached for his weapon and Elias reacted. Filled with the sun's radiant energy, he focused it, and redirected it, into the confiscated supply mound. There was yelling and more men came running. The commander turned to run the length of the dock toward the ship. His eyes were fixed on Elias and Kovan's location when the explosion happened. The heap of crates concussed and detonated from Elias's energy surge. The sound compressed in a double boom and was deafening. The force of the blast tipped the ship steeply in the water, nearly toppling it, catapulting the men on the field out into the sea. There was a panic on board, but the captain hollered out orders to secure the ship and refocused the crew's attention. Behind them they could see the blast had provided the possibility of escape and given them a head start on the open water. The people and soldiers ashore at the tidal point scrambled to put out lingering fires. Gradually the scene faded into the background along with the city of Adalon beyond it. The morning sun reflecting brightly off the buildings transitioned to waves of sparkling light.

# CHAPTER THIRTY-ONE

## AQUOM (KOVAN)

THE SHIP DOCKED IN THE SOUTHEAST OF AQUOM AT THE MORNING Harbor. Captain Morales had expertly navigated through the Sea of Sorrows and the shattered Zuvo islands. A treacherous course even for the most skilled and experienced skippers to traverse. Technically, Aquom was just a collection of islands, and the Zuvo Islands on the eastern reach were merely an extension of Aquom. It was said that Aquom was shattered by the gods long ago and now slowly drifted out to sea. Zuvo plotted that spread. Even the places where the expanse between land masses grew widest, was dangerous. The wrong course could capsize most ships or puncture the hull. The seas between the islands were relatively stable waters, but there was so much unknown rock below the surface it was much safer to simply sail around. Which is what most ships did. The simpler way was through the Neck, but the main canal was heavily taxed.

To navigate through you had to know the route and the tides by heart. There were numerous shoals hidden in the high tides. Some were sandbars, but some were gravel packed and consisted of large rock and coral. Capitan Morales had obviously memorized a way and showed uncommon expertise in steering his ship, the I'Varrin through.

Kovan could tell Elias was contemplating an excuse to get inside the Captain's chambers to see his personal map of the area. Kovan suspected it was more detailed than most. Cartography was still a relatively new profession. The Sagean Empire had simply reproduced the most commonly accepted maps for general use. These maps were in some instances completely erroneous. Even after the New World was discovered, for two hundred years it failed to appear on any map until after the fall of the Empire. Since then, new maps had been commissioned and printed by the Guild. Still, the most exacting and intricately detailed were scarce. The finest maps remained in private collections. Their creators kept them close, and they became like family secrets. Only blood gained you access to them, either inherited or spilled.

Kovan knew no one more captivated by maps than Elias, he coveted them. It was a side effect of his explorer's obsession. Witnessing the I'Varrin slip around the shores of the Sea of Sorrows unscathed, was confirmation that Capitan Morales possessed one of the best maps of the Tavillorean coast and possibly the entire Anamic Ocean. No doubt Elias recognized this as well, but he never pushed to find out more. A surprising transformation as far as Kovan could tell. Maybe his friend had changed.

The entire voyage on the I'Varrin had taken two full days. Luckily, they were able to lend their now callused hands to the crew's efforts and reduced the fee for their passage. The morning of the third day greeted them with a brilliant sunrise. Both Tali and Elias were already awake and on deck, when Kovan had managed to pull himself off the pile of grass he was using as a bed below deck. They had been rising early each morning to meditate together and Elias was intent on giving her instruction whenever they had a free moment. The ship never betrayed a change in tide or weather, and he slept soundly for the first time in a month. When they pulled into the Morning Harbor and disembarked, Captain Morales seemed sad to say goodbye to Tali but glad to be rid of them. Kovan had the sense that without Tali, Captain Morales would have handed them over in Adalon.

At the harbor they rambled around until they were able to commission a smaller cadowa ship to tender them the rest of the way into Aquom. The small vessel slowly passed through the slim canals toward the interior main city. Cadowas were slender bodied boats with one main sail that sliced the sky in a towering sharp point. The triangular sail was roughly twice as tall as the boat was long. The thin body shape made them ideal for navigating along the canals but handling the sea craft was tricky and required a long sweep to balance and steer.

They quickly drifted from the outer banks in the south, where the waters were full of weeds and large seagrass spread to the shacks on the outskirts of the splintered city. When the palms and dripping oaks became thick the shoreline quickly turned into an endless snaking dock. It served as the water's edge sidewalk. There, seaside walls were water stained and worn. Kovan knew the waters well, but the richer center of the city was obvious to anyone, once the wood docks disappeared altogether for the cut stone piers.

Aquom was bisected from north to south by a main canal, called the Neck. The west side was referred to as the Stone Bank. The buildings there were rubblestone and the streets cobbled. The east end of the city was called The Narrows. The wood structures there were stacked high and interconnected. In some spots, they tottered and tilted, with makeshift support poles partially submerged in the waters. Building after building was built atop one another, often over the waterway streets. Rickety bridges of wood and rope criss crossed buildings and wood stairways.

That was where they would find Tavish. As far as Kovan knew, he was still making a living as a wrecker, scavenging the many shipwrecks the Sea of Sorrows birthed.

Kovan let the driver know to stop. Using the sweep, the driver slowed their drift and maneuvered the vessel gently against the stone walk. They paid the man and set out into the Narrows.

THE FRAYED DOOR WAS TILTED CROOKED IN ITS FRAME. THEY STOOD huddled and surveyed the storefront with suspicion, but Kovan was sure this was the place. The entrance to the Diver's Catch was tucked behind a twisted alleyway with a simple sign swinging on two chain links attached to a rough-cut wood standoff above their heads. The cobbled path that led them there was grungy and wet with plots of puddles and a grim sludge in the stone gaps. It had been many years since Kovan had been in this part of the world, and he hadn't missed it much. Especially not the thick, ever-present smell like everything around you had been ruined by water and left to rot.

Elias stood stoically behind him with Tali surveying everything behind Elias. Kovan stepped forward and rapped loudly on the door. A small light through the grim crusted window steadily grew as someone inside approached the door. After a moment, it opened slightly and the kid inside stood a foot below the threshold. The floor there was sunken below the street level and Kovan found himself speaking to the top of the kid's black hair. The kid hardly bothered to even glance up at them, and instead preferring to stare at their boots.

"Yes?" the young man said in a slow, whimpered voice.

"Are you open?" Kovan asked hesitantly.

"No, we're closed. Come back tomorrow," he answered, and he slowly moved to shut the door. Kovan placed his hand around the edge to halt its movement.

"Is Tavish here?" Kovan asked in a stronger tone.

The young man looked up finally and took a moment to judge the peculiar cohorts standing before him. Kovan could tell he had a fair collection of blades on him. From the look of the back of his thin coat, there were two twin reapers tied to his back belt, along with the dirk that was obviously strapped to his right hip side. No doubt he contemplated drawing them to intimidate their departure, but the kid must have thought better of it. Instead, he drew the door open for them to come inside. He locked it after they had stepped down from the street.

Shuffling inside they found themselves standing in a short hall, where what insignificant light there was reflected off the cramped wood walls. The young man squeezed past them and motioned for them to follow. His small tin lantern held chest high. Kovan could see when he passed that he was older than he had first thought, and definitely beyond schooling age. His face was scarred all over by small gashes, probably from diving and some certainly from steel. The Narrows were notorious for knife fights among the lowest order rabble. Waifs like him were common in Aquom, striving to make their way with odd jobs and taking on whatever work that came their way, often nefarious and illegal. To survive on the clustered jetties of the Narrows was to live a hard life.

"Follow me," The young man said.

From the short hall, the room opened up but only to reveal a cramped space consisting of two lanes of trinket-filled aisles. A vast collection of useless and priceless scraps alike was scatter stacked on shelves or hanging on ropes. They walked beyond the knickknacks to a door in the side wall.

Inside, there were large tables and a man working under a hanging lantern at a stand-up bench. He was impassively cleaning a piece of metal with a filthy-stained cloth that looked like it was once white. At their sudden presence, Tavish looked up from his work. His initial shock was masked quickly and replaced by a grimace of exhaustion.

"Thanks, Ludoc, you can go home. See you tomorrow," he said to the young man and then turned back to his cleaning. He lowered a small lens from a band around his head to inspect the finer details, "You look old, Van," Tavish remarked.

"I am old."

"That's true. Did you bring me my dragon glass?" Tavish asked in his gruff voice.

"No."

"You know brother that word of your exploits in Adalon has already spread?"

They looked at one another, but it was not terribly surprising. Shiplocked for days, they had not thought about news of their flight from the city outpacing them on the wire.

Tavish noticed their quick exchange and smiled. He placed his things down and stood up.

"Ha, how in the thorny hell are you, brother?" Tavish said and Kovan put his arm out for greeting. Tavish took it and pulled him into a quick hug, patting Kovan's back and laughing in a deep barreled bark.

"It's been a long time," Tavish said to Elias.

"It has. How's the wreckage diving business lately?"

"Busy. Some new ships in the water. These captained ships for the Prime are headless. If they're going to take over the world, they'll need some better seadogs, I can tell you. These shodders drive ships aground daily. Which is good for business. Before the Prime took over the Coalition was trying to get a piece of my action. So, what do you need Van? I assume you're still the desperateer you have always been, extremely desperate to come here. You know you're not as charmed as you think, brother."

"We're looking for a ship that would have been docked here last month."

"In the Narrows? You're torquing with me, that could be a thousand ships. What else you got, you have a name for me, a cargo, how about a description?"

"It would have been docked on the Stonebank and not in the Narrows. We don't think. The name we have is the Meroha Uvari."

At the sound of the name. Tavish looked startled and slammed the rag down that was strung over his shoulder. He tried to pass over his blatant recognition and moved back to his bench, "I don't know why I didn't expect that, I'm losing my touch. So predictable," Tavish grumbled to himself.

"Spill it, Tavish. What do you know?" Kovan pressed.

"It's not a ship, you mudfoot. It's a person," Tavish said.

"How do you know this?" Kovan asked.

"You remember how it goes around here. I'm not really supposed to know anything, but of course, this is the Narrows. About a month ago a passenger arrived on a ship from the south. The Black Sails were asked to step in and hide her off the manifest from the Port Warden. They were supposed to shelter her for a few days until her handler came. But no one ever came," Tavish explained.

"Do you know where she is now? How can we find her?" Kovan asked, stepping closer.

"Last I heard, they had her at Philion's Wharf."

"She was a refugee then, but from where?" Kovan asked.

"I don't know everything, brother. Baragon and the Black Sails have done their best to keep her an unknown. They're a bit scared of her, I think," Tavish said.

"Why?" Kovan asked.

"The crew from the ship she came in on were all imprisoned and later hung."

"The bonemen?" Kovan asked.

"Must have been. They're everywhere you must have noticed. I'm sure sneaking around them isn't easy. Though they keep their boots on the Stonebank as you'd expect. Been busy shipping and managing lots of boat movements throughout the Zulu. So, why are you looking for this girl?" Tavish asked with squinted eyes.

"Following a thread, my friend. When was this?" Kovan pried.

"That dog don't bark, following a thread, ha. They were hung by the authority, these new bonemen, in the swamps about a week ago. Nasty business the hangings. More suffering by half than a firing squad."

"Not for the ones doing the firing," Kovan remarked.

"Indeed," Tavish said.

"Any ideas how we might go about getting this girl, then? I suppose asking politely isn't going to work?" Kovan asked.

"You know it ain't," Tavish said.

Kovan turned to Elias and Tali to get their input, "What do you two think?"

"We could steal her," Elias offered.

"The Black Sails are thieves and it's very tricky to steal from a thief. So, unless you're going to ride in and out on lightning, that idea is washed?" Kovan said.

"I could bend the light and cloak our way in and out," Elias said.

"Maybe," Kovan said, but their options weren't great. Dealing with the Black Sails was risky as they only did transactions to their advantage.

"What are they protecting her for, do you think? Is it a secret or a commodity they're protecting?" Tali asked.

"Probably their relationship and trade with the New World, seeing as that was the handler they're waiting to deliver her to," Kovan answered.

"Maybe we could just convince them to let us have her. If they heard about the incident in Adalon maybe we can convince them we were sent to pick her up for Danehin," Tali suggested.

"My worst fear is more to fear? It's not a bad play, Kovan," Elias agreed.

Suddenly the watches on Tali and Elias's wrists lit up. Ellaria was sending them a message. They read the eerie glowing dial and looked up.

"What is it?" Kovan asked.

"Seems like we're not the only ones with a problem," Elias said.

Tavish took an unmistakable interest in what he had just seen. When Kovan turned to him. Tavish's eyes looked transfixed on Tali's watch. No doubt he was perplexed and intrigued.

"Tavish," Kovan said loudly to redirect his attention.

"Yes," shaking in place, his husky form, wobbled.

"Will it work?" Kovan asked.

"I think so. They know the girl is a liability. We can convince them it's in their best interest to hand her over."

"We?"

"Yes, a'course. If I go with you brother, the chance of success certainly triples."

Kovan couldn't argue with that. It had been a long time since he had dealt with the Band of the Black Sails and he honestly couldn't recall if they were in good standing or not.

"Are you sure brother? I think we're headed for bad weather," Kovan asked.

"Is there any other kind?" Tavish asked.

"Not in this lifetime," Kovan said.

"What do I need to know about these Black Sail thugs?" Tali asked

"You're not going and he's definitely not going," Kovan said pointing toward Elias. "Every time he helps things go boom. If you haven't noticed this entire city is one gigantic pile of kindling. No, you both need to hang back, so we can get out of here as soon as we have the girl."

"How are we getting out?" Elias wondered.

"Tavish?" Kovan asked

"How have you survived so long without me brother?" Tavish said.

# CHAPTER THIRTY-TWO

## SURGE OF ENERGY (ELIAS)

THEY SAT TOGETHER ON THE SHIP. IT SLOWLY LIFTED AND TIPPED WITH THE waters, before it dipped back down. Small splashes of salty spray tapering onto the side boards. They tied off Tavish's small cadowa boat at the end of the dock, which extended out from a main street rising up the hill beyond. A lone bright lamp at the top of the hill cast light to either end. The brightened hilltop gave way to dark harbors below.

The docks were never completely deserted here, but tonight there was a calm and quietness to the surrounding area. When Elias and Tali repositioned the boat, the dock was packed with people. Now the sun had set, and the sea traffic was emptying out.

"You're sure Remi can find me?" Tali asked, for the third or fourth time.

"I promise, he's fine. It might take him a while, but he'll find his way. They are very special animals," Elias assured her.

Kovan and Tavish had been gone for what was starting to seem like a long time now. Elias could tell by Tali's fidgeting with her hands and sleeves, that she felt it too. Her eyes fixed at the top of the hill for any sign of them.

"What is taking them so long?" she asked.

"Not sure. Kovan can sometimes talk his way in and out of anything."

"Sometimes?"

"Well, he always talks his way in, but sometimes he has to shoot his way out," Elias said, and concern flashed across her face. To which Elias nodded his head in agreement of the precariousness of the situation.

276

"Shouldn't we wait at the top of the hill? I don't like just sitting here," Tali said.

"I don't like our position either. I thought it might be best to stay out of sight in case they weren't alone when they came back. My presence tends to make people like the Band of the Black Sails panic," he said and then reached for the dock. He lifted himself out and held out a hand for Tali. She took it and stepped up next to him.

"Let's go to the end of the street and wait. That way we can help if needed," Elias suggested. Tali smiled and they strolled slowly down the dock, their boots lightly clapping on the wood slats with each step. At the streets end, they paused to linger and stare up toward the hill. Elias hadn't fully appreciated how dark of a night it was. The moon was just a sliver, and the surrounding buildings were mostly dark. The structures were complicated stacked wood shacks, and any lamps inside didn't project their light into the streets. Up the main road, there were mounds of crates that congested the sidewalks. Lanterns hanging from a few of the doors, cast faint glows. The grime encrusted stone road seemed to swallow the light, more than reflect it.

There was still no sign of them.

Elias was beginning to contemplate at what point he would need to go after them when two forms crested the hill. What looked like a smaller slender form walking with short fast strides, followed by Tavish, who bumbled his way on the road. He was continually looking back. His form, with his short and stocky build was unmistakable from Kovan's. The girl was with him, but she was more like a young woman, and they were walking briskly, and where was Kovan?

When Tavish and Meroha were within twenty feet of them. Elias went to meet them.

"Come on," he urged Tali to follow. "Get Meroha to the boat," he told her.

Tali met the young woman up on the road. She shied away slightly at being approached, but Tali said something to calm her and they kept moving back toward the docks.

"Tavish! Tavish, where's Kovan?" Elias called out. Tavish hurried over and was visibly out of breath.

"He's . . . coming"

A loud, shattering crack, crashed beyond the hill on the far side. A moment later Kovan's hat appeared bouncing on the dark horizon and Kovan was there running., periodically turning and firing his pulsator behind him.

Elias quickly decided Tavish was no good in a fight and told him to get to the ship and get it ready for them to jump in. Elias sprinted up toward Kovan. Kovan was waving for him to stop and turn back. Elias paused and waited as instructed. They had fought together for too many years not to listen to each other. At the top of the hill a small band of bonemen were suffocating the road.

They opened fire and Kovan and Elias each dove for cover at the sidewalk, finding barrels to hide behind.

"So, everything went well. I see?" Elias asked.

"Yep. I haven't lost my touch," Kovan replied.

When the bursts of fire paused for the charging recoil and reload, Elias and Kovan jumped up and took aim. Kovan hit three bonemen rapidly, but only one took a lethal wound. Elias sensed only small traces of resting energy he could manipulate and decided his best course of action was to pull and push out upon the capacitor gems in the bonemen pulsator guns. At their distance and being such minute points of energy, the flash of power wasn't enough to injure the men, but the small explosions ruined their weapons for a moment.

A second squad started to file in from the side streets. They fired waves of charged rounds at Kovan and Elias. Taken by surprise, they both huddled back down again for protection. Ricocheted fragments hit Elias. The blasts were very close, and their cover was quickly being decimated. It wouldn't last much longer.

From across the road, a small figure came running in. Tali's cloak whipped rapidly as she ran. When she reached the middle of the street she stopped and looked at each three-man squad down the side streets. Out of shock or confusion the bonemen ceased their fire. Tali had a menacing look to her face. Elias realized she was going to lash out and jumped to his feet to stop her.

"Tali!" he called out, but it was too late.

Tali pushed both arms out from her sides. Suddenly, all the nearby lamps went out. The buildings went dark, and a cold chill prickled against Elias's forearms. Tali's closed fists changed to open palms with a flexing stretch of her hands. Her chest lowered an exhaled breath, and white light burst forth from her fingers. She hurled a massive amount of kinetic force and light at the soldiers. The bonemen flew high into the air. Most were thrown so far, they disappeared into the darkness of the night. It sounded to Elias that a few must have been thrown through buildings.

Tali screamed an ear-piercing bellow of anguish. Elias felt the air contracting and a surge of heat from her. She screamed into the night with her hands clutching against her face. She gripped her eyes with agony, as light burst through the gaps in her fingers. Then she passed out.

Kovan rushed to her side and lifted her into his arms. There were wisps of smoke drifting off her closed eyes. He was yelling at Elias, who stood transfixed at what he had just seen. Kovan's calls quickly snapped him out of his trance and they ran toward the boat.

The sea, which had been still before, was now churning and choppy. The litany of boats in the harbor were rocking up and down on the jetty. Kovan looked frantically until Elias pointed.

"The end of the dock!"

They ran to the cadowa. From the look on Tavish and Meroha's faces, Elias knew they were frightened by what they had witnessed. Kovan and Elias got aboard and Tavish pushed off down the canal. Kovan gently laid Tali down on the deck.

"Elias, help her!" Kovan demanded.

He reached into his satchel for a small leather pouch and proceeded to pull out four crystals.

"Is she going to die?" Kovan asked.

"No. But we need to act quickly, or she will lose her eyesight."

"What do you need?"

"Clean water and a few long strips of cloth to bandage her."

Kovan grabbed his small pack and rummaged through for his tin of water and cut his shirt sleeves to make long strips for Elias. Elias took the first strip of cloth, soaked it in water and placed it gently over Tali's eyes and forehead. Her breathing was labored and erratic. He checked her pulse but found it to be strong. Elias placed a clear quartz crystal atop each eye. He scribbled a sigil inscription into a piece of cloth and wrapped it over the crystals and around her head. He did something similar to each wrist but used two small pieces of rose crystal.

"That's all you can do?" Kovan asked frustrated with his own lack of healing ability, as well as Elias's.

"Yes."

Tavish steered them west through the canal instead of out to sea as they had planned. They all thought it too risky, and predictable to take a large ship out to sea. Of course, that was when they thought they would be evading the Band of the Black Sails, not bonemen. Kovan explained as they drifted along, that the kid Ludoc, from Tavish's shop, had gone directly to the Black Sails after leaving them. After some convincing, they let Meroha go with Kovan but then double-crossed them, calling in the bonemen to ambush them. They had hoped to collect the reward for his capture and eliminate their liability at the same time.

Now the five of them had nothing left to do but sail to the Uhanni River and follow it into the valley and up north. They were expecting to meet Ellaria and the others in Polestis in a week. The timing didn't worry Elias, as much as the prospect of fellow travelers and river-raiders. The river being a major source of travel through Tavillore. The other ships sharing the river could become an obstacle to keeping their anonymity. They would have to change vessels.

# CHAPTER THIRTY-THREE

## THE ARCHIVES (WADE)

The next day following their flight from the meeting at the Skyline restaurant they sat waiting in a reading room of the archives. After escaping unfollowed through the city, they had regrouped at Ellaria's place and planned out their mission to steal the Alchemist's Codex from the Archive's vaults. Learon came through the door with an unusual grin on his face. His usual upright posture filled the passageway, and he held up his hand with the shining bronze key in his grasp.

"No way! You blumdog, you got it?" Wade asked.

Ellaria laughed slightly as Learon sat down at the small table. He handed the key over to her, while Wade struggled to extinguish his look of bewilderment.

"I told you I could get it," Learon beamed.

"That you did. I have to admit I had my doubts," Wade said.

"Well done, Learon," Ellaria told him admiring the interwoven circles of the key and its latching trips, "And you're sure this is the key?"

"It's the same one she used to unlock this reading room. I was watching when she used it. What locks it opens beside the outside door and these reading rooms, I don't know," Learon said.

"I guess that means I lost so I'm waiting. What room should I hide in?" Wade asked

"Honestly, one of the larger rooms would be your best bet. They're least likely to be checked out. You should be safe this evening," Ellaria said.

"So, I wait until tonight and then let you guys inside. Easy, but how do we get past the restricted section door?" Wade asked.

"The restricted section has magical seals," Ellaria explained.

"And that doesn't worry you?"

"Not in the least. I designed them."

"Oh, right," Wade said.

"One other thing," Learon said, "I asked her for more volumes on the excavation of Ash Field. Um, as my reason for talking with her. Anyway, she couldn't find any."

"Is that weird?" Wade asked.

"Well, when I was here the other day there were six or seven different articles on the subject. She told me this sometimes happens when all the manuscripts on one subject are pulled to be relocated to the restricted section. And that they just haven't replaced her cards yet."

"That is odd, but Learon, I don't think you're going to find anything. Your father's journal was probably the only thing written down that diverged from other verified accounts. That's why they wanted it and pursued you and your mother. I'm not trying to deter you from looking. I'm only trying to set your expectations. I believe your father and the entire team were murdered, I just don't think you're going to find the evidence to support your claim," Ellaria explained.

"I'm sure you're right, but I thought I should mention it in case it meant someone has added to the security of the place," Learon conceded.

Wade could tell Learon was becoming obsessed with researching anything he could find about his father's last work and the shipwreck, and he couldn't blame him really.

They waited a little while longer in the room before leaving their small reading nook. They walked up a flight to the fourth floor, where they began opening doors to find one of the larger unoccupied rooms. On their third try they found an eight-person room. It had a larger meeting table in the middle and two large soft chairs positioned in a slight alcove.

"Probably should have asked earlier, but do you need to use the bathroom?" Ellaria asked Wade.

Wade simply grunted a growl of annoyance at them and waved them away. Waiting around an empty room with nothing to do was an odd test of his self-control, of which he knew he had very little. They should have used Semo, but if he was caught, at least he could make an excuse that he had fallen asleep. Semo would be thrown in jail.

"Don't get too comfortable, you probably don't want to fall asleep," she told him.

"What should I do for six hours?" Wade asked.

"I don't know, count the stones?"

They left Wade inside to go and get ready before returning that night. Wade found a spot in the back corner and watched the light fade. Filling the room with an orange glow, still surprised he had lost the bet.

THE DARKNESS IN THE ROOM WAS ABSOLUTE. WADE STRUGGLED TO KEEP his eyes open and kept checking his watch over and over again. Trying to will time to move faster, but it was not helping. It seemed like he had been stuck in the room a lot longer than six hours. Finally, the time had come. He got up to leave. Having memorized the spacing before the light died out he crossed the room swiftly and reached the door without running into anything. It was easier than it probably should have been considering he couldn't see his own hand in front of his face.

He slowly turned the latch and stepped out onto the landing. Quickly, he realized he did not have an innate sense of direction around the archives, and he cursed himself for not spending more time here over the past year.

Slowly, he crept down the winding stairs to the main lobby. He felt his way along the stone walls as he went. The visibility was only slightly better in the stairways. A small amount of ambient light trickled up from the main lobby and helped guide his way. His steps on the tumbled tile stairs made a distinct, shuffling clap. It rang out louder than he would have liked, but it was unavoidable. Everything was magnified in the empty stairwell, including the sound of his own breathing. Wade was unsure how to judge the volume of noise he was making.

He exhaled when he reached the last step and swiftly crossed the main room to the garden entrance doors. He peered through the glass and spotted the others walking the gardens at a leisurely pace. Stalking around in the dark was more suspicious than simply walking around like you belonged. Wade couldn't help feeling like they would have been better off pulling this stunt with Tali than Learon. The kid was swift on his feet, but Wade feared this task was too personal for Learon. His increased intensity and his hunger to get inside the restricted section had the potential to jeopardize the mission.

Wade let them inside, and they silently passed by while he held the door for them. Semo was cloaked in black, but underneath, Wade could see his usual flowing fabrics. They all headed directly for the restricted section and rushed down the stairs in a rhythmical pattern of four sets of boots echoing out.

At the bottom, Semo lit his lantern and Wade could finally see. The room opened up into a large circular space. A short distance from the stairs was a greeting station and beyond that a great silver door. It was ten feet wide and nearly as tall as the ceiling.

The door was a large circle that overlapped a solid panel on the right. In the center was a depression, and a second smaller circle about the size of a hand. This circle seemed to be a natural rock of some kind. The stone was a swirl of color, a frozen stream of dark green and bright red.

Ellaria stepped close to it. She reached inside her cloak and pulled out a black disk of similar size.

"What is that?" Learon asked, referring to the stone inset into the door.

"It's called blood stone," Ellaria said as she drew a knife from her sleeve. It was a short slender blade, but Wade was impressed. He hadn't noticed the weapon until she drew it. "This is obsidian," she told them of the stone she held. Then without warning she ran the knife across her skin and cut a small gash into the top of her left arm. She winced with the pain.

"What are you doing?" Learon asked in a panic. Though Wade knew better by now than to doubt Ellaria, he was also worried.

"Creating a key," she said.

They all watched as she used the butt end of her knife to collect blood from the dripping wound and then use it as ink to draw on the disk. Wade couldn't make out what she had drawn, but even if he could see it clearly, he was sure he wouldn't recognize the mark.

Ellaria finished and tipped her plate into the depression in the door. Then she pressed her right hand onto the blood coated stone. A slight sound of stone on stone slipping together was all that appeared to happen. Ellaria stood motionless with her eyes closed. Suddenly her hand pressed deeper into the hole. The stone plate became soft like it was made of a black mud, and her hand pushed into the solid door without resistance. It was almost repulsive.

When her hand was wrist deep, she started to clutch something solid, and she rotated her hand to the left. A loud depressing whoosh resonated inside the door, followed by a gushing sound of air pressure being released. The large circular slab began to roll easily out of position and to the left, revealing a second door behind it.

Ellaria wheeled the first door away into a pocket in the frame and removed her hand. As she did so, she touched the bottom of the obsidian disc and tipped it out. Catching what was now a solid stone again, she tucked it away into her shoulder bag and moved to the second door.

"What did I just see?" Wade asked.

"I'll explain later," she said.

This second door looked simpler. It was lightly stained thick wood, with two keyholes about chest high on each panel. Semo moved in to examine the lock. He turned to Ellaria.

"I cannot pick two locks at the same time," he told her regretfully.

"They have to be done simultaneously?" Ellaria asked.

"Yes," he verified.

"Walk me through it. I can do the second lock," Learon offered and stepped up to the door next to Semo.

Semo handed him some thin needles of metal and began to investigate the lock in front. He slipped in two long pieces, and then a third. He held all three with one hand and then instructed Learon on what to do.

"The latching has three pins. First the furthest notch is to the bottom and fully left. The second is at the top left."

"I don't feel anything," Learon complained.

Wade closed his eyes and began to worry about time. Their presence would not go unnoticed forever. Sooner or later, someone would find them. He could hear them arguing when his eyes popped open.

"Try the opposite," Wade told Learon. "Do the opposite of what Semo says. If they are synchronized counter locks, then they probably have—"

"Opposite latching," Learon finished.

Learon readdressed the lock and followed Semo's instruction again. He placed the needles this time at the opposite points. They counted down and unlocked the door together.

A wheel and knob on the adjacent wall, spun rapidly. The door mechanism beyond clicked, and they heard the sound of metal sliding across metal. The doors pulled free. On the interior of the doors there were large, exposed metal gears and two holes in the floor where steel bars were now sunken in. Wade figured the wheel and crank outside must position the bars into place and notching into the gears and locking each panel. The doors gave way to a chamber beyond, dimly lit by vapor filled glass spheres. Their first steps inside crossed over an emblem on the floor similar to an alchemist's mark. Ellaria quickly knelt down to it. The three men paused to watch her. She put her hand to her arm and pulled it away with blood at her fingertip. She then drew lines over the floor art and pressed her palm upon the drawing, whispering something. The inlaid design changed colors from green to grey.

She wiped the blood clean with her sleeve, stood up and looked to them, "Let's be quick."

Inside the simple stone room, there were two floor to ceiling bookcases. Both shared the middle of the chamber. A few desks and chairs lined the perimeter walls, and there was a larger table at the back. A few stacks of books still lingered on some of the surrounding table tops.

"We only need the one book for Elias. Let's find it and get out of here," Wade said, but it was almost like Learon and Ellaria had their own agendas. They each rushed to began searching without acknowledging what he had said. Ellaria seemed to be counting the books instead of searching for something in particular. Learon disappeared behind to the other side. After a few long minutes, Ellaria appeared between the bookcases holding a faded gold and black book. It was larger than Wade had imagined.

"Got it!" Ellaria said and she rushed back. "Let's go."

But Learon was still looking for something and didn't concede to her findings.

"Learon!" Ellaria tried again.

"Not yet. I've only found one so far," Learon grumbled from the far side.

"Just go, we'll catch up," Wade told her. She eyed him sternly with her patented scowl. "I promise. I'll drag him out if I need to," Wade assured her.

"Hurry," Ellaria said, and her and Semo started back. Semo handed his lantern to Wade. He took it and scrambled to help Learon. There was no telling how much security the place now had under the Prime and they had already stayed longer then was warranted.

"Can I help?" Wade asked.

"Yes. I need the light," Learon said.

"We need to go, Learon," Wade said.

"I can't. I have to know who killed my father!" Learon said frantically, continuing to talk while he pulled book after book free from the shelves, "You don't understand, this may be my only chance. I've lost nearly everything he ever gave me."

"Fine. Did you check the stacks on the tables?" Wade asked.

"Where?" Learon said, spinning around and finding a large stack behind him. He clawed through them quickly. Scanning the covers, before discarding a book firmly aside. Sometimes he paused to skim a few pages before moving on.

"Learon, we don't have that kind of time."

"Sorry, I'm not sure what some of these are even about."

Wade, growing more frustrated, made a rash decision. He could either wait until Learon eventually found the string of manuscripts that he was looking for or they could take everything they could carry.

"Time's up. Any longer and you're going to have to ask to read these in jail. Let's just take anything you haven't looked through yet," Wade said. Learon paused a moment to look at him as though he might argue but didn't. Wade took Learon's bag and held it open, "Just throw some in and let's go."

They went from table to table and Learon moved faster. If he was unsure, he simply threw it in the bag. They weren't taking everything, but the bag was getting heavy.

"Maybe these," Learon said, when they reached a stack on the other side of the room.

"Great, grab them. I'm sorry to be insensitive here but I don't care, we're leaving," Wade demanded.

Learon placed the books in the pack, and they scrambled out. They made it to the top of the steps to the main hall and hurried across the room to the outside doors. There was a shape moving in the terrace beyond. Someone was coming towards the building. Wade extinguished the lantern and pushed Learon out the door. Hoping the foliage of the park would disguise their exit. Almost instantly, they heard a man call out.

"Who's there?"

Wade grabbed Learon and pulled him back. Forcing him to crouch behind the nearest bushes just steps from the archives entrance. He put his fingers to his lips to motion for Learon to be quiet. Then he flashed into the pathway.

"Just me, sir," Wade called back, stepping forward. The shape in the darkness spotted him immediately and moved closer. Wade was still unsure who was coming toward him. So, he moved slowly toward the man to close the distance between them. When the trees and gardens opened up and some more of the night's light illuminated the area. Wade finally recognized the man.

"Professor Mathis, it's a nice night, don't you think?" Wade said.

The man eyed him suspiciously, "It's very late, Mr. Duval. Why are you stalking around the gardens at this hour?" he asked, while peering past Wade to see if he was alone. Wade resisted the urge to ask him the same question.

"I wasn't stalking, sir. I've been working late on my project in the Crafter's shop. I came up here to get some air and clear my head. How about you?"

Professor Mathis tilted his head slightly to the side like he was deciding how hard he wanted to make Wade's life. Then straightened. "I was helping Professor White in the lab. School is out, does Professor Rhodes know you use the *tinker's* shop this late?" he asked. The word tinker's was spoken with a modicum of disdain that Mathis intentionally didn't hide.

"Of course. That's who gave me a key," Wade said.

"And what are you working on that's so taxing to your mind that it required clearing?" the professor asked.

"Well, it's a set of wings, sir."

"Wings, Mr. Duval?"

"Yes, I had this idea for a mechanical set of wings, that you could strap to your back."

"That sounds like an exceedingly overt way to injure yourself. Are you planning their use for a showman's troupe?"

"I guess," Wade said.

"Well, I'm sure I don't need to tell you, young man, but gravity is not so easily bested by tinkers' gadgets."

"I'm realizing that sir."

"A gadget that you no doubt want to hide from public scrutiny."

"Yes, sir. That's why I've been working on it at night."

"Fine. I suggest you go home, young Wade. And so we are clear. I will be discussing the shop's use this late at night with Professor Rhodes," the professor said sternly and turned on his heel and strode away.

Not wanting to alert the Professor to anything odd. Wade simply walked to the nearest stairway down to the street level. Whistling the tune of the 'Redeemer' as he did so. Halfway down the steps he sat and waited for Learon who came scurrying over after a short time. The look in his wide eyes matched Wade's sentiment. Wade bounded down the steps and watched as Learon leapt from the landing to the lamp's plinth and down to the path. Learon meet Wade's astonished look with a smile. Neither of them commented though, instead choosing to sprint away from the spires as quickly as they could, careful not to instigate any more attention.

Back at Ellaria's apartment, Wade explained the incident with Professor Mathis to Ellaria's dismay. She paused, from the scolding she was giving them over the number of books they had taken, to listen.

"Haden Mathis was walking around the campus that late, and he said he was working with Professor White?" she clarified.

"Yes," Wade said.

"I wonder if he means H.B. White, the physicist?"

"I'm not sure."

"It's curious, but this!" she pointed to the open pack of books laying at their feet, "This complicates things."

"How so?"

"We will need to leave the city immediately. One book might have gone unnoticed for a month, but ten books. That will be discovered this morning and you can bet the Guild will be required to report it to the greencoats," Ellaria said.

"And the greencoats will tell the Prime?" Learon said.

"Exactly."

"Fine, but I need to go back to my room first," Wade said.

"I'm not so sure that's a good idea. You will be their first stop."

"I have to," Wade said. Ellaria's jaw clenched and she threw up her hand.

"I swear to the Blue! I was never this stupid. Fine. Meet us at the Sun Bridge in an hour," She demanded and Wade took it as a win and left before she changed her mind. Ellaria was writing with the engraved pen, messaging the others as he closed the door.

Wade packed what he could as quickly as he could, all the while wondering what he had gotten himself into and why he was willing to go any further. A smarter man would have walked when Qudin, or Elias, whatever he wanted to be called, offered the way out. The presence of soldiers throughout the city was disturbing and if the news was true that Anchor's Point was in ashes, then things had escalated to a level Ellaria and her friends couldn't defeat on their own. More than any of that, the thing weighing on his mind was his sister. He still had yet to hear any word about her and was clinging to the idea that Ellaria would help him.

He needed to decide how far he was willing to go for her. Already he had broken into the Citadel and now the Arcana Archives, surprising himself each time he had agreed.

This time there was a witness connecting him to the incident. His involvement with Ellaria and her conspiracies had moved beyond dangerous. He supposed the danger was understood, but he hadn't paused to think about it. The real crisis remained; he was in serious danger of eliciting Stasia's wrath. She was going to be furious when she found out that he had disappeared. He needed to leave her a note and let her know what was happening. He was at the point now that he feared he would reach the line of keeping her safe and keeping her in the dark. It was no longer safe for her to be oblivious of the mounting danger as events were accelerating, but he still couldn't risk bringing her along.

He wrote her a letter explaining the situation and could only hope she would forgive him. He grabbed everything and walked across the campus to her room. The city was beginning to awake, and he needed to drop the letter off and get out of there. He was ashamed that he was too scared to actually face her, but he knew she would never let him leave. He badly wanted to bring her into this mess just to get an injection of her unwavering level headedness to the proceedings. Protecting her, in the end, was more important.

He reached her door and tried to slip the note below and under the sill, but it jammed up in the doors weather stripping. The dirt and grime at the threshold marked and damaged the paper. He quietly cursed to himself and decided to jam the note into the side near the handle. When he was satisfied that it would stay in place, he raced away.

Traveling from the center of Adalon to the south bridge took longer than he thought, but the others were still waiting when he arrived. All three sat on horses and Learon held an almost entirely white mare by the reins. It looked tantalizingly close to tearing away and Wade approached her with uncertainty.

"This is Ghost," Learon said, handing him the reins. For a second, he almost thought the horse seemed to anger slightly at the sight of him. It took Wade three attempts before he was able to get on. Apparently, not his imagination.

"Whose horse is this, anyway, Kovan's?" he asked.

"No, it was Elias's. Seems she doesn't like anyone else. I had a thorn of a time getting her here. She likes to run so I think she'll lighten up once we are away from the city."

The four of them left the city of Adalon for the west, with the sun rising off the sea, Semo and Ellaria in the lead. Wade was almost instantly uncomfortable and dreaded the next week. His complaining was going to be constant and grating.

# CHAPTER THIRTY-FOUR

## THE RIVER (KOVAN)

THE FIRST FEW DAYS FOLLOWED WITHOUT A CHANGE IN TALI'S CONDITION. Her breathing normalized, and the color was slowly coming back to her face. Her skin had turned ashen despite her temperature, which was still running far too high for Kovan's taste. He continually checked her forehead throughout the day with the underside of his wrist. Mostly, she was peaceful and slept. Even when she awoke, it was only for short bleary bursts. Kovan hated those times. She would say odd, obscure things that were mostly intelligible. They would give her water and in quick order she would rest again. Elias assured him it was normal, but he couldn't see past his worry. Sometimes her words sounded like an unfamiliar language.

On the third day, they were all tired of the tiny cadowa. It was a small drifter meant for cargo and maneuvering through thin canals. It was not ideal for a river like the Uhanni, or passengers holed up on it for days. They stopped for a few hours every day to eat and rest on the shore, but it was reckless to linger. He had to assume the bonemen would be following, though they had yet to see any sign of a chase.

Once the splintered canals from Aquom eventually met up to the Uhanni River, the river traffic increased tenfold. Some took notice of the overcrowded cadowa in their mists. Others, the river lifers, couldn't care less. They only saw another ship with nothing to trade. Navigating the larger river was difficult for the tall, sailed drifter. The larger barges flowed by at greater speeds and threw harsh wakes in their passing.

Steam powered paddle rollers were nearly all passenger ships these days. They found a fair share of those too. They spotted a maroon and white painted ship the night before. A sign they were nearing the port at Midway.

Tavish was intending on getting off there and they would take the cadowa further north to Anchor's Point, or what was left of it.

Gradually, the river widened when they came upon the port city of Pardona. It marked the midpoint on the river from Marathal to the Zulu Sea. Kovan helped unfurl the sail and tie it off, so the ship could slow. So far, the wind had favored them going north, which was exceedingly rare. Kovan finished what he was doing and walked to the back platform.

"Are you doing that?" he asked Elias as he sat down.

"Doing what?"

"Directing the wind?"

"No. I can't do that."

"You sure?"

"Definitely. I'm redirecting some of the force of river flow against us, to draw us up the river faster. But the wind, no."

Kovan gave him a crooked look and shook his head.

"I got word from Ellaria," Elias said.

Kovan was not happy about splitting up. He almost feared to ask, "And?"

"They have the book and are leaving this morning. She thinks they will be pursued all the way to Polestis."

"That should put them a day behind us. I would think."

"We'll see."

Tavish at the head of the boat lowered his pole into the river to steer. Meroha had said almost nothing since they had retrieved her. She obviously thought she was safer with them or she wouldn't have left the Band of the Black Sails. Still, she kept quiet and sat next to Tali. It surprised Kovan she wasn't more afraid of Tali after the light show she had put on in the harbor. It wasn't as though they were kidnapping her, but Kovan struggled to discern the difference. Meroha was younger and more wide-eyed than Tali, but Kovan sensed she was far more openly suspicious.

They had yet to press her for anything and they were avoiding making her feel trapped. But they needed to learn everything she knew, and Kovan hoped it would be at her will and not against it.

Elias had his nose in a book or wrote in his journal the entire trip. At different points, Kovan could see he was trying to work something out. A few glimpses of his journal revealed drawings and scribbled maps. Sometimes, he would make a drawing and Kovan would see him cross it out a short time later. He wasn't sure what he was trying to figure out, but it was probably something to do with the Ancients or his ever-elusive Tempest Stone.

Tavish pulled off to the bank and tied off onto a wobbling jetty. He rounded on Elias and Kovan.

"You owe me, Van. I mean you still owe me that dragon glass right, but now you *really* owe me," Tavish said.

"I'm grateful."

"How about you let me take that crazy wristwatch the girl wears?"

Kovan was insulted by the request and stood up abruptly. Was his friend really asking if he could steal from a sick young woman? He rested his hand on his pulsator and eyed his oldest friend with derision.

"Wow, Brother, I didn't mean anything by it," Tavish said.

"Kovan, relax," Elias said, placing his hand on his shoulder as he rose off the platform, "I don't think he meant any harm."

"Right. I'm just curious. I've never seen something like it is all," Tavish explained. Kovan's eyes told him his oldest friend was asking for a simple payment, but all he could see was a weasel standing in front of him. Tavish had made a comment about the watches a day ago, and Kovan hadn't missed how his eyes had lit up back at his shop the first night. In fact, Tavish only became interested in helping them when the watches lit up. Kovan seldom missed people's body language, it helped him anticipate their actions and reactions. He had hoped that his friend's provocation was simple curiosity, but he knew different. Tavish asking for it straight out revealed his desperation. He must have calculated that stealing it would be too difficult. What with Meroha sitting vigilantly by Tali's side, day and night. Outright robbing Kovan and the Quantum Man would be suicide. So, he went the direct route.

"Tavish, my friend. I know you. Please put it out of your mind," Kovan warned him, trying to remember their long history together, "The young woman invented them. When we are safe, and all of this is behind us. I'm sure she can make you one," he told him.

"Yes, thank you. We could go into business together maybe if she is as skilled as that device appears."

"Tavish," Kovan said in a drawn-out breath of warning.

"I'm just saying I know a lot of great craftsmiths who could not create such a thing. Anyway, safe journey to you all. I shall catch another vessel and be on my way."

"No. Change of plans," Kovan said.

"Change, what change?"

293

"We will find a ship to take us the rest of the way. You can take your cadowa and get back wherever you need to be."

"That works for me," Tavish said.

Kovan was sure his pivot had taken Elias by surprise, and to his credit he simply went along with him like it was decided beforehand. Kovan left the boat and found transport on a barge. They left Tavish on the dock waving farewell. Kovan carried Tali in his arms. They boarded the barge and silently found a spot to rest. The crew cast curious glances but went about their work undeterred. He laid her down in a bed of hay under a small curtain of cloth. Kovan pulled his arm free from under her heavy head, and she stirred, trying to speak.

"Kovan?" she whispered in a weak but clear tone.

"I'm here," he assured her.

"Good," she said, and she rolled to her side again.

# CHAPTER THIRTY-FIVE

## NIGHTMARES (TALI)

Tali was falling, and her stomach clenched, but she didn't awake, and suddenly she wasn't falling anymore but drowning in a sea with eyes that stared at her. She panicked and turned away from the depths. She walked out of the water and into a room that was cavernous and echoed every sound. It was full of a thousand men in armor, their faces menacing and ready to kill. They guarded something and their eyes sparkled and vibrated until they became steam. A scream ruptured in her ears and she ran to the far side, where a wall of symbols pulsated and glowed. They were important but she couldn't focus on a single one. A gale of wind knocked her off her feet. It passed over her head and into a red sky. A phantom lurking behind her breathed energy and smiled. Its form concealed in smoke and ash, and a great fire danced and pulsed like a living thing in its eyes. The ash was in her hair and she backed to the edge of a balcony and put her hand out to catch flecks of ash, but each evaporated like a snowflake. Melted in place and the droplets ran back down her palm to her wrist. Where the line became a gash in her skin and the pain burst at the wound, and darkness was everywhere but for a single opening. She crossed through and found herself alone on a mountain ledge. The endless sea frozen below and the ground gave way. She staggered in terror and a hand of blue skin reached for her, and tears came to her eyes. The world became bright and images flickered all around. Her eyes were gone, they ached, they throbbed with her heartbeat. And a cascade of stomps closed in on her with voices calling her name.

"Tali!" Kovan said.

She heard him and sat up more quickly than she intended. A heavy bandaging awkwardly shifted from around her eyes. She went to grab it but felt Kovan's hands gently repositioning it. She couldn't quite tell, but there was something wrapped around her wrists too.

"Tali, just sit back and relax. I'm going to go get Elias," Kovan said, and she could hear him shuffling to stand. "Meroha, don't let her do anything, please," he said in an unusually kind and pleading voice. She was having trouble recalling just who exactly Meroha was at the moment.

Her eyes hurt, but more than that, her entire body ached. She stretched her fingers out and placed them blindly on the ground. There was a thin bed of hay needles prickling her fingertips, but below wasn't dirt. She wasn't sitting on the ground, but slatted wood sanded smooth. She used her arm to lift herself to sit up.

"What are you doing? The gruffy one said you shouldn't move," a soft feminine voice told her.

"Oh, I don't think I could go anywhere if I wanted to. If one's the gruffy one, what is the other one?" Tali asked.

"The quiet one. He scares me."

"Why?"

"His eyes. He comes now," she said, and Tali heard a rapping of footsteps coming their way.

"Tali, how do you feel?" Elias said sitting next to her.

"I'm tired and sore."

"Would you mind if I felt your forehead?"

"Of course not."

Elias shimmied closer and put his hand to her head. He kept it there for a count of ten seconds and withdrew. "Your fever is gone," he announced.

"Great, can I get these bandages off then?" Tali said, slowly raising her hand to pull off the one around her head. Elias stopped her.

"I'll do it," he said.

Elias slowly peeled back the wrapping. After the third pass, two lumps fell free from her eyes.

"Huh," Tali inhaled sharply.

"It was only two small heart stones I placed there."

"Oh, I thought it was . . . I was afraid it was my . . ." but she couldn't bring herself to say it. With her eyes and face completely numb the ghosted sensation felt like her eyeballs had fallen from the sockets.

"I know," he said and unwrapped the last of the cloth from her face. The last layer clung to her skin but gaveway at Elias's gentle pulling. The fresh air felt good, but with the pressure alleviated, a dizziness came on. Her eyelids were shut, and she was afraid to open them.

"So, what were the stones for?" Tali asked, still maintaining her eyelids in place.

"Heart stone, they're a healing stone that cleanses the blood."

"Oh."

"Tali?" Kovan said.

"Yes?" she answered in her most laid-back tone.

"Don't worry. I think the bloodstones worked," Kovan said, trying to reassure her.

"How do you know?" she whispered back. Her voice faltered.

"They are glowing slightly," Kovan said, and he placed them in her hands.

Instinctively, she opened her eyes to look at them. The light blurred and hurt. The air in her eyes burned with a sting like freshly chopped onion.

"Ow," she yelped. She blinked over and over and the slow moistening was helping, but something was wrong.

"I can't see." she said.

"What do you see, just blackness?" Elias asked her.

"No, just light. Shimmering but soft actually."

"That's good. Does it hurt?"

"Yes, kind of. It hurts to have my eyes open. The air is irritating, but it doesn't hurt to see. If that makes any sense at all."

"Tali, I'm going to wash your face and the skin around your eyes. I think it's important that you keep trying to use your eyes. Your eyesight will come back," Elias explained to her.

"I can do it," the girl with them said. It had taken a while, but her memory was coming back and Tali recalled who the girl was now.

"Are we still on the splinters or the Uhanni now?"

"The Uhanni," Elias said, and he unwrapped the bandages at her wrists. Then he got up.

"It's good to see you up and talking again, young Raven," Kovan said.

"Thanks, Kovan. Elias was that the luminance surge?" Tali asked.

"Yes, now get your rest. I'll be back to check on you again."

When the night came, Tali could tell by the surrounding sounds. A song of crickets and locusts replaced the birds. The smell of smoke that had begun that evening had been growing steadily thicker the further north they traveled. It was now almost to the point of making her cough.

She could hear Van and Elias talking some distance away, but she was struggling to place things in space. Often when she thought a sound was coming from one direction, it turned out to be coming for a completely different one. The sensation was startling and nauseating.

"Meroha, are you there?"

"Of course, Miss Tali."

"Can you see Kovan and Elias?"

"Yes, they are standing near the sidewall."

"Can you take me over to them?"

"Yes."

Meroha's hand softly held her own, and she led Tali out of their spot. She had walked once before during the day, but her legs still weren't steady. There was a weariness to her bones. Her steps across the ship were made in short clips, but it was all she could do. She wanted to avoid using Meroha as a crutch. Tali was sure it looked completely foolish, and a sudden ping of embarrassment made her cringe.

After what she counted as twelve paces. They reached the side wall. Meroha transferred Tali's hand to the rail and made sure she was gripping firmly before moving her hand away.

"Everything alright, Raven?" Kovan asked her.

"Yes. What's going on? Where are we?"

"We are coming up on Anchor's Point. It's almost completely burned to the ground. Some buildings collapsed into the river, otherwise we would have docked by now," Kovan said.

"Is it still on fire?"

"There's a smoldering still in some areas," Elias said.

"Is anything still standing?"

"Very few buildings along the river, some of the town beyond looks to have been saved. Fort Verdict is decimated," Kovan said.

"I would have thought the river side ones would have fared better."

"It looks like the people did all they could to save the west end of the fort and the homes beyond. Hopefully we can find passage still to Polestis. Otherwise, we need to head all the way to Marathal," Elias said, but from his voice Tali could tell he did not favor that route.

"What's the matter with going to Marathal, it's supposed to be the richest city in the world?" Tali asked.

"And the most heavily guarded," Elias said.

The barge lurched under her feet, and her grip tightened onto the rail. Tali heard gangplanks slamming down and assumed they had docked. At least there was a place still to dock.

"We'll be back, you two wait here. We won't be far," Kovan said.

Tali waited on the ship with Meroha. They sat, listening to the crew unload cargo. They were talking boisterously about the rumors they had heard of the Quantum Man's return. How he had wiped out a legion of bonemen in Aquom. This after destroying part of the harbor in Adalon where he had fought his way out. By the time they started to load and store new cargo, Elias had returned. They had secured a carriage for the four of them, and it was waiting to take them to Polestis.

With Elias's help, she traversed the city. From the dock to the main road, it took an agonizing amount of time. She had heard stories of people who had lost their sight, and then their other senses became enhanced. If her eyes never came back, she was going to need a miracle like that. As it was, she felt vulnerable, and it was not a feeling she enjoyed. At times, walking through the city she heard the tiniest trickle of embers still crackling. The city was eerily quiet, but she knew it was still packed with people. She could hear their footsteps and shuffling. All this because of ideological anger.

"How bad is it?" she asked.

"Consider yourself lucky you can't see it," Elias told her.

She couldn't see it, but she certainly could smell it and the aroma of char was pungent and sickening. She recalled running around the boardwalk and seeing the colored banners strung above. The savory and spicy meal they all had and devoured had been a cherished relief to the previous night's horror at the Fork. Mostly, she was reminded of the overwhelming dread and helplessness as they watched the boardwalk go up in flames from their ship, and Aramus's cold voice as he spat lies and incited the crowd.

When they reached the carriage, Meroha helped her inside. She wiped a tear from her eye and felt around for the seat. Kovan's powerful hand found hers and helped her the rest of the way. It was calloused and less slender than Elias's.

From the sounds of horses were huffing all around her. They were apparently leaving with an entire caravan. She sat back against the leather cushions and vowed that one day, she would return to put right what had gone terribly wrong here.

# CHAPTER THIRTY-SIX

## ELIAS'S VAULT (TALI)

THERE WAS A CHILL IN THE MORNING THROUGH THE NORTH MOUNTAINS, even in the summer. The cold permeates through the thin air, where it moves freely. At night, it seeps into the dense landscape, until it clashes with the sun at dawn. Polestis had taken three and a half days to reach from Anchor's Point. They had maintained an unrelenting pace, only stopping when they had to rest the horses. Even so, they pushed them to exhaustion the first day by riding straight from the river to Thelmaria, where they traded out for a fresh group. From there they ascended into the mountains fully and finally over Talon's Pass. Elias told her how treacherous the pass could be in the winter, when snow drifts built up so high it became insurmountable. There was a reason Skyvier was always willing to stand alone from the Coalition. Most of their cities were highly protected, and unreachable by an invading army. None more so than the capital city of Polestis.

It was said to be the most beautiful land in all of Territhmina and Tali, for now, could only imagine it. Her eyesight still had yet to return. Elias said she was just lightblind and stressed that she needed to give it time. There was a slight change a day ago from gradations of white to a shifting brightness with depth. It gave her hope, but her patience was waning.

The carriage came to rest on the fourth day in Polestis. She exited and stretched her legs. That was when the cold air hit her skin. Tali still hadn't bothered to wear a cloak for some time. In most of the mainland, it was the zenithal now and the heat on the river could get muggy and suffocating. Here, the air was gloriously crisp and fresh. Her senses were under full assault now. She threw her head back and took it in. Fresh scents of the surrounding forests filled the air, but there was a lovely smell of cooking fires and food. Whatever she was smelling was making her mouth water.

There was a sweeping chatter, as though people were moving about all around her. Horses' hooves beat the gravel and conversations passed and dissipated. The sounds were pleasant though, and not overwhelming. Tali figured it was because of the early hour. It was also like the noise was free to move and not reverberate against large buildings. The space felt expansive and open. As she turned her head to each sound, shapes formed in her vision. Not with any clarity, but she could definitely make out forms of people like bright mists flowing through a blurry cloud. She had come to realize a stronger connection to all the energies surrounding her. It seemed when her eyes stopped distracting her, she could feel the vibrations Elias spoke of.

Meroha grabbed her hand and startled her slightly. Not to lead her anywhere. She just liked to hold Tali's hand. Meroha told her that in her culture it was common to hold hands with your friends. Tali found it sweet. From what Elias had told her about Aquom, Tali was surprised the girl wasn't afraid of her. Tali, for the most part, couldn't remember much.

It turned out Meroha had escaped from Kotalla. That much she had gotten out of her. That and her age. She was fifteen. Four years younger than Tali and a refugee alone in a strange land with possibly the most dangerous people in the world. It was the least Tali could do to hold her hand. She inspired Tali. Still, she shied away from talking about herself and conversation in general. Tali didn't press her.

The stop in Polestis was brief. Soon they were making their way on a trail through the mountains. Tali road behind Kovan and Meroha behind Elias. They had traded their things for supplies and kept two horses for the trek to Elias's home. Tali slumped onto Kovan's back. The constant moving had her trying not to fall asleep while holding on. The path there must have been tricky as Kovan complained multiple times. Especially when they originally left the trail.

When they reached Elias's home, nobody was sure they had reached anything. Elias dismounted and told them to do the same.

"This is just the edge of a cliff," Kovan said.

"It's this way," Elias assured them.

They walked over to what Kovan described to Tali, as a small shack in the middle of a grouping of trees. Once inside, they walked down a long flight of stairs. At some point, they went through a set of doors and Tali could tell then the air had changed. They were inside his home now. To Tali's eyes, the dark tunnel of the stairway was a blur of blackness. Then, drastically, it became brighter with each step. Like she had stepped outside again.

"Kovan, what am I looking at?"

"You're standing in front of a tall floor to ceiling window facing out over the mountainside. There's a small grass courtyard just a couple of paces deep, outside of the glass and then a drop off," Kovan said.

"Tali, there's a chair just to your right if you would like to sit. It's one of Merphi's favorite spots," Elias told her.

She reached out until she felt the chair's armrest. She was excited to meet Merphi. She missed Remi since leaving Adalon. She sat and sunk deep into the soft cushions. She could see why it was the mystcat's favorite. Moments later she heard a soft meow and a cat jumped up to her lap to greet her. The cat's fur was softer than a rabbit and Merphi purred and kept crashing into Tali, before propping herself up over Tali's legs. Tali stared at the cat shape in her vision and suddenly she was looking at a beautiful white cat with spots of gold and gray—"Ah!" Tali gasped loudly.

"What's going on, what's wrong?" Kovan asked, bounding from the other room.

"I can see!" Tali exclaimed. She wanted to jump up and down and celebrate, but the cat anchored her down.

"What?" Elias said.

"Yes. I started seeing shapes today and variations of light and dark. Merphi jumped up on me and poof. Is this your home, Elias?" Tali said awestruck.

"Yes. It took me years to carve out this spot on the side of the mountain. I would come up here to meditate, and one day I found this perfect ledge on the mountainside," Elias explained.

The cat jumped down at the raised tones and went to Elias's feet. To weave in and around them for comfort. Tali went to look around now that she had her eyes back.

There were two levels, each nestled into the mountain. With an open end toward the drop off. The main level had a large room with a fireplace in the middle of it and a circular stone hearth all the way around. The ceilings were not very high, and the entire thing looked made of stone, but Elias had lush carpets scattered all around to warm the space. Outside the glass wall was a small patch of natural grass over hard rock, a few trees and bushes to walk around before you fell off the edge. She was now fully snooping around, admiring Elias's art and photograms. There were a lot of chairs with small tables, and each one had books or papers piled on them. She shuffled through a stack nearest to her and noticed that Kovan and Elias were grabbing their weapons and heading out.

"Where are you going?" she asked.

"We are going to go do a sweep of the area in case anyone followed us," Elias said.

Before they left, Kovan came over to her and gave her a hug. "It's good to see you smile again, Raven."

They walked up the stairs and disappeared in the mountain above. Tali continued to look around. The lower level was smaller. There was a bedroom with a photogram of a young beautiful women with brown hair and though the image was faded, it looked like she had pointy ears. There was a locked door she couldn't find a key for. So she searched further, and eventually came upon a long hallway beyond the stairs, that went deeper into the mountain. Along the wall were orbs fixed in place. They were spaced out about every eight feet and looked like solid rock, but they gradually lit up an almost harsh, blue color, when she neared them and then they would gently fade when she passed. One after another until she reached what she thought was a dead end at first. The stone wall at the end of the hallway was slightly ajar, so Tali pressed upon the face. The cold surface moved, with a crunching sound of stone sliding on stone. The wall pivoted to the side more easily than she expected.

The room beyond illuminated at her entering. Four steps in, and she stood on a small balcony overlooking a cavern within the mountain. There were more of the orbs placed around the room. These had a softer, more pleasant yellow color to them. As each orb came alive, she could see the room was full of statues, old weapons, and trinkets. It was Elias's own private collection of historical curiosities.

Tali took the short flight of steps down to inspect the treasure. There had to be more pieces in this room, then in any other singular place she knew of. The Scholar's Guild would sometimes have exhibitions of their collections, but they were rare and usually not open to the public. The entire collection between the four universities might only double this. Elias's collection looked to be almost all from the Ancients. The Guild's exhibitions mostly included a lot of Sagean artifacts.

She strolled around everything. Some pieces seemed impossible to even be there. They should have weighed far too much for any man to move. There were smaller items like weapons of ornate design, some with jade handles and some with obsidian blades. There were animal bones from beasts she didn't recognize and smaller locked boxes. Throughout the space there were slabs of thin crystal tablets, remarkably pristine. She counted four like it around the room. One table had jewelry, and another had random disks of stone with markings on each piece.

Near the back was a brilliant obsidian plinth block. It had three smooth sides and a triangular relief cut out of the top. The place where something used to rest. The top of the stone block stood just above her waist. She reached her hand out to feel the stone surface.

"Careful. It shocked me the first time I touched it," Elias said from the balcony.

Startled by his presence, Tali put her hand away. She trembled slightly in her stance. She couldn't tell by his tone if he was mad, she had intruded.

"Sorry," was all she could think to say, and shuffled back.

A slight movement amongst the artifacts slowed Tali's wandering feet. Her eyes tried to track the motion, but the light, and scattered arrangements of pieces, big and small, threw shadows around the room in layers. She paused to listen and could hear a small repeating squeak. She could not locate the source of the sound, until the squeaking emerged in form, and a small dark bat flapped furiously over her head, before landing on the plinth in front of her. It proceeded to chirp and jabber at her in a scolding reminiscent of an angry mother. For an instant she thought of her own mother, but she quelled the worry before it could take hold. This spirited bat had its eyes fixed and glaring at her. They sparkled like green gems and Tali could see its body and head were not merely black fur, but in fact, colorful and shiny flakes. Yet something was off. Squawking furiously, it fell from the pillar and landed amazingly on its face. In a huff it flopped to its feet and crawled back to the plinth top triumphantly. Immediately rounding back on Tali to continue its scolding, and she realized what it was.

"Oh, don't mind Jules, she's just protective," Elias said.

"It's a machine?" She asked, "I've seen something like it in Ravenvyre, but this one is more lifelike."

"That's where I got her actually. I like to think she is alive."

"You modified or tinkered with the design?"

"You could say that. She had a tendency to break so I fixed different parts every time I put her back together. Over time, I added the jade plates and sigils to expand on her abilities."

"So now she's some kind of house guardian?"

"She seems to think so. She is why I have to keep the library locked. She likes to catalog everything endlessly."

It flew to Elias's shoulder and cocked its head still chirping, but almost under its breath now, apparently agitatedly at Tali's presence.

She shook off the surprise and looked at Elias, "I am sorry."

"Nothing to be sorry about. I forgot you could enter here."

"What do you mean?"

"There are wards in the hallway that would prevent most people from entering."

"Wards? You mean the orbs?"

"Yes. I would ask you how you did it, but I assume you got past them without meaning to," Elias said. Tali nodded coyly. The feeling like she had intruded was growing stronger. So, she decided she should leave until Elias invited her back.

"This place is amazing," she said, climbing the stairs to exit.

"Thank you, it took me a lifetime to collect it all."

"Ellaria is going to lose her mind when she sees this."

"I hope not. I need her to solve the riddles that have eluded me."

"Did you find all these things yourself?"

"Sometimes I worked with small teams of archeologists, but a lot of it yes."

"What's it like, to find something so valuable and buried?"

"There's a magical moment where you discover something that hasn't been touched or seen by anyone since the moment it was lost. An instant feeling like you have brought the past back to life. Still, there is also great sadness. You are inadvertently ruining everything at the same speed in which you are discovering it."

"What do you mean?"

"The air and the elements are trying to kill what you have found. They attack immediately. You have discovered something preserved from the past, but don't mistake that for saving it. It was safe. You are endangering it. Now there is a substantial burden to protect what you have exposed."

"Can I ask you, why did you never get Ellaria's help before?"

"I… I don't know. I guess my best explanation is that it's easy to lose yourself in your own mind. Sometimes your expectations have a way of manifesting the reality you project. You assume people will react a certain way and they do, but there's a possibility that had your expectations been different– so too would their reactions have been."

They walked down the hallway back to the rest of the hideaway. The orbs were now all the same soft yellow as the room they just left. Suddenly both of their watches lit up blue, with an incoming message from Ellaria.

Jules chirped and flew away from Elias's shoulder back into the vault, and Tali flipped aside the top face of her watch to see what was happening.

*We will arrive in Polestis shortly*

"Come, we should tell Kovan he needs to go meet them in the city and you and I have things to do," Elias said.

"Things?"

"Training, but this time with my elum blade."

# CHAPTER THIRTY-SEVEN

## POLESTIS REFUGE (LEARON)

KOVAN MET THEM AT THE CENTER OF THE CITY. THEY FOUND HIM WAITING by a large bell tower. The city of Polestis was hard to quantify. It sprawled up and down the mountainside, and in and out of the nearby valley. Like a meandering village that wouldn't stop growing. The architecture was similar to Atava in that it was all wood-built and sided structures. However, the style was more complex and dynamic. A combination of steep shed roofs from the ground and outward, with unexpected building shapes– predominately triangles or pyramids, and very few squares. The color tones of grays, blues, and browns were more calming than drab, the color somehow muting the structural severity of the forms. Though the city was as old as Atava, the buildings were in much better condition.

They crossed a few streets of dirt or crushed stone, but the major roads were stone laid with large slabs and moss growing between the spacings, maintained to clean overgrowth. The center of the city where they found Kovan was a switch backed street, stretching uphill with shops lining the sides. It was no wonder this was the place Elias had hidden from the world in. It was the perfect seclusion.

Kovan greeted them and led them from the center of the city deeper into the mountains. Traversing mostly over rough trails and lightly trampled paths. They veered off the trail which itself was vaguely followable, about two hours into the mountains.

Learon clinched again in pain as Remi dug his claws into his side. The cat had preferred to ride in his saddlebag for most of the trip, but had shifted inside to his coat as the night had fallen. He couldn't believe the cat's willingness to go with him. If there was a bond between Tali and this cat, then it was strong and unwavering– even across half the country. Remi had found Learon the morning they left Adalon at the horses' stables, preferring to sleep near Tali's horse when it couldn't find her. The cat somehow knew that Learon was taking him to her.

For Learon, the cat helped ease his time on their trip west. Wade's incessant complaining was wearing thin. He tried to read the books he had taken from the archives but found himself too fatigued at night to devote any time to them. They pushed through the country at a rigorous pace. At first, he worried about Ellaria, but she was as tough as they came. She said little and never complained. She was quick to spot the best cover and camp sites too. True to form, she directed them along the way and was the ever present decision maker. Learon appreciated her ability to command and could see how she had led forces into battle during the war. She was decisive and had a clarity to her thoughts unlike anyone he had ever met. It was natural to follow her because you quickly came to believe she always knew what she was saying, thought out the options and could trust her. It was amazing she ever fell for Kovan. He must have driven her mad.

Along their trip, wherever she was, Semo was. He was her guardian for reasons that weren't entirely clear to Learon, more than that, Learon could tell Semo respected her. Semo was always his stoic self but was far more helpful than Wade. He could set up camp quickly and get the fire going for protection from the beasts. A few mornings Semo and he had found fresh tracks of something watching their camp, but nothing ever attacked, and they couldn't find any evidence they were being followed.

Semo kept watch more often than any of them combined; he said very few words. Wade got him to tell a story one night about his Darkhawk training and his last trial; The survival trek through the Zenoch's land in the highlands of the New World. On his trial there were ten cadets who went into the highlands for a month. Only four returned to attain the shield. Of the other six, half came back maimed and the other half were never seen from again. During his time, he never saw the blue-skinned Zenoch or one of their famed elite soldiers, the Duskmen, but he knew that they saw him. Semo had survived on small rodents and fish. He purposefully stayed away from any of the larger animals, as not to steal meals the Zenoch people relied on. His brother had told him that was the secret to his survival, and that was how he was to survive the land. He went quiet at the mention of his brother, and Semo moved back to his post to watch for enemies. That was the same night Semo failed to wake anyone else for a shift. Instead, he had stayed vigilant the entire night.

Learon could see him hiding it, but the trip had exhausted Semo—as much or more than any of them.

As they neared their destination, they were all weary and beaten. Twisting through trees in a forest Learon didn't know, had quickly disoriented him. Learon prided himself on being an experienced woodsman, but he only had experience in the forrest near West Meadow and White Hawk mountain. This place was foreign, and the land confused him. They stopped at a cliff side and Kovan dismounted.

"We have to lead the horses on foot from here, down the slope. Elias has a stable there," Kovan said.

Remi must have sensed the way. He became excited and jumped down from Learon and darted away. They followed, pushing their aching muscles to navigate the track down. They got their horses settled and entered Elias's home through a stone wall cut into the side.

Inside, they entered a short hallway that was also a supplies area. Past that, the room opened up into a large open area with pockets of different seating. The center fireplace was open on all sides and Elias stood near it, adding new wood to it. The chimney was hammered metal, that funneled up to the ceiling. The open space had an arrangement of timber posts and beams with a wood ceiling, all holding up the earth of the mountain above. While most of the walls were stone, the entire left wall was an expanse of glass. Tali sat in a chair, nestling her face into Remi's and looking out toward the view beyond. Elias's cat was at her feet. At their arrival, she looked up and rushed over to meet them. Learon was happy to see her.

Before he could greet her, Ellaria barged in front and hugged Tali tightly, "Elias sent a message about what happened. Are you alright Dear?" Ellaria asked.

"I'm better now. Thank you," Tali said, and when they pulled away and Tali smiled they could see some red scaring flaring off from her eyes. She noticed them looking at her scars and she touched the lines with her finger. "The surge left a little reminder. I've decided I like them."

"Actually, you can't really see them. They just disappeared entirely," Ellaria said astounded.

"Yeah, they do that. The visibility is tied to my energy. You should see them when I am training with Elias."

Just then Wade entered the room saying something under his breath about Ghost, and he dropped his packs down.

"Hi Wade," Tali said and smiled.

"Hi Tali, what did I miss, this is new?" Wade said using his finger he pointed to his own eye, referencing her scars, "I like it."

"I was just explaining. They're a remnant of my illumination surge."

"Awesome," he said, and Tali's smile widened.

"What about this girl, Meroha. I know she has been through a lot. Will she talk to us?" Ellaria interrupted.

"Yes. She will. I'll go get her, she's in prayer," Tali said and before she walked away she went up to Learon and hugged him.

"I'm glad you're back. Try not to leave me alone with those two again, please," she told him.

"I won't."

# CHAPTER THIRTY-EIGHT

## REVELATIONS (ELIAS)

T&#72;EY GATHERED AROUND THE OPEN ROOM IN CHAIRS ALL TURNED TO HEAR the girl's story. Elias stood looking out the expanse of glass to the dark canyons beyond while Kovan fiddled with the fireplace behind him. Ellaria got Meroha a glass of water and then went and sat near Tali who was curled up on the big chair with both cats again. Kovan had dubbed this common occurrence around the house as, 'cat soup'. Elias turned back and sat by the hearth as Meroha began.

"We lived in a small gobo in the west fields of Kotalla, where my father worked at the capitol and my mother was a toolmaker. She was a quiet person, but also very strong. My father was very friendly and worked his way up from a carpenters' job to the capitol's prominent position as the voice of the people in the king's court. As the Prolaten, he came to have many friends throughout the city. When the culling started, he was able to keep us safe."

"The culling?" Ellaria asked.

"I'll get to that, but I wanted to explain a little bit about my country. Until I came to this land, I was completely unaware of the outside world's view of Kotalla. We are a relatively cheerful people, sustained by our life as much as any population of people. It's true we live under strict rules and tyranny. But we are also people with reverence for the Sagean faith. Our laws and society are guided by the strict adherence to the teachings of the Sagelight. Recently there was a shift in my country. A devision, between what people are willing to do in the Sacred Light's name.

"It started last winter when a stranger came to Kotalla and was accompanied by the head priest. Understand, it is very rare for foreigners to get through the King's Perimeter, the Kotalla Wall. What was most curious was how he was immediately given a private audience with King Rouloch and General Deraska. Soon after that, everything changed. The crystal mines, which were always steadily foraged, went into high production. Manpower was doubled and soon tripled. At first, people were happy for the extra work. My country rarely offers opportunities to work beyond the allotted hours or compensation. Then the culling began. The Kotalla Authority started requiring citizens to submit for testing. They went systematically through the city and then spread out to the larger countryside. When word of the nature of the testing spread, there was a revolt. Somehow, they anticipated the people's reaction, because suddenly the entire country was flooded with soldiers in metal and gold faceplates. Like they had come from the darkness. You call them the bonemen. It turned out they were electrocuting every citizen inside a custom-built chamber. That was the test. The Authority called it the 'Culling of Light'. They tested everyone. The old and young and many old people were not healthy enough to survive the test."

"Why didn't your people put a stop to it?" Ellaria interrupted.

Meroha paused, her youth was clear as she sat in front of them all. Not that she was a child, but among this group she looked young. Her slight frame curled up in the chair. She held her knees in her hands as she spoke to them. With obvious pain in her eyes, she continued.

"By this point, half of my people had decided what the Authority was doing was the right thing to do. The king and head priest told the people it was the will of the Light. A lot of people believed that the sacrifice of the old was for the greater good. It would strengthen our people. Very quickly, a dissenting voice became treason. This continued for months. Last month, a farmer came to our house. He was frantic and he demanded to see my father. When my father met with him, the man began ranting about the Authority experimenting on people. That they were taking people from their homes in the night to experiment and torture them. He said they took his wife. He found her days later wandering aimlessly in the field. She wasn't the same person, something was wrong with her mind. That was all I heard before my mother took me from the room. It was only a few days later that my father came home unexpectedly after the blue, in a panic. He told my mother to grab the bags and go to the Northsider pier. A man there would take us to Tavillore. My mother already had bags packed and was ready to leave. I can't explain how disoriented I was, but I clung to the fact that we would be together."

Meroha stopped again and sobbed. Tali rose from her chair and approached her. She whispered something in her ear and then sat down next to her on the floor. Meroha took a few long breaths to compose herself and then looked up.

"We were nearly out of the door when I told my Uhna I forgot my necklace," Meroha said, and she pulled a dark chain free from under her shirt. At the end of the chain was a bloodstone. It was held in place by an ornately shaped piece of turquoise. "It was my grandmother's, and I would not leave without it. My mother went back to my room to find it with me. When we reached my sleeping chamber, we heard a loud crash in the main room outside. My mother looked outside of the door and quickly locked it. She rushed me over to the window and opened it up. There was only one level to our gobo, so I climbed out to the ground outside. With my head in the window, looking inside the room, I could hear my father in the next room pleading with someone. My mother grabbed my hand, and I went to help her out, but she stopped. She looked at me and told me to run. I couldn't breathe, and I wasn't sure I had heard her correctly. Then she turned from me to go to my father. I held tight to her hand to keep her from leaving, but I couldn't hold on. Almost at the same instant that our hands unlocked, someone came into the room where my mother was. I pushed off from the wall and ran to fields. It was a dark night. The mists from the Avaleer Mountains were drifting into the fields. I thought if someone followed me, I could lose them in the fog. I made it a long way before I heard them."

At that moment a loud pop emanated from the fireplace and everyone's attention was startled and they turned to look. Elias wanted to start asking questions but decided to let the girl finish, "Please go on Meroha."

"Yes, well after what must have been an hour, I heard my pursuers closing in. I scrambled in the darkness and found a berm. Where I lay down with my stomach in the mud trying to hide. I don't know what I saw that night. Whatever was in the field looking for me was not human, that I am sure of. I could tell they were very tall, but all I could see were their eyes. They glowed a dark orange, almost red, and they held beasts on leashes as they searched the field. Terror completely froze me in place. I put my face into the mud and waited to be found. I'm not sure how much time passed. An hour or hours, but eventually the silence gave me strength to get up. When I did, I ran straight to the pier. There I found a man named Berona, or he found me wandering the docks. I told him what had happened, and he hid me on his ship. He waited until the morning before we left the harbor. I did not know I was supposed to be meeting up with a man named Danehin until much later. In Aquom, when no one was there to meet us, Berona got worried. He smuggled me off the ship with the Band of the Black Sails for help. I was there a few weeks before you showed up to retrieve me."

Everyone in the room was silent. Kovan got up and brought Meroha some tea and thanked her. Tali, still next to her, with her black cat curled in her lap, was holding Meroha's hand. They somehow had an instant bond that Elias didn't understand yet.

They gave her a moment before asking questions, and Elias could tell Ellaria was as eager as he. He signaled for her to go ahead.

"Meroha, thank you for telling us your story. Do you mind if we ask you a couple of questions?" Ellaria asked.

Meroha gave a silent nod, yes.

"Did you ever see this stranger in person?" Ellaria asked.

"No. I heard others say he was handsome, and he had odd looking eyes. I never saw him."

"Do you know why they increased mining and crystal production?" Ellaria asked.

"The Authority wanted as many large and pristine blue joule-stones they could get. Father never said why, though."

"Meroha, I have never heard of beasts existing on Kotalla before. Are they common like here on Tavillore?" Elias asked.

"No. They are rare. We started killing some gigantic wolves this past spring, at the first thaw. They were the first ones anyone had ever seen on Kotalla."

"You are a very brave person, Meroha. We are glad you trusted Tali enough to accept our help. We will do all we can to make sure you are safe. This man here. His name is Semodarian. He is one of Danehin's special guards. Your father wanted you to go to the New World, Semo will take you. We believe that what happened in Kotalla may be happening here. We are determined to stop it. Is there anything else you can tell us? Anything at all that would help us?" Elias asked.

Meroha squeezed Tali's hand and reached into her pocket. She pulled out a small, tightly rolled parchment the size of her finger.

"There was one more thing. I found this note in my bag, on the ship while crossing the Zulu Sea. My father must have placed it inside. I don't know what it means," she said, and delicately she unrolled it to read aloud. "The Sagean's madness grows. He needs the Sagean's Testament to complete the binding tempest and then the Wrythen will live again."

Elias stood abruptly; his eyes transfixed on the Meroha. His mind wandered a moment until Ellaria's voice snapped him out of it.

"Elias. Elias. What is it?" Ellaria asked.

"Do you know where this Testament is?" Tali asked.

"No," Elias replied.

"I assumed it to be a reference to the scripture. In the Book of Light, it says that all Sageans go into the light with the testament for rebirth," Meroha said in her soft tone. They all turned back to register what she had said.

"That's right, the endless soul. That's part of the mythology of the Sageans promise to return," Ellaria said.

"So, the Sageans of old are buried with this testament, but where are they buried?" Learon asked.

"Well, nobody knows where the tomb is located exactly. Only the Sagean and his closest acolytes were allowed inside," Elias said.

"Wait, I thought it was in the city of Marathal?" Tali asked.

"No, that's just a shrine. I've been there," Ellaria said.

"Isn't it guarded?" Kovan asked.

"It is. By the Legion of the Light. Probably taken over by the bonemen now."

"Have you ever been there, Elias?" Tali asked.

"To the shrine, no."

"Could you tell if there was a tomb there? I mean, if you went there. Could you tell?"

"Maybe. Yes, I think I could."

"Does Marathal city fit a description for possible locations of another gate?" Ellaria asked.

"It's a better place to look than most. It is one of the oldest cities, and texts describe a city on a lake, protected by mountains on all sides. But they also talk about a dueling waterfall. Which is the only hiccup, because the great falls at Marathal are an entire mountain cliff, not dual streams," Elias reasoned.

"But it's called the city of rejuvenation, maybe the tomb is there," Ellaria said.

"Maybe," Elias agreed. He had to admit, Marathal was high on his list to go next, but taking this group there was more dangerous than going back to Adalon. Though not as dangerous as breaking into the Citadel, which Ellaria had already done.

"Maybe - is good enough for me," Kovan said, snapping his fingers, "It's only a couple days' ride, let's go have a look around."

"Going to one of the most protected cities in the world to look around might be madness," Elias suggested.

"Yeah, it is. But it's our kind of madness," Kovan said.

The room's leaning was clear. With their eyes on him like he was a beacon of hope, Elias reluctantly nodded his head in agreement. He had to go against his own reservations, because he saw no other way, even if it meant he was leading everyone to their deaths.

# CHAPTER THIRTY-NINE

## ILLUMINATIONS (TALI)

SHE WALKED ALONG THE RIDGE, BALANCING ELIAS'S ELUM SWORD IN HER hand, carefully placing one foot in front of the other to manage the rock's jagged pale edge. She leapt and attempted to relinquish the energy she held before landing, trying to ease her momentum like Elias had shown her. Instead, she splashed into the lake's icy waters again. She lifted her head out of the water. Her hair was drenched and heavy across her face. Tali peeled it away and looked over toward the others where they sat watching her fail repeatedly.

She couldn't tell what they were saying, but if she found them laughing, she was going to storm over there and throw them both into the lake. Instead, she found Wade had an ear-to-ear grin and held a small coin up he had apparently just won off of Learon. It could have been worse, she hadn't let go of the sword this time, and been forced to dive to the bottom to get it. Tali rolled her eyes at the juvenile nature of her friends but flashed a smile toward Meroha, who sat further from them, just watching Tali's continued attempts.

She swam to the edge and pulled herself up onto the rocky shore. The boulders were slimy and hard to grip, but it was faster than walking out of the shallow end where the boys and Meroha sat.

"You're just wasting your money, Learon! I'm never going to do it!" she called over to them.

"You got this, try again," Learon reassured her.

"Are you meaning to fall in the water or is the sun blinding you?" Wade asked, smiling, "I'm asking so I know how much to wager on your next attempt."

"Oh, be quiet, Wade. I can't believe you're betting against me," Tali replied.

"I'm pragmatic, besides the goal is what exactly? To not get wet jumping into a lake?"

"Something like that," Tali muttered.

She climbed the path through the lower brush, ducking around a few tree limbs and up to the top slope. The cream-colored shale that was scattered up atop the ridge was slippery. Tali steadied herself there. Her body aimed toward the lake, she focused on the ground in front of her. Water dripped and rolled off her feet in a cold trickle onto the dirt. There was fifteen feet from her wet toes to where the land projected out over the lake below.

She felt her chest rise and fall with slow, deliberate breaths. She put the blade out in front of her to practice the methods Elias had shown them. She tried to think about Elias's words and pinpoint what she was doing wrong. He had insisted she learn to fight with the sword, since her control of energy was dangerously weak. Unlike a pulsator, the blade felt right in her hands, even if she was still not very good with it. In her mind, she was at least more graceful than Wade or Learon, though both were much better with the pulsators than she was. Wade refused to part with his gauntlet blade, even after Elias showed how easily he could be defeated with it.

She walked forward, swirled the blade and spun on her high-shuffling feet. She understood the balance necessary, and she liked that the sword's size fit her natural movements. The balance and weight of the blade felt good, and her grip and control came instantly. Her issue was her speed with the forms and poor instincts. Elias stressed that instincts came later. As she neared the edge, Wade's words struck her. It was incredibly sunny here. The afterblue sun blazed throughout the area, and the surface of the lake reflected the light and heat. An abundance of light was bouncing off and back at her. Suddenly, she felt just how much heat was being reflected by the surfaces around her. Not just by the lake, but the slightly silver rocks on the shore, and even from the small sparkling chips in the shale. She could feel it, and the power in it vibrated in a slow continual beat.

She leapt again.

Before hitting the water, she exhaled. She pushed the energy she could sense and directed it to the surface below. The water exploded out in a ring, like a giant ball was slowly descending into the pool. The water rushed up and away.

Suddenly she thought she was going to crash into the lake bottom. Tali flailed in the air and her fear took over. She closed her eyes and braced for a collision, but none came. She opened her eyes and found herself suspended in the air below the surface of the surrounding water, in some sort of protective energy bubble. It reminded her of the stone stopping above the river in Elias's test.

She released her flow of energy and fell into the water. The surrounding lake crashed back into itself above.

When she emerged this time and looked over toward the others, they were drenched, and the surrounding ground was wet almost twenty feet beyond the lake's edge. Water receded back into the lake at their feet, and they were all standing and shouting. Serves them right, she thought as she swam toward them.

When she reached the shore, she stood and walked out. A sudden worry that she may have drenched her watch caused her to sprint toward where she left it and past Meroha, whose brown hair was pulled up and revealed her thin, high cheekbones. Her eyes were bright and wide.

"What?" Tali asked.

Meroha put her hands together in front of her face and whispered a prayer.

"Please stop that," Tali said.

"I… I just can't believe it. You are a Sagean," Meroha said.

"No, I'm not, please don't call me that."

"But…"

"I'm just Tali. Has anyone seen my watch? I thought I left it on this rock, but it's gone?"

"I have it," Learon said.

Tali looked over to see him holding the watch out for her. She grabbed it and thanked him. Checking for any moisture, she found he had saved it. The time on the front face however shocked her.

"Oh, we need to go. I promised Elias we would be back to continue going over the manuscripts."

"Come on, more reading?" Wade said, taking off his wet shirt.

"What are you talking about? You haven't been reading anything," Learon said.

Wade scowled, wrung out his shirt and moved his hand through his wet hair, pushing it back. Tali unwillingly gawked.

Learon audibly cleared his throat. Tali broke her brief focus on Wade to find Learon shaking his head at her, with a slight smirk on his face.

"Let's go," Tali said and stepped past them. The small lake was not far from Elias's place, but through rough terrain. Her shoes were wet, and she had no choice but to walk in them. Small clips from the water to the ridgeline, on mostly boulders was one thing, traversing the mountain barefoot was not something she wanted to try.

"How's your search going, Learon?" Tali asked.

"I've found almost nothing yet. But I still have a stack to go through," he answered.

"I'm sorry," Tali said.

"It's fine. I'm probably grasping at smoke," Learon said.

"Don't give up. Have you talked with Ellaria about it?" Tali asked.

"No. She was less than happy with me and Wade when we came back with a bag of books."

"Hey now, don't lump me in with your nefarious actions," Wade complained.

"Are you saying she didn't yell at you too?" Learon asked.

"Oh no, she lit into me like a thunderstorm. You know how she is?" Wade said, throwing his hand up.

"No, I don't. I haven't spent much time with her, to be honest. I want to, though. Out of everything written about the Great War, her exploits are probably talked about the most. She's obviously a force," Tali said.

"She's something all right," Wade agreed, and Tali rolled her eyes.

"What?" Wade asked

"You think she's sparkling, don't you? You know she's like sixty, right?" Tali asked.

"She's fifty-six. I think and even Learon would admit the years have been kind to her," Wade said with a shrug.

"Don't bring me into this," Learon said, and Meroha giggled from behind.

When they arrived back at the house, they passed Semo standing guard outside. His unbreakable jawline was tense as always. He looked intimidating with his hand on the hilt of his sword and his shaved head. Though Elias told him it wasn't entirely necessary, Semo insisted and was not easily talked out of anything he saw as duty.

Inside, the main level was empty. Tali made her way down the stairs to the lower level, assuming they were in Elias's museum. At the last step she could see light creeping out of the door at the far end. They were in the room Tali had found locked two days before. The door now stood slightly ajar and the three veterans inside were intensely conversing over something. Tali paused before going in, trying to listen to the details of the conversation. She wasn't sure what she expected to overhear, but the whispers inside evaporated instantly as Wade and Learon came bounding down the stairs behind her. Tali pushed the door, knocked slightly and entered.

"Are you guys in here?"

"Tali, dear, you're soaked," Ellaria told her.

Tali looked down at her outfit and shoes, they still sagged and dripped from the lake– even after the trek back. Then she took in the room and realized she needed to change.

"I should change," Tali said.

"Please and then come back we have a lot of work to do," Ellaria told her.

Tali scampered back to the room she was sharing and tried to change as quickly as she could. Peeling her wet clothes off and laying them flat to dry. She dressed and dashed back to Elias's library, where Wade and Learon had now gathered too.

In the center of the room, was a great big table with an intricately detailed map of the world. Easily the most detailed map of Territhmina that she had ever seen. It was meticulously drawn and noted extensively with names and symbols. Some of which she didn't recognize. What she found more amazing was that it contained a great deal of information about the New World. There was also an elaborate bookcase at the far wall, with pocketed windows near the ceiling wrapped in the wood casement.

"Did you figure out what the symbols in the Alchemist's Codex mean?" Tali asked as she entered.

"I think we have. They refer to the Guardians of Light," Elias said.

"I thought you could decipher the language?" Learon asked.

"Only partially," Ellaria said slightly defeated.

"What about the vault? Can you find these same symbols in there?" Tali asked.

"We haven't been back in the vault today, let's go look," Ellaria said.

"That's a good idea," Elias said and he led them out of the library and down the hallway of orbs. At the end of the hall he placed his right palm on a metal plate near the opening. Tali had originally walked right past it. Ellaria was interested in the orbs themselves as they walked. Tali noticed the others followed tentatively. Upon entering the room of artifacts they waited as the orbs inside began to glow.

"I can't see this and not stand breathless before it every time," Ellaria said as they stood before the treasure. She descended the stairs both eager and completely absorbed in her surroundings. Elias's guardian, Jules the mechanical bat, emerged at Ellaria's presence. Tali expected her to get the same welcome she received, but Jules sat on Ellaria's shoulder, like they were old friends. "These are all so wonderful, Elias. Thank you."

"It was a life's work. I'm glad to share it with you."

"Why are you thanking him?" Tali asked.

"Because, he has saved all these things from death. Resurrected them from the past. Every piece in here represents a lot of hard work. It takes time to save these things. It's not a job for a machine. It must be done by hand and with great care."

"That is true. I admit I was very lucky to make friends long ago with a great digger named Bogavesh. He had come from a family of diggers in the south. They searched for all kinds of things."

"Including the Tempest Stone?" Ellaria said.

"Yes."

Ellaria wandered around to the very back and returned. "Where do we even start? Look at all this. Elias, you're after something more than just a stone. Whatever it is, now is the time to tell us. We can't keep chasing our tail," Ellaria said.

"She's right, Elias. We all saw your reaction to Meroha. You're not searching for the Ancient's knowledge on illumination, are you?" Tali submitted.

"No,"

"You're searching for knowledge about this Wrythen," Kovan asked, suddenly interested in the conversation.

"What?" Ellaria asked.

"The Wrythen, you've seen it, haven't you?" Tali pressed.

"I have."

"When?" Kovan demanded.

"Forty years ago, on the top of the Dragon's Spine," Elias admitted.

"The night you killed the Sagean?" Tali said.

"The Wrythen appeared that night as I fought the Sagean. It grew from the ground like black smoke and its eyes came alive first— orange and then bright white. It took the shape of a man, but moved like a phantom, and laughed at us. I was near to being defeated as it was, and at first, I thought the Sagean had conjured something to finish me. But it mocked me in a voice that echoed in my head more than my ears. It told us that the power of our charged souls would bring it out of the shadows. Together we were the binding tempest, a storm of energy that breaches the void, and through that breach It could return to this world. Somehow, in that moment of pure terror, I realized the Sagean was as shocked and scared as I was of this thing. I used the distraction and brought forth all the energy I could feel around me and released it at both of them. The world exploded in light and I fell from the ridge. When I came to, I climbed up to the top again, and the Sagean was gone. So, too, was this entity that had appeared to us. I searched the mountain but found no tracks or sign of the Sagean."

"You never saw a body? You told us he was dead!" Kovan fumed.

"It was a kindness to you both. I could sense his energy was gone."

"Why didn't you tell us? By the Light, Elias we could have helped. Why have you always been so determined to walk alone?" Ellaria said.

"I have no great excuse. I knew it was up to me to defeat the Sagean, and afterward I couldn't tell either of you the truth. I saw the relief in your eyes, and I couldn't take that from you."

"Right, your classic overtures of nonsense," Kovan said.

"You would never have believed me, Van."

"What about our daughter? Did this Wrythen kill her?" Kovan was shouting now.

"No. I don't know!" Elias fired back.

"Could you have saved her?" Kovan asked.

"No."

"After she died, came to us in the middle of the night and you told us that this being you called a Wrythen could come for us. Why? And why are you afraid to use your powers? Don't think we all haven't noticed," Kovan demanded.

"I…" Elias struggled to respond. Then Kovan suddenly drew his weapon out. His eyes blazed with venom like Tali had never seen.

"Van, Stop!" Ellaria yelled. Kovan looked to her and paced away, holstering his gun. His hand forming a tight fist as he paced. Ellaria watched him stalk away before readdressing Elias, "Please explain."

"At first I started to see it when I would use the luminance, then, in the shadows, and then in my dreams. I became convinced it was after me. So, I stopped using my powers for a long time and it went away. Shortly before your daughter died I had a dream that something terrible was going to happen. After she died. I became wrought with worry. It hung on me like a noose. So, I sent my dear Mia away and told her to go into hiding far from me. I warned you, and I disappeared. I figured that I might have to face this thing one day. I stopped using my powers almost completely and set out to find out anything I could. I had always been curious about my abilities. Who wouldn't be? But there was no one to explain anything to me. I went and met with the Tregoreans for answers and their healer helped me. He didn't know much about the Wrythen, just that it existed. It was healing just to know I wasn't crazy. Then he told me to find the Tempest Stone, that the Ancient Luminaries had faced this being before."

"Do you still see it?" Ellaria asked.

"No. Until recently I had gone years without using my abilities."

"So that's why you left and why you sent Mia into hiding?"

Elias nodded his head and kept staring at the floor. Kovan kicked a stone statue over with a crash, and a shiver ran through Tali's spine. Elias didn't even look up. Tali had been standing by with her arms crossed watching the argument between her heroes play out but something stirred in her and she couldn't take it anymore.

"Stop it! We need to find out what this thing is and how to defeat it. We are all here now. We'll find something or we'll find this Tempest Stone, but we can't do it if we're fighting each other," Tali cried out.

"This is my fight," Elias said.

"It's everyone's fight. You need to trust someone for once in your life, Elias," Tali said.

"She's right. You never trusted the Guild; you never trusted me or Kovan with any of this. For forty years! Thorns, Elias! You don't even trust the world with your own name," Ellaria said, and she went over and embraced her friend, "If we can't trust each other we can't stand against this."

"What can we do?" Elias said.

"We take action, we do something. Because evil succeeds, when good men do nothing."

# CHAPTER FORTY

## DECODING THE PAST (ELLARIA)

SPREAD OUT ON THE MAGNIFICENT TABLE WAS AN ARRANGEMENT OF BOOKS, manuscripts, and journals, with slips of parchment scattered everywhere in between. Each scrap contained Elias's random thoughts and scribblings. His own disciplined mind unraveled the language of the ancient texts. He had pieced together words and phrases that might connect, but often with confusing results. Ellaria could see the task had obviously overwhelmed him, it had overwhelmed her in only a day. She knew he had amassed a collection to rival any of the universities, but in reality, Elias's collection of original texts and artifacts was more valuable than any singular hold outside of the Guild's own archives.

The journal was enlightening. Elias had deciphered a great deal of it, but not all – and most with questionable accuracy. It was a wonder he could pinpoint likely locations for the gates. Translating the other texts in his library was proving difficult. Already they had run into roadblocks. There were three of them poring over everything in Elias's library. Learon was busy digging into his own stacks. Wade, Semo, and Kovan spent the time outside training. Kovan was still struggling to be in the same room as Elias.

The first day had yielded very little to the others' consternation, and Ellaria felt her old eyes wearing fast. When the sound of a book slapped closed it shook her focus back into place.

"I can't make sense of this," Tali fumed, "Every time I think I've settled on a translation, I read the passage back and it makes no sense. Are you sure about your groupings, Elias?"

"I can't be positive. There are many meanings for every word. For instance, the journal uses the words energy, life and light interchangeably."

"Could we be accidentally doing this with other words?" Ellaria asked.

"I would say undeniably we are."

"Huh!" Learon exclaimed from his seat.

"Did you find something?" Tali asked.

"Maybe, it's from a ledger on the Ash Field excavation. They have included an account by the site foreman. He filed a grievance on behalf of his team. A man named Hogmar, argued for his workers' pay even though they were furloughed for the day. Listen to this. On day eleven the workers were called off and sent home, back to their tents for the day but it turned into three days. Then he argues later with the manager that they changed the site conditions. He is told the delay is for worries over the temple's structural integrity, but no expert is ever brought in to inspect."

"Does it say how the site was changed?" Elias asked.

"Hogmar claimed there was a mural of symbols that was destroyed. They brought an artist in for detailing, but she only made drawings of one, as they had reduced the second mural to dust. He also says there were a lot of high order individuals around that seemed to all be in charge, but who were arguing amongst themselves. This Hogmar is the only one I've found, other than my father, who spoke out about the suspiciousness surrounding a seemingly simple and fruitless excavation. Sequestered scientists sworn to secrecy, a ruined mural, a mysterious cloaked man, reports of the Citadel's presence, missing artifacts and closed sites, and of course the laboratory explosion and a shipwreck. It's a joke. Why wasn't the Guild managing this?"

"Missing artifacts, does he say what?" Elias inquired.

"Hogmar, in his grievance describes an entire room full of objects that they cataloged and then he says someone altered his ledger. Apparently, they were paid a bonus for each item that was recovered. Among the items he says went missing was a chest with a broken locket, a glove, and coins of colored glass. I believe these are the things my father did further research on. Also, he says there was a set of large clay pots with colored symbols. They were full of a salt like substance and Citadel guards removed them. The workers never saw them again."

"That's it!" Elias got up suddenly to retrieve something off his shelf.

"What is it?" Ellaria asked.

He came back to the table with a long glass vase. It had a black rubber stopper on one end and inside Ellaria could see a parchment scroll. He pried the stopper loose. It resisted moving, like it was glued in place. The vase made a popping sound like carbonated wine when the cork came. He reached in and pulled the scroll from inside.

"I found this scroll years ago in a clay pot like the one you just described, Learon. It seems the substance it was buried in helped preserve the parchment. However, it quickly deteriorated the longer I exposed it to air. So, I encapsulated it in this."

Elias unrolled the scroll, and it was filled with a small, delicate script. Three columns of ancient lettering and symbols. Elias placed weights at the corners and together they reviewed the document. Each of them leaned across the table to see as much as they could.

"I have never transcribed it," Elias said.

"This section. This looks like a repeat of the section I transcribed from another text," Tali offered.

"What do you think it says?" Elias asked. Tali looked down at her notes and read them off.

"The protectors of the storm and black energy, spectrum promise, the five furies of light, united below in force for the old one hungers for unlimited light."

"You're right, that doesn't make sense, and I don't like the sound of it, whatever it means," Learon said.

"Can I see that?" Ellaria asked

Tali handed the slip of paper to her. The passage was rewritten, and below she had scribbled her translation with various words crossed out. Ellaria was realizing that they needed to adjust their thinking to read the ancients scripts. The ancients wrote in a faster style that included more complicated symbols in combination with words, symbols with multiple meanings. Staring at Tali's translation, she noticed the flaw. The symbols and script in its original form were not spaced out like their own sentence structure would be. The Ancients connected the strokes of ink from one symbol to the next, from the top of the page to the bottom. This made the entire text its own power and meaning. With that in mind, Ellaria retranslated the passage. One of Tali's crossed out words stuck out at her and she couldn't ignore its implication, the *soul*.

The key was you had to look at the individual piece, but also, and more importantly at the whole. The meaning became discernible through the flow or connected lines similar to alchemy sigils. The others slowly watched her as her pen made scratches on sheet after sheet of parchment. Until she settled on the right translation, finally she exclaimed, "I got it."

"What does it say," Elias urged.

"The guardians of life wielded the tempests of darkness and light.

The Gradient Pact, of five luminary orders united under an edict to defeat the Old One from feeding on the energy of souls."

Elias stared at her and stepped away to pace, while Tali grabbed the parchment to examine how Ellaria had done it.

"That's easier to understand, but it sounds like things just got worse," Learon said.

"I don't disagree. It would appear to be a historical account. It's one of the oldest references I've ever seen to the Guardians and further evidence of the luminary divisions that existed before the Sagean Empire. Each of the luminary division's symbols align with the symbols Elias found in the temple and the ones in the Alchemist's Codex," Ellaria said.

"If this Old One and the Wrythen are one and the same . . ." Tali asked.

"Then we need to translate this scroll completely. Maybe it might tell us how to defeat this thing," Ellaria said.

"If they found scrolls at Ash Field. I wonder if they were the same?" Learon asked.

"Who knows? The Ancients had many mysteries. The Tempest Stone, the wave gates, the amulets, the Atlas Tablet, all of them have remained unknown for centuries. What's more important is if the Prime and his team can translate them."

"If they did find a scroll, couldn't it just be crop ledgers or trading records?" Learon asked.

"Possibly, but I doubt anyone would go through the effort to preserve the scrolls for that purpose. Considering, the broken amulet, my best guess is that the scrolls may be about them. Or if they discovered the pots beneath the mural of the Tempest Stone, the scrolls could be about it. There's no way of knowing," Elias counseled.

With a new singular focus, they divided the three columns of the scroll for each of them to decipher. Tali and Learon worked together in the middle section. Elias and Ellaria split the left and right sides. They worked into the night, with the others checking on them routinely. It was very late when Ellaria finished her section. Even so, she was the first to complete the translation. She moved on to help the others. With the entirety of the scroll translated, they sat back and examined its contents.

It was clear the scrolls were written a generation after the fall of the Ancient World and the Eckwyn age. The first column explained the scrolls' purpose. It was one in a series of scrolls called the Providence Papers. Each spoke of the failures of the Luminaries. The goal was to preserve the history and legacy of the Luminaries. A brief history detailed the takeover of the other factions by the Sageans. First, persecution and banishment of all nonhuman peoples; The Tregoreans, the Menodarins and the Zenoch were exiled. Then, the Sagean Order betrayed the other luminary factions and took hold of the world. This scroll was the history of the fallen orders and their beliefs. Elias and Ellaria could only assume other scrolls were yet to be unearthed.

The middle section and right column were an account of the Wrythen and the War of Luminaries. The Old One had appeared to the leaders of each faction. At first, they ignored the warning, unsure why the prophets had not foreseen the coming threat or shared the visions. A darkness took hold and enslaved people like the walking dead. They called this entity a plague at first. Soon they realized it was a being of power older than their records. They formed an Order of Guardians, made up of chosen warriors from each faction to find and defeat this being. Entrusting each with a powerful amulet to aid them on their quest. However, the Guardians failed.

"Listen to this," Ellaria said reading from the section on the war, "The Luminary war led to experimental magic that combined luminance powers with everything that was known about alchemy. The greatest example of this was the Tazrus Shroud. The luminary Tazrus gave his life to enact a spell. A spell that hid the greatest achievements of the era from the memories of all who lived. Many things were forgotten and lost and the whispers that remained live on as myth and legend. The Sageans soon took control of the rival temples and decimated the lands– beginning their reign."

"Well, this is depressing," Learon said after they had finished going through it.

Tali tapped the bottom section of the middle column with her finger, "This part is interesting. It says the being seemed to be known to a small tribe of cave dwellers that lived in the land of the deadly wind. It was the land of the one people. It says here that their leader, a wiseman, came to convene with the factions of luminaries. He knew of a power within the laws that govern the furies, and could destroy the Wrythen. That the Light entrusted his people to protect the west boundary. The wiseman left and said his people would return when the endless night was brought to bear," Tali said.

"You're right, dear, it seems to be the loose end in this account. And this word for the one people, Wanvilaska," Ellaria said.

"It sounds familiar. It says they lived north beyond the killing wind," Elias said. He put his hand to his chin, mulling over the possibilities.

"Do you know this place?" Ellaria asked.

"It could be the Dead Lands west of Wainbro. It's a desolate waste, where the winds are said to be deadly. It's a no-man's-land," Elias said.

"Even sailors from Ravenvyre avoid that area. They say the coastline is a death trap and the west winds carry ships, smashing them into the cliffs," Tali said.

"Well, if you want to know how to defeat this Wrythen, then your answer may be there," Ellaria said.

"We don't know if anything is there," Learon said.

"No, but this scroll says the amulets were created for each of the champions of the luminaries with the purpose to defeat this thing. Seeing as we don't have any amulet, finding this lost tribe may be our only hope," Tali said.

"This scroll is what, more than a thousand years old? This lost tribe is dead," Learon argued.

"Probably, but maybe they left something behind that can help us. How far away is Wainbro?" Tali asked.

"It's not far. It's a day to the west. But it is in the opposite direction of Marathal. What do you think, Ellaria?" Elias said.

Somehow, she knew it would come back on her to decide. It always did, but this time she thought the path forward was clear, "We have to try," she said. Knowing it meant that they would split up again.

They devised out a plan and started packing. Ellaria, Kovan and Wade would go to the city of Marathal, while Elias would take Tali and Learon to find this Wanvilaska. Kovan and Elias both agreed that it was better to stagger their arrivals in Marathal, anyway. Ellaria wasn't sure it was going to matter. The bonemen would look out for all of them and the Whisper Chain would hear word of them arriving sooner rather than later. Still, it was good to have them speaking to each other again.

# CHAPTER FORTY-ONE

## WANVILASKA (ELIAS)

THEY SAID GOODBYE IN THE MORNING, IN THE DARKNESS AND PARTED AT the base of the mountain. Elias thought Meroha would never let go of Tali. After much debate, they decided she would stay at Elias's home, instead of going with Semo. Her promise to look after both cats was tough to pass up. Though Elias suspected Remi might follow Tali, being so young still. Semo was agreeable to it because he wanted nothing slowing him down. He was returning to Illumeen to report in person to Dalliana and carried a letter from Ellaria. She also gave him strict instructions to avoid any altercations. With a mission beset upon him, Semo was eager to leave, and he set out before dawn that morning. Semo was always vigilant, and an excellent soldier and they would miss him. Hopefully, not when they needed him most.

"Send us word when you reach this, Wanvilaska," Kovan said.

"You do the same when you reach Marathal, my friend," Elias said.

"Are you sure you can find this place?"

"I will or I will die trying."

"That's what I'm afraid of. Remember Elias, There's no meaningful death, only a meaningful life."

"I'll remember, until we meet again, safe travels," Elias said.

"You too," Kovan said and turned his horse to Tali, "Young Raven, you keep him out of trouble, understand?"

She nodded, and the two groups turned from each other in the road and moved in opposite directions.

Elias could tell Ghost was happy to have him back. She was going to hate him once they got closer to Wanvilaska, and the wind pummeled them. First, they needed to reach Wainbro over the mountain pass. It would be nightfall before they arrived. They took the western trail out of Polestis into the tall peaks. Once beyond Brighteyes Pass, the lands to the west of Warhawk mountains became harsh, wind stripped and desolate. It was not a frequently traveled area, even amongst explorers.

"Elias, do you have any idea where we are going?" Learon asked.

"I have been to Wainbro many times on my way to Ravenvyre. I have never traveled north from there. Few do."

"What do you think? Is it possible Wanvilaska is out there?" Tali asked.

"I don't know. Everything we found says yes. I'll say this, I'm glad for the zenithal sun. If the land north of Wainbro is impassable. I would rather try in the summer than not."

"Worse than the Frostlands?" Learon asked.

"We'll see."

The roads before the pass were not as friendly to travelers. The biggest deterrent was that the distance between cities was greater, combined with harsh weather and more beasts, people didn't voyage through there other than in large convoys. Even the outskirt cities tried to coordinate departures to protect travelers when they could. Most routed their trip through Parado, along the pass of the Hawk's Neck. Given all that, Elias expected the road from Polestis to Wainbro would be empty, and it was.

When the sun moved out of the blue overhead, they had crested the Brighteyes Pass. The descent out of the mountains was swift and easier, but they rode with the sun in their eyes. Learon was obviously an accomplished rider. He was comfortable with his horse and rode with his bow thrown over his shoulder. Tali, he could tell, despised the ride, but she never complained. Elias knew she would never stop too, she had a searcher's spirit he understood.

He couldn't help but think that their time together was running out, and he hadn't taught her a thing. Most of all, how to live with being a luminary. As an outsider, shielding her abilities from those who would see her as a threat. Part of him wanted to keep her as far from all this as possible. He knew that if the Prime and the Sagean found her, she would be in great danger. She would constantly be on the run and in fear of who was closing in, the only solution to protect her was to defeat the threats first.

During the night, while they all packed for the trip, Kovan had spoken with Elias about it. They both felt protective of her. Not because she was helpless. She was far more capable than either of them at her age, and possibly even now. They had a responsibility to her. Kovan felt like he had brought her into this mess and Elias had committed to guide her. They had each made a promise to her and had to see it through.

They reached Wainbro in the night with the howls of wolveracks crying in the surrounding wilderness. Elias had never known the beast to be so vocal about their position. Nor could he remember a time when the wolveracks were ever a big problem in this area.

Wainbro was a simple town. It was a small, walled circular city, with three towers on the perimeter and a single gate entrance.

When they arrived at the gate, it was closed. Elias dismounted and approached the speak-through and knocked on the shutter. A guard opened the shutter on the third knock.

"Yes."

"We need a place to stay for the night."

"How many in your party?"

"Three."

"Give us a moment. Please walk your horses in as soon as we open the gate."

Elias returned to Learon and Tali and motioned for them to get down.

"Is there a problem?"

"I'm not sure. It's unusual for their gates to be closed. Be on your guard."

Behind him the gate creaked to life, as the guards inside pulled it open for them to pass through.

"Don't linger, you three. Hurry," the guard said.

They each pulled their horses along and past the gate. Elias stopped when he was inside to talk with one guard on duty.

"What's going on?"

"We've had attacks on the wall every night for the past ten days."

"Attacks?"

"The wolveracks have been testing the wall all around the city. We have killed almost two a night."

"What about the protection fires?"

"They don't seem to work. The beasts go right past. We can tell it hurts them, but they don't care. What's your business here?"

"We are looking for a friend that came through here," Elias lied.

"We haven't had many visitors in some time. Talk to Banner at the inn. He would know."

"Thank you."

Elias came back to the others and directed them to the inn near the center of the town. It was one of the larger buildings in this small city. The corner entrance was a thirty-foot-tall stone tower. They tied off their horses and passed under the stone arch vestibule. Elias remembered staying here once in his youth, but the proprietor was named Goya. The main lobby had a small bar and eatery, just past the front desk.

"Get us a table," he told Learon

Elias crossed the room and rang a bell. A young man came to greet him.

"Can you tell me where can I find Banner?"

"Mr. Banner tends the bar at night. Do you need a room?"

"Yes, but just for the night. Two beds."

The kid checked him in, and Elias moved on to the bar. An older man with a full gray beard sat on a stool behind the counter, sipping something hot out of a tin cup. The steam wafting up from the surface.

"Mr. Banner?"

"That's me, youngster."

Elias smiled at being called young, "I was told you're the man to talk to in this town," he said.

"Well, I've been living in Wainbro for seventy years. There's not much I don't know. Which is good, cause I'm too old you see and I ain't got time to be learning nothing new. What is it you want to know?"

"For starters, what's the story with the beasts?"

"Cut right to it, huh. Not sure what's driving them to attack. I admit I never saw that, but I know I'm worried those towers will be overrun. They're not prepared to kill beasts inside the walls."

"They don't have any charged guns or rifles?"

"Not in this town, son," Banner said.

"Do you know, are there any settlements north of here?"

"There's nothing north of here, but death and wind."

"I heard a tale that there's a village out there."

"Ahh, the bat people, you're talking about the cave dwellers."

"Cave dwellers?"

"Yep. Them and the drizars are the tallest of tales this area has. Them bat people are supposed to be demons. With skin as pale as a ghost and they speak in hisses like snakes."

"Really? What are the drizars?"

"They're large lizard like beasts that roam the plateaus."

"You ever seen them? The bat people or these drizars?"

"No. I met a man once who pulled an odd-looking skeleton out of the north. Drug it out of the wild. It was real enough, and it didn't look like any beast I know of. No, the only tale around here that's real is the one about the Quantum Man."

Elias was taken back, "What would that be?"

"The Quantum Man stayed here one night forty years ago. Hiding out from the Legion. The way the old timer that used to run this place, Goya, used to tell it, his wife had to patch him up. He was wounded and had a great fever for three nights, like a living fire. Still, he somehow cloaked this whole building in light and hid it from the men chasing him. Some folk think he sent the building to another world. Now when people stumble or an accident happens, they say it's an echo of the energy he left behind."

"That is a tale."

"It's the Light's truth. I saw the thing disappear in the middle of the day."

"When was this?"

"Not long after the Sagean was said to have been killed."

Elias thanked the old man and tipped him a small amber. Then joined the others at their table. He silently sat down, trying his hardest to recall anything that matched the story he just heard. Try as he did, he couldn't reconcile the past with the present.

"Everything alright, Elias?" Learon asked.

"Um. Yes. Sounds like there's a history of people seeing things in the north. We'll head out in the morning toward the plateaus and the canyons. We should get some rest. Here's a key: we have a room upstairs. I'm going up now. Oh, and don't step on me. I'll be asleep on my bedroll in the middle of the floor," Elias said and retired to the room.

He laid down, and troubled by fading memories, stared at the ceiling until he fell asleep.

THE HILLS BECAME MORE DRY AND CRACKED THE FURTHER THEY PRESSED on. The rifts in the land rose above them, and they found themselves walking the floor of an ancient, eroded valley, like the crevasse of an evaporated estuary. Elias looked for a mercy from the wind and headed for the jagged cliffs, where they would be surrounded by plateaus. He felt something guiding him along, but he couldn't say what. The gusts picked up in intensity before the rifts opened up, and the horses were struggling to walk. For the last league, it forced them to push through on foot. They led the horses through turbulent gusts that left them all blind and unable to hear each other. Elias trusted Ghost to get them beyond the blinding swirls, but while his horse kept moving, something was spooking it. Elias wondered if there wasn't something else provoking and agitating her. He couldn't rule out the possibility the horse had sensed something he didn't. They could recognize a predator, beast or man, before he saw one coming. The sheer number of wolveracks that had been attacking Wainbro was alarming. The beasts dispersed into the cover and shadows of the mountains by dawn, but Elias knew they were still out there.

Gradually the rising side walls of the canyon blocked the wind, and an odd tranquility settled into place. The cliff faces were a hard-red clay with weeds and dead trees puncturing the rock. In the canyon's mouth, they could finally hear each other again. Tali wore an expression of trepidation, while her eyes darted from corner to corner. Learon stalked stiffly beside her. His free hand clenched tightly in a fist. The canyon was eerily calm.

There was no telling how far these rifts would take them. Some of them led all the way to the Brovic Ocean. About five hours into the winding canyon, he spotted tracks in the valley floor.

Elias handed Ghost's reins over to Tali and inspected the ground. They had come across tracks before, but all belonging to smaller animals. This depression– soled and flatfooted. The shape was human, but it did not have boot or shoe tracks to it. There weren't many, and he couldn't tell where they went. They kept moving deeper into the canyon, which was fully twisting to the west now.

More time passed when suddenly there was a low rattle in the wind. Elias pulled them all to a stop to listen, and it was gone.

"Did you hear that?" he asked the others.

"What?" Learon asked.

"Yes, that rattling?" Tali whispered.

"Yes. It was almost like a clicking sound."

All three of them looked around them but could see no sign of movement. The wind from time to time would hiss and whistle above, but mostly it was quiet. In fact, their voices carried a great distance in the canyon, making any sound difficult to pinpoint and account for.

They hiked thirty feet farther when he felt them.

A tinge of energy collecting on their position altered him. Elias searched for the energy and found vibrations moving in the plateaus above. He turned to Learon and Tali.

"Throw your weapons to the ground."

"What?"

"Do it now!"

They followed his instruction. Elias laid the tip of his sword in the dirt and let the hilt go. Learon dropped his bow and unbuckled his pulsator, letting it fall. Tali did the same.

Almost at the same instant, wild looking warriors appeared all around them. They were pale skinned, almost ashen white, but they looked dirt covered and worn. Their clothes were tightly sewn in a manner that the larger cities would consider lewd and all wearing colors that blended with the ground. A few of the warriors had a roll of black fabric connecting the entire length of their sleeve and back to their body. All of them had markings on their face, in what Elias understood to be a war paint. They had colored feathers interwoven in their long hair and animal bones adorning their weapons. Most were carrying bows, but a few had curious looking double-bladed knives.

They seemed satisfied to just watch them for the moment. Studying the odd group who had ventured into their territory with the same scrutiny as he had done to them. Then a woman in the valley in front of them made a clicking sound with her mouth and moved her hands in odd motion. Signaling two men on the top plateau, they responded with hand movements. With each movement, they could hear a light rattle. It was a much more sophisticated form of hand language than Elias had learned in the Darkhawks. Elias could tell the woman was the commander. In addition to feathers, she wore a headdress made up of red vines and she was the only one with a short blade made of jade.

For a tense moment, Elias wondered if he had made a huge mistake. Then the rhythmic prattle of a horse's hooves echoed through the chamber of rock. Three people approached riding atop animals slightly smaller than horses, but with bodies similarly proud and full of coarse hair. They had long necks and a small head with wide set eyes and antlers. Elias had never seen them before but knew them by description to be lameers. A Frostland species near extinction, that experts believed were a cousin to the llama. Staring at them in person the resemblance was obvious, except the antlers.

Two of the riders were men. They dismounted immediately and helped the third rider down. An old woman with nearly twice the amount of covering then the others. She wore her hair spun above her head, held in a sort of headdress with feathers. The high collar of her coat was a colored fur and came up above her ears. She walked toward Elias with an agitated expression on her face.

"Why have you come to seek us out?" the women spoke, but not out loud. The sounds bloomed in his head just the same, Elias shook his head. The sensation was peculiar. Elias didn't want to be rude, but for the moment he struggled to respond. He blinked his eyes forcefully a few times.

"We are looking for Wanvilaska. The united people."

"But we were not looking for you or your kind."

"My kind, do you mean humans?"

"I see no human here. No, I speak of you and the young woman. You are both luminaries, are you not?"

Elias caught slightly off guard by her assessment, "How do you know this?"

"Still too seduced by the power of energy to understand its delicacy, I see."

She had avoided the question with a statement and Elias continued, "We have come seeking that understanding."

"I don't trust you, luminary. Your energy is a storm I don't care for."

"Please. We need your help."

The old women took a deep breath and studied the faces of each of them. Her brown eyes were brilliantly bright and powerful.

"Come. My people will lead you the rest of the way."

THEY TOOK THEM ANOTHER TWO LEAGUES FURTHER INTO THE CANYON. The top plateaus soared higher and reached three hundred feet above the crevasse floor. The Wanvilaska village was at a point where the canyon widened and split around a small flat-topped mound in the middle. On the surrounding sides, the cliffs had rows of holes stacking one atop another, with rounded doorways into the cliff dwellings.

There was a system of skinny stairs cut into the vertical rock that climbed from tier to tier with a crisscrossing array of ladders anchored to the stone. Some homes required complicated routes to access them.

Here, the rock face was smooth and near vertical, like a slot canyon. The striations swirls in the chiseled stone surface looked almost unnaturally cut.

Elias had learned that the One-People's leader's name was Unaharra. She had told him, as they rode into her village, by sending her voice into his head as she had done before. She wasn't their ruler, for the One-People had no ruler. They were a unified people, and she their guide.

Her people brought Tali and Learon into a cave in the mountain for food. They had to duck their heads as they passed through the opening and disappeared from Elias's view. He followed Unaharra to the middle of the canyon. Where she climbed a path of steps to the flat mound top.

"So, you have found us. What is this desperation I sense from you?"

"First, can you tell me, why did you agree to meet with us? You seemed ready to turn us away."

"I liked the young woman's spirit. It spoke to me more clearly and with more sway than I care to admit," Unaharra left it at that, and Elias quickly caught on that she was not a woman to press to explain herself.

"Well, I thank you. You may not know, but my world has changed from the one I think you suspect it is. The age of luminaries is past. We are very rare now among our people."

"This is true. Though, not as rare as you think."

"How could you know?"

"We know. You should remember that we know. Your people have sought us before. A small group similar to yourself came many ages ago to meet with my ancestors. Seeking our wise man. They spoke of a purge and a Sagean Empire oppressing the world of humans. My people turned them away, told them to solve their own problems. I will probably tell you the same."

"We are on the verge of war once again. This is true. But our battle I fear is with a force greater than another luminary."

"You speak of the Old One?"

"I do. We have also heard him called the Wrythen. I have searched much of this world for a way to defeat this being. Or anything about it, and you are my last hope."

"Then hope is lost, Elias Qudin."

"Why? I know your ancestors tried to help mine before in this battle."

"They did, and your people refused to listen."

"I cannot be a better person for people who have passed. I can only be a better person than I was the day before."

"Are you better today than the day before?"

"No, I can't say that I am."

"Finally, you speak honest words. I've decided I will tell you what I know of the Old One. Based on your spirit, I see you have confronted it before?"

"Yes. That's the second time you have mentioned my energy. What's wrong with it?"

"You must decide that. I can only tell you it feels twisted. How do you understand energy but not human energy? It's a link as real as your link to electricity. Similar to how a lightning strike connects the sky to the land. The energy of beings binds them together. Even from a great distance. This is the eternal nature of entanglement."

"Is this how you communicate?"

"Yes, however, some are skilled, others are not. Some may only feel the empathic pulls. Hate or sadness, even sickness or enlightenment. The great ideas are created with collaborative minds if they are singularly focused. Now tell me how did the Old One appear to you?"

"Like a breathing being of black smoke."

"Were you near death?"

"Yes, why?"

"Its very nature is bound to dark energy. However, it is strongly drawn to the opposite energy, like a magnet, it is pulled to the energy of the soul. When it connects to the spirit, it drains that energy. Turning it to its will."

"Why the soul?"

"Your spirit, your soul is energy. But unlike the energy of light or heat, it is free. Many wars have been fought over the currency of souls."

"This Old One, what is it?"

"The universe is alive with light and darkness. There is significant power in both."

"The darkness?"

"Oh yes. There's an incredible power to the darkness. The darkest matter is so consuming it dominates the void. This is the essence of the Old One. It is the darkness. But it is still energy."

"Where does it come from?"

"If it has a name, I don't know it."

"Well, why is it here? What does the Wrythen want?"

"There is no motive beyond its own nature. Like gravity, it is part of the structure of existence."

"Then can it be killed?"

"No, energy doesn't die, all energy transforms, it exists to change."

"In the account I read, It said your ancestor offered a way. The Wrythen told me we would bring it to life by the power of the opposites. The force of opposites. Can that be wielded against this being?"

"No, but the power of opposites is not the strongest force. The strongest energy is that of the Protagen. The force of two identical energies. It is this which my ancestors believed could defeat the Old One."

Elias contemplated her words and gazed into the canyon. Breathing deeply, before turning his eyes back to Unaharra.

"Thank you for sharing your knowledge, Unaharra."

"You are a seeker, Elias Qudin. But be careful, your mind is singularly focused on the past. Please tell me, Elias. How did the young woman find you?"

"It was a friend that found her, our meeting was coincidental."

"You must protect her. If I am drawn to her, the Old One will be as well. She has shown great power, I assume?"

"She has, why?"

"She is what my people call the Unova. They would mark her to take my place were she born here. And the boy?"

"He found me and saved me. For a time, I thought he was also a luminary. You said he wasn't human?"

"He is not. They have a connection, those two."

"She has that ability, I think, to make powerful allies of anyone she meets."

"The boy is hiding something from you. You know this?"

"I do, but I do not know what he is."

"I sense the blood of others in him, but I cannot say for certain. However, I would not let it worry you. His spirit is kind, like the young woman's."

On the ridge line above, a wild call echoed out. A scout relaying something to the others. Others repeated his call in the village. Learon and Tali emerged from the cave to see what the commotion was. Another warrior on the plateau top called something and then ran at full speed to the cliff's edge and off. He flung his arms out wide and a taut fabric between his arms and body caught the wind. The warrior sailed majestically across the canyon to the scout on the other side. Unaharra looked at Elias with a serious expression and grabbed his arm.

"We need to go inside."

"What's happening?"

"They have spotted a drizar on the plateaus."

"Can we help?"

"No. It is their duty. They hunt the drizar for food and sport. We are safe."

He didn't argue. They retreated off the mound and into the cave where Learon and Tali waited. It was lit inside by lanterns pocketed into small carved out niches. The ceiling was full of draped furs, and they made the furniture of woven husks of an indigenous plant.

"What's happening?" Learon asked.

"They're hunting a beast on the plateaus. A drizar," Elias told him.

In the early night, the warriors returned with their kill. There was a great commotion and different groups were carrying litters back to the village. The first two were full of the beast's body they had killed. The drizar had a red scaly skin and a giant head, with a wide enough mouth to eat a man. Judging by the size of the kill, the drizars were twice the size of a horse.

The last group was carrying a wounded warrior. A woman not much older than Tali. Elias spotted small wounds on some others in the hunting party, but this looked serious. Unaharra rushed out to meet the convoy. Elias was a few steps behind her. He didn't want to intrude, but he wanted to help.

They took the woman to a cave on the second level. Elias stood in and out of the opening, awkwardly in the way. There were four people inside scrambling around to clean and wrap the wounds. Elias could see they were beyond their capabilities to mend. One warrior from outside clasped his hand around Elias's arm and tugged. Elias met the man's eyes with a stare. The warrior recoiled slightly, and Unaharra's voice sounded in his head.

"You cannot help her, Luminary."

"I can. I–I have an ability for healing."

"Let it serve you well in the future, but my people won't allow it."

"She will die if I don't."

"Maybe, but her spirit will transform and live on."

"I– I understand," Elias said. He relented and left with the guard, to the man's apparent relief.

The One People treated the kill as a grand celebration. They ate and played a rhythmic music of percussion instruments. There were rattles, drums, and dancing. The people's syncopated singing was joyous, the meat was chewy. Unaharra joined later, after everyone had eaten. Elias stood to greet her, and she shook her head to let him know the woman had died.

The One People allowed Elias, Tali, and Learon to stay for the night. They stationed guards at the entrance to the small cave they had provided. In the morning, they saddled their horses to leave and met with Unaharra one last time. Elias gave her a charged gem as a gift. She clasped her hands over the gem and his palm.

"Thank you for allowing us to share a meal," Elias said.

"Shift your focus, Elias Qudin, may we meet again."

They strolled through the canyon shadows at a slow trot. Elias wasn't sure he had gained anything, but he was better to have come. There were trials ahead of them, and their willingness to face them, improved their ability to prevail.

"You know, for a hidden community cut off from the larger world, they were better to us then we probably deserved," Learon said.

"How is it they can talk without words?" Tali asked.

"I'm unsure, but I mean to figure it out," Elias said.

"It was a weird feeling to communicate with thoughts," Tali said.

"That's an understatement," Learon chimed in.

"Did you both have conversations with her?" Elias asked, surprised.

"Yes."

"Yes."

Elias didn't know what to make of that but decided not to press either of them on it. They exited the canyon into the blistering wind and broke out into a gallop. Elias knew they would have to drive hard for Marathal. They had wasted enough time. The Tempest Stone was all that mattered.

# CHAPTER FORTY-TWO

## MARATHAL (WADE)

THE CITY ON THE LAKE WAS NEAR LOCK DOWN. ARMED BONEMEN WERE
stationed on each of the surrounding village shores and troops guarded
the many bridges that connected to the lake's island city. Wade lost count,
but their numbers were greater than he had seen in Adalon. Ellaria paced
in her small patch of the sidewalk. She was getting more and more
worried by the hour for the others and their ability to enter the city. After
receiving word from them that they were enroute, she had become
agitated and short with Wade and Kovan. If that wasn't enough, there
were wild rumors around the city that the king of the New World,
Danehin, had resurfaced. This news had put Ellaria into a frenzy to verify
its validity, but so far, they had come up empty.

She already had Wade place some messages out to her contacts in the
south to see what they knew of the development, but all her inquiries had
failed to return information.

Wade just wanted the others to arrive already and at least set Ellaria's
worry aside. The principal city was on an island on the massive lake, but
the entirety of the outlying shoreline was built up and highly populated.
The bridge system interconnecting the shorelines was extensive. Some
bridges spanned a thousand paces. Typically, people took a ferry from
shore to shore, but Kovan said the lake was more heavily guarded than he
remembered. Specifically, noting that there was an abnormal amount of
cargo barges rolling in, and with them a lot of authority ships monitoring
the piers. In the three days they had been there, Kovan said he had
counted nine supply drops. When Ellaria sensed Kovan wouldn't let it go,
she sent him to the pier to ask around and to find out what he could.

Wade and Ellaria were waiting for him in the southern markets. The sweltering heat made waiting worse in the overcrowded streets.

The typical mass of pedestrians on Marathal Island was clogging the sidewalks. No matter where you stood, you were close enough to smell every stranger's breath that moved through the throng. The increased presence and influence of the Prime had not affected tourism. However, the additional people had afforded them a level of inconspicuousness they hadn't counted on. They were able to set up in a good inn and go unnoticed when they toured the falls with a group the day before. There they had spotted to their curiosity a few ground hammers beyond the falls in the north woods. Kovan assured Ellaria the congestion would be enough to allow Elias to get into the city.

Staring at the marina below, Wade spotted Kovan returning up the street with a worried look. When Kovan closed the distance, he motioned for them to walk. They fell in beside him and they continued up the hill, Kovan weaving them between the crowd.

"What's going on? What did you find out?" Ellaria asked with her arms firmly planted on her waist.

"There are a lot of large crates, all with the Prime's insignia inscribed."

"How large is large?" Wade asked, trying to keep pace.

"Big enough that they are building special carts to pull them through town."

"What do you think it is?" Ellaria asked.

"I don't know, but I asked around, and they all came from Andal."

"The Citadel?" Ellaria confirmed.

"That's my guess."

"If we didn't need to meet Elias, I would go have a look at the Whisper Chain headquarters," Ellaria said flatly.

"Why?" Kovan asked.

"This is supposedly the location of their melodicure machine. I would like to know what kind of security the Prime has there, It might be the only way we have to find Danehin," she explained.

"I'll go. You two head back and I'll go," Wade offered, taking the opportunity to get relief from Ellaria's escalating paranoia. Ellaria and Kovan looked at each other. Ellaria crushed her lips together but threw her hands up.

"Fine," she finally said, "But you're there to just look around and report back. You can't get in without a medallion, so don't try. You'll only tip them off."

"Wouldn't dream of it," Wade said.

He left them as fast as they would allow and crisscrossed through the hills of the city. Following Ellaria's directions he arrived at the location, but had to wrap around the block twice before deciding that the nondescript building he was looking at was it. He watched the entry door for a while but saw no one enter or leave for the entire stretch. He switched to watching another door at the back.

Anyone watching him probably saw him doing hand calculations trying to determine that this was in fact the rear of the building. The street was narrow and the door he kept his eye on was one of a few on the block along a plain white stucco wall. Wade leaned back near a shadowed section of another building. It was one of many connecting streets and provided the clearest view of the door without being obvious. This access point was a lot more active, with people in cloaks coming in and out regularly. Possibly in intervals, but Wade didn't have a watch to time it. Frequently, random commotions caught his attention from the busy market nearby. Turning his eyes on the door and eventually he spotted a file of four bonemen going inside.

"Don't I know you?" A woman's voice sounded from the top of the street behind him. Wade's heart bounced, and he shook in his own stance. Snapping his head to the voice, he found a familiar warm smile. Tali was coming toward him with her satchel draped over her shoulder and her pulsator concealed beneath her green cloak. She was looking more and more like her two mentors every day.

"Tali! What are you doing here?" he said with relief.

"What are you doing creeper?"

"I'm . . ." Wade realized his standing in the shadows was hard to explain, "It's not like that. Where are the others?"

"We found the inn, and they stayed back to eat. I had to see this city. It's so vibrant. I love all the blue cobalt glass everywhere. Kovan said I should go look for some new parts for one of the pulsators. Anyway, what are you doing?" she asked suspiciously.

"I came to look at the Whisper Chain headquarters for Kovan and Ellaria."

"So really, you are creeping?"

"Right, but for the right reasons."

"Headquarters?" Tali asked curiously. Positioning herself next to him on the wall to see the door. Her head inches away from his. Again, close enough to smell, but he liked her smell. It was sweet and flowery, like lavender and fruit.

"That's what they said, why?" Wade said.

"If it's their headquarters. I think that means the Melodicure machine is in there. See anything interesting yet?"

"Actually, I just saw a group of bonemen go inside."

"Really? We should go in."

"Are you crazy?"

"No, I still have my chain issued cloak. I can get inside and see what's going on."

"And then what? Act like you're lost?"

"Sure. I could make up some excuse."

"No way. Ellaria would skin me alive, and I don't even want to think about what Kovan would do to me."

Tali scrunched her nose and eyes together in her version of being annoyed. Wade found it charming.

They stood and watched a short time more, before heading back together. Tali told him of her voyage past the Deadlands and into the Stormdark Plateaus. A wild story about giant lizards, he believed she exaggerated. However, the flying man piqued his interest. Tali had her dark green short cloak on and her hair pulled high off her face. The red lines at her eyes weren't visible at the moment, but Wade looked anyways. He wasn't lying when he said he liked them, but when she was practicing at the lake he witnessed the full fury of them come alive. It was an intimidating and frightening sight he never wanted to be on the wrong side of.

They walked through the merchant filled streets and admired the many curiosities of such an opulent city. They watched a man steering his steam powered lonerider come through. The clipper was propelled by a rolling track encased in a bronze metal shell, and the man rode at the back with his goggles down. A lot of the people in Marathal wore goggles. The fashion in general was of finer quality than Adalon. The men had top hats and long tailed coats. The women had dresses in bold stripes and accentuated sleeves or necklines. Tali shopped at a tinker's store and came out with a new set of transfer tethers for Kovan, and they decided to return to the inn.

Outside of the inn, Ellaria met them at the threshold.

"There you are!" she said to him, "Oh, hi, Tali, go on inside the others are waiting."

"What's going on?" Wade asked.

"I think I recognized some members of the Guild walking up the block. Can you run into them?"

"And say what exactly?"

"Just say you're on vacation."

"I guess so. Why?"

"I need to know why they're here."

Wade turned to leave, and she tugged him back.

"Try to figure out who everyone is."

"I can do that," he said and went to walk, but she pulled him again.

"And ask about Danehin," her hand was still gripping his sleeve.

"Anything else, or do you want me to go shirtless?"

His quip drew a scowl from her, and she released him. Wade lightly jogged up the block to catch the group she saw. He found them five minutes later. There were about eight people in their group. He ran through them and acted like he was on his way somewhere. He approached them and jutted his arm wide to nick a man in a fine coat as he passed.

"Oh, I'm so sorry," Wade said to the man, but he didn't recognize him and stood there awkwardly trying to think of a follow-up.

"Mr. Duval," Delvette said. He knew her as the Guild's Regent, but never recalled her calling him anything other than Wade.

"Hi."

"What are you doing here?" she asked in a cold monotone.

"I'm here with my friend's family. I was heading to meet them, actually. What are you doing here?" he asked and recognized a few of the others, "Hello professor Deroo."

"It's our annual Guild conference," Delvette said.

"In Marathal? I thought they did it in Adalon?"

"We changed venues this year, Mr. Duval," she said. Again, her voice and manner were colder than usual, "There are people looking for you, boy. They say you broke into the archives."

Wade's pulse quickened, and he nervously wet his lips. He had completely forgotten about that. "What?"

"You were seen outside of the archives the night it was broken into," Delvette said.

"I'm sorry, what happened?" Wade asked.

"Professor Mathis talked to you in the gardens that night in question and said you were being very suspicious."

"Me! I was working on something in the shop. I always work late at night because it's a lot quieter, and the foundry makes the room boil during the day," Wade said. This was going horribly. He didn't anticipate defending himself.

"Why run off?"

"My sister went missing. I went home to see my family. When my friend Ander asked me to come here, I thought it would be good for me to get a break. Is Professor Mathis here? I could straighten all this out."

"He was, but I believe he returned to Adalon," Delvette said.

"Delvette, let the kid go. He's obviously not a person who would steal books from the restricted section," headmaster Knox said.

"You're right, Edward," she said in agreement, "Good day to you, Mr. Duval."

"One more thing, is it true they found Danehin?" he asked. He knew he was pressing his luck.

"I'm not aware he was ever missing. Goodbye, Mr. Duval," she said dismissively.

"Good day, Professors," Wade said, and he jogged a further three blocks before starting his way back to the inn. Once there, Ellaria riddled him with questions. He explained what happened to her obvious consternation.

"Really? That doesn't sound like Delvette at all. She is never combative. Actually, she is meek and sweet," she said. Tapping her nails, her eyes were darting around like she was chewing on something.

"I have never known her to treat me that way. When I started last year I had trouble with funding and she helped me get settled," Wade said.

"Something is very strange," Ellaria said.

"I am more disturbed by the bonemen taking control of the Whisper Chain," Kovan said.

"Thank you, Wade. Go on up to the room. We'll wait down here for Elias," Ellaria said dismissing him.

Wade took the excuse to leave. He grabbed some bread from the kitchen for Tali. Assuming she would be hungry and hit the stairs two at a time.

# CHAPTER FORTY-THREE

## BURDENS (TALI)

Tali stood transfixed, looking out the window to the falls beyond. The volume of water pouring over the cliffs streamed in a brilliant white. The mountain was easily two thousand feet wide, with water crashing down from various points, but the bulk of it at the top. In the center was a giant glass pyramid constructed by the second Sagean Emperor to mark the Shrine of the Sageans and claim the falls as a monument to the faith. Seeing the crystal-like glass sparkle in the sun, glowing above the crashing water, was awe-inspiring. She couldn't take her eyes off it, like it was drawing her attention.

Wade came through the door and handed her some bread. She was hungry and quickly tore a chunk off to eat.

"Thank you," she said, through a mouthful of bread. He smiled and sat down next to Learon at the foot of the bed. Learon repositioned from leaning back against the headboard to give him more room.

"Where did Elias go, anyway?" Wade asked.

"Kovan told him about the machines they saw in the woods beyond the falls, and he wanted to go see them for himself," Tali said.

"What do you think they're going to decide to do?" Learon asked.

"Something insane, no doubt," Wade suggested.

"I think Elias is determined to go to the falls tonight," Learon said.

"That's fine. I think I'm going to the chain," Tali said, turning from the window.

"You are crazy," Wade said.

"I can handle myself in a fight, thank you," Tali fired back.

"I mean, you're crazy if you think Kovan is going to go along with that idea."

"He has to. Wade, do you get what's going on here? They are not afraid that a war is coming. They are afraid we have already lost the war. The Prime took command and has since systematically taken military control over the largest cities in Tavillore. The new Sagean merely has to show himself, and we are back under the rule of the Sagean Empire. And that's not the worst of it. Elias, he's not scared of them. He is only afraid of this Wrythen."

"Do you think this Wrythen thing exists?" Wade asked.

"I do. Learon and I have been with Elias almost a month now and I can tell you he's not scared of anything. Kovan is calculating and quick to action, but he's not as calm under pressure as Elias. But this thing he says he saw, it terrifies him. I've seen it in his eyes."

"Well, you're braver than I am. I can't even look at his eyes."

"Oh, Wade," she moved across the room and kicked him in the side of his foot. She didn't want to admit that she was afraid her eyes would change too.

"What was that for? I'm just saying sometimes his eyes do that thing where the color looks like it's draining out."

"I know, Wade. Don't you think *I've* noticed?"

Wade looked at her, confused with why she was getting upset. He looked to Learon for help. Learon motioned with his eyes back toward Tali. "I'm sorry, Tali. I didn't mean. I didn't know what I meant; I'm just frustrated. Ellaria couldn't find out anything about my sister Tara. It's one of the reasons I agreed to help. I believed if anyone could find my sister it was Ellaria. I will help Ellaria if she needs me, but someone should be searching for all these missing people. What about you, Learon? You still feel you owe Elias?"

"For saving my mother? No. It's my father that keeps me going. They killed him for protecting something from the Sagean and the Prime. I don't intend to let that go to waste."

She didn't want to push but she felt a shift to Learon's tone that made her ask, "What was he protecting?"

Learon took a deep breath and exhaled. His arms sagged, and he reached for his bag on the floor. He dug into the bottom and pulled out a package wrapped in leather and tied in crossing knots of twine. "This," he said.

"What is that?" Wade asked. Leaning in to get a closer look.

Learon slipped the knots free and unwrapped the leather. Holding out a folded piece of worn golden cloth. It was unlike any material Tali had ever seen. When it unfolded, she realized it was a glove of some kind, "Is that fabric?" she asked.

"It's some kind of metal, I think, but it's extremely light," he dropped it on purpose and instead of falling to the bed it drifted in the air like a feather, "And it can't be damaged. Look," Learon pulled a sheathed hunting knife out and tried to cut it.

"Don't!" Tali called out, suddenly afraid he would damage it. She had no idea what it was, but she knew it was important and ancient.

"Don't worry, watch," Learon put the point of the blade into the middle, but no matter how hard he pressed, nothing happened. He held it close for Tali to see no mark or scuff. Which was odd because it looked worn like it had aged in the sun. He handed it to Tali and the touch of it made her feel power and almost made her vomit. She dropped it immediately.

"Are you alight?" Learon asked.

"Yes, where did you get this?" she breathed.

"My father smuggled it out of their examination facility and hid it in his cabin. I sat reading his journal for months, over and over again before it dawned on me where he had hidden it. I finally realized he was referencing the lake by his cabin when he called it the pool. I went there to retrieve it the same day I saved Elias."

"Your father dug this up at Ash Field?"

"Yes. In his journal he said he was afraid of letting this man with a dragon ring get it. I've read probably everything there is about the excavation and came across only a single mention of it."

"You think someone killed your father for it," Tali asked.

"Definitely."

"But you haven't shown it to Elias yet? Why?" Tali asked.

"At first I didn't trust him, but . . ." Learon trailed off and he bowed his head not wanting to explain.

"But what?" Tali urged him to continue.

"This stupid glove is all I have left of him."

"What about the journal you talk about?" Wade asked.

"I lost it," Learon said solemnly.

Tali inhaled shapely

"Where? When?" Wade asked.

"At the Fork. I knew I had dropped something, but with all the wolveracks around I didn't stop to make sure I had everything."

"I'm so sorry, Learon," Tali said.

"Me too," Wade said.

"Part of me knows I must give it to Elias eventually, but I'm just not ready to part with it," Learon looked up, "Does that make sense?" Learon said and he wrapped the thing back up.

Abruptly, there was a knock on the door, and they all turned. Kovan didn't wait for them to answer before coming inside. Tali watched Learon tuck his possession into his vest. The three veterans filed into the room, looking weary. Ellaria spoke first.

"Tali, dear. Do you really think you can get inside the headquarters of the Whisper Chain?"

"Yes. Absolutely. I can do it."

"Good. That's what I needed to hear. You, Kovan, and I will go there this evening. We need to discover what's going on there and if we can trust their services or not. More than that, we want to gain access to their Melodicure machine. It is supposed to locate anyone anywhere in the world. We want to use it."

"To find out where Danehin is?" Tali asked.

"Yes, and the Prime and the new Sagean and Wade's sister too."

"Really, it can do that?" Wade asked.

"That's the rumor."

"I'm not sure my cloak will get me that far inside, especially if it's being protected by bonemen."

"I have something in my bag that could work. A small vial of dreamers haze."

"What's that?" Tali inquired.

"It creates a smoke similar to shadow dust but the gases inside render those who inhale it unconscious."

"Wouldn't I in danger too?"

"Yes!" Kovan answered from the corner, where he stood with his arms folded.

"No," Ellaria corrected him, throwing her scowl his way, "I have an antidote you can take. It's not a full protection, but it will buy you time to run."

"If you can't talk your way in to see the machine, call for help. I come in and we shoot our way in and out," Kovan said.

"Let's call that Plan B, but I don't want it to come to that," Ellaria said.

"Me neither," Tali agreed.

"Are we going too?" Learon asked.

"No, I'm taking you two with me to the falls," Elias said.

"A trek through the woods at night, great," Wade complained.

"No. We're going by boat. I need you two to row. I want to go through the falls to the other side."

"How's that?" Wade said, tilting his head as though he misheard.

"Skinny, has a point, Elias," Kovan said, pointing to Wade, "How are you doing that, with patrol boats out there?"

"I was thinking of doing the Sea Watch Cove maneuver again," Elias said. Kovan put his fingers to the bridge of his nose.

"And what's this now?" Wade asked skeptically.

"Just a trick we pulled years ago," Kovan said, talking over Wade and redirecting Elias, "You can disguise the boat in the night?"

"The boat, yes, but not the wake. However, I expect the water to be churning that close to the falls. It shouldn't be a problem."

They had all agreed to this fight and now was the moment to make the moves to win. While the evening came on, they finalized their plans and left the inn going in opposite directions again. Tali watched them walk down the street to the north, biting her lip. The last rays of sunlight gleaming off the buildings and reflected in the blue glass. She should have been worried about how she was going to get past a group of secret keepers, but she found herself more concerned for her friends. She was growing tired of being separated at every turn.

# CHAPTER FORTY-FOUR

## THROUGH THE FALLS (ELIAS)

THE MIST WAS EVERYWHERE AND THE WAVES FOUGHT AGAINST THEIR advance. A thousand feet of falling water, spraying into the night and drenched them as they approached. The lake was exceedingly dark once you were far enough outside the radiance of the shoreline villages. It had allowed them to make it farther to the falls than Elias expected before garnering attention, at which point, he began warping the light around their small boat. To the patrol lookouts, they would see a darkness that blended in with the night.

The crash of the falls was deafening, and Elias went over a series of hand gestures to communicate to one another. He signaled for Learon and Wade to turn slightly to the north. As it was, the water was almost impossible to navigate with the surface churning violently. Elias needed them to get as close as possible before attempting to pass through the pounding downpour. At the moment, his entire focus was on masking their boat from the patrol ships. Eventually, Elias would have to shield them from the crushing force. Since he could not do both at the same time there would be a moment where, if a patrolling ship was watching closely enough, they would be seen passing through the falling water. Elias was relying on the watcher's complaisance as much as anything else to carry them by unnoticed.

Wade and Learon paddled the boat, while Elias bailed the rising water from inside. It was a hopeless battle— more and more, the boat was taking on water. He couldn't keep up without help, but it took both Learon and Wade to propel the boat forward against the current.

When he couldn't take it any longer and they were close to sinking.

Elias released his grip on the light cloaking and redirected his energy into shielding them from the pouring water by throwing his drenched arms out front. Both Learon and Wade cringed instinctively, as though he had hurled something at them. It took a moment to form, but a bubble of kinetic energy formed around the ship. They watched the crushing weight of the falling water hit the top of the invisible bubble and splash away. Elias urged them to keep rowing.

To Elias, it felt like an exceptionally long stretch of time, to get through the curtain of water. The veiled inside was devoid of light, the curtain blocked even the moon and whatever ambient light there had been was lost. They rowed on blindly, and Elias had to fight his instinct to illuminate their way for the moment.

Beyond the falls and back toward the lake, something they had done had caused the patrol to notice. A ship closed the distance with speed propelled on by steam jets. The lights of a ship pulled close to the falls. They projected a watchmen's lamp into the falls. The light winking in and out of existence through gaps in the flow. They had been seen, but the patrol's inspecting was turning up nothing. Having breached the vertical flow, Elias, Wade and Learon were safely hidden from view. The light from the ship stopped seeping through the endless stream of water and they assumed the ship lost interest.

When the turbulent rumble below the boat subsided, Elias released his protection. He hoped they had passed the pull of the plunge pool. The boat faithfully continued to move deeper into the suffocating void. The noise had increased somehow on this side as it ricocheted off the underside. They were traveling blind and Elias pulled out an orb of light. With the smallest trickle of electricity, the orb began to glow a soft orange. He held it up with his hand and cast it into the air in front of them to light their way. No sooner had it passed beyond the stern of the boat, and Elias was yelling at the boys to change course to avoid a massive pillar rising out of the water.

Abruptly, Learon stood up, practically tipping the boat over. Elias and Wade scrambled to counterbalance the sway and avoid capsizing. At the last moment, Learon used his paddle to stop them from crashing. He pushed hard against the stone to veer them to the side and clear. The boat scraped hard against the rising pillar, but maintained its line.

With the orb of light floating higher, the glow illuminated a sea of ruins buried in the water, multiple points of jagged stone and rubble pierced the surface. Waves cast from the falls, lapping hard against the graveyard of broken stones. When the light reached the surface of the wall, they could see distinct lines of a facade carved into the mountain, something manmade. It was an ancient temple, forgotten and in a constant state of degradation and collapse. Large chunks of the building were now the splattered contents of the lake. The overhang of stone above their heads propped the headwaters up and projected the cascading runoffs proud of the mountain and edifice underneath. From this vantage, Elias could see various points where water chutes were actually spraying through ancient arched window openings. The water's attempt to drown the whole building still incomplete.

Gazing at the collection of submerged building fragments, obviously a great castle or fortification had existed here long ago. Something must have shifted the land upstream, altering the natural flow of water and causing a massive overflow to the falls in perpetuity. It had turned dual streams into a full plunging onslaught that had destroyed whatever stood before. Toppling it into the lake and sweeping away the past, drowning it.

Near the base of the edifice the shape and design become clearer. Large, ornately fluted, columns held up beams with a full length frieze of figure carvings. There were three stacking levels to the facade with the fourth level demolished by the overflow. At the foot of the columns, a vast set of stairs were at the waters edge. The stairway of stone tampered down to the depths of the lake.

Bumping into the stone, the boat reached the edge of the steps and stopped. If they were concerned about being wet, that was a battle lost long ago. Each of them was soaked from head to toe. Learon threw back dripping hair from his face and jumped from the boat to the steps in the lake and pulled the tie-line with him. With no obvious choice, he eventually wrapped the rope around a column to secure the craft.

"I will never be dry again," Wade shouted, though they barely heard him. The curtain of water came down with a constant ear-splitting crash, made worse by the echoing stone surface, baffling their hearing.

Standing beneath the columns, each of them stood restlessly in pools of water at their feet. Wade wrung the bottom of his shirt free of the excess. The water splattered in large amounts to the floor, another sound that went unheard. Elias watched as some slide water, gliding down the face of bedrock and stone, had eroded what once was an intricate exterior mosaic. Elias drew the orb back to his hands and proceeded inside.

The first room they entered was some sort of gathering chamber. To each side of them were grand staircases built into the walls and leading up to rooms above. Learon ran a few steps up one of the stairs and came back down.

"It's blocked, it's completely caved in up there," he said.

Elias looked at Wade and pointed to the second stairway. Wade hesitated, then reluctantly ran up the other stairway, slipping on the marble surface at the landing turn. He issued a curse that echoed out, but Elias and Learon couldn't hear it. He came back shaking his head, "It's too dark up there to see, it's mostly caved in."

At the back of the room were three ten-foot-tall arched doors in a row. They had a similar inscribed text in the surrounding frame, the meaning of which eluded Elias's ability to translate. One door was broken and slanted in the opening, almost falling down. Learon and Wade instinctually approached it to pass. Wade crawled under the angled gap and Learon climbed over the teetering top gap. They both slipped in the process, Learon falling onto Wade with crash. Elias instead opened a perfectly functioning adjacent door. He looked over to see them pulling themselves off the floor.

Inside this room, the roar of the falls was dampened and nearly muted. Somehow, they designed the chamber to restrict any transference of noise. Likewise, they could now hear their footsteps and each other's labored breathing.

The ceiling here was taller than the previous chamber. The room was large but seemed empty. There was a mosaic design in the floor they couldn't get a full picture of to understand. At the sides was an arcade of columns with a raised walkway. Elias's light only cast light in a small radius and it was hard to tell, but something large stood at the back. Small particles of dust drifted in the eerie light from his orb and they progressed deeper.

When at last they came to the back of the room, they found a large dais. Elias knelt to investigate and found symbols inlaid at the edge.

"It's here," he mumbled, surging light into the orb. The glow brightened rapidly until it fully illuminated the hauntingly still features of an ancient archway.

"What is that?" Wade asked.

"That, kid, is a wave gate," Elias said and for a time they stared transfixed at the gate. It rested alone and awaiting life to surge through it once more. Elias stepped up atop the dais and began studying all the symbols he could see. The platform itself was far more intricate than he knew. There was an intricately carved endless symbol in the main stage of the dais itself. Like interwoven lines of circles and dashes. It reminded Elias of degree lines on a compass. There were also five equally spaced symbols at the outer edge. Though oddly, he could have sworn the text specified seven. He searched until he found the same symbol he had activated before. That fateful moment in the Cracked Lands seemed like a long time ago now. Without paper, he tried to commit the symbols to memory so he could explain them to Ellaria when they returned.

"I thought we were going to find the Sagean's Tomb?" Learon asked.

"It's here, I'm sure of it," Elias said.

"Where?"

Elias pointed to the ceiling, "Above us."

"Above? You're sure?" Wade asked.

"Yes," he said and jumped down from the platform and headed back toward the entrance, "That's what they did. Destroy, appropriate, and build on top of the past. That's why there's a shrine at the top, and that's why the Prime is digging with ground hammers further to the north. They know it's here too, and they're looking. But they think it's located further north, where there are smaller ribbon falls that feed the main. The Sageans recognized the site was sacred, but they had forgotten why and they built atop the rubble."

"Without bothering to search the ruins?"

"Correct. If they cared about history, they wouldn't have tried at every turn to erase it. Once someone shows you who they are, believe them. They were not searchers, they were never interested in enlightenment, only ruling, self-preservation and power."

"What now?" Wade asked.

"Now we go back, get changed, and in the morning, we unbury the dead."

# CHAPTER FORTY-FIVE

## WHISPERS (TALI)

Tali moved through the street swiftly and determined, with Ellaria and Kovan trailing behind. The city she loved in the day was even more stunning at night, with the lights on every shoreline sparkling in the lake around them. Instead of trying to top the scenery, the structures on the shoreline existed inside it. The most fantastical architectural element were the various bridges connecting shoreline to shoreline. That, and the cobalt infused glass that marked some of the more important buildings.

She needed to see if she could talk her way past the front desk. Part of her knew it was an impossibility. The door was as inconspicuous as Wade described. A single step off the sidewalk to an unremarkable wood slab door. The chain's symbol was engraved in the small plaque outside the door. Tali lifted her hood over her head and knocked.

The door man gave her an awkward scowl but let her inside without a word. The interior smelled wonderfully studious and mechanical. The room was a long hall with no adornments. Past there, it opened up into a small cove with chairs and a desk behind a geometric lattice screen. Flanking the desk were two-armed bonemen.

Tali did her best to ignore the guards and approached the golden bronze countertop resolutely. She reminded herself to think like Ellaria. The tender looked up and she could tell he was quizzically trying to understand who she was.

"Are you a runner? If you're a runner, you shouldn't be here. Please meet your link where they designated," he said with a dismissive wave. Tali remained undaunted.

"I am here to inspect the melodicure," Tali said. The request must have been the only one like it the tender had ever received, because his expression was part panic and part total confusion.

"I'm sorry, you are?"

"I am the Prime's personal dispatch. Surely you were told I would be arriving?" Tali said, and she produced Elias's coin, holding it up as if it were some sort of badge. He looked at it unimpressed until she trickled a slight amount of energy and the coin gleamed around the perimeter.

"Umm. No," he stammered. Tali couldn't believe that this was working. She tried to suppress a smile from her face. While the man paused, trying to think of a way to dismiss her request, "I cannot let you in," he managed.

"Why?"

"I don't have access."

"Well, of course, you don't have access. Please show me to someone who does," Tali said putting her arms to her side in her best imitation of Ellaria.

"I can take you to the Overseer."

"Please do."

The tender came around the side and opened the gate for her. Tali passed by the guard without making eye contact. She was taken to a back hallway that wrapped around the desk station. At the end of the hall they went through a door that opened up into a warehouse and a set of cascading stairs. There was the main metal walkway they were on and a stairway down to a message receiving area. Clerks in small single desks were feeding notes through small machines. Silver tubes deposited notes from the front office to a station near the wall. There was a second set of clerks working magnotype machines. Each desk seemed to field messages from different corners of the globe.

They passed through the workroom on the raised walkway to the other side and a glass office that overlooked the area. A woman with silky blonde hair stood watching the floor below. Her eyes were intense and without empathy. She was tall for a woman and had an athletic build that suggested she was more than an Overseer. With one look, Tali knew it was over. Plan B was up.

"Who are you?" the Overseer asked.

"I am here to inspect the melodicure machine."

"You are not tinkersmith, or a machinist. Amasten, why did you bring her back here?"

"She produced credentials, or something," Amasten said.

"Show it to me, girl," the Overseer demanded.

Tali reached into her cloak until she found the vial, she hoped was the right one. She pulled it free. All their eyes were on her closed palm. Tali opened her hand to see the green vial and then tilted it. The vial fell to the ground. The Overseer's eyes grew wide. It hit with a tap and remained intact. A smirk crossed the lady's lips.

Tali drew a shawl over her face and slammed her foot down on the glass vile. It ruptured with a tiny blast and the room filled with smoke.

The Overseer grabbed for Tali's cloak, but her strength waned. Amasten stumbled out of the door and collapsed.

Tali ripped herself away and ran for the edge of the walkway. Ellaria said the smoke would pool for some time and the antidote would only sustain her for so long. Tali reached the edge and jumped to the work floor below. At the moment before landing, she expelled energy to slow her momentum. She landed clumsily and with more force than she could counter. She hit her feet but stumbled to the ground face first.

The clerks all pushed back from their chairs at the sudden ruckus. Someone yelled — "Smoke!" And a small paniced scramble ensued. The throng of people pushed toward the backstreet exit, filing past two of the guards coming toward Tali. The smoke continued to billow above the rafters.

Tali's right arm ached, and her feet and legs felt jammed up. She rolled to her back and slowly tried to get up. The bonemen were on her quickly. One of them put his foot on her shoulder and shoved her to stay down. The other went to bound up the steps. No one had the sense to sound an alarm yet.

The soldier looming over her released the charging mechanism on his rifle and aimed it at her. Then three shots rang out.

The first took the soldier covering Tali in the head, killing him and throwing his lifeless body back. The other two met their mark, killing the bonemen on the steps.

Ellaria came rushing over and helped Tali to her feet. Kovan crept around them in the room. His pulsator hummed and his eyes darted all over.

"Good timing," Tali said, getting to her feet.

"Plan B?" Kovan asked.

"Yes," Tali admitted.

"I always liked Plan B better anyway," Kovan said.

"I think the machine is through there. I can sense a cluster of energy emanating from behind that door," Tali said, pointing to a large metal door. The tall metal doors hung on sliders and it took every ounce of strength Kovan had to pry them apart.

The machine inside filled the room, and there was a man sitting at a chair in front of it. He wore a set of goggles over his eyes and a second set atop his head. He was as old as Kovan, but looked filthy and exhausted. He reacted slowly to their intrusion and stood.

"Get out of here. Who are you?"

Kovan ran over to him and rapped him across his temple. The man fell in a lump to the stone floor.

The melodicure machine was a giant contraption with a jumble of a thousand parts interwoven and moving. There were revolving gears and pistons on rotating wheels at the surface and many more beneath. The device looked like it was alive. Puffs of steam burst free at various exhaust points in a syncopated rhythm. Various tubes and cords mixed with a metal framing to look skeletal. At closer inspection, Tali could see sigils were inscribed into all the workings. A series of power lines stretched over the face and connected all around a center grid expanse. The middle grid was above the desk and was made up of tiny metal rods. The polished metal rods were all partially sticking proud of the machine. Directly below the screen of metal pins, was a black plate with a depression in the middle. Something that went there was missing.

Tali searched the desk.

"What are you looking for?" Ellaria asked.

"Something that powers the machine."

"Is this it?" Kovan tugged a crystal in the man's palm free and handed it over to her. It was a quantum stone. A capacitor gem that could be electrically recharged. Tali placed the gem into its resting position, on the black plate. The cranks and gears roared to life. Something inside started to rattle and decompress repeatedly, and the tiny metal rods moved chaotically in and out. Finally, the pins settled. Most of them deposited back into individual recessed holes. The remaining rods formed the words:

Ask me

They looked at one another, confused.

"Is this machine talking to us?" Kovan asked, and he raised his weapon to it, suddenly fearful of the contraption of metal parts. There was more rattling noise and more movement in the metal pins. Ellaria took a step back.

Yes

"Wait, it can hear us?" Tali said. They looked around, dumbfounded what to do.

"Well, ask it some questions, and let's get out of here," Kovan said.

"Where is Arno Danehin?" Ellaria asked.

Exhaust puffed out and gears rotated in one direction and then another. Then the pins went wild until settling:

The City of Andal
Yes
No

"Which one is it?" Tali said to Ellaria, confused.

"Is there a new Sagean?" Ellaria asked a second question.

The pins of graphite sinking and reeling stopped again:

Yes

Somewhere in the facility they could hear stomping. Kovan sprinted to the door to look out and rushed back.

"We have to go, Ellaria," Kovan said. Tali and Ellaria started to leave, but Tali stopped.

"Wait," She said and she turned back and stepped closer to the machine, "Tara, is Tara Duval alive? Where is she?"

No
Yes
The Mainsolis Sea

Kovan reached in and snatched the gem off the plate. The device ground to a halt. An excess of steam burst from various points.

"Run!" he said.

They ran for the exit. In the workroom, a squad of bonemen were up on the ramparts shouting. Ellaria threw two vials of shadow dust wildly. The first burst on the walkway. The second in the middle of the room. The bonemen opened fire, but it was aimless in the cloud of black smoke. Kovan emerged firing his pulsator into the soldiers.

They scrambled out the door into the empty alley. Two bonemen charged at them from up the road. Before Tali had even registered the

365

threat, Kovan had drawn and fired his gun twice, killing both men. One of the shots shattering the soldier's faceplate. They ran into the night, through the alleys and the jumbled streets of the island. Kovan leading them to twist and turn every two blocks. The sounds of more pursuers continued at their heels.

# CHAPTER FORTY-SIX

## THE RENDERED (KOVAN)

A FOG ROLLED ACROSS THE ISLAND AS THE NIGHT GREW DARKER AND THE streets more and more scarce. They had been running around the meandering city and its alleyways for an hour but couldn't shake their stalkers. They couldn't go directly back to the inn either. The mist would help, or at least Kovan hoped it would. While they jogged, Kovan became very cognizant of the noise they were making. Boots in unison clacking on the stone path. They would have to slow their retreat, as the haze settled in and thickened. The chase became a game of sound over vision. Most of these bonemen soldiers were poor shots and even worse trackers. Their skills were in following orders and blind allegiance. Oddly, there was practically no presence of greencoats, even on routine patrols.

They turned up a small market street. A narrow connecting street with multiple storefronts and decorated the windows. The jumble of awnings, angled posts amid staggered building fronts, provided cover to stop and catch their breath. Kovan thought maybe they had eluded their tail.

"Can we make it back to the inn?" Ellaria whispered breathlessly. Kovan nodded that they could. They were roughly five blocks away now, and their trackers had disappeared.

Suddenly, they heard a disturbance across the island. At first it was mechanical and ringing, but the sound soon turned into a stomp. It was distant but closing on their position. Kovan feared somehow their enemy's numbers had grown. He placed a finger to his lips for the others to remain quiet.

The sound of something large walking on the connecting street was tough to distinguish. He stared down the road, trying hard to focus on whatever movement he could through the fog. A tall, metal figure appeared and passed from their view. The procession of mechanical noise continued.

Kovan instinctively pulled both Ellaria and Tali lower to the ground and out of sight. He still stared down the street to understand what he had just seen – blinking and squinting for his eyes to prove themselves. Another one passed, and then a third. Each one tall and holding a small light high in the air. Their movements were rigid, and each step was producing a powerful crunch of stone. Still, they were too far off to make out.

Unexpectedly, the watches on both Ellaria's and Tali's wrists lit up with a blue glow in the night. The light bounced off the sidewalls and casted into the fog like a beacon. Kovan spun on them. Motioning wildly for them to shield the light. He turned his attention back to the top of the alley. One of the figures had stopped and turned. The light had drawn their attention.

The closer it came, the more Kovan was unsure of what exactly he was seeing. His eyes and mind were arguing about the reality in front of them. He pulled back and huddled closer to the other two. He drew his weapon free, the familiar weight held tight. The thing was nearly upon them.

When it was fully in view, he could feel Ellaria slightly recoil and Tali's fingers on his shoulder trembled.

A being of animated metal stood before them and seemed to breathe with metallic lungs. Its height was staggering and at its head was a pair of glowing eyes. Kovan had mistaken them for a lantern's flame. A long, single vein stretched from its neck to its ankle and glowed red like its eyes. There was an unmistakable sound of a mechanical pump working, and small jets of steam burst from ports in its shoulders. A series of tubes wrapped from the back to each arm and to the mouth of its metal face. Still, the thing was clothed, with a cloak that humped high behind its head. The bronze figure stopped to scan the area and then continued to move. Kovan fought his urge to fire upon the thing, he was honestly unsure of where to target. Instead, he watched its movements to get an idea of what they were up against. The thing crept along and passed them. It held a gem charged, circulating rifle unlike any he had seen before. It was a modified rifle, that was part spear. The spear shaft looked like spilt barrels and had bindings from the hand mount to a short blade at the tip. A second grip guard was the rifle handle and trigger, an impossibly bulky weapon no man could practically weld. This thing gripped it tight and easily with articulating thin metal fingers.

Somewhere in the city a woman screamed, and the metal moved to the noise. It wasn't a run, but it didn't need to. With its height, it could cover distance quickly, and it was nimble, but it moved in a slinking creep.

When it turned at the top of the block. Kovan motioned for Tali and Ellaria to move. He led them to the other end of the street, slowing at the connection and scanning for any more of the metal men. With nothing but fog consuming the road, he took them north.

Tali whispered, "What was that?"

To which Kovan could only throw his hands up in confusion, "No idea. What did Elias want?" he asked, curious why the watches had lit up.

"He found a gate," Ellaria said.

"Good, we may need to use it to get the thorny—death out of here and away from those things."

He turned them again on a more direct route to the inn. They moved swiftly down the empty road, but found the way blocked by three sets of glowing eyes. The things didn't seem to speak, but one of them spat out an odd bark in alarm, like the cry or caw of an animal. The hair on Kovan's arms prickled from the sound. He tugged on Ellaria's shoulder and pointed to another alleyway.

"There," he said, and they dashed away.

At the corner Kovan turned and blasted the first one in the group, but the tungsten rounds had zero effect. Where was Elias with that damned sword of his? The bronze monsters crept toward them, their glowing eyes almost pulsing in the mist. Kovan aimed for an eye and fired. The shot found its mark and the thing staggered. When it regained its balance, smoke was flowing out of the opening, and tiny sparks were firing deep in the socket. It pressed in toward them. The other two closed in faster.

Kovan fired repeating blasts. The charged rounds hurdled through the fog in pointed bolts of fire.

"Run!" he called out, and they retreated to another alleyway. A being of rendered metal barreled in after them. Its hulking form dominated the space. Kovan fired again and again. It's two rendered friends charging in behind it.

"Kovan!" Tali screamed from behind him.

"A little busy, young Raven."

"It's a dead end!" Ellaria shouted back.

Kovan turned to look and cursed at the sight of the stone wall rising between the angled buildings. Still, they continued deeper into it with the passage narrowing. Currently, the limited space held the beings back.

The closest one took a swipe with the bladed end of his weapon. Kovan ducked and rolled back, firing rounds at its head. The spear sliced hard across the stone floor, and the thing faltered slightly from Kovan's blasts.

A form fell out of the sky. At first Kovan feared it was another attacker. Until the shape spun on the rendered metal men and Kovan caught the sight of a silver flash in the mist. Loud clangs rang out as Elias's elum blade slashed at the bronze shell. The huge being flinched at the pressed attack. Most of the effort Elias put forth did nothing but confuse the thing until Elias's blade found a weak spot and cut clean through the glowing vein. The blade whirled and sparks erupted out along with a glowing liquid. The figure fell with the liquid flowing out of the severed vein. Elias ran on top of it and hurled himself in an impossible leap. The sparks gathered around him as he jumped. Elias flew directly at the other two. His blade glowed hot, and he came down on the first with a crash. The red blade slammed down into the neck of the metal beast. The force knocked Elias back and to the ground. His blade was still lodged in the machine. The third rendered beast came. With one eye, it fired its rifle. The blast pierced the air and hit the ground near Elias. Kovan fired rounds into the last good eye, and the thing fell when the third shot found the light. Elias picked himself up and retrieved his sword. He came striding back to Kovan.

"Show off," Kovan told him with a smile. Elias smiled back, but his steps faltered. Kovan rushed to his side to keep his friend from collapsing. He got there just in time. Elias's weight sagged in his arms, "Elias."

"I'm fine, just old," Elias said, but his hand was bloody.

Kovan dragged his friend back to the wall where the others were now climbing up. Learon and Wade stood atop the rampart helping Ellaria and Tali get over. Kovan stood beside Elias near the wall. Elias put a bleeding hand to the surface to steady himself, but it was obvious he didn't have the energy for the climb. Learon jumped down to them.

"Help me," he said to Kovan, and together they lifted Elias up, Learon doing most of the work. With Wade's help at the top, they were over to the other side and moving again. Just in time, as Kovan could hear more of the machines stomping where they had just been.

"Where to now?" Wade asked.

"We need to get out of this city. I fear the ships we have been watching come in are bringing these things with them. Elias, can we make it to the gate?"

"Yes, but we should take the mountain roads. The small boat we used can't take all of us, and I have no energy to cloak two ships on open water."

"Fine, it would be our luck these machines could swim, anyway."

Instead of weaving through the jungle of streets, they made their way to the bridge where the fog was thickest. They moved in a line over the bridge and across the lake to the west. Crouching at the edge as they went, with Kovan at the lead. They were forced to stop once for a three-man patrol of bonemen. Kovan could have taken them out, but the aim was to cross over undetected. Once they were on the west bank, they crossed through the outskirts of Sun Ray Village and into the wilderness and closer to the roar of the Marathal falls.

# CHAPTER FORTY-SEVEN

## THE TOMB (ELIAS)

THEY MOVED SILENTLY IN THE DARKNESS ACROSS THE FOREST FLOOR. There was an exhaustion to the group from the weeks of travel that was catching up to them. They were struggling to hike the mountain with any speed. Most of the forest was lush, but there were occasionally large boulders that blocked their way. They had to scale them in tandem. So far, Elias kept climbing higher with no one questioning his navigation, yet. At some point during the night, they had climbed above the fog line. Below them, they could see it rising off the lake and into the surrounding forests.

"Why did you have us come this way, Elias? You planned this, didn't you? We need to get to the gate, but we seem to be heading to the shrine above the falls," Ellaria asked.

"I have to search the shrine before we leave."

"Why?"

"For an entrance to the tomb. I may not have another chance. With their drilling and digging, eventually they will find it, Ellaria, and if they find the stone first, we will lose everything we have fought for. It will all crumble. You have seen what they have created. Those beings of metal they somehow rendered alive. I'm afraid of what law of nature they defied to create them."

"And you're sure it's here?"

"Yes."

"Would you two shut it!" Kovan said, putting a finger between them, "We're not going to do anything but die if you two keep talking. We are going for the stone while we have the chance. Elias is right. The stone is all that matters."

Ellaria agreed, but Elias knew she was holding a concern for the others.

Eventually, they reached the gushing torrent of the river's edge as it toppled over the cliff to the lake below. Changing course, they began moving upstream to the shrine entrance. It was situated at a patch of land where the river forked around before falling off. With the white stone platform in view, Elias took them to a higher vantage point to oversee the area.

Placing his hands on the rocks and weeds beneath the low tree bows, Elias crawled to the edge of the hill overlooking the shrine entrance. With Kovan next to him, they assessed the defenses. The shrine was an arena of terraced water fountains and a center stairway of white stone. The wide steps went down to a circular platform with a series of sweeping archways overhead. At the edges of the space were jagged cut rock formations, each with its piercing point angled toward the falls and the great glass pyramid, sparkling at the center. It dawned on Elias that it was possible the tomb entrance wasn't inside the shrine. But he thought it was a bad time to mention it.

Elias counted four sentinels guarding the area. He and Kovan watched the patrol movements for a minute before they returned to the others, but they found Ellaria alone. She rolled her eyes at their mutually dumbfounded looks, before moving to point for them to turn around.

The other three, Wade, Learon and Tali were already approaching the shrine. With their backs against the side rocks, they were busy scheming something. Tali handed Learon a small red crystal, which he immediately tied to an arrow, then he pulled back on the drawstring and swept his bow high, as though he was shooting a star, and released. The arrow flew awkwardly but far up the mountain. Tali's gaze following the arch of the shot, threw her hand out, and the arrowhead erupted into flames. It streaked down into the forest. The guards responded and all of them scurried to investigate the streaming fire from the sky. Frantically, Tali waved for the old veterans to come quickly, while the diversion was still working.

They jumped down to the main platform and ran beneath the archways to a set of ornately molded bronze doors. Kovan bent down to pick the lock, with everyone huddled in tight. It wasn't working.

"Oh, forget it," Elias said, and he pulled free the sword at his hip. The others backed away at the sight of the blade. He concentrated on the metal and directed energy and heat down the length of the palladium's edge. The metal had an extremely high melting point and kept its form. He slammed it in between the brass doors and sliced through the lock. Then he withdrew the blade and the energy. Kovan shoved the doors open, and they dashed inside.

INSIDE, THE SHRINE WAS AS ELLARIA HAD DESCRIBED, FULL OF IMMACULATE mosaics and paintings. Everything depicted either the Sagean's ideology or Sagean emperors of the past. Small flames burned in stone pockets randomly around the walls and cast a flickering light to the space. The first room was a small, circular vestibule with a connecting hallway at each side. The hall simply wrapped around and back, like a gallery. Elias thought they would step inside and be staring at the base of the glass pyramid. The shape of the hall was instead wrapping around it.

"What is this place?" Wade asked.

"A memorial to the Sageans," Ellaria said.

"Right, but why don't they allow anyone inside?" Wade asked.

"You're right, Wade," Elias said, "This is more than a shrine for believers to worship at. This is an elaborate tombstone. A grave marker, and that means the tomb is below our feet."

"Are you sure this isn't it?"

"Like I said in the gate room, I think they found the ruins of the lost city, and instead of discovering what was possibly inside they built on top of them. We saw the sealed passageways below. What I'm positive of is that their book of light talks about rebirth and they would have left a passageway for their energy to escape and transform. There's a false door in here somewhere. We are looking for something out of place or possibly a symbol. Spread out and look around," he told everyone.

"Could it be a symbol of the energies?" Tali asked.

"Yes. Why? Where do you see that?"

"Under each portrait there is a symbol for different energies," Elias looked at what Tali was pointing to.

"Anyone see these repeated anywhere?" he said.

"Over here, Elias," Ellaria called out.

He dashed over to Ellaria, who stood in front of an engraving in the stone wall. It was a depiction of a person bending the energies of life around them. Elias examined the wall with his fingers until he could sense something. His hand crossed over a symbol and the wall behind it felt different beyond his touch. He opened his eyes on the stone and the symbol beneath— the everlasting energy. The symbol for the soul. He pressed the symbol, and it sank into the stone. A pressure valve released somewhere in the structure's cavity and followed by a chorus of clanging sounds. He rotated the symbol and a plain section of cut stone blocks released from the wall and dust fell from the joints. It moved out of the way and revealed a dark passageway. The others stared in wonder as he walked over and ducked inside.

They pressed on through the passage. A dampness permeated the air and their presence felt intrusive. A dim light at the end of the tunnel lit the way, but the tunnel was only wide enough for them to walk in a single file line. The floor was smooth and gently sloped down as they progressed further. Walls were rough to the touch, but Elias couldn't find any joinery marks. The passage led them deeper into the mountain. The scuffing sound of their footfalls scratched at the stone. Finally, the hall ended at a wall with orbs similar to the ones Elias had back in the vault. There was a door to one side and at the other, an opening to a second passage switching back on itself. Kovan opened the door.

Inside was a small room with odd tools hung on the wall and a single long table. There was a large floor drain in the middle. The ground was grimy, and the lighting was actually brighter inside than in the hallway.

"What is this place then?" Wade asked.

"I believe this is where the acolytes prepped the bodies for the afterlife," Ellaria said, and Elias nodded his agreement.

"Lovely," Wade said.

"What happened to the acolytes? Were they killed or captured in the war too?" Learon asked.

"We don't know. My team captured one and he took his own life instead of talking to us. We never found the others," Kovan explained.

"Let's keep going," Elias said and headed down the second passageway. This second route was shorter, and they quickly came to a large double door. It opened with a single push by Learon. Beyond was a large balcony overlooking a vast room. They all stepped to the balcony without a rail. Learon braved a look over the edge and backed away. The sound of water flowing was greater in here than the previous passages. There didn't appear to be a way down.

"How are we getting down there?" Kovan asked.

Elias examined the platform they all stood on. The edges notched around copper channels that extended to the floor below. A small groove surrounded the outside perimeter and marked a transition of material in the floor. Elias realized the platform had an inset disk that would move if made to. Only a luminary could go further.

"Everyone get inside the black circle. I have to lower us down."

They huddled together in what quickly felt like tighter confines than the space suggested. Slowly, the platform fell in a smooth motion to the bottom floor.

While it descended, they gaped at the chamber beyond. It was like a grand theatre. Row after row passed on the side walls with hundreds of individually carved alcoves, each occupied with bronze statues. Mostly soldiers with inlaid crystal eyes but some simply stood proud in their armor. While others, like the archers, brandished weapons or pointed bows and quivered arrows at the pathway. Running the length at the foot of both walls were small, still pools. The room was incredibly large and most of the light came from the far side.

"What is that at the back of the room?" Kovan asked. It was a good question. From this distance it looked like a curtain of smoke in the middle of an arched opening, almost as tall as the room itself. The archway appeared to be iron and there was a blacked edge to it, like scorch marks.

"I don't like the look of their eyes," Learon said, referring to the statues. Their crystal eyes sparkled in the light and the setup gave the statues a sense of movement. Elias didn't either. Something was tugging at him about the room.

The platform came to rest at a turquoise stone floor. A reverberation emanated and the sound of something colliding in the walls followed. Then, the hum of an engine working began.

"Can you feel that?" Tali asked. Kovan looked to her, confused. Elias could feel the energy too, and he put his hand out to hold Kovan back from entering the room.

"What is it?" Kovan asked.

"I don't know. Something's not right. Nobody leaves this platform," Elias told them. Something about Learon's observation disturbed him. He repositioned his satchel to go through it. Tossing the flap back, he rummaged around until he found what he was looking for. He put the goggles on, with a reception of odd looks from the others. Gazing into the room, he could see what was tugging at his senses. A torrent of pinpoint beams of light were streaming out of all the crystal eyes. They flooded the room with a massive amount of energy, but no heat.

He gestured for the others to stay, as he slowly crept away from the platform to the center aisle. With each cautious and soft step forward, his boots clacked against the floor in a slight echo in the great chamber. His presence stirred the wrath of the bronze guards, as their crystal eyes sparkled and smoked, and thin beams of light hit him with a violent shock. Elias fell to his knees, the flood of energy raged a moment and receded.

"Elias!" Ellaria called out, but a loud boom instantly concealed her voice, and the archway at the end of the hall burst into a curtain of fire. Everyone left on the platform dove to the ground at the sudden inferno.

Elias could feel the waves of light enveloping him as he got up and continued to walk closer to the arch of fire. Most of the initial energy he felt was now raging in the flames. The heat made him sweat, and the closer he got the harder it was to breathe. The fire he realized would consume the breathable air in the room in short order. It was imperative he solved the problem, and fast.

He could consume the energy of the light waves, but that much energy might kill him. He tried to imagine how a Sagean accessed the tomb when another was placed in eternal rest. They would have known of the security measures and had a simple way to get passed them. He told himself to focus on the problem: the wall of fire.

The light and the fire were not the source of the energy, he realized, only the product. This entire underground structure was a machine. There had to be a way to turn it off. In order to get through the opening, he would have to take on the heat and transform it. He stopped himself and thought maybe there was another way, maybe he only needed to redirect it. Elias looked again to the edge basins of water. He knew time was running out and didn't question the simplicity of his decision. He threw both his arms out wide toward the two walls of bronze figures. Using himself as a conductor, he pulled the heat of the flames into himself and simultaneously channeled it into the pools of water. The air rippled and moved in swirls. The flames dissipated, and the water boiled, producing hot steam that filled the room. He didn't stop to consider the result and moved through the opening. On the other side, there was a stone ledge overlooking another large chamber, and there was a lever in the floor. With relief he tugged it back, and the light and heat ceased.

Elias waved for his friends to come through.

Turning back to assess the next challenge before them, he noticed the sounds of the falls were much greater here. So too, was the humming sound he had heard throughout the depths of the site. The walls of the wide chamber were all covered in the luster of a silver-gray substance. *Possibly a metallic*, Elias thought. The ledge he stood on ended at a pool of water that encompassed the entire room. A path of pillars rising just proud of the water's surface, laid out like stepping stones. The path crossed over the pool to a rounded wall and a set of copper doors. Elias believed he was staring at the Tomb of the Sageans and he exhaled a breath he had held for almost forty years. He suddenly felt his age, and the weight of all the years of searching, like heavy chains he was dragging to the end.

Water flowed in at four different points along the walls above him. As it fell, it collided and continuously turned wheels embedded in the walls. The tomb's architect had taken advantage of the water in the construction of the facility, and Elias was certain it was providing a source of energy for the tomb's inner workings. At the outer wall to his right, about two feet above the pool's surface, was a remnant of the former temple that once stood. A great circle window of blue glass, in a frame of honed white stone remained while the chamber around it had been rebuilt and repurposed. Through the glass, Elias could see the falls raging beyond.

"Are you hurt?" Ellaria asked when everyone reached him at the edge of the chamber.

"No," Elias said flatly.

"Tell me you have a key to those doors?" Kovan said, staring across the room, "Or do you have to do some other impossible feat?"

"Let's find out, but don't touch the water," Elias said.

"Why not?" Wade asked.

"Somehow the surface is still, even with the water flowing in at the sides. It may be nothing. Let's just say I don't want to find out," Elias said, and together they crossed the pool. Stepping from one pillar top to the next, like floating stones on a pond. Outside the doors there was a landing with barely enough room for all of them to stand. Elias now saw there was a bright ruby in the center where the doors met.

"Nobody touch the doors. Especially not the center," Elias warned.

With their distorted images reflecting in the surface, Elias began to examine the copper doors. They would not open without a key, but Elias didn't believe it required a physical object. Perhaps a phrase spoken correctly or an energy signature, but he couldn't be sure. He blinked his eyes in disbelief, recalling the similar feeling at the gate in Merinde. Elias reached his hand into his satchel and put his goggles on. His vision changed and symbols appeared on the door. Removing the goggles, he handed them to Ellaria. She took them with an unsteady hand.

"Tell me what you see," Elias asked.

"Each door panel has a symbol in it and the lines of one cross over into the other. The markings bridge over the seam as though the entire door is sealed by one symbol," Ellaria said.

"There is a triangle shape of brushed copper at the center where the panes connect. Is there anything written in the triangle?" Elias asked. He leaned in and blew the dust out of the grooves.

"Yes! There's a small inscription underneath."

"Can you translate it?" Elias asked.

"What does it say?" Kovan asked.

"Pass with the hand of light and enduring energy," Ellaria said, and she handed back the goggles for Elias to look.

"What does that mean?" Wade asked, his eyes still fixed on the surface of water in the chamber, like he was waiting for a monster to come alive and grab them.

"My question is, what is this silvery stuff all over the walls?" Learon asked.

"I don't know, it's a metal coating, maybe cobalt," Elias said.

"But why?"

"My best guess is it's another safeguard," Elias said.

"In case we fail to unlock this thing correctly?" Wade said tapping his knuckles on the wall. The taps pinged loudly, and Ellaria slapped him over the head.

"Wade!" Tali moaned.

"Sorry, I forgot, but you know let's not fail."

"The Hand of Light," Tali repeated aloud. Then her eyes widened, and she looked to Learon at her side—"The glove, Learon."

Elias looked at them quizzically, unsure what was happening. Learon's shoulders slumped slightly as he starred at her. Tali nodded her head yes and Learon agreed. He reached into his pocket and removed a compact bundle with twine. Learon removed the leather wrapping and handed a light piece of reflective fabric to Elias. The moment Elias took hold of it, there was a pull of power to it. He reluctantly took his eyes off it and set them back to Learon for an explanation. "My father found that at Ash Field. I don't know what it is, but if it can help us. It's yours," Learon said.

"What is it?" Ellaria asked, and Elias unfolded it to see the shape of a glove.

"I think it's a sagemitter gauntlet," Elias said.

"Is it metal?"

"I believe it's the original form of phifer cloth."

"Well, whatever it is, put it on and let's crack this egg," Kovan said.

Elias took a deep breath and slipped his injured right hand gingerly through the sleeve. The glove only partially extended past his knuckles, leaving his blood-stained fingers free. The material was cold and smooth, and almost instantly healed his hand. But it was pulling energy on its own from somewhere.

"That's it?" Wade asked, looking at Elias's hand. They all turned to him, "Sorry, I just thought the way you hesitated that something might happen when you put it on."

Elias inspected the glove more closely. The mesh had a distinct stitching to it that made the gauntlet look like strips of a bandage, but the stitching itself was almost an unending sigil. What it meant; he couldn't say.

"Try it," Ellaria said to him.

With his palm wrapped in the sagemitter, he pressed his hand and fingers flush to the triangle. They heard a hiss, like the sound of air rushing to escape, and the hum stopped. Whether a trick of the light or his imagination, but for a moment he thought he saw the inscription light up and then the doors unsealed.

THE DOORS TO THE TOMB MOVED FREELY AND SWUNG INWARD WITH EASE. The first thing he saw inside was the bottom of the glass pyramid fixed into the ceiling of the space. A small amount of light was flooding the compartment as the dawn was breaking above them. Elias stepped inside first and looked around.

The burial vault was larger than he expected. Inside the crypt, individual geode alcoves surround the room. Each alcove had a body wrapped in blue cloth and laid on a bed of white fur beneath the crystalline formations. All of them had something precious that rested by their side. A staff, a scepter, jewels, even a deck of cards, but no amulets and no books that Elias could see. The geodes themselves varied from emperor to emperor. Some rested under purple amethyst and others blue azurite or jade. Elias was curious how it came to be which stone each would lie beneath for the afterlife. There were empty spaces too, but all total Elias counted eight Sagean emperors. A small number considering their reign of over a sixteen hundred years. The center of the room, beneath the pyramid, was an open floor space except for a small table with a wood box atop it. The floor itself was inlaid with gems in an indiscernible pattern.

Elias hurried over to the box and noticed he was alone. He looked back to the door and found them all still staring at him from the opening. No one else had ventured inside yet. He smiled and waved them in. They crossed in hesitantly and investigated the contents. Elias studied the wood chest. It was a simple yet perfectly crafted wood box. No script, symbols or markings other than the carpenter's finely crafted joinery.

"Another test?" Kovan asked.

"I don't think so," Elias said, and he lifted the lid, and set it aside to the floor with care. He heard someone's breath catch before he set eyes to it. The Tempest Stone resided alone in the soft furred interior. It was a brilliant milky white, with sparkling crystal chips flashing in the light. Elias gently removed the stone from the box. The pyramid shape was roughly larger than his hand, and the edges of the stone were fine and unblemished.

"If that's the Tempest Stone then where is the Sagean's Testament? Shouldn't it be here, in this chamber somewhere?" Ellaria asked, her face next to Elias's as they stared at the stone.

"I thought it would be?" Elias said, puzzled.

Kovan stepped between them, "Nice rock, Q. I think it's time we get the thorns death out of here."

Elias didn't argue the point. Retracing their path through the series of chambers and passageways would take time. They rounded up everyone to leave.

"Let's go Wade," Ellaria said. He was looking at the various emperors and had been transfixed by one in particular. Tali was doing the same, but each was mesmerized by a different one, "Tali?"

Tali turned at her name being called and went to get Wade.

"Did you see that. I think that guy had an original deck of Reckoner cards?" Wade said.

Ellaria waved them out and Elias followed last for one final look. They emerged from the tomb and stepped out onto the ledge to head back. Elias closed the door and backed up into someone as they were all still crowded together on the landing. The odd hum began again, but then he heard the sound of a primer-charge activate on Kovan's gun, and from beyond the burial vault, Elias heard a voice.

"Thank you so much for unlocking the vault, Qudin Lightweaver."

Elias turned to find the first chamber of bronze statues was now full of bonemen soldiers. Their guns all raised and aimed on them. At the head of them, at the ledge just beyond the smoking archway, were two men. Elias assumed the one in white was Rogan Malik, the Prime and the other his general, Lavic Dunne. Though he didn't recognize either man, but with a glance he was sure that neither were luminaries.

With everyone crowded on the landing step, Elias swiftly hid the stone in the first place he could find and stepped forward.

"Don't bother fighting, Qudin. I have fifty soldiers inside, another two files waiting outside the shrine, and a legion of automatons. Just like the ones you saw in the city. You will never escape," Malik said, and then he appraised the entire group, "Well, you may, but your friends will not. I can promise you that."

"I like a challenge," Kovan said.

"As I recall, Van, you know when you have been outmaneuvered," Malik said.

"Your recollections must be torqued Malik, otherwise you would remember that only my friends call me Van," Kovan spat back.

"You mean these friends you have led to death? I heard you lost a step Kovan, but I didn't think you were so old that you needed the help of a young girl. But I must say, I am most disappointed in you, Ellaria. I never thought you would allow students under your charge to be so reckless. And now they will die with you as traitors to the unified realm," Malik said and his face darkened.

Elias could see the muscles in Kovan's jaw tightening and knew his eyes were trying to calculate how to win. Elias was about to unleash a torrent unlike anything these adversaries had seen before when they heard someone else speak.

"Stand down, Malik," the voice said from the shadows. The group of soldiers turned, and a man emerged in a sweeping black cloak that flowed out behind him. Malik and Dunne both backed away for the newcomer who swiftly advanced. He wore spectacles, and he held his hands in front of him oddly, with his thumbs touching and his forefingers crossed. On his left hand was a unique bone ring that stretched the length of his finger in the shape of a dragon. The dragon had ruby eyes.

Elias knew instantly this was the new Sagean lord. His posturing and Malik and Dunne's reaction said as much.

"Plan B?" Kovan whispered to Elias.

"Plan C," Elias said back to him and shifted his head slightly to the left and the blue glazed window.

The man stepped to the ledge next to the Prime and Dunne. Elias was about to say something when he heard Ellaria's breath catch. She recognized him.

"Professor?" Wade said, also recognizing the man, but he kept blinking like his eyes were struggling to identify the man and image before him.

"Edward is that you? You are the Sagean?" Ellaria said as equally confused as Wade.

The Sagean removed his hat in a tip of hello, a shimmering ripple of air enveloped him and his appearance changed. Ellaria eyes grew wide obviously recognizing the new appearance even more and she stared dumbfounded.

"But you voted against the Prime, you stood up for me, you warned me . . ." Ellaria muttered.

"I was hoping you would lead me to Qudin. I knew Qudin would get us through the vault. He may be the only one alive who could," Edward said and his appearance warped back.

"Then why were you trying to kill him?" Ellaria probed.

"I never ordered my men to kill him. I had held out hope that through our mutual love of history, he and I could come to an agreement. That together, we could find the Sagean's Testament. You see, he has a significant advantage in his years of research and training. Only a fool wouldn't try to use that knowledge. Had I known sooner that he was reluctant to use his powers, I might have approached him myself at Anchor's Point. My beasts told me that during the attack at the Fork, Qudin waited until the last moment to use his power and I saw it for myself at Fort Verdict. Sure enough, there again, he held back. Otherwise, he would have stopped the men from burning the city down. Once I learned that he was afraid of his own power, I decided he had less to teach me than I wished to learn..." Edward stopped when his eyes found the sagemitter gauntlet on Elias's hand. His eyes arched together in a flare of envy, he pointed his finger at the glove, "Where did you get that?" Edward demanded of Elias, and sparks of electricity crackled in the Sagean's hand. The mild-mannered and monotone person dissolved to his more rapacious nature.

Elias raised his hand in the air, "You've seen this before?" he asked, and to his side Learon stirred in his stance. His breathing came faster. All three of these men before him were responsible for his father's death, and Learon knew it. Elias hoped he would keep his cool.

"It belongs to me!" Edward said through gritted teeth.

With his sagemitter covered hand still raised, Elias closed his fingers to a fist. Suddenly the wall of flames burst into place again inside the archway. The men on the ledge dove to the ground, fearing Elias had attacked them.

Without warning, Elias grabbed Kovan's hand and put it to the plate on the tomb door. The hum throttled louder, and he heard Edward scream at his soldiers. Both Malik and Dunne tried pulling on the lever to turn the flames off, but Elias was fighting against their attempts. Edward, recognizing the situation, walked undaunted to the edge of the pool and lashed out with a burst of lightning from his hands, and aimed at Elias's heart. Instead of hitting any of them, it flung high into the rock above and traveled around the room. Before zapping out of existence.

Edward looked wide eyed at Elias, obviously unsure what had just occurred. At first Elias thought it was Tali who had done it, but something was happening in the chamber.

The pool of water had started to tremble all over in wild, tiny vibrations. The room oscillated, and Elias felt an abrupt onset of nausea. All of them staggered in their stance on the landing, and Ellaria vomited onto the stone. In the chaos, Elias could no longer hold back the lever. The noise of the rushing falls seemed amplified, and Tali screamed at an unseen pain.

"What's happening?" Kovan yelled.

"It's the safeguard. Quick, shoot the window out, that's our escape," Elias yelled back. Kovan fired three rounds at the window, but none made it there. Each one flew in wild arches up above their heads and fell flat. Beyond the chamber Elias could see the army coming to join the others, but there was a haze between them at the edge of the two rooms.

The pool trembled madly and then went still. Droplets of water vapor rose into the air and swirled around. Elias's elum blade started to pull away by an unknown force. He looked to Edward at the ledge and he was shouting orders. Then the bonemen unleashed an onslaught of gunfire at them. Instinctively, they all ducked, but every slug hit the barrier and fell to the floor without penetrating through.

"Shoot the window, again," Elias said.

Kovan shot four rounds, and this time Elias helped guide them to the mark. The glass shattered and split into the air in various directions. The curtain of water falling beyond started to draw into the room.

"Go," Elias told them.

"Into the pool?" Ellaria shouted.

"Yes!" Elias yelled and pointed to the tungsten slugs sitting still on the water's surface.

Learon placed his foot to the water, but it didn't go under. He looked back at them in complete terror. Whatever was happening inside the chamber had increased the surface tension of the pool so much that

Learon could stand on it. Elias urged them to keep going. He wasn't confident how much longer they would survive inside alive. He was sure the chamber had turned into a powerful magnetic field. If it was strong enough to stop tungsten rounds, then they didn't have much time before they would start to melt like chocolate bars in the sun.

They all ambled to the window in slow motion. Any faster felt like they would slip through the water's surface and the air was turning at such a rapid rate that running would likely knock you off your feet. It was like walking in a hurricane.

Learon reached the window and looked back. He yelled something but Elias was too far away to make it out. Wade stood up next to him and looked down. Elias could see him shake his head no over and over.

When Elias got there, he helped Ellaria to climb up to it. The circular window was actually quite massive and held all three. Learon leaned down to talk to Elias.

"We're still like a hundred feet above the lake from here!" he shouted.

"I don't care! If we stay, we die!" he waved his hands wildly, "Jump!"

Learon turned and dove off the sill into the raging waterfall. Wade shook his head, grabbed his nose, and jumped. Ellaria helped Elias up and squeezed his hand. She was trembling. Her fear of heights had her paralyzed.

"You'll make it," Elias mouthed and nodded his head. She took two deep breaths, turned, and dove off on the third.

Elias turned back to help Tali and check on the Sagean. Edward had restarted the fire and was drawing energy from it. Elias watched, enraptured to see what he was going to try. The Sagean flung a stream of flames into the chamber. The heat rolled around the room and singed Elias's hand. Next, Edward took off anything metal he had. Throwing his spectacles to the floor. He then stepped through the barrier. Immediately he staggered to the ground. When he stood, Elias could see him channeling his energy into the turning water wheels in the walls.

With great effort he stopped the wheels from spinning, and the magnetic field wavered. Tali and Kovan fell into the pool. Elias reached out and grabbed Tali. Pulling her out before being blasted back by a force. He slammed into the windowsill and toppled over it into the falls. Glimpsing a grin on Edward's face as he fell.

# CHAPTER FORTY-EIGHT

## THE COST OF KNOWLEDGE (TALI)

Elias's body flew out of the window, knocking him around as he hurdled through. Tali clutched to the sill and watched the Sagean smile and run toward the vault door. She pulled herself up onto the ledge. The unbearable noise had died away, and whatever was happening in the room had faded. She could hear the rushing water again and her body didn't feel like it was being torn apart anymore.

Kovan lifted himself out of the pool and looked at her. They were both soaked and looked out into the endless stream of falling water. Yet, she felt lighter than she should. Her bag was missing. She jerked her head and looked around for it instinctively, but decided it was meaningless, and prepared to jump without it. Kovan noticed her looking and he too searched for it.

"There," he said. He spotted it caught up on the wall, clinging to the rock instead of sinking to the bottom of the pool. He reached for it.

"Forget it, Kovan. Let's go!" she said, pleading with him. When he couldn't get at it, he jumped back into the pool, grabbed the satchel and swam back. At the ledge she took the bag from him and slung it over her shoulder.

"Now, let's keep moving," he said with a smile, using Tali's grip to leverage himself up on the sill. When he was climbing up by her side he tried to say something but her words were cut off by yelling at the ledge behind them, followed by blasts of gunfire suddenly blaring in the cavernous space. Kovan, still gripping Tali's arm to get to his feet, yanked her into the pool. She flopped in with a splash, and with her head submerged, the sounds of the shots muffled. When she resurfaced the gunfire had ceased, and Kovan was still on the sill trying to stand up, but he sagged to the side. He placed a hand on the side of the frame to support himself and left a smear of blood. Tali gasped and Kovan's eyes found her. With a far off and drowsy gaze, he wobbled in his stance as Tali scrambled to reach him. Kovan's chest shuttered and sighed heavily. He winked at her and collapsed through the window opening, out into the endless rush of water, flipping freely in the downpour all the way to the bottom.

Tali tried to scream out his name, but no words formed, and she shook uncontrollably all over. Her voiceless breath, held captive in her mouth, finally gave way to a piercing scream, long after Kovan had disappeared from her sight. She pulled herself to the sill's edge and looked out, but through the rush of water there was nothing to be seen.

Her eyes found more evidence of blood at her feet and she looked back at the squad of soldiers. Their rifles pointed at her; she unleashed a hold of her fury. Blinded by grief and rage, her other senses compensated. She could feel the vibrations of all the colliding energies around her, and she sifted through the flows until she found what she wanted. She gripped tightly to the spirit of the soldiers themselves and started to rip the life's energy from the bonemen's bodies. The surge of energy was beyond anything she had touched before, but the feel of it made her tremble and she released it instantly. The men fell where they stood and life slowly returned to them. More soldiers approached the ledge and Tali reacted and channeled pure heat into each one. Light burst from their eyes and mouths and they all dropped lifeless to the stone.

The Sagean looked up from studying the vault door to stare in curious amazement. Tali screamed again, flooded the chamber full of light, and threw the remaining men in the room against the stone walls. The Sagean, Malik, and Dunne were pummeled into the cobalt covered rocks.

The exertion staggered her to her knees, and she gripped the side of the window. Satisfied that no one was attacking her, but not sure of the damage she had caused, she turned toward the lake and dove off into the water far below.

She fell faster than she could breathe. With more force from the waterfall than she wanted, she crashed into the cold turbulent lake at the plunging downpour. Her momentum taking her down, and down, and deep into the depths of the lake. The falls were still pummeling into her far below the surface and driving her deeper. Her limbs and body spun out of her control. Finally, she felt her feet touch the rocky bottom of the lake and she frantically kicked up. Wildly, she swam for the breath she desperately needed.

When she reached the surface, she gulped madly for air and choked on mouthfuls of water. Coughing uncontrollable, a hand snatched her by the shoulder and towed her away. Someone was saving her from being drawn back under by the pull of the spill point.

Learon lifted her out of the lake and laid her down onto a stone floor. She blinked rapidly, wiping her face free of water. Her body convulsed and she leaned over to her side and retched up a mouthful of lake water.

When her senses returned, she stood up slowly and found Learon and Ellaria there by her side.

"Where's Kovan?" Tali said when she could finally speak, but they looked at her confused.

"Wasn't he with you?" Ellaria said, her eyes widening.

"They shot him, and he fell."

"What? He was shot?" Ellaria said with panic.

"Yes, didn't you see him?"

"No dear, but if he fell on the outside of the falls, we wouldn't have. We just barely saw Elias. There's Wade with him now," Ellaria said pointing. Wade was helping Elias get to the stone steps. Having gone through the falls pouring blast to retrieve him.

"Go back. Kovan is out there," Tali said to them.

"We didn't see him. He fell through the falls?" Wade answered.

"Yes! I don't know. They shot him. Elias, he's hurt terribly, please," she implored. Elias nodded and turned to Learon.

"Show them where the gate is. Make sure we're alone down here and come back."

Learon and Ellaria turned to go into the temple they found themselves standing in front of. Wade and Elias jumped back into the water and swam for the plunging pool. Tali walked partly inside the structure but stopped and watched the water, waiting for any signs of them returning. She wanted to be there when they dragged Kovan ashore. *He was hurt, she knew he was hurt. But he was still alive. He had to be alive.*

Finally, Tali spotted them swimming back. She thought they were towing Kovan with them, but he wasn't there. Wade reached the steps, clutching onto Kovan's jacket. It was bloodstained and had several holes. Elias was still swimming for the steps.

"I'm sorry, Tali, this is all we found," Wade said, unable to look her in the eyes.

"What?" Ellaria said, emerging from the temple.

Elias reached the steps and got out, waving at them. He coughed and coughed and couldn't speak.

"What is it?" Ellaria said. Her eyes were full of tears.

"Run!" Elias yelled at them, "Run, those rendered automatons are coming! Go to the gate," Elias said.

"What about Kovan!" Tali yelled at them.

"We have to go, child. If Kovan is alive, he is on the other side. The Light be with him. We can't help him," Ellaria told her.

"He's alive, Ellaria! He can't be dead."

"I know, dear," Ellaria said, and pulled Tali into a tight embrace, "I know," She held Tali, but pulled back slightly and wiped the tears streaming down Tali's face, "Listen, there is no one in this world harder to kill than that man. If he's alive, he will find a way back to us. He always does."

"Come on. Keep moving," Elias said, placing his hands on her shoulder.

He sprinted into the darkness of the gate room. Halfway inside, Elias pulled a small ball from his bag. It bloomed and glowed in his palm. He ran to the gate and searched the dais for something.

"Here," he said, "This is the symbol I activated that took me to the cave beyond Hawk's Perch."

"Fine, let's go," Ellaria said.

"Stand back," Elias said, and put his palm on the symbol and the design ignited in a red glow. The gate creaked and moaned. Then it burst alive with energy. Lightning sparked and slapped the air. Bolts arched to the ground and rolled up the walls. They all backed away from the discharges.

"Is this thing safe, because it doesn't look safe?" Wade said.

"It's safe. Don't worry, it's over in a heartbeat. It will feel like every part of your being is being pulled forward, and then it will feel like you're falling. It's like riding a wave, but halfway across the world in a matter of seconds," Elias assured him.

"Great . . ." Wade said.

They watched the gate and the metal arches begin to slowly move, and shots rang out from the lake. Two of the rendered had risen out of the water and started firing their rifles, as the waterlogged barrels allowed. One breached through a set of the arched doors, throwing the panels out in a crash. Learon began shooting at it and Elias ran in with his blade. He toppled the automaton but was under heavy fire from more in the main hall. They ran to help.

Wade flipped a switch on his gauntlet and a blade sprang free. Learon pulled his gun out, but when Tali reached for hers it was missing. It must have come out in the fall.

Elias noticed her weaponless and passed her his elum blade, strappings and all. She wrapped the awkward sheath around her and held the blade like he had taught her.

"Wait, won't you need this?" she asked.

"No, I have this," Elias answered, raising his hand up and showing her the odd glove.

Tungsten rounds fired again into the room, but Elias stood with his head bowed, breathing calmly. Then he raised his chin, and the color of his eyes evaporated. Lightning rolled and sparked along his body until it collected at his right hand. In a flash of light, and a roar of sound, a sword of light burst from his sagemitter.

It was shaped similar to the elum blade, but the intensity was too bright to look at. It illuminated the entire room. He moved the sword in the air, getting a feel for the weapon and then he ran toward the machines.

"That's really not fair," Wade said to them. But then he charged after Elias.

Elias cut down the first rendered he saw. The blade sliding through the machine without resistance in a blaze of heat and steam.

More came from the water. They looked like they weren't swimming as much as they were walking the lakebed.

A rendered came at Tali and swung its lumbering limb to attack her with its spear. The point of the spear slammed down near her. She dodged the attack, but it took her to the ground hard. Wade bounded in to help. He slashed unsuccessfully at the bronze shell. One of its massive hands reached down and picked her up. The thin fingers were sharp and cut into her shoulder. Tali reeled back in pain and tried to manipulate the energy inside it. It was hard to grasp, but just the attempt caused the thing to drop her to the stone. She looked up, aware of what Elias had meant about the things feeling wrong. They were alive by more means than mechanical energy. There was a spirit energy bound in them. Wade sprinted close and cut the main vein. The rendered fell awkwardly.

"Wade!" Learon yelled and he threw his gun over. Wade caught it and climbed atop the machine. He fired successive rounds of charged slugs into the thing until it ceased to move.

They destroyed a wave, after wave of rendered. Learon was an excellent shot, but unless he was perfect, the slugs did minor damage.

Ellaria had eventually ran out of firespark and hung back behind cover. Tali and Wade mostly distracted them until Elias could cut them down, but Elias was struggling to keep up with every one that crawled out. The sagemitter was a magnificent weapon, but it was slowly taking its toll on Elias.

In a moment of brief relief from their attacks, they looked at each other from across the forum of scattered machines. Tali saw Elias grab Learon by his shirt and tell him something. They argued. but Learon eventually shook his head in agreement and ran to her and Wade.

"We're going. Now!" Learon said.

"Isn't Elias coming?" Ellaria asked, but Learon just looked at her like she already knew the answer to her own question. Ellaria came over and held her hand out. Learon hesitated but handed her his pulsator gun.

"No!" Tali protested, but Ellaria just smiled at her and tapped her watch.

"It's time to go, dear. We'll contact you when we're safe."

Learon tugged at her sleeve and led her away. At the gate, Learon and Wade did a quick round of gun, knife, or cloak. Learon chose cloak, and Wade knife. Wade smiled widely. Learon slapped his arm and stepped up to the dais. He looked back at them both and then gestured toward Tali. Silently telling Wade to make sure she got through. Then Learon walked into the light.

Still, she couldn't go. She turned and ran back to help Elias, but Wade caught up to her. Getting in her path before she reached the doors.

"We have to keep moving," he said, and his words stopped her. "Don't look back, Tali."

Beyond Wade, she could see Elias fighting the rendered. He retreated a few steps and looked at them. He was yelling something at her, but she couldn't understand what. Then he pointed again to the gate, and Wade grabbed her arm. She shrugged it off violently and attempted to throw more energy at the rendered rising by the dozens at the lake's edge. Elias turned and pointed frantically, this time she followed his motion to look at the ceiling. There were massive cracks forming in it, and it looked ready to collapse. Wade picked her up as she looked on in disbelief and carried her to the gate and put her down.

She looked at him furiously and wanted to hit him, "We can't leave them!" she scolded him.

"We have to!" he yelled back and holding her hand he urged her to jump. Tali looked up into his eyes, where his honest concern for her was real and staggering. She nodded; she was ready. Wade pointed toward the light, "Ladies first."

Tali stilled herself from a final look back, let go of Wade's hand and stepped into the shimmering vail.

THE WHIRLING PROPULSION OF IMPOSSIBLE VELOCITY THROUGH MATTER and space terminated in a flash with impunity, dispatching her heavily to the ground. Her bag slid out in front with a knock, as it clattered away from her. Tali's body ached and she could feel the coarse stone below her, but she couldn't see it. Her eyes were refusing to work. She rubbed them feverishly, fearing she had lost her vision again.

"Tali, I'm here. Don't worry, it wears off," Learon said, and he reached down and helped lift her to her feet. She thanked him and turned back to the gate. Blinking rapidly until the blur faded away from her vision. Her eyes adjusted in time to see Wade tumble into the room from the pool of light.

"I think I'm going to be sick," Wade said, picking himself off the floor.

With her vision restored completely, Tali could see they were in an ancient room. Unlike the previous one, this room had various sections with streams of light filtering through from above. Hundreds of thin stone columns filled the expansive space. Each column arched over from one to the next, dividing the room. The carved marble pillars were ornately fluted and completely different then the ones inside the Marathal temple they had just left.

Tali turned her attention back to the steady drone and vibration of the gate. Waiting for Elias and Ellaria, but the gate's power was slowly subsiding. No one else was coming through.

Unexpectedly, the gate flung off a slew of wild bolts of lightning, crackling loudly and illuminating the hollow even more. They each backed away from the blast of sparks that popped and lashed out. A burst hit at Learon's feet and he lunged backward into a toppled block of black stone. The gate's center oculus was almost closed, but the discharges of electricity didn't seem to stop. Another wild burst dislodged a section of stone from the ceiling, and it fractured, falling to the floor between them.

They looked at each other and then for an exit. An opening of light at the far end of the room suggested a way out. Wade and Learon headed there and Tali grabbed her bag and darted out after them. Clutching tightly to the strap, she surged out onto the mountainside. Her momentum nearly took her over a cliff edge.

Where there should have been a walkway, there was only a drop off. Whatever had been there before, floor or bridge, it had long ago broken free and disintegrated to the ravine below. A final blaring crack was echoed from the temple interior, followed by the sound of more stone colliding with the floor. A cloud of dust billowed out of the entrance around their feet. The gate went silent and the sounds of the mountain returned.

Tali gulped the fresh air of the mountainside in heaps. Then she gawked at the endless landscape of mountains and hills stretching out below them. An endless sea of cliffs and trees spread out before them, with larger snow capped mountain peaks beyond. Dread washed over her. *What were they to do next? Where would they go?* She checked her watch. Unsure if it still worked. The top face had gone still, but the communicator's plate underneath looked intact. She suspected it was too soon to contact them. Though she wanted to, she would wait until nightfall.

To her right, Learon climbed up the rocks to the higher ridge point, to look out upon the eastern route. Tali thought it best to stick together and moved to join him. She slung the satchel over her shoulder. The weight hit her hard in the hip, and she cried out softly. Her muscles hurt all over. She lifted her still wet shirt and found her side badly bruised from the night's fight. She threw back the to flap of her pack to look inside. The contents immediately caught the light and sparkled. She lifted the pyramid shaped stone free and into the sunlight. She had never seen a crystal like it; the milky-white effervesce was nearly blinding. Tears streamed down her face and the boys came to her side.

"Are you alright?" Wade asked. Tali nodded that she was fine.

"Look at that," Learon said. Tali turned her gaze from the stone to the odd light shining into the sidewall. The rays of sunlight were bouncing through the Tempest Stone like a prism and casting a strange collage of colors on the wall. Small specks of crystal in the wall surface shimmered.

With the stone held in her palm a jolt of recognition flooded her mind, and a memory of Elias's artifact room became clear. Soundlessly, she rushed back into the ancient structure.

"Tali, what is it?" Wade called out after her and followed her back to the cave.

Inside the burrow, she jogged around the scattered broken stone and over to the corner of the room where the black plinth rested on the floor. She placed her things down and tentatively tapped it with her fingers. Remembering Elias's warning that it could shock her. Only the tiniest trickle pricked her finger, and she moved her weight and tried unsuccessfully to lift it. It was unimaginably heavy.

"Help me," she called out to the guys as they darted toward her. It took the two of them to lift it. Seeing it in front of her, even in the darkness, she was sure it was the same as the one she had seen before. Something was still off, though. She looked around and inspected the shaft of light hitting the floor nearby.

"Guys move it into the light," she directed them.

"This thing is heavy, you know. Are you sure you wouldn't like it by the entrance, you know to greet guests as they arrive? I mean, as long as we're redecorating, let's make it nice," Wade said.

"Just do it, Wade," she answered impatiently.

When they stationed it fully in the rays of light, Tali wiped the dust off and placed the Tempest stone into the grooved track where it belonged. She stepped back, and the light flared alive around them in small broken fragments of stone at their feet and one larger chunk still living in a spot on the wall.

Learon picked up a piece off the floor, "It's a quartz crystal," he said.

They moved closer to inspect the fragment still on the wall. Inside the crystal there were a thousand tiny images. Not sparks of light, but actual images of drawings, and text. Tali touched the crystal and light flickered all around them. The images appeared like translucent ghosts, floating between them. Only a few formed fully, while most simply continued to flicker.

"It's like a book, but one you can literally step into," Wade said with astonishment.

"Not just one book, it's an entire library of books. This shattered crystal tablet was a storage system for their collective knowledge. Each tablet is a database. The Tempest Stone isn't a singular source of knowledge it unlocks the knowledge of these crystal tablets."

"I guess we need to get some more of these tablets," Wade said.

"I know where we can find four or five of them," Tali told them.

"Where?"

"Elias's home in Polestis. He had a plinth just like this and four or five crystal tablets in his artifact room. He said that the things in there, he had found all over the world, and that a few pieces were even from the Sagean's palace."

"The Sagean Testament they're looking for. It's not a book. It's a piece of crystal?" Learon surmised.

"Yes, I think you're right," Tali agreed.

They collected the pieces they could salvage from the room and packed it away. Leaving the darkened temple behind they climbed the ridge across to the eastern horizon. Hungry, searching, and forever entangled, they stepped toward the sun, mindful that they needed to keep moving. Fate had brought them together and together they would go forward, because no one makes it through this world alone. Light moves mysteriously and so would they, this time with the wind at their back.

## THE END OF BOOK ONE

# EPILOGUE

VIBRANT GREEN AND TURQUOISE WINGS FLUTTERED THROUGH AND DOWN the open well. It was there that a set of winding stairs descended the interior far below the ground. The warbird moved in flashes until it landed at a stone sill on one of the many arched openings along the spiraling stairway. Verro Mancovi stepped to the archway to retrieve the warbird messenger. The artificer's creation bounced on its tiny legs in waiting and Verro gently picked the bird off of the stone sill and whispered to it.

The birds beating wings moved rapidly and then stilled. The metal breast of the hummingbird opened up, and a small scroll that rested inside fell out. Verro took the message and placed the bird down. He tapped a point on its mid-back, and the warbird lifted to flight again. Verro suspected he already knew the contents of the message, so he restrained from reading it. He strode down the steps to the meeting chamber near the lowest depths and pushed through the heavy old wooden doors. The panels creaked at first but swept in smoothly. The top arches of the towering door whispered clear of the stone ceiling. The overhead caliber stones illuminated the large room, and he found the others around the long table awaiting his return. All except Aylanna Alvir, who stood admiring the gems of honor in the pool of ghost sand. She too, turned at Verro's entrance and found her seat.

"What does it say?" Theomar Kyana asked. Always one in need of instant information.

"What we suspected," Verro said, handing Herod the message before sitting.

"But you haven't even opened it?" Shirova asked.

"I don't have too. I keep telling you Shirova, the Orb of Delawyn, is never wrong."

Shirova took his response with a scowl. Herod unfurled the message and read it, before passing it along.

"The rogues have entered the tomb and Knox is preparing to capture them," Herod reported to the seven.

"He will fail, of course," Batak hissed.

"But why? We trained Edward as the great book instructed and he is powerful. Are we so sure he will fail?" Harrimon asked.

"Yes, we can be sure. Qudin is superiorly gifted and if our reports can be believed. He has also found an apprentice," Aylanna said.

"He will fail, because he was meant to fail, we knew Knox couldn't defeat Qudin, but he will survive, and now that the chamber has been opened, we can continue with our plan," Batak said, tossing the message to the center. At the same time the doors to the chamber's creaked open. Two guests came through the opening. However, it was only Rotha Durrone and Helona Knox, two members of outsider families, so none of the seven paid them much mind.

"But the Tempest Eye is surely gone though," Harrimon said.

"Perhaps but it matters not. With the tomb opened, we now have access to the Temple of Ama," Verro said.

"What if they took the scepter?" Shirova asked. Always looking for a flaw in their plan.

"Highly unlikely. No, Qudin believes the past is sacred he wouldn't desecrate any of the tombs. He would have left the scepter in the hands of Sage Corinsura, blessed be her light," Verro told them.

"We have also just received word that our agents in Polaris have located the mountain site," Helona Knox said, from a side chair.

"Excellent. Send word back to Marathal; inform your son that the time is near for the Culling of Light and he should return to the Dragon's Well for rest. We need Knox strong to raise all of us and we will all be equal to Qudin," Verro instructed her.

"Soon you will all be luminaries and the world will once again be beneath the rule of the Sages," Batak said.

"You are confident as always old friend. You still intend to give your spot to Delvar?" Herod asked.

"Yes, my son will rule long after I am gone," Batak said, tapping his fingertips on the table in slow waves. "And why shouldn't I be confident? With the blockade in place in the Anamic, we can control the waters and our legion grows strong as the Lionized convert more everyday."

"And if these Rogues, as you call them, raise another army against you? What then?" Queen Rotha Durrone asked from her side chair.

"Impossible," Batak sneered.

"If you recall, we thought it impossible forty years ago too. Let us not underestimate Qudin again," Aylanna said. A few fists pounded the table in agreement, and Batak shook his head.

"Which leads me to ask. What did you do with the Peace King?" Aylanna redirected to Verro.

"He was re-sintered and is on his way to the Red Spear to await our ascension," Verro said.

"Your determination to have his spirit will be the end of you," Shinova warned.

"No my old friend, the chamber will be the end of us all and then it will be our rebirth," Verro said.

# GLOSSARY

*Note: The current date is the 24th of Jovost in the 54th year of the 23rd epoch.*

**Acarite:** A bright blue crystal, also called the soul crystal. Prized for its blue color, which many nations see as sacred.

**Afterblue (The afterblue, the blue hours, blue sun):** The atmosphere of Territhmina is clear and thin enough that when the sun reaches the highest point in the sky the sun turns a blue color. For the Sagean faith this time is spent in worship. Afterblue refers to the moment the sun leaves the apex of the sky and the color of the sun returns to normal. The thin atmosphere contributes to a high volume of water vapor in the air.

**Age of Eckwyn (ek-win):** The time before the Sagean Empire, spanning the 2nd to the 6th epoch, when the people of Territhmina were unified. See also **Ancients**

**Alchemist's Codex, the:** Written by Xand Zosimus. It is the oldest and most extensive book on alchemy ever found.

**Amadazumi (ah-ma-daz-ew-me):** The name of the God of the northern region, near the Gray Sea.

**Amatori Market:** The great market in Ravenvyre. The market established a wider notoriety because of the large contingent of crafters, tinkers and alchemists found in Ravenvyre, who sell their gadgets and potions there.

**Amber Coins:** The common currency of the world are stamped amber coins. The amber has an odd bluish tint from pyrite inclusions. Each coin is marked with a symbol denoting the location of its origin.

**Ancients, the:** The common term for the forgotten Age of Eckwyn. A time lost to history. All that is known is that the civilization that existed before the Sagean Empire was advanced and divided. See also **Eckwyn Age**.

**Anthracite:** A black stone used in fires to ward off the beasts. It burns blue.

**Artificer:** A machine maker of small lifelike devices, such as mechanical butterflies, bats, spiders and owls.

**Ascendency Tower:** The main government seat and headquarters for the Coalition of Nations and the Councils Court.

**Band of the Black Sails:** A crime syndicate that mostly operates out of Aquom. They plunder and pirate the Mainsolis Sea and the Zulu Sea.

**Bogdrin:** A swamp creature with a tentacled face. They are a rare creature known to exist in the blood marshes off the western coast of Nahadon. They have been seen as far north as the swamps of Aquom.

**Bonelark:** A large, featherless flying beast. Though rare, these creatures eat human flesh and bone. They first appeared during the Great War. It is believed they don't hunt in numbers and stay close to their nests.

**Bonemen, The (The Bloodless, the Bone Army):** The Sagean's personal army. The bonemen or also known as the bloodless or the bone army. They derived their name as a representation of last servitude beyond death. For even bones remain after the blood is gone and the flesh has decayed.

**Cadowa:** A slender boat with a very tall single sail. Used predominantly in Aquam to navigate the shallow and thin canals and waterways.

**Calendar Year:** The Territhmina year is 396 days long and divided into 12 months. Summer (Jovost, Savon, Shadal), Fall (Deluarch, Harven, Faden), Winter (Emberheart, Hazune, Souludal), Spring (Anander, Thawrich, Reesee). The New Year begins on the first day of summer and is the longest day of the year.

**Capacitor gems:** Any stone or crystal capable of energy.

**Cloaked Knife:** An elite group of mercenaries trained at the Citadel. This special military unit grew from the remnants of the Ultrarians.

**Cloudparter:** Enormous metal airships that transport people and supplies across the mountains and throughout Tavillore.

**Confidence chairs:** Attendees at the council's court in support of the ambassador who called them there.

**Craftcore, The:** The center for scientific development in Adalon.

**Craftsmith:**  A crafter of objects not associated with a blacksmith.

**Crime Syndicates:**  There are six known crime syndicates around the world. Most of them originated after the fall of the Sagean Empire. They are: The Deviants Core, The Insurgents Guard, The Shield, The Reckers, The Broken Flame, The Devisors and **The Band of the Black Sails**.

**Crystals, Jewels & Gems:** Crystals are categorized into five groups based on their use: Energy stones, Power stones, Protection stones, Healing stones and Lore stones. Lore stones are rare or considered myth in some cases.

*Energy Stones:*
>>Quantum Stone: a capacitor gem that recharges continually until the stone's integrity eventually degrades, (Extremely Rare).
>>Caliber Stones: orb stones used as lights by luminaries, (Extremely Rare).
>>Joulestone: crystals that can hold electrical charges. Fragments are used throughout the world to power small gadgets, guns, (Common).

*Power Stones:*
>>Turquoise: strength and stamina.
>>Blue Acarite: spirit, energy and clarity.
>>Ruby: added skill and movement and agility.
>>Topaz: inspiration.
>>Emerald: luck and reflexes.

*Protection Stones:*
>>Obsidian: protection and clarity of mind.
>>Blood stone: protection and cleansing.

*Healing Stones:*
>>Jade: healing and wisdom.
>>Clear Quartz: healing and memory.
>>Rose Quartz (love stone or heart stone): love bond, and blood cleansing.
>>Amethyst: calms the spirit, dispels anger and fear, grief and stress.
>>Sun Stone: healing of wounds and internal aliments.
>>Bismuth crystal: stomach aches and headaches.

*Lore Stones: A lore stones are considered myth and legend.*
>>The Elder Stone: ultimate protection stone and stone of wisdom.
>>The Dream Stone: provides a connection to dreams.
>>Mistinite Crystal: crystal prisms of a glittering milk like luster. Reveals hidden realms.
>>Gemstar Stone: an asteroid fragment used to power the wave gates.

**Court of Dragons:** A rumored organization of great power and influence. Their members, origin, and organization are unknown.

**Daraku (dare-ah-kew):** The dark lord's son.

**Darkhawks:** Elite group of fighters located to the New World.

**Dawning gale:** A morning songbird of the Warhawk Mountains.

**Day of Light:** The New Year begins on the first day of summer, and the longest day of the year. It is the most celebrated holy day in the Empire.

**Dire, the:** A small grouping of islands in the Brovic Ocean, seven leagues off the Coast of Rodaire, beyond which no one dares travel. It marks a point of no return in the Brovic Ocean. All who have sailed beyond it have died or never returned.

**Dreamer's smoke:** An alchemist's dry potion that produces a cloud of white mist and renders all who inhale it asleep.

**Drizar:** Large reptiles that live in the deadlands.

**Drooping pine bark:** A common tree in Tavillore, its bark is used in fires and wards off the Sagean's beasts. It burns blue.

**Egregore mind:** An ability of the One people of Wanvilaska to share each other's thoughts.

**Elegan Language:** An ancient undecipherable language of the Eckwyn Age. It's use predates the Territhian language instituted by the Sagean Empire.

**Elum Blade:** A sacred sword of the Shadowyn. With a short thin blade, it is holstered upside down and is only 2 and half feet long, including the long hilt. The technique and material used to make the blade are unknown.

**Encumbrance, the:** People's term for the Coalition of Nations. Referring to both the corruption and game of politics.

**Emberbroth:** A spicy burning alcoholic drink, served both hot and cold.

**Eruptor:** A power charged rifle, that fires electrical bolts. It is nearly three times stronger than a pulsator.

**Firespark:** A thick red liquid, an alchemist's potion created during the Great War. It explodes in a burst of fire once in contact with air.

**Furies:** A term used by alchemists to describe the known and unknown forces of nature.

**Gas discharge lamps:** Sealed airless glass tubes, with a local capacitor, producing an electrical current that charges a chemical inside, producing light. Oxygen is white, sodium vapor is bright yellow, or orange and krypton is blueish white or green when low.

**Great War, the:** The Great War spanned for 990 days. It began on the 1st of Emberheart in the 15th year of the 23rd epoch and ended on the 1st of Jovost year 18 of the 23rd epoch.

**Greencoats:** The organized policing force of protectors and law enforcement throughout the world. Also known as peacekeepers.

**Guardian amulets:** The amulets said to be constructed by the ancient Luminaries to protect the world. The number of amulets made, and their individual powers are unknown.

**Guardians of Illumination, the:** A book written by Orin Ioka. It is the oldest account of the Luminaries in existence.

**Hammer blast rifle:** A powder ignited projectile gun for long range accuracy. Discontinued manufacture and use following the Great War and the invention of charged ammunition.

**Hellfiend:** A mutation of the bear family. This beast is very rare, seen only once during the Great War. Tracks have been found in both the Sun Mountains and the Soaring Mountains.

**Horse types:**

> *Cold blooded horse:* a larger horse used to pull carts. These horses are harder to scare and used by military forces.

> *Hot blooded horse:* a fast and slim horse used for speed. They are known to scare easily.

> *Light horse:* a racing breed

> *Warm blood:* a mix of cold and hot blooded horses. They are athletic and strong and the most commonly used for travel.

> *Nyrogen:* a rare breed of horse from the southern regions of Rodaire. They are temperamental, but considered the fastest horse in the world.

**Illumination surge:** The moment a luminary's powers are truly born inside them. It is the point when the luminary's ability to store energy that they've unconsciously gathered is released. This may occur at any time, but the later in life it takes to occur, the stronger and deeper the luminaries well for energy will be.

**Imperial Road:** A white stone road arrayed throughout Tavillore, connecting the major cities. The stone road has four grooved tracks to allow wagon wheels to stay in position. Most major settlements and cities are along the track. Also known as the stone track.

**Joulestone:** See **crystals**.

**Joybird:** A performer in a showman's traveling circus.

**Legion of Light:** A group of zealots and believers in the teachings of the Sagean faith. Disbanded after the Great War and the fall of the Sagean Empire.

**Lionized, the:** Contemporary zealots of the Sagean faith. A radical organization rising up with fall of the Coalition and the appointment of the Prime Commander. They long for the return of a Sagean Emperor.

**Luminaries:** A special race of humans with the ability to sense, control, and manipulate energy. This process is referred to as binding. The flows of energies they sense are referred to as the tempests. Once, they were common and collectively ruled the world under separate factions. The separate factions were divided based on their world views, and beliefs. Each faction — its own religion. For reasons lost to history, the Sagean faction took control in the 6th epoch. Most of the other factions were killed or died off. During the reign of the Sagean Empire, their own numbers of luminaries also dwindled.

**Luminance Squad:** A squad appointed by the Prime Commander to hunt down and capture Qudin Lightweaver.

**Magnetometer:** A device that measures magnetism—the direction, strength, or relative change of a magnetic field at a particular location.

**Magnotype:** A typewriter machine with intricate gears and an ink well. It uses magnetic displacements of a needles and gears they are used to communicate messages across the world.

**Melodicure machine:** A gem powered machine of unknown origin and construction, in use by the Whisper Chain. It aids the Chain in finding people throughout the world.

**Menodarians:** A race of beings that once existed mostly in Merinde. They are known for their slender, tall forms and their intellect. They have flat faces and were known to be closely guarded and distrustful of other races.

**Meiyoma blade:** The common sword in Rodaire. Characterized by its long gentle arching blade with two hand length handles. Handles range from plain wood to decorated jade. The hilt is commonly in the shape of a crescent moon.

**The Moonstalkers:** A guild of organized bounty hunters.

**Monarch trees:** Extremely large trees that grew to incredible heights. Only known grove exists on the island of Hazon.

**Moonstone dust:** An alchemist's dry potion. A fine powder that protects against evil spirits.

**Mudfoot:** A slang term or derogatory reference to river folk who live along the banks of the Uhanni River. They are known to attack or rob small ships and vessels.

**Mystcat:** A special breed of cat that is unusually attracted to the gifted. They search out and bond to luminaries and other gifted beings. They are quizzical, sneaky, and very loyal. They love heights and their fur is usually white and gray, all gray, or black. With black being the most rare. Their eyes can be green, blue & yellow and they produce a low harmonic purr. They also bend their ears in patterns of anthropomorphic communication. Additional powers remain unknown.

**Ovardyn (O-var-din):** The lord of darkness and ruler of The Nothing and the realm of Evil Spirits.

**Nothing, the:** The domain of Evil Spirits. It is the realm where the demon Ovardyn dwells.

**Nowarin Basilisk:** Large sand snakes in the Nowarin dessert. They can grow to be the size of whales, but are mostly unseen, as the desserts are uninhabited.

**Paravin Schools:** Small schools of higher learning in some of the cities. An alternative to the larger Guild run universities. With the aim to teach trade crafts.

**Peace King:** The Free Cities of The New World were instrumental in the Resistance's success in the Great War. Lead by Arno Danehin, the fourteen-year-old son of Bara Danehin who was killed in the battle of Axern. Arno Danehin railed the troops to win the battle and for the rest of the war assumed the leadership of the armies of the New World. After the war, he was named the Peace King of the Free New World.

**Phifer cloth:** A cloth of scientifically engineered material that is microscopically fused metal with alchemic symbols sometimes engraved into the weaving. It is impact resistant, highly conductive and so light of weight that it floats on water or even would fail to crush a dandelion. The lithium mesh coat is typically worn by soldiers. Gold colored or black, depending on the rank. Its nickel phosphorus alloy lattice acts as a thermal insulator, acoustic and vibration dampening.

**Prolaten:** A government official in Kotalla that is the voice of the people.

**Protagen force:** An eternal fury of bound elements more powerful than the opposite pulls of magnetic energy.

**Pulsator:** A handheld, charged gun or projectile weapon that fires charged tungsten rounds or bolts. It replaced the less powerful and inaccurate powder firing guns. They are notoriously expensive, and the many components are sought after for various modifications and customizations.

**Quandinium:** A metal found in abundance across the world. It is most often used in building construction for its strength and lack of conductivity. Other characteristics include: corrosion resistant, a high melting point, ferromagnetic.

**Quarter Day Festivals:** There are four festivals at the quarter marks of the year. One in each season; Brighden (spring), Alustra (summer), Harven (fall), and Solstar (winter).

**Ravenhawk:** The nickname of war hero Ellaria Moonstone. A general of the Resistance in the Great War. The name was derived from her service as both a general and a spy during the war.

**Raven's breath:** An alchemist's potion, truth serum.

**Ravinors:** The most feared of all the Sagean's beasts. These rare monsters retreated mostly to the south swamps of Tavillore and into the jungles of Nahadon after the war. They are the most intelligent and dangerous of all the beasts. They are lizard like humanoids, walk on two legs and have long snouts with exposed sharp teeth. Sharp claws on their hands and short spiked tails. They are presumed to be reptilian but have many anthropomorphic traits and social behaviors.

**Reckoner:** A card game played in the major cities. The deck of cards is housed in an action turner that counts down the individual turn meter. Starting after the third turn the reckoning can appear on the turner — ending the game. Anywhere from 2 to 8 people can play, but rules vary. The cards have individual strengths and weaknesses, represented by figures and objects throughout Territhmina history. The object is to field the strongest set of cards to defeat your opponent. The game evolved from the Eckwyn Age and was outlawed for eighteen hundred years until the Empire issued a new and revised deck of cards featuring Sagean Lords. As a way to quell the prominent families forming an uprising in the 19th epoch. A reprint of the original pre-Empire deck was made during the Great War, but an actual fully intact set of original cards has never been found.

**Rendered:** Automaton beings or machine hunters built by the Sagean.

**Risen World, the:** The realm of souls ascended to a plane of existence of pure energy. Where they reside in peace and harmony until they are called upon for a new life.

**Sagean (Saw-Gee-in):** The luminary leader of the Sagean faith and Emperor. According to believers of the faith, the Sagean is the living manifestation of the God of Light. The Sagean Empire ruled the world uncontested from the 6th epoch until the 23rd epoch, when the empire was overthrown during the Great War. The last Sagean Emperor, Mayock Kovall, the ninth line of the Sagean progression was defeated by Qudin Lightweaver in the battle of Dragon Spine. The Sagean luminaries can control energy, and were known to manipulate the minds of others, control animals, and alter their appearance.

**Sagean's Consortium, the:** The name for the remaining army that continued to wage war for the Emperor after the Sagean's death at the Battle of Dragon's Spine. The Consortium waged war and continued to cause conflicts until they were defeated, almost three years later, at the Black Spire of the Citadel.

**Sagean Testament:** A book guarded by the Sagean ruler passed down to each in line. Its contents are unknown to anyone outside of the lineage of Sageans and their closest acolytes.

**Sagelight, the:** Can refer to the Sagean faith or the sacred religious text itself.

**Sagemitter gauntlet:** A glove. It is light as a feather, and only partially covers the fingers. Made of phifer cloth, it allows a luminary who wears it to easily harness and form the energy they sense and bind it into solidified objects.

**Scholar's Guild, the:** An organization entrusted with control over education, curation of history, all publications and select institutes of higher knowledge. Including supervision over alchemists, machine patents, inventions, civil planning and architecture.

**Shadow dust:** A fine powder that blooms into a cloud of black mist. Created by alchemists during the Great War.

**Shadowyn, the:** A small province hidden in the mountains. They train a group of elite warriors for protection from the outside world. Known for their stealth and ability with swords.

**Shodders:** A common term for cheats, cheaters, grifters, halfwits and anyone who tries to swindle someone with faulty goods, false claims or bad products.

**Silver six gun:** An old powder fired handgun. The predecessor to the pulsator. These, like all powder powered guns, were discontinued after the Great War.

**Sintering:** The pressing, molding or binding of elements together.

**Stonebank, the:** The affluent section of the city of Aquom.

**Tazrus Shroud:** During the luminary wars, the ancient luminary Tazrus produced a spell so powerful it concealed the great advancements of the Eckwyn Age from all who lived. Including the wave gates.

**Tempest Stone:** An ancient artifact said to contain the collective knowledge of the ancients.

**Territh:** The name for the land or below the surface of the ground. Interchangeable with soil, dirt or ground.

**Territhamy:** Scientific study of the land.

**Territhian language:** The common language throughout Territhmina. Instituted by the Sagean Empire in the 9th epoch. It is the universal language.

**Territhmina:** The name of the world. The origins of the name predate the Age of Eckwyn.

**Territh Driver:** Pyramid constructed ground hammer or pile driver used to excavate the ground.

**Tinkersmith:** A skilled technician with small machine parts, gears, gadgets and workings.

**Trancing sand or Ghost sand:** Alchemist powder used in sigil spells.

**Tregoreans:** A race of beings who are known to live in the mountains and jungles of Nahadon, a providence they have lived in untouched throughout the Sagean Empire. They are recognized by their pointed ears and pristine facial appearances. They have been reported to commonly wear tight clothing that camouflages into the surrounding forests and jungles. Very little is known about them, as they do not let outsiders in and are very protective of their lands. It is believed that they live twice the length of time of humans.

**Tune of the Redeamer:** A famous song.

**Tungsten Carbide:** Metal used in military weapons due to its extremely high melting point.

**Ultrarians:** An elite special forces unit established by Kovan Rainer, the war hero, near the end of the Great War. This force tracked and defeated the final remnants of the Sagean supporters called the Consortium.

**Underdeath:** A slang term meaning worse than death. Meaning something as horrible or revolting as a corpse.

**United Coalition of Nations:** The collective governing body of Territhmina. Established, following the Great War, a pact for peace, unity, law and order was signed by all the nations of the known world. While every nation signed the treaty, only a select number of ambassador seats were granted for inclusion on the Coalition Council based on population and land size. At the time the New World was given only one chair represented by their King.

**Varium Crystal:** A small, hollow, delicate crystalline glass jewel that can be filled with an alchemist's concoction, like firespark.

**Vazey:** Aloof or evasive.

**Viper Lords:** The five coastal cities of Nahadon are controlled by individual rulers.

**Wave Gate or Acuber magnetic wave gate:** Ancient stone and metal gates, constructed with gemstone stars. They were once used by the luminaries to travel instantaneously around the world. Their locations are unknown. Texts suggest they utilize special matter to warp space, allowing objects to pass at speeds faster than light on a gravitational wave to another gate through a unique magnetic connection.

**Wavelifers:** Term used to describe people who make their living sailing the Anamic Ocean or Zulu Sea.

**Winddrifter:** A smaller airship typically built from a modified sailboat. It uses a steam powered engine and a large air balloon along with large sails to navigate the skies. Sizes, styles and colors vary.

**Whisper Chain, the:** An organization for the delivery of secret messages, started during the Great War as a secret courier service. They have since expanded their organization to every major city. Their offices are often indistinguishable and hard to locate. Access to the organization and their services is exclusive to its members.

**Wolveracks:** A beast from the great war once controlled by the Sagean. They are a solitary animal with the size and features of a very large wolf. They have pointed ears and long fang-like teeth. Their upper mane is very full and wiry, but their hind legs are muscular and shorthaired. They have a tough hide and strong tails that grow up to five feet in length. Their eyes can glow yellow when they are aggressive. They don't live in packs, but sometimes hunt in them. Considered very dangerous and aggressive, they become ravenous by the smell of blood.

**Wraith or The Night Wraith:** A mystical spirit believed to be the hand of death and the messenger and guide to the Nothing.

**Wrythen, the:** A dark spirit entity that appeared to Qudin on the Dragon's Spine just before he vanquished the Sagean Lord. It seems to be drawn to luminary powers.

**Xand Zosmos:** The author of the greatest book of alchemy that the Scholar's Guild owns. It surfaced sometime before the Great War.

**Zacaren language:** A thick dialect spoken throughout Nahadon, but mostly in Zawarin. The language includes a lot of words considered non-territhian.

**Zenoch:** A race of beings in the northern mountains of the New World. They are recognized by their blue skin. They are very secretive and considered extremely dangerous. The government of the New World has not tried to expand into their lands. Instead choosing to section off various points as border stops to prevent people from wondering too far.

**Zinithal:** The summer season is commonly referred to as the zinithal season. In reference to the sun.

KOVAN'S PULSATOR

CHARGED CRYSATAL SADDLE

SHOCK GUARD PLATE HOUSING
CATHALITIC TRANSFORMER
CURRENT DISPATCHER

AMP COMTROLS

ELECTRON FLASH TUBE
SILICA GLASS
(ZERO THERMAL EXPANSION)

POWER TRANSFER
TEATHER

SILVER MAGNETIC
FLUX INDUCTOR

REACTOR CHAMBER

EXHAUST PORT

AMMUNITION
POWER SHIFTER

AMMUNITION SPPLY
CHARGED TUNGSTEN
CARBINE SLUGS

BARREL
STABILIZERS

MUZZLE FLASH
SURPRESSOR

# ABOUT THE AUTHOR

Steven Rudy studied architecture and creative writing at the University of Colorado at Boulder. Currently he lives with his wife and three children in Colorado and works as an architectural designer.

This is his first novel.

You can find him at https://stevenrudybook.com/

.....or on social media

Made in the USA
Monee, IL
03 June 2021